TARGET ZERO

Jack Mars is the USA Today bestselling author of the LUKE STONE thriller series, which includes seven books. He is also the author of the new FORGING OF LUKE STONE prequel series, comprising three books (and counting); and of the AGENT ZERO spy thriller series, comprising six books (and counting).

ANY MEANS NECESSARY (book #1), which has over 800 five star reviews, is available as a free download on Amazon!

Jack loves to hear from you, so please feel free to visit www. Jackmarsauthor.com to join the email list, receive a free book, receive free giveaways, connect on Facebook and Twitter, and stay in touch!

TARGET ZERO

(An Agent Zero Spy Thriller—Book #2)

JACK MARS

CONTENTS

Agent Zero – Book 1 Summary (recap sheet to be included in book 2)

A college professor and father of two rediscovers his forgotten past as a CIA field agent. He fights his way across Europe to find the answer of why his memory was suppressed while unraveling a terrorist plot to kill dozens of world leaders.

Agent Zero: Professor Reid Lawson was kidnapped and an experimental memory suppressor was torn from his head, allowing his forgotten memories to return as CIA Agent Kent Steele, also known the world over as Agent Zero.

Maya and Sara Lawson: Reid's two teenage daughters, ages 16 and 14 respectively, are unaware of their father's past as a CIA agent.

Kate Lawson: Reid's wife and the mother of his two children passed away suddenly two years earlier from an ischemic stroke.

Agent Alan Reidigger: Kent Steele's best friend and fellow field agent, Reidigger helped him have the memory suppressor installed in the wake of a deadly rampage by Steele to track down a dangerous assassin.

Agent Maria Johansson: A fellow field agent and Kent Steele's former love interest in the wake of his wife's death, Johansson proved an unlikely but welcome ally as he recovered his memory and unearthed the terrorist plot.

Amun: The terrorist organization Amun is an amalgamation of several terrorist factions from around the world. Their masterstroke of bombing the World Economic Forum at Davos while authorities are distracted by the Winter Olympics was thwarted by Agent Zero.

Rais: An American expat turned assassin of Amun, Rais believes it is his destiny to kill Agent Zero. In their fight at the Winter Olympics at Sion, Switzerland, Rais was mortally wounded and left for dead.

Agent Vicente Baraf: Baraf, an Italian Interpol agent, was instrumental in helping Agents Zero and Johansson to stop Amun's plot to bomb Davos.

Agent John Watson: A stoic and professional CIA agent, Watson rescued Reid's girls from the hands of terrorists on a New Jersey pier.

PROLOGUE

"Tell me, Renault," said the older man. His eyes twinkled as he watched the coffee bubble in the cap of the percolator between them. "Why did you come here?"

Dr. Cicero was a kind man, jovial, the sort who liked to describe himself as "fifty-eight years young." His beard had turned gray in his late thirties and white in his forties, and though usually neatly trimmed, it had grown wispy and unruly in his time on the tundra. He wore a bright orange parka, but it did little to mute the youthful light in his blue eyes.

The young Frenchman was slightly taken aback by the question, but he knew his answer immediately, having rehearsed it in his head many times. "The WHO contacted the university for research assistants. They, in turn, offered it to me," he explained in English. Cicero was native Greek, and Renault from the southern coast of France, so they conversed in a shared tongue. "To be honest, there were two others given the chance before me. They both turned it down. However, I saw it as a great opportunity to—"

"Bah!" the older man interjected with a simper. "I'm not asking about academics, Renault. I've read your transcript, as well as your thesis on forecasted influenza B mutation. It was quite good, I might add. I don't think I could have written it better myself."

"Thank you, sir."

Cicero chuckled. "Save your 'sir' for boardrooms and fundraising. Out here, we are equal. Call me Cicero. How old are you, Renault?"

"Twenty-six, sir—uh, Cicero."

"Twenty-six," said the old man thoughtfully. He warmed his hands over the heat from the camp stove. "And nearly finished with your doctorate? That's very impressive. But what I want to know is, why are you *here*? As I said, I've reviewed your file. You're young, intelligent, admittedly handsome..." Cicero chuckled. "You could have gotten an internship anywhere in the world, I imagine. But these four days you've been with us, I haven't heard you once talk about yourself. Why here, of all places?"

Cicero waved a hand as if to demonstrate his point, but it was wholly unnecessary. The Siberian tundra stretched in every direction as far as the eye could see, gray and white and utterly empty, save for the northeast where low-lying mountains sprawled lazily, capped in white.

Renault's cheeks turned slightly pink. "Well, if I am being honest, Doctor, I came here to study by your side," he admitted. "I am an admirer of yours. Your work in hindering the Zika virus outbreak was truly inspiring."

"Well!" said Cicero warmly. "Flattery will get you everywhere— or at least some Belgian dark roast." He pulled a thick mitten over his right hand, lifted the percolator from the butane-powered camp stove, and poured two plastic mugs of steaming, rich coffee. It was one of the very few luxuries they had available in the Siberian wilderness.

Home, for the last twenty-seven days of Dr. Cicero's life, had been the small encampment established about a hundred and fifty meters from the shore of the Kolyma River. The settlement was comprised of four domed neoprene tents, a canvas canopy enclosed on one side to protect from the wind, and a semi-permanent Kevlar clean room. It was under the canvas canopy that the two men currently stood, making coffee over a two-burner camp stove amid the folding tables that held microscopes, samples of permafrost, archaeology equipment, two rugged all-weather computers, and a centrifuge.

"Drink up," said Cicero. "It's nearly time for our shift." He sipped the coffee with his eyes closed, and a soft moan of pleasure escaped his lips. "Reminds me of home," he said softly. "Do you have someone waiting for you, Renault?"

"I do," answered the young man. "My Claudette."

"Claudette," Cicero repeated. "A lovely name. Married?"

"No," Renault said simply.

"It's important to have something to long for, in our line of work," said Cicero wistfully. "It gives you perspective amid the detachment that is often necessary. Thirty-three years I've called Phoebe my wife. My work has taken me all over this earth, but she is always there for me when I return. While I'm away, I pine, but it is worth it; every time I come home it is like falling in love all over again. As they say, absence makes the heart grow fonder."

Renault grinned. "I would not have pegged a virologist for a romantic," he mused.

"The two are not mutually exclusive, my boy." The doctor frowned slightly. "And yet...I don't believe it is Claudette that haunts your mind most. You're a pensive young man, Renault. More than once I've noticed you staring at the mountaintop as if looking for answers."

"I think you may have missed your true calling, Doctor," said Renault. "You should have been a sociologist." The smile dissipated from his lips as he added, "You are right, though. I have accepted this assignment not only for the ability to work at your side, but also because I have dedicated myself to a cause...a cause predicated on belief. However, I have fears of where that belief might take me."

Cicero nodded knowingly. "As I said, detachment is often necessary in our line of work. One must learn to be dispassionate." He put a hand on the young man's shoulder. "Take it from someone with some years behind him. Belief is a powerful motivation, to be certain, but sometimes emotions have the tendency to blur our judgment, dull our minds."

"I'll be wary. Thank you, sir." Renault grinned sheepishly. "Cicero. Thank you."

Suddenly the walkie-talkie squawked intrusively from the table beside them, shattering the introspective silence of the canopy.

"Dr. Cicero," said a female voice edged with an Irish brogue. It was Dr. Bradlee, calling from the nearby excavation site. "We've unearthed something. You're going to want to see this. Bring the box. Over."

"We'll be there momentarily," Dr. Cicero said into the radio. "Over." He smiled paternally at Renault. "It seems we're being called in early. We should suit up."

The pair of men set down the still-steaming mugs and hurried to the Kevlar clean room, stepping into the first antechamber to dress in the bright yellow decontamination suits the World Health Organization had provided. Gloves and plastic boots went on first, sealed at the wrists and ankles, before the full-body coveralls, hood, and finally, mask and respirator.

They dressed quickly but quietly, almost reverently, using the brief interim as not only one of physical transformation, but mental as well, from their pleasant and casual banter to the somber mind-set required for their line of work.

Renault disliked the decontamination suits. They made movement slow and the work tedious. But they were absolutely necessary to conduct their research: locate and verify one of the most dangerous organisms known to mankind.

He and Cicero stepped out of the antechamber and made their way toward the bank of the Kolyma, the slow-moving icy river that ran south of the mountains and slightly east, toward the ocean.

"The box," said Renault suddenly. "I'll fetch it." He hurried back to the canopy to retrieve the sample container, a stainless steel cube fastened shut with four clasps, a biohazard symbol emblazoned on each of its six sides. He trotted back to Cicero, and the two resumed their hasty trek to the excavation site.

"You know what occurred not far from here, yes?" Cicero asked through his respirator as they walked.

"I do." Renault had read the report. Five months ago, a twelve-year-old boy from a local village had fallen sick shortly after fetching water from the Kolyma. At first it was thought that the river was contaminated, but as symptoms manifested, the picture became clearer. Researchers from the WHO were mobilized immediately upon hearing of the illness and an investigation was launched.

The boy had contracted smallpox. More specifically, he had fallen ill with a strain never before seen by modern man.

The investigation eventually led to the carcass of a caribou near the river's banks. After thorough testing, the hypothesis was confirmed: the caribou had died more than two hundred years earlier, and its body had become a part of the permafrost. The illness it carried froze with it, lying dormant—until five months ago.

"It is a simple chain reaction," said Cicero. "As the glaciers melt, the river's water level and temperature rise. That, in turn, thaws the permafrost. Who knows what diseases might lurk in this ice? Ancient strains the likes of which we have never seen before . . . it is entirely possible that some might even predate mankind." There was a tension in the doctor's voice that was not only concern, but an edge of excitement. It was, after all, his livelihood.

"I read that in 2016 they found anthrax in a water supply, caused by a melted icecap," Renault commented.

"It is true. I was called to that case. As well as the Spanish flu found in Alaska."

"What became of the boy?" the young Frenchman asked. "The smallpox case from five months ago." He knew that the boy, along with fifteen others in his village, had been quarantined, but that was where the report had ended.

"He passed," Cicero said. There was no emotion in his voice; not like when he spoke of his wife, Phoebe. After decades in his line of work, Cicero had learned the subtle art of detachment. "Along with four others. But out of that came a proper vaccine for the strain, so their deaths weren't for naught."

"Still," Renault said quietly, "a shame."

Less than a stone's throw from the river's shore was the excavation site, a twenty-square-meter patch of tundra cordoned by metal stakes and bright yellow procedural tape. It was the fourth such site the research team had created over their investigation so far.

Four other researchers in decontamination suits were inside the cordoned square, all hunched over a small patch of earth near its center. One of them saw the two men coming and hurried over.

It was Dr. Bradlee, an archaeologist on loan from the University of Dublin. "Cicero," she said, "we've found something."

"What is it?" he asked as he crouched low and sidled under the procedural tape. Renault followed.

"An arm."

"Pardon?" Renault blurted.

"Show me," said Cicero.

Bradlee led the way to the patch of excavated permafrost. Digging into the permafrost—and doing so carefully—was no easy task, Renault knew. The topmost layers of frozen earth commonly thawed in the summer, but the deeper layers were so-called because they were permanently frozen in the polar regions. The hole that Bradlee and her team had dug was nearly two meters deep and wide enough for a grown man to lie down in.

Not unlike a grave, Renault thought grimly.

And true to her word, the frozen remnants of a partially decomposed human arm were visible in the bottom of the hole, twisted, nearly skeletal, and blackened by time and soil.

"My God," Cicero said in a near-whisper. "Do you know what this is, Renault?"

"A body?" he ventured. At least he hoped that the arm was attached to more.

Cicero spoke quickly, gesticulating with his hands. "Back in the 1880s, a small settlement existed not far from here, right on the banks of the Kolyma. The original settlers were nomads, but as their numbers grew, they intended to build a village here. Then the unthinkable happened. A smallpox epidemic swept through them, killing forty percent of their tribe in a matter of days. They believed the river was cursed, and the survivors vacated quickly.

"But before they did, they buried their dead—right here, in a mass grave at the shore of the Kolyma River." He pointed into the hole, at the arm. "The floodwaters are eroding the banks.

The melting permafrost would soon uncover these bodies, and all it would take after that is some local fauna to pick at them and become a carrier before we could be facing an all-new epidemic."

Renault forgot to breathe for a moment as he watched one of the yellow-clad researchers, down in the hole, scrape samples of the decomposing arm. The discovery was quite exciting; up until five months ago, the last known natural outbreak of smallpox had occurred in Somalia, in 1977. The World Health Organization had declared the disease eradicated in 1980. Yet they now stood at the edge of a literal grave known to be infected with a dangerous virus that could decimate the population of a major city in days—and their job was to dig it up, verify it, and send samples back to the WHO.

"Geneva will have to confirm it," Cicero said quietly, "but if my speculation is correct, we have just unearthed an eight-thousand-year-old strain of smallpox."

"Eight thousand?" Renault inquired. "I thought you said the settlement was in the late nineteenth century."

"Ah, I did!" said Cicero. "But the question then becomes, how did they—an isolated nomadic tribe—contract it? In a similar fashion, I would imagine. Digging the ground and stumbling upon something long-since frozen. This strain found in the thawed caribou carcass five months ago dated all the way back to the start of the Holocene epoch." The older virologist could not seem to take his eyes from the arm jutting from the frozen dirt below. "Renault, fetch the box, please."

Renault retrieved the steel sample box and set it in the frozen earth near the edge of the hole. He unlocked the four clasps that sealed it and lifted the lid. Inside, where he had stowed it earlier, was a MAB PA-15. It was an old pistol, but not a heavy one, weighing about two pounds fully loaded with a fifteen-round magazine and one in the chamber.

The gun had belonged to his uncle, a veteran of the French Army who had fought in Maghreb and Somalia. The young Frenchman, however, disliked guns; they were too direct, too discriminate, and far too artificial for his tastes. Not like a virus—nature's perfect machine, capable of wiping out entire species, both systematic and uncritical at the same time. Emotionless, unyielding, and precipitate; all of which he needed to be in the moment.

He reached into the steel box and wrapped his hand around the gun, but wavered slightly. He did not want to use the gun. He had, in fact, grown rather fond of Cicero's infectious optimism and the twinkle in the older man's eye.

But all things must come to an end, he thought. *The next experience awaits.*

Renault stood with the pistol in his palm. He toggled the safety and dispassionately shot the two researchers on either side of the hole, point-blank in the chest.

Dr. Bradlee let out a startled shriek at the sudden, jarring report of the gun. She scrambled backward, covering two paces before Renault fired twice into her. The English doctor, Scott, made a feeble attempt to climb out from the hole before the Frenchman made it his grave with a single shot into the top of his head.

The shots were thunderous, deafening, but there was no one around for a hundred miles to hear them. Almost no one.

Cicero was rooted to the spot, paralyzed with shock and fear. It had taken Renault only seven seconds to end four lives—only seven seconds for the research expedition to become a mass murder.

The older doctor's lips trembled behind his respirator as he attempted to speak. At long last he stammered a single word: "Wh-why?"

Renault's icy gaze was stoic, as detached as any virologist would have to be. "Doctor," he said softly, "you are hyperventilating. Remove your respirator before you pass out."

Cicero's breath came ragged and quick, outpacing the respirator's ability. His gaze flitted from the gun in Renault's hand, held casually at his side, to the hole in which Dr. Scott now lay dead. "I...I cannot," Cicero stuttered. To remove his respirator would be to potentially subject himself to the disease. "Renault, please..."

"My name is not Renault," said the young man. "It is Cheval—Adrian Cheval. There was a Renault, a university student who was awarded this internship. He is dead now. It is his transcript, and his paper, that you read."

Cicero's bloodshot eyes widened further. The edges of his vision grew fuzzy and dark with the threat of losing consciousness. "I don't... I don't understand... why?"

"Dr. Cicero, please. Remove the respirator. If you are going to die, would you not prefer it to be with some dignity? Facing the sunshine, rather than behind a mask? If you lose consciousness, I assure you, you will never wake up."

Fingers quivering, Cicero slowly reached up and tugged down the tight yellow hood from over his white-streaked hair. Then he gripped the respirator and mask and pulled it off. The sweat that had beaded on his forehead chilled instantly and froze.

"I want you to know," said the Frenchman, Cheval, "that I truly do respect you and your work, Cicero. I take no pleasure in this."

"Renault—or Cheval, whoever you might be—listen to reason." With the respirator off, Cicero regained enough of his faculties to make a plea. There could be only one motivation for the young man before him to commit such an atrocity. "Whatever it is you are planning to do with this, please, reconsider. It is extremely dangerous—"

Cheval sighed. "I am aware, Doctor. You see, I was indeed a student at Stockholm University, and I truly was pursuing my doctorate. Last year, however, I made an error. I forged faculty signatures on a request form to obtain samples of a rare enterovirus. They found out. I was expelled."

"Then... then let me help you," Cicero pleaded. "I-I can sign such a request. I can assist you with your research. Anything but this—"

"Research," Cheval mused quietly. "No, Doctor. It is not research I am after. My people are waiting, and they are not patient men."

Cicero's eyes welled. "Nothing good will come of it. You know that."

"You're wrong," said the young man. "Many will die, yes. But they will die nobly, paving the way for a much better future." Cheval looked away. He did not want to shoot the kind old doctor. "You were right about one thing, though. My Claudette, she is real. And absence does indeed make the heart grow fonder. I must go now, Cicero, and so must you. But I respect you, and I am willing to grant a final request. Is there anything you would like to say to your Phoebe? You have my word I will deliver the message."

Cicero shook his head slowly. "There is nothing so important to tell her that I would send a monster like you into her path."

"Very well. Goodbye, Doctor." Cheval raised the PA-15 and fired a single round into Cicero's forehead. The wound frothed as the older doctor staggered and collapsed onto the tundra.

In the stunning silence that followed, Cheval took a moment and, kneeling, murmured a brief prayer. Then he set about his work.

He wiped the gun clean of prints and powder and hurled it into the flowing, icy Kolyma River. Next he rolled the four bodies into the hole to join Dr. Scott. With a shovel and pick, he spent ninety minutes covering them and the exposed, decomposing arm with partially frozen dirt. He disassembled the excavation site, pulling out the stakes and tearing down the procedural tape. He took his time, working meticulously—no one would even attempt to contact the research team for another eight to twelve hours, and it would be at least a full twenty-four before the WHO sent anyone to the site. An investigation would certainly yield the buried bodies, but Cheval was not keen to make it easy on them.

Lastly, he took the glass vials containing the samples from the decomposing arm and carefully slid them, one by one, into the secure foam tubes of the stainless steel box, all the while keenly aware that any single one of them had the power to be staggeringly deadly. Then he sealed the four clasps and carried the samples back to the encampment.

In the makeshift clean room, Cheval stepped into the portable decontamination shower. Six nozzles sprayed him down from every angle with steaming hot water and a built-in emulsifier. Once finished, he carefully and methodically peeled off the yellow hazmat suit, leaving it on the floor of the tent. It was possible that his hairs or spittle, identifying factors, could be in the suit—but he had one last step to perform.

In the back of Cicero's all-terrain jeep were two rectangular red gasoline canisters. It would take only one for him to reach civilization again. The other he dumped liberally over the clean room, the four neoprene tents, and the canvas canopy.

Then he lit the fire. The blaze went up quickly and instantly, sending black, oily smoke roiling skyward. Cheval climbed into the jeep with the steel sample box and drove away. He did not speed, and he did not look in the rearview mirror to watch the site burn. He took his time.

Imam Khalil would be waiting. But the young Frenchman still had much to do before the virus was ready.

CHAPTER ONE

Reid Lawson peered through the blinds of his home office for the tenth time in less than two minutes. He was growing anxious; the bus should have arrived by now.

His office was on the second floor, the smallest of the three bedrooms of their new home on Spruce Street in Alexandria, Virginia. It was a welcome contrast to the cramped, boxy closet of a study he had in the Bronx. Half of his things were unpacked; the rest were still in boxes that lay scattered across the room. His bookshelves were constructed, but his books lay stacked in alphabetical order on the floor. The only things he had taken the time to completely build and organize were his desk and computer.

Reid had told himself that today was going to be the day that he finally got it together, nearly a full month after moving in, and finished unpacking the office.

He had gotten as far as opening a box. It was a start.

The bus is never late, he thought. *It's always here between three twenty-three and three twenty-five. It's three thirty-one.*

I'm calling them.

He snatched his cell phone from the desk and dialed Maya's number. He paced as it rang, trying not to think of all the awful things that could have happened to his girls between the school and home.

The call went to voicemail.

Reid hurried down the stairs to the foyer and pulled on a light jacket; March in Virginia was considerably more favorable than New York, but still a bit chilly. Car keys in hand, he punched

1

in the four-digit security code on the wall panel to arm the alarm system to "away" mode. He knew the precise route the bus took; he could backtrack it all the way to the high school if he needed to, and ...

As soon as he pulled the front door open, the bright yellow bus hissed to a stop at the end of his driveway.

"Busted," Reid murmured. He couldn't very well duck back into the house. He had undoubtedly been spotted. His two teenage girls stepped off the bus and down the walkway, pausing just shy of the door that he now blocked as the bus pulled away again.

"Hi, girls," he said as brightly as possible. "How was school?"

His eldest, Maya, shot him a suspicious look as she folded her arms across her chest. "Where you going?"

"Um ... to get the mail," he told her.

"With your car keys?" She gestured to his fist, which was indeed gripping the keys to his silver SUV. "Try again."

Yup, he thought. *Busted.* "The bus was late. And you know what I said, if you're going to be late, you have to call. And why didn't you answer your phone? I tried to call—"

"Six minutes, Dad." Maya shook her head. "Six minutes isn't 'late.' Six minutes is traffic. There was a fender-bender on Vine."

He stepped aside as they entered the house. His younger daughter, Sara, gave him a brief hug and a murmur of, "Hi, Daddy."

"Hi, sweetheart." Reid closed the door behind them, locked it, and punched in the code to the alarm system again before turning back to Maya. "Traffic or not, I want you to let me know when you're going to be late."

"You're neurotic," she muttered.

"Excuse me?" Reid blinked in surprise. "You seem to be confusing neurosis with concern."

"Oh, please," Maya retorted. "You haven't let us out of your sight in weeks. Not since you've been back."

She was, as usual, right. Reid had always been a protective father, and he had grown more so when his wife and their mother, Kate, died two years earlier. But for the past four weeks, he had become a veritable helicopter parent, hovering and (if he was being honest) perhaps being a tad overbearing.

But he wasn't about to admit that.

"My dear, sweet child," he chided, "as you blossom into adulthood, you'll have to learn a very hard truth—that sometimes, you are wrong. And right now, you are wrong." He grinned, but she didn't. It was in his nature to try to diffuse tension with his kids using humor, but Maya wasn't having it.

"Whatever." She marched down the foyer and into the kitchen. She was sixteen, and staggeringly intelligent for her age—sometimes, it seemed, too much so for her own good. She had Reid's dark hair and penchant for dramatic discourse, but lately she seemed to have gained a proclivity toward teenage angst, or at the very least moodiness... likely brought on by a combination of Reid's constant loitering and obvious misinformation about the events that had occurred the month before.

Sara, the younger of his two, trudged up the stairs. "I'm gonna get started on my homework," she said quietly.

Left alone in the foyer, Reid sighed and leaned against a white wall. His heart broke for his girls. Sara was fourteen, and generally vibrant and sweet, but whenever the subject came up of what had happened in February she clammed up or quickly vacated the room. She simply didn't want to talk about it. Just a few days earlier, Reid had tried to invite her to see a therapist, a neutral third party that she could talk to. (Of course, it would have to be a CIA-affiliated doctor.) Sara declined with a simple and succinct "no thanks" and scurried out of the room before Reid could get another word in.

He hated keeping the truth from his kids, but it was necessary. Outside of the agency and Interpol, no one could know the truth— that barely more than a month ago he had recovered a portion of his memory as an agent in the CIA under the alias Kent Steele, also known to his peers and enemies as Agent Zero. An experimental memory suppressor in his head had caused him to forget all about Kent Steele and his work as an agent for nearly two years, until the device was torn from his skull.

Most of his memories as Kent were still lost to him. They were in there, locked away somewhere in the recesses of his brain, but they trickled in like a leaky faucet, usually when a visual or verbal prompt jarred them loose. The savage removal of the memory suppressor had done something to his limbic system that prevented the memories from returning all at once—and Reid was, for the most part, glad for it. Based on what little he knew about his life as Agent Zero, he wasn't sure he wanted them all back. His biggest trepidation was that he might remember something that he wouldn't want to be reminded of, some painful regret or awful act that Reid Lawson could never live with knowing.

Besides, he had been extremely busy ever since the activities in February. The CIA helped him relocate his family; upon his return to the US, he and his girls were sent to Alexandria in Virginia, a short drive from Washington, DC. The agency helped to secure him a position as an adjunct professor with Georgetown University.

Ever since then had been a whirlwind of activity: getting the girls enrolled in a new school, acclimating to his new job, and moving into the house in Virginia. But Reid had played a large part in keeping himself distracted by creating plenty of busywork for himself. He painted rooms. He upgraded appliances. He purchased new furniture and new school clothes for the girls. He could afford to; the CIA had awarded him a healthy sum for his involvement in stopping the terrorist organization called Amun. It was more than he made annually as a professor. They were delivering it in monthly installments to avoid scrutiny. The checks hit his bank account as a consulting fee from a fake publishing company that claimed to be creating a series of forthcoming history textbooks.

Between the money and his copious amounts of free time—he was only doing a few lectures a week at the moment—Reid kept himself as busy as he could. Because pausing for even a few moments meant thinking, and thinking meant reflecting, not only on his fractured memory, but on other equally unpleasant things.

4

Like the nine names that he had memorized. The nine faces he had scrutinized. The nine lives that had been lost because of his failure.

"No," he murmured quietly, alone in the foyer of their new home. "Don't do that to yourself." He didn't want to be reminded of that now. Instead he headed into the kitchen, where Maya was digging through the refrigerator for something to eat.

"I think I'll order some pizza," he announced. When she said nothing, he added, "What do you think?"

She closed the fridge with a sigh and leaned against it. "It's fine," she said simply. Then she glanced around. "The kitchen is nicer. I like the skylight. Yard is bigger, too."

Reid smiled. "I meant about the pizza."

"I know," she replied with a shrug. "You just seem to prefer avoiding the topic at hand lately, so I figured I would too."

He recoiled again at her brashness. On more than one occasion she had pressed him for information about what had happened when he disappeared, but the conversation always ended in him insisting that his cover story was the truth, and her getting angry because she knew he was lying. Then she would drop it for a week or so before the vicious cycle began anew.

"There's no need for that kind of attitude, Maya," he said.

"I'm going to go check on Sara." Maya spun on her heel and left the kitchen. A moment later he heard her feet pounding up the stairs.

He pinched the bridge of his nose in frustration. It was times like these that he missed Kate the most. She always knew just what to say. She would have known how to handle two teenagers who had been through what his girls had been through.

His willpower to continue with the lie was growing weak. He couldn't bring himself to recite the cover story yet again, the one the CIA had supplied him with to tell his family and colleagues where he had vanished to for a week. The story went that federal agents had come to his door, demanding his assistance on an important case. As an Ivy League professor, Reid was in a unique position

5

to help them with research. As far as the girls were aware, he had spent most of that week in a conference room, poring over books and staring at a computer screen. That was all he was allowed to say, and he couldn't share details with them.

He certainly couldn't tell them about his clandestine past as Agent Zero, or that he had helped stop Amun from bombing the World Economic Forum in Davos, Switzerland. He couldn't tell them that he had singlehandedly killed more than a dozen people in the course of only days, each and every one a known terrorist.

He had to stick to his vague cover story, not only for the sake of the CIA, but for the sake of the girls' safety. While he was away dashing madcap all over Europe, his two daughters were forced to flee New York, spending several days on their own before being picked up by the CIA and brought to a safe house. They had very nearly been abducted by a pair of Amun radicals—a thought that still made the hairs on Reid's neck stand on end, because it meant that the terrorist group had members in the United States. It certainly lent to his overly overprotective nature as of late.

The girls had been told that the two men who tried to accost them were members of a local gang that was abducting children in the area. Sara seemed slightly skeptical of the story, but accepted it on the grounds that her father wouldn't lie to her (which, of course, made Reid feel even more awful). That, plus her total aversion to the topic, made it easy to skirt the issue and move on with life.

Maya, on the other hand, was downright dubious. Not only was she smart enough to know better, but she had been in contact with Reid via Skype during the ordeal and had seemingly gathered enough information on her own to make some assumptions. She herself had witnessed firsthand the deaths of the two radicals at Agent Watson's hand, and she hadn't been quite the same since.

Reid was at a complete loss about what to do, other than to try to continue with life with as much normalcy as possible.

Reid took out his cell phone and called the pizzeria up the street, putting in an order for two medium pies, one with extra cheese (Sara's favorite) and the other with sausage and green peppers (Maya's favorite).

As he hung up, he heard footfalls on the stairs. Maya returned to the kitchen. "Sara's taking a nap."

"Again?" It seemed that Sara had been sleeping a lot during the day lately. "Is she not sleeping at night?"

Maya shrugged. "I don't know. Maybe you should ask her."

"I tried. She won't tell me anything."

"Maybe it's because she doesn't understand what happened," Maya suggested.

"I told you both what happened." *Don't make me say it again,* he thought desperately. *Please don't make me lie to your face again.*

"Maybe she's scared," Maya pressed on. "Maybe because she knows her dad, who she's supposed to be able to trust, is *lying* to her—"

"Maya Joanne," Reid warned, "you want to choose your next words carefully…"

"Maybe she's not the only one!" Maya didn't seem to be backing down. Not this time. "Maybe I'm scared too."

"We're safe here," Reid told her firmly, trying to sound convincing even if he didn't fully believe it himself. A headache was forming in the front of his skull. He retrieved a glass from the cupboard and filled it with cold water from the tap.

"Yeah, and we *thought* we were safe in New York," Maya shot back. "Maybe if we knew what was going on, what you were really into, it would make things easier. But no." Whether it was his inability to leave them alone for twenty minutes or her suspicions about what had happened didn't matter. She wanted answers. "You know damn well what we went through. But we have *no* idea what happened to you!" She was nearly shouting now. "Where you went, what you did, how you got hurt—"

"Maya, I swear…" Reid set the glass on the counter and pointed a finger of warning in her direction.

"Swear what?" she snapped. "To tell the truth? Then just tell me!"

"I *can't* tell you the truth!" he yelled. As he did, he threw his arms out at his sides. One hand swept the glass of water off the countertop.

Reid didn't have time to think or ponder. His instincts kicked in and in a rapid, smooth gesture he bent low at the knees and snatched the glass out of the air before it could crash to the floor.

He immediately sucked in a regretful breath as the water sloshed, barely a drop spilled.

Maya stared, wide-eyed, though he didn't know whether her surprise was at his words or his actions. It was the first time that she had ever seen him move like that—and the first time he had ever acknowledged, out loud, that what he told them might not have been what had happened. It didn't matter if she knew it, or even just suspected it. He had blurted it out, and there was no taking it back now.

"Lucky catch," he said quickly.

Maya slowly folded her arms across her chest, with one eyebrow raised and her lips pursed. He knew that glare; it was an accusatory look she had inherited directly from her mother. "You may have Sara and Aunt Linda fooled, but I'm not buying it, not for a second."

Reid closed his eyes and sighed. She wasn't going to let him off the hook, so he lowered his tone and spoke carefully.

"Maya, listen. You are very intelligent—definitely enough to make certain suppositions about what happened," he said. "The most important thing to understand is that knowing specific things could be dangerous. The potential danger that you were in for that week I was away, you could be in all the time, if you knew everything. I can't tell you if you're right or wrong. I won't confirm or deny anything. So for now, let's just say that…you can believe whatever assumptions you've made, so long as you're careful to keep them to yourself."

Maya nodded slowly. She stole a glance down the hall to make sure Sara wasn't there before she said, "You're not just a professor. You're working for someone, government-level—FBI, maybe, or CIA—"

"Jesus, Maya, I said keep it to yourself!" Reid groaned.

"The thing with the Winter Olympics, and the forum in Davos," she pressed on. "You had something to do with that."

"I told you, I won't confirm or deny anything—"

"And that terrorist group they keep talking about on the news, Amun. You helped stop them?"

Reid turned away, glancing out the small window that looked out over their backyard. It was too late, by then. He didn't have to confirm or deny anything. She could see it on his face.

"This isn't a game, Maya. It's serious, and if the wrong kind of people knew—"

"Did Mom know?"

Out of all the questions she could have asked, that one was a curveball. He was silent for a long moment. Once again his eldest had proven herself too smart, maybe even for her own good.

"I don't think so," he said quietly.

"And all that traveling you did, before," Maya said. "Those weren't conferences and guest lectures, were they?"

"No. They weren't."

"Then you stopped for a while. Did you quit after … after Mom …?"

"Yes. But then they needed me back." That was enough of a partial truth for him to not feel like he was lying—and hopefully enough to sate Maya's curiosity.

He turned back toward her. She stared at the tiled floor, her face etched in a frown. There was clearly more she wanted to ask. He hoped she didn't.

"One more question." Her voice was nearly a whisper. "Did this stuff have anything to do with … with Mom's death?"

"Oh, god. No, Maya. Of course not." He crossed the room quickly and put his arms around her tightly. "Don't think like that. What happened to Mom was medical. It could have happened to anyone. It wasn't … it had nothing to do with this."

"I think I knew that," she said quietly. "I just had to ask …"

"It's okay." That was the last thing he wanted her to think, that Kate's death was somehow linked to the secret life he had been involved in.

Something flashed across his mind—a vision. A recollection of the past.

A familiar kitchen. Their home in Virginia, before moving to New York. Before she died. Kate stands before you, every bit as beautiful as you remember—but her brow is furrowed, her gaze is hard. She's angry. Shouting. Gesturing with her hands toward something on the table...

Reid stepped back, releasing Maya's embrace as the vague memory spurned a dull headache in his forehead. Sometimes his brain tried to recall certain things from his past that were still locked away, and the forcible retrieval left him with a mild migraine at the front of his skull. But this time was different, stranger; the memory had clearly been one of Kate, some sort of argument they had that he couldn't recall having.

"Dad, you okay?" Maya asked.

The doorbell rang suddenly, startling them both.

"Uh, yeah," he murmured. "I'm fine. That must be the pizza." He looked at his watch and frowned. "That was really quick. I'll be right back." He crossed the foyer and glanced through the peephole. Outside was a young man with a dark beard and a half-vacant gaze, wearing a red polo shirt bearing the pizzeria's logo.

Even so, Reid checked over his shoulder to make sure Maya wasn't watching, and then he snaked a hand into the dark brown bomber jacket that hung on a hook near the door. In the inside pocket was a loaded Glock 22. He clicked the safety off and tucked it into the back of his pants before he opened the door.

"Delivery for Lawson," the pizza guy said, monotone.

"Yup, that's me. How much?"

The guy cradled the two boxes with one arm as he reached for his back pocket. Reid instinctively did too.

He saw movement from the corner of his eye and his gaze flitted left. A man with a military buzz cut was crossing his front lawn in a hurry—but more importantly, he was clearly wearing a holstered gun on his hip, and his right hand was on the grip.

CHAPTER TWO

Reid held up his arm like a crossing guard stopping traffic.
"It's okay, Mr. Thompson," he called out. "It's just pizza."

The older man on his front lawn, with his graying buzz cut and
slight paunch, stopped in his tracks. The pizza guy glanced over
his shoulder and, for the first time, showed some emotion—his
eyes widened in shock when he saw the gun and the hand resting
upon it.

"You sure, Reid?" Mr. Thompson eyed up the pizza guy
suspiciously.

"I'm sure."

The delivery guy slowly pulled a receipt from his pocket. "Uh,
it's eighteen," he said, bewildered.

Reid gave him a twenty and a ten and took the boxes from him.
"Keep the change."

The pizza guy didn't have to be told twice. He jogged back to
his waiting coupe, jumped in, and screeched away. Mr. Thompson
watched him go, his eyes narrowed.

"Thank you, Mr. Thompson," Reid said. "But it's just pizza."

"I didn't like the look of that guy," his next-door neighbor
growled. Reid liked the older man just fine—though he thought
Thompson took on his new role of keeping a watchful eye on the
Lawson family just a bit too seriously. Even so, Reid decidedly preferred having someone a bit overzealous to someone lackadaisical
in their duties.

"Never can be too careful," Thompson added. "How are the
girls?"

"They're doing fine." Reid smiled pleasantly. "But, uh … do you have to carry that around in plain sight all the time?" He gestured to the Smith & Wesson at Thompson's hip.

The older man looked confused. "Well … yes. My CHP expired, and Virginia is a legal open-carry state."

"… Right." Reid forced another smile. "Of course. Thanks again, Mr. Thompson. I'll let you know if we need anything."

Thompson nodded and then trotted back across the lawn to his house. Deputy Director Cartwright had assured Reid that the older man was quite capable; Thompson was a retired CIA agent, and even though he'd been out of the field for more than two decades he was clearly happy—if not a tad eager—to be useful again.

Reid sighed and closed the door behind him. He locked it and activated the security alarm again (which was becoming a ritual every time he opened or closed the door), and then turned to find Maya standing behind him in the foyer.

"What was *that* about?" she asked.

"Oh, nothing. Mr. Thompson just wanted to say hi."

Maya crossed her arms again. "And here I thought we were making such good progress."

"Don't be ridiculous." Reid scoffed at her. "Thompson is just a harmless old man—"

"Harmless? He carries a gun everywhere he goes," Maya protested. "And don't think I don't see him watching us from his window. It's like he's spying on—" Her mouth fell open a little. "Oh my god, does he know about you? Is Mr. Thompson a spy too?"

"Jeez, Maya, I am *not* a spy …"

Actually, he thought, *that's exactly what you are …*

"I don't believe this!" she exclaimed. "Is that why you have him babysit us when you leave?"

"Yes," he admitted quietly. He didn't have to tell her the unrequested truths, but there wasn't much point in hiding things from her when she was going to make such accurate guesses anyway.

He expected her to be angry and start throwing accusations again, but instead she shook her head and murmured, "Unreal. My dad is a spy, and our next-door nut-job is a bodyguard." Then, to his surprise, she hugged him around the neck, almost knocking the pizza boxes from his hand. "I know you can't tell me everything. All I wanted was some truth."

"Yeah, yeah," he muttered. "Just risking international security to be a good dad. Now go wake your sister before the pizza gets cold. And Maya? Not a *word* of this to Sara."

He went into the kitchen and took out some plates and napkins, and poured three glasses of soda. A few moments later, Sara shuffled into the kitchen, rubbing sleep from her eyes.

"Hi, Daddy," she mumbled.

"Hey, sweetheart. Have a seat. Are you sleeping okay?"

"Mm," she murmured vaguely. Sara plucked up a piece of pizza and bit off the tip, chewing in slow, lazy circles.

He was worried about her, but he tried not to let on. Instead he grabbed a slice of the sausage-and-pepper pie. It was halfway to his mouth when Maya intervened, snatching it out of his hand.

"What do you think you're doing?" she demanded.

"…Eating? Or trying to."

"Um, no. You have a date, remember?"

"What? No, that's tomorrow…" He trailed off, uncertain. "Oh, god, that is tonight, isn't it?" He nearly smacked himself in the forehead.

"Sure is," said Maya around a mouthful of pizza.

"Also, it's not a date. It's dinner with a friend."

Maya shrugged. "Fine. But if you don't go get ready, you're going to be late for 'dinner with a friend.'"

He looked at his watch. She was right; he was supposed to meet Maria at five.

"Go, shoo. Get changed." She ushered him out of the kitchen and he hurried upstairs.

With everything going on and his continual attempts to elude his own thoughts, he'd nearly forgotten about the promise to meet with Maria. There had been several half-baked attempts to get together over the past four weeks, always with something getting in the way on one end or another—though, if he was being honest with himself, it was usually his end that made the excuses. Maria had seemed to finally grow tired of it and not only planned the outing, but chose a spot halfway between Alexandria and Baltimore, where she lived, if he would promise to see her.

He did miss her. He missed being around her. They weren't just partners in the agency; there was a history there, but Reid couldn't remember most of it. Barely any, in fact. All he knew was that when he was around her, there was a distinct feeling that he was in the company of someone who cared for him—a friend, someone he could trust, and perhaps even more than that.

He went into his closet and pulled out an ensemble he thought would work for the occasion. He was a fan of a classic style, though he was aware that his wardrobe probably dated him by at least a decade. He pulled on a pair of pleated khakis, a plaid button-down, and a tweed jacket with leather patches at the elbows.

"Is *that* what you're wearing?" Maya asked, startling him. She was leaning against the door frame to his bedroom, munching casually on a pizza crust.

"What's wrong with it?"

"What's wrong with it is that you look like you just stepped out of a classroom. Come on." She took him by the arm back to the closet and began rooting through his clothes. "Jeez, Dad, you dress like you're eighty…"

"What was that?"

"Nothing!" she called back. "Ah. Here." She pulled out a black sport coat—the only one he owned. "Wear this, with something gray under it. Or white. A T-shirt or a polo. Get rid of the dad-pants and put on some jeans. Dark ones. Slim fit."

At the behest of his daughter, he changed his outfit while she waited in the hall. He supposed he should get used to this bizarre role reversal, he thought. One moment he was the overprotective father; the next he was caving in the face of his challenging, astute daughter.

"Much better," Maya said as he presented himself anew. "You almost look like you're ready for a date."

"Thank you," he said, "and this isn't a date."

"You keep saying that. But you're going for dinner and drinks with a mysterious woman that you claim is an old friend, even though you've never mentioned her and we've never met her..."

"She *is* an old friend—"

"And, I might add," Maya said over him, "she's quite attractive. We saw her get off the plane in Dulles. So if either of you are looking for something more than 'old friends,' this is a date."

"Good god, you and I are *not* talking about that." Reid winced. But in his mind, he was panicking slightly. *She's right. This is a date.* He had been doing so many mental gymnastics lately that he hadn't paused long enough to consider what "dinner and drinks" really meant to a pair of single adults. "Fine," he admitted, "let's just say it's a date. Um... what do I do?"

"You're asking me? I'm not exactly an expert." Maya grinned. "Talk to her. Get to know her better. And please, try your best to be interesting."

Reid scoffed and shook his head. "Excuse me, but I am plenty interesting. How many people do you know that can give an entire oral history of the Bulavin Rebellion?"

"Only one." Maya rolled her eyes. "And do *not* give this woman an entire oral history of the Bulavin Rebellion."

Reid chuckled and hugged his daughter.

"You'll be fine," she assured him.

"You will too," he said. "I'm going to call Mr. Thompson to come by for a while..."

"Dad, no!" Maya pulled away from his embrace. "Come on. I'm sixteen. I can watch Sara for a couple of hours."

"Maya, you know how important it is to me that you two aren't alone—"

"Dad, he smells like motor oil, and all he wants to talk about is 'the good ol' days' with the Marines," she said exasperatedly.

"Nothing is going to happen. We're going to eat pizza and watch a movie. Sara will be in bed before you're back. We'll be fine."

"I still think that Mr. Thompson should come—"

"He can spy through the window like he usually does. We'll be okay. I promise. We have a great security system, and deadbolts on all the doors, and I know about the gun near the front door—"

"Maya!" Reid exclaimed. *How did she know about that?* "Do *not* mess with that, do you understand?"

"I'm not going to touch it," she said. "I'm just saying. I know it's there. Please. Let me prove I can do this."

Reid didn't like the idea of the girls being alone in the house, not at all, but she was practically begging. "Tell me the escape plan," he said.

"The whole thing?!" she protested.

"The whole thing."

"Fine." She flipped her hair over a shoulder, as she often did when she was annoyed. Her eyes rolled to the ceiling as she recited, monotone, the plan that Reid had enacted shortly upon their arrival in the new house. "If anyone comes to the front door, I should first make sure the alarm is armed, and the deadbolt and chain lock are on. Then I check the peephole to see if it's someone I know. If it's not, I call Mr. Thompson and have him investigate first."

"And if it is?" he prompted.

"If it's someone I know," Maya rattled on, "I check the side window—carefully—to see if there is anyone else with them. If there is, I call Mr. Thompson to come over and investigate."

"And if someone tries to force their way in?"

"Then we get down to the basement and go into the exercise room," she recited. One of the first renovations Reid had made, upon moving in, was to have the door to the small room in the basement replaced with one with a steel core. It had three heavy deadbolts and aluminum alloy hinges. It was bulletproof and fireproof, and the CIA tech that had installed it claimed it would take a dozen SWAT battering rams to knock it down. It effectively turned the small exercise room into a makeshift panic room.

"And then?" he asked.

"We call Mr. Thompson first," she said. "And then nine-one-one. If we forget our cell phones or can't get to them, there's a land-line in the basement preprogrammed with his number."

"And if someone breaks in, and you can't get to the basement?"

"Then we go to the nearest available exit," Maya droned. "Once outside, we make as much noise as possible."

Thompson was a lot of things, but hard of hearing was not one of them. One night Reid and the girls had the TV on too loud while watching an action movie, and Thompson came running at the sound of what he thought might have been suppressed gunshots.

"But we should always have our phones with us, in case we need to make a call once we're somewhere safe."

Reid nodded approvingly. She had recited the entire plan—except one small, yet crucial, part. "You forgot something."

"No, I didn't." She frowned.

"Once you're somewhere safe, and after you call Thompson and the authorities...?"

"Oh, right. Then we call you right away and let you know what's happened."

"Okay."

"Okay?" Maya raised an eyebrow. "Okay as in, you'll let us be on our own for once?"

He still didn't like it. But it was only for a couple of hours, and Thompson would be right next door. "Yes," he said finally.

Maya breathed a sigh of relief. "Thank you. We'll be fine, I swear it." She hugged him again, briefly. She turned to head back downstairs, but then thought of something else. "Can I get away with just one more question?"

"Sure. But I can't promise I'll tell you the answer."

"Are you going to start... traveling, again?"

"Oh." Once again her question took him by surprise. The CIA had offered him his job back—in fact, the Director of National Intelligence himself had demanded that Kent Steele be fully reinstated—but Reid hadn't yet given them an answer, and the agency hadn't yet demanded one of him. Most days he avoided thinking about it altogether.

"I...would really like to say no. But the truth is that I don't know. I haven't quite made up my mind." He paused a moment before asking, "What would you think if I did?"

"You want my opinion?" she asked in surprise.

"Yes, I do. You're honestly one of the smartest people I know, and your opinion matters a lot to me."

"I mean...on the one hand, it's pretty cool, knowing what I know now—"

"Knowing what you *think* you know," Reid corrected.

"But it's also pretty scary. I know there's a very real chance that you could get hurt, or...or worse." Maya was quiet for a while. "Do you like it? Working for them?"

Reid didn't answer her directly. She was right; the ordeal that he'd been through had been terrifying, and had threatened his life more than once, as well as the lives of both his girls. He couldn't bear it if anything happened to them. But the hard truth—and one of the bigger reasons why he kept himself so busy lately—was that he *did* enjoy it, and he did miss it. Kent Steele longed for the chase. There was a time, when all this started, that he acknowledged that part of him as if it were a different person, but that wasn't true. Kent Steele was an alias. *He* longed for it. He missed it. It was a part of him, just as much as teaching and raising two girls. Though his memories were fuzzy, it was a part of his greater self, his identity, and not having it was like a sports star suffering a career-ending injury: it brought with it the question, *Who am I, if I'm not that?*

He didn't have to answer her question aloud. Maya could see it in his thousand-yard gaze.

"What's her name again?" she asked suddenly, changing the subject.

Reid smiled sheepishly. "Maria."

"Maria," she said thoughtfully. "All right. Enjoy your date." Maya headed downstairs.

Before following, Reid had a minor afterthought. He opened the top dresser drawer and rummaged around in the rear of it until he found what he was looking for—an old bottle of expensive cologne, one he hadn't worn in two years. It had been Kate's favorite. He sniffed the diffuser and felt a chill run down his spine. It was a familiar, musky scent that carried with it a flood of good memories.

He spritzed some on his wrist and dabbed each side of his neck. The scent was stronger than he remembered, but pleasant.

Then—another memory flashed across his vision.

The kitchen in Virginia. Kate is angry, gesturing at something on the table. Not just angry—she's frightened. "Why do you have this, Reid?" she asks accusingly. "What if one of the girls had found it? Answer me!"

He shook the vision loose before the inevitable migraine came on, but it didn't make the experience any less disturbing. He couldn't recall when or why that argument had happened; he and Kate had rarely argued, and in the memory, she looked scared— either scared of whatever they were arguing about, or possibly even scared of *him*. He had never given her a reason to be. At least not that he could remember...

His hands shook as a new realization struck him. He couldn't recall the memory, which meant that it might have been one that was suppressed by the implant. But why would any memories of Kate have been erased with Agent Zero?

"Dad!" Maya called from the bottom of the stairs. "You're going to be late!"

"Yeah," he muttered. "Coming." He would have to face the reality that either he sought a solution to his problem, or that the occasional resurfacing memories would continuously struggle forth, confusing and jarring.

But he would face that reality later. Right now he had a promise to keep.

He went downstairs, kissed each of his daughters on the top of their head, and headed out to the car. Before making his way down the walkway, he made sure that Maya set the alarm after him, and then he climbed into the silver SUV he'd bought just a couple weeks earlier.

Even though he was very nervous and certainly excited about seeing Maria again, he still couldn't shake the tight ball of dread in his stomach. He couldn't help but feel that leaving the girls alone, even for a short time, was a very bad idea. If the events of the previous month had taught him anything, it was first and foremost that there was no shortage of threats that wanted to see him suffer.

CHAPTER THREE

"How are you feeling tonight, sir?" the overnight nurse asked politely as she entered his hospital room. Her name was Elena, he knew, and she was Swiss, though she spoke to him in accented English. She was petite and young, most would say pretty, even, and quite cheerful.

Rais said nothing in response. He never did. He merely stared as she set a Styrofoam cup on his bedside table and set about carefully inspecting his wounds. He knew that her cheerfulness was overcompensation for her fear. He knew that she did not like being in the room with him, despite the pair of armed guards behind her, watching his every move. She did not like treating him, or even speaking to him.

No one did.

The nurse, Elena, inspected his wounds cautiously. He could tell she was nervous being that close to him. They knew what he had done; that he had killed in the name of Amun.

They would be a lot more afraid if they knew how many, he thought wryly.

"You're healing nicely," she told him. "Faster than expected." She told him that every night, which he took as code to mean "hopefully you'll leave here soon."

That was not good news for Rais, because when he was finally well enough to leave he would likely be sent to a dank, horrible hole in the ground, some CIA black site in the desert, to sustain more wounds while they tortured him for information.

21

As Amun, we endure. That had been his mantra for more than a decade of his life, but that was no longer the case. Amun was no more, as far as Rais knew; its plot in Davos had failed, its leaders had been either detained or killed, and every law enforcement agency in the world knew about the brand, the glyph of Amun that its members burned into their skin. Rais was not allowed to watch television, but he got his news from his armed police guards, who talked often (and at great length, often to Rais's annoyance).

He himself had sliced the brand from his skin before being taken to the hospital in Sion, but it ended up being for naught; they knew who he was and at least some of what he had done. Even so, the jagged, mottled pink scar where the brand had once been on his arm was a daily reminder that Amun was no more, and so it only seemed fitting that his mantra change.

I endure.

Elena took the Styrofoam cup, filled with ice water and a straw. "Would you like something to drink?"

Rais said nothing, but he leaned forward slightly and parted his lips. She guided the straw toward him cautiously, her arms fully extended and locked at the elbows, her body reclined back on an angle. She was afraid; four days earlier Rais had tried to bite Dr. Gerber. His teeth had scraped the doctor's neck, not even broken the skin, but still it warranted a crack across the jaw from one of his guards.

Rais did not try anything this time. He took long, slow sips through the straw, enjoying the girl's fear and the tight anxiousness of the two police officers who watched behind her. When he'd had his fill, he leaned back again. She audibly sighed with relief.

I endure.

He had endured quite a bit in the past four weeks. He had endured a nephrectomy to remove his punctured kidney. He had endured a second surgery to extract a portion of his lacerated liver. He had endured a third procedure to ensure that none of his other vital organs had been damaged. He had endured several days in the ICU before being moved to a medical-surgical unit, but he never left the bed to which he was shackled by both wrists. The nurses turned him and changed his bedpan and kept him as comfortable as they were able, but he was never allowed to rise, to stand, to move around of his own volition.

The seven stab wounds in his back and one in his chest had been sutured and, as the night nurse Elena continuously reminded him, were healing well. Still, there was little the doctors could do about the nerve damage. Sometimes his entire back would go numb, up to his shoulders and occasionally even down his biceps. He would feel nothing, as if those parts of his body belonged to another.

Other times he would wake from a solid sleep with a scream in his throat as searing pain ripped through him like an angry lightning storm. It never lasted long, but it was acute, intense, and came irregularly. The doctors called them "stingers," a side effect sometimes seen in those with nerve damage as extensive as his. They assured him that these stingers often faded and stopped entirely, but they could not say when that would happen. Instead they told him he was lucky there was no damage to his spinal cord. They told him he was lucky to have survived his wounds at all.

Yes, lucky, he thought bitterly. Lucky that he was recovering only to be thrust into the waiting arms of a CIA black site. Lucky to have had everything he worked for torn away in the course of a single day. Lucky to have been bested not once, but twice by Kent Steele, a man whom he hated, loathed, with every possible fiber of his being.

I endure.

Before leaving his room, Elena thanked the two officers in German and promised to bring them coffee when she returned later. Once she was gone, they resumed their post just outside his door, which was always open, and resumed their conversation, something about a recent football match. Rais was fairly well-versed in German, but the particulars of the Swiss-German dialect and the speed with which they spoke eluded him at times. The day-shift officers often conversed in English, which was how he got much of his news about the goings-on outside his hospital room.

Both men were members of the Swiss Federal Office of Police, which mandated that he have two guards on his room at all times, twenty-four hours a day. They rotated in eight-hour shifts, with an entirely different set of guards on Fridays and the weekend. There were always two, always; if one officer had to use the restroom or get something to eat, they would first have to call down to have one of the hospital's security guards sent to them, and then wait for their arrival. Most patients in his condition and this far along in their recovery would likely have been transferred to a lower-level trauma center, but Rais had remained in the hospital. It was a more secure facility, with its locked units and armed guards.

There were always two. Always. And Rais had determined that it could work to his advantage.

He had had a lot of time to plan his escape, especially in the last several days, when his medication levels were decreased and he could think lucidly. He ran through several scenarios in his head, over and over. He memorized schedules and eavesdropped on conversations. It would not be long before they discharged him—a matter of days, at most.

He had to act, and he decided he would do it tonight.

His guards had grown complacent over the weeks posted outside his door. They called him "terrorist," and they knew he was a killer, but besides the minor incident with Dr. Gerber a few days prior, Rais had done nothing but lie there silently, mostly unmoving, and allow the staff to perform their duties. If no one was in the room with him, the guards barely paid any attention other than to occasionally glance in on him.

He had not tried to bite the doctor out of spite or malice, but out of necessity. Gerber had been leaning over him, inspecting the wound on his arm where he had sliced off the brand of Amun—and the pocket of the doctor's white lab coat had brushed the fingers of Rais's shackled hand. He lunged, snapping his jaws, and the doctor leapt back in fright as teeth grazed his neck.

And a fountain pen had remained firmly clutched in Rais's fist.

One of the officers on duty had given him a solid smack on the face for it, and in the moment the blow landed, Rais slid the pen under his sheets, stowing it beneath his left thigh. There it had stayed for three days, obscured under the sheets, until just the night before. He had taken it out while the guards chatted in the hall. With one hand, unable to see what he was doing, he separated the two halves of the pen and removed the cartridge, working slowly and steadily so the ink did not spill. The pen was a classic-style gold-tipped nib pen that came to a dangerous point. He slipped that half back under the sheet. The back half had a gold pocket clip, which he carefully pried back and away with his thumb until it snapped off.

The restraint on his left wrist allowed a little less than a foot of mobility for his arm, but if he stretched his hand to its limit he could reach the first few inches of the bedside stand. Its tabletop was simple, smooth particle board, but the underside was rough as sandpaper. Over the course of a grueling, aching four hours the night prior, Rais gently rubbed the pen's clip back and forth along the table's underside, careful not to make much noise. With every motion he feared the clip might slip from his fingers, or the guards would notice the movement, but his room was dark and they were deep in conversation. He worked and worked until he had sharpened the clip to a needle-like point. Then the clip disappeared beneath the sheets as well, next to the nib tip.

He knew from snippets of conversation that there would be three night nurses on the med-surg unit tonight, Elena included, with another two on-call if need be. They, plus his guards, meant at least five people he would have to deal with, and a maximum of seven.

No one among the medical staff liked to attend to him much, knowing what he was, so they checked in fairly infrequently. Now that Elena had come and gone, Rais knew he had somewhere between sixty and ninety minutes before she might return.

His left arm was held with a standard hospital restraint, what professionals sometimes refer to as "four-pointers." It was a soft blue cuff around his wrist with a tight, white, buckled nylon strap around that, the other end firmly attached to the steel railing of his bed. Because of the severity of his crimes, his right wrist was handcuffed.

The pair of guards outside were conversing in German. Rais listened carefully; the one on the left, Luca, seemed to be complaining that his wife was getting fat. Rais almost scoffed; Luca was far from fit himself. The other, a man named Elias, was younger and athletic, but drank coffee in doses that should have been lethal to most humans. Every night, between ninety minutes and two hours into their shift, Elias would call the night guard up so that he could relieve himself. While away, Elias would step outside for a cigarette, so that with the bathroom break meant he was usually gone between eight and eleven minutes. Rais had spent the last several nights silently counting the seconds of Elias's absences.

It was a very narrow window of opportunity, but one for which he was prepared.

He reached beneath his sheets for the sharpened clip and held it in the fingertips of his left hand. Then, carefully, he tossed it in an arc over his body. It landed deftly in the palm of his right hand.

Next would come the hardest part of his plan. He pulled his wrist so that the handcuff chain was taut, and while holding it that way he twisted his hand and worked the sharpened tip of the clip into the keyhole of the cuff around the steel railing. It was difficult and awkward, but he had escaped handcuffs before; he knew the catch mechanism inside was designed so that a universal key could open nearly any pair, and knowing the inner workings of a lock meant simply making the right adjustments to trigger the pins inside. He had to keep the chain taut, though, to keep the cuff from clanking against the railing and alerting his guards.

It took him nearly twenty minutes of twisting, turning, taking short breaks to alleviate his aching fingers and trying anew, but finally the lock clicked and the cuff slid open. Rais carefully unhooked it from the railing.

One hand was free.

He reached over and hastily unbuckled the restraint on his left. Both hands were free.

He stowed the clip under the sheets and removed the top half of the pen, gripping it in his palm so that only the sharp nib was exposed.

Outside his door, the younger officer stood suddenly. Rais held his breath and pretended to be asleep as Elias peered in on him.

"Call Francis, would you?" Elias said in German. "I've got to piss."

"Sure," Luca said with a yawn. He radioed down to the hospital's night guard, who was ordinarily stationed behind the front desk on the first floor. Rais had seen Francis plenty of times; he was an older man, late fifties, early sixties perhaps, with a thin frame. He carried a gun but his movements were slow.

It was exactly what Rais had been hoping for. He didn't want to have to fight the younger police officer in his still-recovering state.

Three minutes later Francis appeared, in his white uniform and black tie, and Elias hurried off to the bathroom. The two men outside the door exchanged pleasantries as Francis took Elias's plastic seat with a heavy sigh.

It was time to act.

Rais carefully slid to the end of the bed and put his bare feet to the cold tile. It had been some time since he had used his legs, but he was confident that his muscles had not atrophied to a state beyond what he needed them for.

He stood carefully, quietly—and then his knees buckled. He gripped the edge of the bed for support and shot a glance toward the door. No one came; the voices continued. The two men hadn't heard anything.

Rais stood shakily, panting, and took a few silent steps. His legs were weak, to be sure, but he had always been strong when needed, and he needed to be strong now. His hospital gown flowed around him, open at the back. The immodest garment would only impede him, so he tugged it off, standing unabashedly naked in the hospital room.

The nib cap in his fist, he took a position just behind the open door, and he let out a low whistle.

Both men heard it, apparent by the sudden scraping of chair legs as they rose from their seats. Luca's frame filled the doorway as he peered into the dark room.

"*Mein Gott!*" he murmured as he hastily entered, noticing the empty bed.

Francis followed, his hand on the holster of his gun.

As soon as the older guard was past the threshold, Rais leapt forward. He jammed the nib cap into Luca's throat and twisted, tearing a berth in his carotid. Blood sprayed liberally from the open wound, some of it splashing the opposite wall.

He let go of the nib and rushed Francis, who was struggling to free his gun. *Unclip, unholster, safety off, aim*—the older guard's reaction was slow, costing him several precious seconds that he simply did not have.

Rais struck two blows, the first one upward just below the belly button, immediately followed by a downward blow to the solar plexus. One forced air into the lungs, while the other forced air out, and the sudden, jarring effect it had on a confused body was generally blurred vision and sometimes loss of consciousness.

Francis staggered, unable to breathe, and sank to his knees. Rais spun behind him, and with one clean motion he broke the guard's neck.

Luca gripped his throat with both hands as he bled out, gurgles and slight gasps rising in his throat. Rais watched and counted the eleven seconds until the man lost consciousness. Without stopping the blood flow he would be dead in under a minute.

He quickly relieved both guards of their guns and put them on the bed. The next phase of his plan would not be easy; he had to sneak down the hall, unseen, to the supply closet where there would be spare scrubs. He couldn't very well leave the hospital in Francis's recognizable uniform, or Luca's now-blood-soaked one.

He heard a male voice from down the hall and froze.

It was the other officer, Elias. *So soon?* Anxiety rose in Rais's chest. Then he heard a second voice—the night nurse, Elena.

Apparently Elias had skipped his cigarette break to chat with the pretty young nurse, and now they were both heading down the hall toward his room. They would pass by it in mere moments.

He would prefer not to have to kill Elena. But if it was a choice between him and her, she would have die.

Rais grabbed one of the guns from the bed. It was a Sig P220, all black, .45 caliber. He took it in his left hand. The weight of it felt welcome and familiar, like an old flame. With his right he gripped the open half of the handcuffs. And then he waited.

The voices in the hall fell silent.

"Luca?" Elias called out. "Francis?" The young officer unclipped the strap of his holster and had a hand on his pistol as he entered the darkened room. Elena crept in behind him.

Elias's eyes went wide with horror at the sight of the two dead men.

Rais slammed the hook of the open handcuff into the side of the young man's neck, and then yanked his arm backward. The metal bit into his wrist, and the wounds in his back burned, but he ignored the pain as he tore the young man's throat from his neck. A substantial amount of blood spattered and ran down the assassin's arm.

With his left hand he pressed the Sig against Elena's forehead.

"Do not scream," he said quickly and quietly. "Do not cry out. Stay silent and live. Make a sound and die. Do you understand?"

A small squeak erupted from Elena's lips as she stifled the sob rising from it. She nodded, even as tears welled in her eyes. Even as Elias fell forward, flat on his face on the tiled floor.

He looked her up and down. She was petite, but her scrubs were somewhat baggy and the waistband elastic. "Take off your clothes," he told her.

Elena's mouth fell open in horror.

Rais scoffed. He could understand the confusion, though; he was, after all, still nude. "I am not that type of monster," he assured her. "I need clothes. I won't ask again."

Trembling, the young woman tugged off the scrub top and slid out of her pants, removing them over her white sneakers, as she was standing in the pool of Elias's blood.

Rais took them and put them on, a bit awkwardly with one hand while he kept the Sig trained on the girl. The scrubs were snug, and the pants a bit short, but they would suffice. He tucked the pistol in the back of his pants, and retrieved the other from the bed.

Elena stood in her underwear, hugging her arms over her midsection. Rais noticed; he plucked up his hospital gown and held it out to her. "Cover yourself. Then get on the bed." As she did what he asked, he found a ring of keys on Luca's belt and unlocked his other cuff. Then he looped the chain around one of the steel railings and cuffed Elena's hands.

He set the keys on the farthest edge of the bedside table, beyond her grasp. "Someone will come and free you after I've gone," he told her. "But first I have questions. I need you to be honest, because if you're not, I will come back and kill you. Do you understand?"

She nodded frantically, tears rolling over her cheeks.

"How many other nurses are on this unit tonight?"

"P-please don't hurt them," she stammered.

"Elena. How many other nurses are on this unit tonight?" he repeated.

"T-two…" She sniffled. "Thomas and Mia. But Tom is at break. He would be downstairs."

"Okay." The name tag clipped to his chest was about the size of a credit card. It had a small photo of Elena, and on the reverse, a black stripe running its length. "Is this a locked unit at night? And your badge, it is the key?"

She nodded and sniffled again.

"Good." He tucked the second gun into the waistband of the scrub pants and knelt by Elias's body. Then he tugged off both shoes and wiggled his feet into them. They were somewhat tight, but close enough to make an escape. "One last question. Do you know what Francis drives? The night guard?" He gestured to the dead man in the white uniform.

"I-I'm not sure. A…a truck, I think."

Rais dug into Francis's pockets and came out with a set of keys. There was an electronic fob; that would help locate the vehicle.

"Thank you for your honesty," he told her. Then he tore a strip from the edge of the bed sheet and stuffed it in her mouth.

The corridor was empty and brightly lit. Rais held the Sig in his grip but kept it obscured behind his back as he crept down the hall. It opened onto a wider floor with a U-shaped nurses' station and, beyond that, the exit to the unit. A woman in round spectacles with a brunette bob typed away on a computer, her back to him.

"Turn around, please," he told her.

The startled woman spun to find their patient/prisoner in scrubs, one arm bloodied, pointing a gun at her. She lost her breath and her eyes bulged.

"You must be Mia," Rais said. The woman was likely around forty, matronly, with dark circles under her wide eyes. "Hands up."

She did so.

"What happened to Francis?" she asked quietly.

"Francis is dead," Rais told her dispassionately. "If you wish to join him, do something brash. If you want to live, listen carefully. I am going to leave through that door. Once it closes behind me, you are going to slowly count to thirty. Then you are going to go to my room. Elena is alive but she needs your assistance. After that, you may do whatever it is you're trained to do in a situation like this. Do you understand?"

The nurse nodded once tightly.

"Do I have your word you will follow those instructions? I prefer not to kill women when I can avoid it."

She nodded again, slower.

"Good." He circled around the station, tugging the badge from the scrub top as he did, and swiped it through the card slot to the right of the door. A small light turned from red to green and the lock clicked. Rais pushed the door open, shot one more look at Mia, who had not moved, and then watched the door close behind him.

And then he ran.

He hurried down the hall, tucking the Sig into his pants as he did. He took the stairs down to the first floor two at a time, and burst out a side door and into the Swiss night. Cool air washed over him like a cleansing shower, and he took a moment to breathe freely.

His legs wavered and threatened to give out again. The adrenaline of his escape was wearing off rapidly, and his muscles were still quite weak. He tugged Francis's key fob from the scrub pocket and pressed the red panic button. The alarm on an SUV screeched, the headlights flashing. He quickly turned it off and hurried over to it.

They would be looking for this car, he knew, but he wouldn't be in it for long. He would soon have to ditch it, find new clothes, and come morning he would head toward the Hauptpost, where he had everything he would need to escape Switzerland under a fake identity.

And as soon as he was able, he would find and kill Kent Steele.

CHAPTER FOUR

Reid was barely out of the driveway on his way to meet with Maria before he called Thompson to ask him to keep watch on the Lawson home. "I decided to give the girls a little independence tonight," he explained. "I won't be gone too long. But even so, keep an eye out and an ear to the ground?"

"Sure thing," the old man agreed.

"And, uh, if there's any cause for alarm, of course, head right over."

"I will, Reid."

"You know, if you can't see them or something, you can knock on the door, or call the house phone..."

Thompson chuckled. "Don't worry, I got it. And so do they. They're teenagers. They need some space now and then. Enjoy your date."

With Thompson's watchful eye and Maya's determination to prove herself responsible, Reid thought he could rest easy knowing the girls would be safe. Of course, part of him knew that was just another example of his mental gymnastics. He'd be thinking about it the whole night.

He had to bring the GPS map up on his phone to find the place. He wasn't yet familiar with Alexandria or the area, though Maria was, thanks to its proximity to Langley and CIA headquarters. Even so, she had chosen a place that she had never been to before either, likely as a way to level the playing field, so to speak.

On the drive over, he missed two turns despite the GPS voice telling him which way to go and when. He was thinking of the strange flashback he'd now had twice—first when Maya asked if Kate knew about him, and again when he smelled the cologne that his late wife had loved. It was gnawing at the back of his mind, so much so that even when he tried to pay attention to the directions he quickly grew distracted again.

The reason it was so bizarre was that every other memory of Kate was so vivid in his mind. Unlike Kent Steele, she had never left him; he remembered meeting her. He remembered dating. He remembered vacations and buying their first home. He remembered their wedding and the births of their children. He even remembered their arguments—at least he thought he did.

The very notion of losing any part of Kate shook him. The memory suppressor had already proved to have some side effects, like the occasional headache spurned by a stubborn memory—it was an experimental procedure, and the method of removal was far from surgical.

What if more than just my past as Agent Zero had been taken from me?

He didn't like the thought at all. It was a slippery slope; before long he was considering the possibility that he might have lost memories of times with his girls as well. And even worse was that there was no way for him to know the answer to that without restoring his full memory.

It was all too much, and he felt a fresh headache coming on. He switched on the radio and turned it up in an attempt to distract himself.

The sun was setting by the time he pulled into the parking lot of the restaurant, a gastropub called The Cellar Door. He was a few minutes late. He quickly got out of the car and trotted around to the front of the building.

Then he stopped in his tracks.

Maria Johansson was third-generation Swedish-American, and her CIA cover was that of a certified public accountant from Baltimore—though Reid thought it should have been as a cover model, or maybe a centerfold. She was an inch or two shy of his five-eleven height, with long, straight blonde hair that cascaded around her shoulders effortlessly. Her eyes were slate-gray, yet somehow intense. She stood outside in the fifty-five-degree weather in a simple navy-blue dress with a plunging V neck and a white shawl over her shoulders.

She spotted him as he approached and a smile grew on her lips. "Hey. Long time no see."

"I … wow," he blurted. "I mean, uh … you look great." It occurred to him that he had never seen Maria in makeup before. The blue eye shadow matched her dress and made her eyes seem nearly luminescent.

"Not so bad yourself." She nodded approvingly at his choice of apparel. "Should we go in?"

Thanks, Maya, he thought. "Yeah. Of course." He grabbed the door for her and pulled it open. "But before we do, I have a question. What the hell is a 'gastropub'?"

Maria laughed. "I think it's what we used to call a dive bar, but with fancier food."

"Got it."

Inside was cozy, if not a bit small, with brick interior walls and exposed wood beams in the ceiling. The lighting was hanging Edison bulbs, which provided a warm, dim ambience.

Why am I nervous? he thought as they were seated. He knew this woman. Together they had stopped an international terrorist organization from murdering hundreds, if not thousands, of people. But this was different; it wasn't an op or a mission. This was pleasure, and somehow that made all the difference.

Get to know her, Maya had told him. *Be interesting.*

"So, how's work?" he ended up asking. He groaned internally at his halfhearted attempt.

Maria smiled with half her mouth. "You should know I can't really talk about that."

"Right," he said. "Of course." Maria was an active CIA field agent. Even if he was active too she wouldn't be able to share details of an op unless he was on it with her.

"How about you?" she asked. "How's the new job?"

"Not bad," he admitted. "I'm adjunct, so it's part-time for now, a few lectures a week. Some grading and whatnot. But it's not terribly interesting."

"And the girls? How are they doing?"

"Eh … they're coping," Reid said. "Sara doesn't talk about what happened. And Maya actually was just…" He stopped himself before he said too much. He trusted Maria, but at the same time he didn't want to admit that Maya had guessed, very accurately, what it was that Reid was involved in. His cheeks turned pink as he said, "She was teasing me. About this being a date."

"Isn't it?" Maria asked point-blank.

Reid felt his face flush anew. "Yeah. I guess it is."

She smirked again. It seemed she was enjoying his awkwardness. In the field, as Kent Steele, he had proven he could be confident, capable, and collected. But here, in the real world, he was just as awkward as anyone might be after nearly two years of celibacy.

"What about you?" she asked. "How are you holding up?"

"I'm good," he said. "Fine." As soon as he said it, he regretted it. Had he not just learned from his daughter that honestly was the best policy? "That's a lie," he said immediately. "I guess I haven't been doing that great. I keep myself busy with all these unnecessary tasks, and I make excuses, because if I stop long enough to be alone with my thoughts, I remember their names. I see their faces, Maria. And I can't help but think that I didn't do enough to stop it."

She knew exactly what he was referring to—the nine people who had been killed in the single successful explosion set off by Amun in Davos. Maria reached over the table and took his hand. Her touch sent an electric tingle up his arm, and even seemed to calm his nerves. Her fingers were warm and soft against his.

"That's the reality we face," she said. "We can't save everyone. I know you don't have all your memories back as Zero, but if you did, you would know that."

"Maybe I don't want to know that," he said quietly.

"I get it. We still try. But to think that you can keep the world safe from harm will make you crazy. Nine lives were taken, Kent.

It happened, and there's no way to go back. But it could have been hundreds. It could have been a thousand. That's the way you need to look at it."

"What if I can't?"

"Then... find a good hobby, maybe? I knit."

He couldn't help but laugh. "You knit?" He couldn't imagine Maria knitting. Using knitting needles as a weapon to cripple an insurgent? Certainly. But actually knitting?

She held her chin high. "Yes, I knit. Don't laugh. I just made a blanket that's softer than anything you ever felt in your whole life. My point is, find a hobby. You need something to keep your hands and mind busy. What about your memory? Any improvements there?"

He sighed. "Not really. I guess I haven't had much going on to jog it. It's still kind of jumbled." He set the menu aside and wrung his hands on the tabletop. "Although, since you mention it... I did have something strange happen just earlier today. A fragment of something came back. It was about Kate."

"Oh?" Maria bit her lower lip.

"Yeah." He was quiet for a long moment. "Things with Kate and me... before she passed. They were okay, right?"

Maria stared straight at him, her slate-gray eyes boring into his. "Yes. As far as I know, things were always great between you two. She really loved you, and you her."

He found it hard to hold her gaze. "Yeah. Of course." He scoffed at himself. "God, listen to me. I'm actually talking about my late wife on a date. Please don't tell my daughter."

"Hey." Her fingers found his again across the table. "It's okay, Kent. I get it. You're new to this and it feels strange. I'm not exactly an expert here either, so... we'll figure it out together."

Her fingers lingered on his. It felt good. No, it was more than that—it felt right. He chuckled nervously, but his grin faded to a perplexed frown as a bizarre notion struck him; that Maria still called him Kent.

"What is it?" she asked.

"Nothing. I was just thinking…I don't even know if Maria Johansson is your real name."

Maria shrugged coyly. "It might be."

"That's not fair," he protested. "You know mine."

"I'm not saying it *isn't* my real name." She was enjoying this, toying with him. "You can always call me Agent Marigold, if you prefer."

He laughed. Marigold was her code name, to his Zero. It was almost a silly thing to him, to use code names when they knew each other personally—but then again, the name Zero did seem to strike fear into many he'd encountered.

"What was Reidigger's code name?" Reid asked quietly. It almost stung him to ask. Alan Reidigger had been Kent Steele's best friend—*no*, Reid thought, *he was* my *best friend*—a man of seemingly unyielding loyalty. The only problem was that Reid barely remembered anything about him. All memories of Reidigger had gone with the memory implant, which Alan had helped coordinate.

"You don't remember?" Maria smiled pleasantly at the thought. "Alan gave you the name Zero, did you know that? And you gave him his. God, I haven't thought about that night in years. We were in Abu Dhabi, I think, just coming off an op, drunk at some hoity-toity hotel bar. He called you 'Ground Zero'—like the point of a bomb's detonation, because you tended to leave a mess behind you. That shortened up to just Zero, and it stuck. And you called him—"

A phone rang, interrupting her story. Reid instinctively glanced at his own cell, lying on the table, expecting to see the house number or Maya's cell displayed on the screen.

"Relax," she said, "it's me. I'll just ignore it…" She looked at her phone and her brow knitted perplexedly. "Actually, that's work. Just a sec." She answered. "Yes? Mm-hmm." Her somber gaze lifted and met Reid's. She held it as her frown grew deeper. Whatever was being said on the other end of the line was clearly not good news. "I understand. Okay. Thank you." She hung up.

"You look troubled," he noted. "I know, I know, you can't talk about work stuff—"

"He escaped," she murmured. "The assassin from Sion, the one in the hospital? Kent, he got out, less than an hour ago."

"Rais?" Reid said in astonishment. Cold sweat immediately broke out on his brow. "How?"

"I don't have details," she said hastily as she stuffed her cell phone back into her clutch. "I'm so sorry, Kent, but I have to go."

"Yeah," he murmured. "I understand." Truthfully, he felt a hundred miles away from their cozy table in the small restaurant. The assassin that Reid had left for dead—not once, but twice—was still alive, and now at large.

Maria rose and, before leaving, leaned over and pressed her lips to his. "We'll do this again soon, I promise. But right now, duty calls."

"Of course," he said. "Go and find him. And Maria? Be careful. He's dangerous."

"So am I." She winked, and then hurried out of the restaurant.

Reid sat there alone for a long moment. When the waitress came over, he didn't even hear her words; he just waved vaguely to indicate that he was fine. But he was far from fine. He hadn't even felt the nostalgic electric tingle when Maria kissed him. All he could feel was a knot of dread forming in his stomach.

The man who believed it was his destiny to kill Kent Steele had escaped.

CHAPTER FIVE

Adrian Cheval was still awake despite the late hour. He sat upon a stool in the kitchen, staring blurry-eyed and unblinking at the laptop computer screen in front of him, his fingers typing away frenetically.

He paused long enough to hear Claudette padding softly down the carpeted stairs from the loft in her bare feet. Their flat in Marseille was small but cozy, an end unit on a quiet street a short five-minute walk from the sea.

A moment later her slight frame and fiery hair appeared in his periphery. She put her hands on his shoulders, sliding them up and around, down his chest, her head coming to rest upon his upper back. "*Mon chéri*," she purred. "My love. I cannot sleep."

"Neither can I," he replied softly in French. "There is too much to be done."

She bit him gently on the earlobe. "Tell me."

Adrian pointed at his screen, displayed on which was the cyclical double-stranded RNA structure of *variola major*—the virus known to most as smallpox. "This strain from Siberia is...it is incredible. I've never seen anything quite like it. By my calculations, the virulence of it would be staggering. I am convinced that the only thing that might have stopped it from eradicating early humanity thousands of years ago was the glacial period."

"A new Deluge." Claudette moaned a soft sigh in his ear. "How long until it is ready?"

"I must mutate the strain, while still maintaining the stability and virility," he explained. "No simple task, but a necessary one.

The WHO obtained samples of this same virus five months ago; there is no doubt that a vaccine is being developed, if one hasn't been already. Our strain must be unique enough that their vaccines will be ineffective." The process was known as lethal mutagenesis, manipulating the RNA of the samples he had acquired in Siberia to increase virulence and reduce the incubation period. At his calculations, Adrian suspected the mortality rate of the mutated *variola major* virus could reach as high as seventy-eight percent—nearly three times that of the naturally occurring smallpox that had been eradicated by the World Health Organization in 1980.

Upon returning from Siberia, Adrian had first visited Stockholm and used the deceased student Renault's ID to access their facilities, where he ensured that the samples were inactive while he worked. But he could not linger under someone else's identity, so he stole the necessary equipment and returned to Marseille. He set up his laboratory in the unused basement of a tailor's shop three blocks from their flat; the kindly old tailor believed that Adrian was a geneticist, researching human DNA and nothing more, and Adrian kept the door secured with a padlock when he was not present.

"Imam Khalil will be pleased," Claudette breathed in his ear.

"Yes," Adrian agreed quietly. "He will be pleased."

Most women would likely not be terribly keen to find their significant other working with a substance as volatile as a highly virulent strain of smallpox—but Claudette was not most women. She was petite, standing only five-foot-four to Adrian's six-foot figure. Her hair was a fiery red and her eyes as deep green as the densest jungle, suggesting a certain irascibility.

They had met only the year prior, when Adrian was at his lowest. He had just been expelled from Stockholm University for attempting to obtain samples of a rare enterovirus; the same virus that had taken his mother's life only weeks earlier. At the time, Adrian had been determined to develop a cure—obsessed, even—so that no one else would suffer as she did. But he was discovered by university faculty and summarily dismissed.

Claudette found him in an alley, lying in a puddle of his own desolation and vomit, half-unconscious from drink. She took him home, cleaned him up, and fed him water. The next morning Adrian had awoken to find a beautiful woman sitting at his bedside, smiling upon him as she said, "I know exactly what you need."

He swiveled on his kitchen stool to face her and ran his hands up and down her back. Even sitting he was nearly her height. "It is interesting you mention the Deluge," he noted. "You know, there are scholars who say that if the Great Flood truly did occur, it would have been approximately seven to eight thousand years ago ... nearly the same epoch as this strain. Perhaps the Flood was a metaphor, and it was this virus that cleansed the world of its wicked."

Claudette laughed at him. "Your constant endeavors to blend science and spirituality are not lost on me." She took his face gently in her hands and kissed his forehead. "But you still do not understand that sometimes faith is all you need."

Faith is all you need. That was what she had prescribed to him the year before, when he awoke from his drunken stupor. She had taken him in and allowed him to stay in her flat, the very same one that they occupied still. Adrian was not a believer in love at first sight before Claudette, but she came to hold many influences on his way of thinking. Over the course of some months, she introduced him to the tenets of Imam Khalil, an Islamic holy man from Syria. Khalil considered himself neither Sunni nor Shiite, but simply a devotee of God—even to the point that he allowed his fairly small sect of followers to call Him by whatever name they chose, for Khalil believed that each individual's relationship with their creator was strictly personal. For Khalil, that god's name was Allah.

"I want you to come to bed," Claudette told him, stroking his cheek with the back of her hand. "You need your rest. But first ... do you have the sample prepared?"

"The sample." Adrian nodded. "Yes. I have it."

There was but a single, tiny vial, barely larger than a thumbnail, of the active virus, hermetically sealed in glass and nestled between two cubes of foam, those inside a stainless steel biohazard container. The box itself was sitting, quite conspicuously, on the countertop of their kitchen.

"Good," Claudette purred. "Because we are expecting visitors."

"Tonight?" Adrian's hands fell away from the small of her back. He hadn't expected it to happen so soon. "At this hour?" It was nearly two o'clock in the morning.

"Any moment," she said. "We made a promise, my love, and we must keep it."

"Yes," Adrian murmured. She was right, as always. Vows must not be broken. "Of course."

A brusque, heavy rapping on the door of their flat startled them both.

Claudette padded quickly to the door, leaving the chain lock on and opening it only two inches. Adrian followed, peering over her shoulder to see the pair of men on the other side. Neither looked friendly. He did not know their names, and had come to think of them only as "the Arabs"—though, for all he knew, they could have been Kurds or even Turkmen.

One of them spoke quickly to Claudette in Arabic. Adrian did not understand; his Arabic was rudimentary at best, limited to a handful of phrases that Claudette had taught him, but she nodded once, slid the chain aside, and granted them entry.

Both were fairly young, their mid-thirties or so, and sported short black beards over their mocha-tinted cheeks. They wore European clothing, jeans and T-shirts and light jackets against the chilly night air; Imam Khalil did not require any religious garb or coverings of his followers. In fact, ever since their displacement from Syria, he preferred that his people blend in whenever possible—for reasons that were obvious to Adrian, considering what the two men were there to procure.

"Cheval." One of the Syrian men nodded to Adrian, almost reverently. "Forward? Tell us." He spoke in extremely broken French.

"Forward?" Adrian repeated, confused.

"He means to ask for your progress," Claudette said gently.

Adrian smirked. "His French is terrible."

"So is your Arabic," Claudette retorted.

Fair point, Adrian thought. "Tell him that the process takes time. It is meticulous, and requires patience. But the work is going well."

Claudette relayed the message in Arabic, and the pair of Arabs nodded their approval.

"Small piece?" the second man asked. It seemed they were intent to practice their French on him.

"They've come for the sample," Claudette told Adrian, though he had gathered that much from context. "Will you retrieve it?" It was clear to him that Claudette had no interest in touching the biohazard container, sealed or not.

Adrian nodded, but he did not move. "Ask them why Khalil did not come himself."

Claudette bit her lip and touched him gently on the arm. "Darling," she said quietly, "I am sure he is busy elsewhere—"

"What could be more important than this?" Adrian insisted. He had fully expected the Imam to show up.

Claudette asked the question in Arabic. The pair of Syrians frowned and glanced at each other before responding.

"They tell me that he is visiting the infirm tonight," Claudette told Adrian in French, "praying for their release from this physical world."

Adrian's mind flashed to a memory of his mother, only days before her death, lying on the bed with her eyes open but unaware. She was barely conscious from the medication; without it she would have been in constant torment, yet with it she was practically comatose. In the weeks leading up to her departure, she had no concept of the world around her. He had prayed often for her recovery, there at her bedside, though as she neared the end his prayers changed and he found himself wishing her only a quick, painless death.

"What will he do with it?" Adrian asked. "The sample."

"He will ensure that your mutation works," Claudette said simply. "You know this."

"Yes, but…" Adrian paused. He knew it was not his place to question the Imam's intent, but suddenly he had a powerful urge to know. "Will he test it privately? Somewhere remote? It is important not to show our hand too soon. The rest of the batch is not ready ..."

Claudette said something quickly to the pair of Syrian men, and then she took Adrian by the hand and led him to the kitchen. "My love," she said quietly, "you are having doubts. Tell me."

Adrian sighed. "Yes," he admitted. "This is only a very tiny sample, not quite as stable as the others will be. What if it does not work?"

"It will." Claudette wrapped her arms around him. "I have every confidence in you, as does Imam Khalil. You have been gifted this opportunity. You are blessed, Adrian."

You are blessed. Those were the same words Khalil had used when they met. Three months earlier, Claudette had taken Adrian on a trip to Greece. Khalil, like so many Syrians, was a refugee—but not a political one, nor a byproduct of the war-torn nation. He was a religious refugee, chased out by Sunnis and Shiites alike for his idealistic notions. Khalil's brand of spirituality was an amalgamation of Islamic tenets and some of the esoteric philosophical influences from Druze, such as truthfulness and transmigration of the soul.

Adrian had met the holy man in a hotel in Athens. Imam Khalil was a gentle man with a pleasant smile, wearing a brown suit with his dark hair and beard combed and neat. The young Frenchman was mildly taken aback when, upon meeting for the first time, the Imam asked Adrian to pray with him. Together they sat upon a carpet, facing Mecca, and prayed silently. There was a calmness that hung in the air around the Imam like an aura, a placidity that Adrian had not experienced since being a young boy in his then-healthy mother's arms.

After prayer, the two men smoked from a glass hookah and drank tea while Khalil spoke of his ideology. They discussed the importance of being true to oneself; Khalil believed that the only way for humanity to absolve their sins was absolute truthfulness, which would allow the soul to reincarnate as a pure being. He asked many questions of Adrian, about science and spirituality alike. He asked about Adrian's mother, and promised him that somewhere on this earth she had been born anew, pure and beautiful and healthy. The young Frenchman took great solace in it.

Khalil then spoke of Imam Mahdi, the Redeemer and the last of the Imam, the holy men. Mahdi would be the one who would bring about the Day of Judgment and rid the world of evil. Khalil believed that this would occur very soon, and after the Mahdi's redemption would come utopia; every being in the universe would be flawless, genuine, and untainted.

For several hours the two men sat together, well into the night, and when Adrian's head was as foggy as the thick, smoky air that swirled around them he finally asked the question that had been on his mind.

"Is it you, Khalil?" he asked the holy man. "Are you the Mahdi?"

Imam Kahlil had smiled wide at that. He took Adrian's hand in his own and said gently, "No, my son. *You* are. You are blessed. I can see it as clearly as I see your face."

I am blessed. In the kitchen of their Marseille flat, Adrian pressed his lips to Claudette's forehead. She was right; they had made a promise to Khalil and it must be kept. He retrieved the steel biohazard box from the countertop and carried it to the waiting Arabs. He unclasped the lid and lifted the top half of the foam cube to show them the tiny, hermetically sealed glass vial nestled inside.

There did not appear to be anything in the vial—which was part of the nature of it being one of the most dangerous substances the world over.

"Darling," Adrian said as he replaced the foam and clasped the lid firmly again. "I need you to tell them, in no uncertain terms, that under no circumstances whatsoever should they touch this vial. It must be handled with the utmost care."

Claudette relayed the message in Arabic. Suddenly the Syrian man holding the box appeared far less comfortable than a moment earlier. The other man nodded his thanks to Adrian and murmured a phrase in Arabic, one that Adrian understood—"Allah is with you, peace be upon you"—and without another word, the two men left the flat.

Once they were gone, Claudette twisted the deadbolt and put the chain back on, and then turned to her lover with a dreamy, satisfied expression on her lips.

Adrian, however, stood rooted to the spot, his face dour.

"My love?" she said cautiously.

"What have I just done?" he murmured. He already knew the answer; he had put a deadly virus in the hands of not Imam Khalil, but two strangers. "What if they do not deliver it? What if they drop it, or open it, or—"

"My love." Claudette slid her arms around his waist and pressed her head to his chest. "They are followers of the Imam. They will exercise caution and get it to where it needs to be. Have faith. You have taken the first step towards changing the world for the better. You are the Mahdi. Do not forget that."

"Yes," he said softly. "Of course. You are right, as always. And I must finish." If his mutation did not work as it should, or if he did not produce the completed batch, he had no doubt that he would be a failure not only in the eyes of Khalil, but in Claudette's as well. Without her he would crumble. He needed her as he needed air, food, or sunlight.

Even so, he could not help but wonder what they would do with the sample—if Imam Khalil would test it privately, at a remote location, or if it would be released publicly.

But he would find out soon enough.

CHAPTER SIX

"**D**ad, you don't need to walk me to the door every time," Maya griped as they crossed Dahlgren Quad toward Healy Hall on the Georgetown campus.

"I know I don't have to," Reid said. "I *want* to. What, are you ashamed to be seen with your dad?"

"It's not that," Maya muttered. The ride over had been quiet, Maya staring pensively out the window while Reid tried to think of something to talk about but fell short.

Maya was approaching the end of her junior year of high school, but she had already tested out of her AP classes and started taking a few courses a week at the Georgetown campus. It was a good jump toward college credit and looked great on an application—especially since Georgetown was her current top choice. Reid had insisted not only on driving Maya to the college but also walking her to her classroom.

The night prior, when Maria had been forced to suddenly cut their date short, Reid had hurried home to his girls. He was extremely disturbed by the news of Rais's escape—his fingers had trembled against the steering wheel of his car—but he forced himself to stay calm and tried to think logically. The CIA was already in pursuit and likely Interpol as well. He knew the protocol; every airport would be watched, and roadblocks would be established on Sion's major thoroughfares. And Rais had no allies left to turn to.

Besides, the assassin had escaped in Switzerland, more than four thousand miles away. Half a continent and an entire ocean spanned between him and Kent Steele.

Even so, he knew he would feel a lot better when he received word that Rais had been detained again. He was confident in Maria's ability, but he wished he would have had the foresight to ask her to keep him updated as best she could.

He and Maya reached the entrance to Healy Hall and Reid lingered. "All right, I guess I'll see you after class?"

She glanced back at him suspiciously. "You're not going to walk me in?"

"Not today." He had a feeling he knew why Maya was so quiet that morning. He had given her an ounce of independence the night before, but today he was right back to his usual ways. He had to remind himself that she wasn't a little girl anymore. "Listen, I know I've been kind of crowding you a bit lately…"

"A bit?" Maya scoffed.

"…And I'm sorry for that. You are a capable, resourceful, and intelligent young woman. And you just want some independence. I recognize that. My overprotective nature is my problem, not yours. It's not anything you did."

Maya tried to hide the smirk on her face. "Did you just use the 'it's not you, it's me' line?"

He nodded. "I did, because it's true. I wouldn't be able to forgive myself if something happened to you and I wasn't there."

"But you're not always going to be there," she said, "no matter how hard you try to be. And I need to be able to take care of problems myself."

"You're right. I will try my best to back off a bit."

She arched an eyebrow. "You promise?"

"I promise."

"Okay." She stretched on her tiptoes and kissed his cheek. "See you after classes." She headed toward the door, but then had another thought. "You know, maybe I should learn how to shoot, just in case…" He pointed a stern finger her way. "Don't push it."

She grinned and vanished into the hall. Reid loitered outside for a couple of minutes. God, his girls were growing up too fast. In two short years Maya would be a legal adult. Soon there would be cars, and college tuition, and … and sooner or later there would be boys. Thankfully that hadn't happened yet.

He distracted himself by admiring the campus architecture as he headed toward Copley Hall. He wasn't sure he would ever grow tired of walking around the university, enjoying the eighteenth- and nineteenth-century structures, many built in the Flemish Romanesque style that flourished in the European Middle Ages. It certainly helped that mid-March in Virginia was a turning point for the season, the weather coming around and rising into the fifties and even sixties on nicer days.

His role as an adjunct was typically taking on smaller classes, twenty-five to thirty students at a time and primarily history majors. He specialized in lessons on warfare, and often subbed in for Professor Hildebrandt, who was tenured and traveled frequently for a book he was writing.

Or maybe he's secretly in the CIA, Reid mused.

"Good morning," he said loudly as he entered the classroom. Most of his students were already there when he arrived, so he hurried to the front, set his messenger bag on the desk, and shrugged out of his tweed coat. "I'm a few minutes late, so let's jump right in." It felt good being in the classroom again. This was his element—at least one of them. "I'm sure someone in here can tell me: what was the most devastating event, by death toll, in European history?"

"World War Two," someone called out immediately.

"One of the worst worldwide, to be sure," Reid replied, "but Russia fared a lot poorer than Europe did, by the numbers. What else you got?"

"The Mongol conquest," said a brunette girl in a ponytail.

"Another good guess, but you guys are thinking armed conflicts. What I'm thinking is less anthropogenic; more biological."

"Black Death," muttered a blond kid in the front row.

"Yes, that is correct, Mister….?"

"Wright," the kid answered.

Reid grinned. "Mr. Wright? I bet you use that as a pickup line."

The kid smiled sheepishly and shook his head.

"Yes, Mr. Wright is right—the Black Death. The pandemic of the bubonic plague started in Central Asia, traveled down the Silk Road, was carried to Europe by rats on merchant ships, and in the fourteenth century it killed an estimate seventy-five to two hundred *million* people." He paced for a moment to punctuate his point. "That's a huge disparity, isn't it? How could those numbers be so far spread?"

The brunette in the third row raised her hand slightly. "Because they didn't have a census bureau seven hundred years ago?"

Reid and a few other students chuckled. "Well, sure, there's that. But it's also because of how quickly the plague spread. I mean, we're talking about more than a third of Europe's population gone inside of two years. To put it in perspective, that would be like having the entire East Coast *and* California wiped out." He leaned against his desk and folded his arms. "Now I know what you're thinking. 'Professor Lawson, aren't you the guy that comes in and talks about war?' Yes, and I'm getting to that right now.

"Someone mentioned the Mongol conquest. Genghis Khan had the largest contiguous empire in history for a brief time, and his forces marched on Eastern Europe during the years of the plague in Asia. Khan is credited as one of the first to use what we now classify as biological warfare; if a city would not yield to him, his army would catapult plague-infected bodies over their ramparts, and then ... they'd just have to wait a while."

Mr. Wright, the blond kid in the front row, wrinkled his nose in disgust. "That can't be real."

"It is real, I assure you. Siege of Kafa, in what is now Crimea, 1346. See, we want to think that something like biological warfare is a new concept, but it is not. Before we had tanks, or drones, or missiles, or even guns in the modern sense, we, uh ... they, uh ..."

"Why do you have this, Reid?" she asks accusingly. Her eyes are more afraid than they are angry.

At his mention of the word "guns," a memory suddenly flashed across his mind—the same memory as before, but clearer now. In the kitchen of their former home in Virginia. Kate had found something while cleaning dust from one of the air conditioning ducts.

A gun on the table—a small one, a silver nine-millimeter LC9. Kate gestures at it like a cursed object. "Why do you have this, Reid?"

"It's ... just for protection," you lie.

"Protection? Do you even know how to use it? What if one of the girls had found it?"

"They wouldn't—"

"You know how inquisitive Maya can be. Jesus, I don't even want to know how you got it. I don't want this thing in our house. Please, get rid of it."

"Of course. I'm sorry, Katie." Katie—the name you reserve for when she's angry.

You gingerly take the gun from the table, as if you're not sure how to handle it.

After she leaves for work you'll have to retrieve the other eleven hidden throughout the house. Find better spots for them.

"Professor?" The blond kid, Wright, glanced at Reid in concern. "You okay?"

"Um ... yeah." Reid straightened and cleared his throat. His fingers ached; he'd gripped the edge of the desk hard when the memory struck him. "Yeah, sorry about that."

There was no doubt now. He was certain he had lost at least one memory of Kate.

"Um ... sorry, guys, but suddenly I'm not feeling so great," he told the class. "It just kind of hit me. Let's, uh, leave off there for today. I'll give you some reading, and we'll pick it up on Monday."

His hands shook as he recited the page numbers. Sweat prickled on his brow as students filed out. The brunette girl from the third row paused by his desk. "You don't look so good, Professor Lawson. Do you need us to call someone?"

A migraine was forming at the front of his skull, but he forced a smile that he hoped was pleasant. "No, thank you. I'll be fine. Just need some rest."

"Okay. Feel better, Professor." She too left the classroom.

As soon as he was alone, he dug in the desk drawer, found some aspirin, and swallowed them with water from a bottle in his bag.

He sat in the chair and waited for his heart rate to slow. The memory hadn't just had a mental or emotional impact on him—it had a very real physical effect as well. The thought of losing any part of Kate from his memory at all, when she had already been taken from his life, was nauseating.

After a few minutes the sick feeling in his gut began to subside, but not the thoughts swirling in his mind. He couldn't make any more excuses; he had to make a decision. He would have to determine what he was going to do. Back at home, in a box in his office, he had the letter that told him where he could go for help—a Swiss doctor named Guyer, the neurosurgeon who had installed the memory suppressor in his head in the first place. If anyone could help to restore his memories, it would be him. Reid had spent the last month vacillating back and forth on whether or not he should at least attempt to regain his full memory.

But parts of his wife were gone, and he had no way of knowing what else might have been washed out with the suppressor.

Now he was ready.

CHAPTER SEVEN

"Look at me," said Imam Khalil in Arabic. "Please."

He took the boy by the shoulders, a paternal gesture, and knelt slightly so that he was eye to eye with him. "Look at me," he said again. It was not a demand, but a gentle request.

Omar had difficulty looking Khalil in the eye. Instead he looked at his chin, at the trimmed black beard, shaved delicately at the neckline. He looked at the lapels of his dark brown suit, by no means expensive yet finer than any clothes Omar had ever worn. The older man smelled pleasant and he spoke to the boy as if they were equals, with a respect unlike anyone else had ever shown him before. For all of those reasons, Omar could not bring himself to look Khalil in the eye.

"Omar, do you know what a martyr is?" he asked. His voice was clear but not loud. The boy had never once heard the Imam shout.

Omar shook his head. "No, Imam Khalil."

"A martyr is a type of hero. But he is more than that; he is a hero who gives himself fully to a cause. A martyr is remembered. A martyr is celebrated. You, Omar, *you* will be celebrated. You will be remembered. You will be loved forever. Do you know why?"

Omar nodded slightly, but he did not speak. He believed in the Imam's teachings, had clung to them like a life preserver, even more so after the bombing that killed his family. Even after being forced from his homeland of Syria by dissidents. He had some trouble, however, believing what Imam Khalil had told him only a few days ago.

"You are blessed," said Khalil. "Look at me, Omar." With much difficulty, Omar lifted his gaze to meet Khalil's brown eyes, soft and friendly yet somehow intense. "You are the Mahdi, the last of the Imam. The Redeemer that will rid the world of its sinners. You are a savior, Omar. Do you understand?"

"Yes, Imam."

"And do you *believe* it, Omar?"

The boy was not sure he did. He did not feel special, or important, or blessed by Allah, but still he answered, "Yes, Imam. I believe it."

"Allah has spoken to me," Khalil said softly, "and he has told me what we must do. Do you remember what you are supposed to do?"

Omar nodded. His mission was quite simple, though Khalil had made sure that the boy had no misgivings about what it would mean for him.

"Good. Good." Khalil smiled wide. His teeth were perfectly white and shining in the bright sun. "Before we part, Omar, would you do me the honor of praying with me for a moment?"

Khalil held out his hand, and Omar took it. It was warm and smooth in his. The Imam closed his eyes and his lips moved with silent words.

"Imam?" said Omar in a near-whisper. "Should we not face Mecca?"

Again Khalil smiled broadly. "Not this day, Omar. The one true God grants me a request; today, I face *you*."

The two men stood there for a long moment, praying silently and facing each other. Omar felt the warm sunshine on his face and, for the silent minute that followed, he thought he felt something, as if the invisible fingers of God were caressing his cheek.

Khalil knelt slightly as they stood in the shadow of a small white airplane. The plane could fit only four people and had propellers over the wings. It was the closest Omar had ever been to one—other than the ride from Greece to Spain, which was the only time that Omar had ever been in a plane, either.

"Thank you for that." Khalil slipped his hand from the boy's. "I must go now, and you must as well. Allah is with you, Omar, peace be upon Him, and peace be upon you." The older man smiled once more at him, and then he turned and stepped up the short ramp onto the plane.

The engines started, whining at first and then rising to a roar. Omar took several steps back as the plane pulled forward down the small airstrip. He watched as it gathered speed, faster and faster, until it rose into the air and eventually disappeared.

Alone, Omar looked straight up, enjoying the sunshine on his face. It was a warm day, warmer than most this time of year. Then he started the four-mile hike that would take him into Barcelona. As he walked, he reached into his pocket, his fingers gently but protectively wrapping around the tiny glass vial there.

Omar could not help but wonder why Allah had not come to him directly. Instead, His message had been passed along through the Imam. *Would I have believed it?* Omar thought. *Or would I have thought it just a dream?* Imam Khalil was holy and wise, and he recognized the signs when they presented themselves. Omar was a youthful, naïve boy of only sixteen who knew little of the world, particularly the West. Perhaps he was not fit to hear the voice of God.

Khalil had given him a fistful of euros to take with him into Barcelona. "Take your time," the older man had said. "Enjoy a good meal. You deserve this."

Omar spoke no Spanish, and only a few rudimentary English phrases. Besides, he wasn't hungry, so instead of eating when he arrived in the city, he found a bench looking upon the city. He sat upon it, wondering why here, of all places.

Have faith, Imam Khalil would say. Omar decided he would.

To his left was the Hotel Barceló Raval, a strange round building adorned in purple and red lights, with well-dressed young people coming and going from its doors. He did not know it by its name; he knew only that it looked like a beacon, attracting opulent sinners as a flame attracts moths. It gave him strength to sit before it, reinforcing his belief so that he would be able to do what must come next.

Omar carefully took the glass vial from his pocket. It did not look like there was anything inside it, or perhaps whatever was in it was invisible, like air or gas. It didn't matter. He knew well what he was supposed to do with it. The first step was complete: enter the city. The second step he performed on the bench in the shadow of the Raval.

He pinched the conical glass tip of the vial between two fingers and, in a small but swift movement, snapped it off.

A tiny shard of glass stuck in his finger. He watched as a bead of blood formed, but resisted the urge to stick the finger in his mouth. Instead, he did as he was told to do—he put the vial to one nostril and inhaled deeply.

As soon as he did, a knot of panic gripped his gut. Khalil had not told him anything specific about what to expect after that. He had simply been told to wait a short while, so he waited and did his best to remain calm. He watched more people enter and leave the hotel, each dressed in lavish, ostentatious clothing. He was very much aware of his humble garb; his threadbare sweater, his patchy cheeks, his hair that was growing too long, unruly. He reminded himself that vanity was a sin.

Omar sat and he waited for something to happen, to feel it working its way inside him, whatever "it" was.

He felt nothing. There was no difference.

A full hour went by on the bench, and then at last he rose and walked at a leisurely pace northwestward, away from the purple cylindrical hotel and further into the city proper. He took the stairs down to the first subway station he found. He certainly could not read Spanish, but he didn't need to know where he was going.

He bought a ticket using the euros Khalil had given him and stood on the platform idly until a train came. Still he did not feel any different. Perhaps he had misjudged the nature of the delivery. Still, there was one last thing for him to do.

The doors whooshed open and he stepped inside, moving nearly elbow to elbow with the boarding crowd. The subway train was quite busy; all of the seats were taken, so Omar stood and held onto one of the metal bars that ran parallel to the train's length, just over his head.

His final instruction was the simplest of all, though also the most confusing to him. Khalil had told him to board a train and "ride it until you cannot anymore." That was all.

At the time Omar was unsure of what that meant. But as his head began to prickle with sweat, his body temperature rising, and nausea rose in his stomach, he began to have a suspicion.

As minutes ticked by and the train rocked and swayed over the rails, his symptoms grew worse. He felt as if he might vomit. The train lurched to a stop at the next station and, as people climbed aboard or disembarked, Omar dry-heaved violently. Passengers skirted away from him in disgust.

His stomach felt as if it had tied itself into a painful knot. Halfway to the next station he coughed into his hand. As he pulled it away, his trembling fingers were moist in dark, sticky blood.

A woman standing beside him noticed. She said something sharply in Spanish, speaking rapidly, her eyes wide in shock. She pointed at the doors and chattered away. Her voice grew distant as a high-pitched whine began in Omar's ears, but he could tell that she was demanding that he get off the train.

As the doors whooshed open once again, Omar stumbled out, nearly falling over on the platform.

Air. He needed fresh air.

Allah help me, he thought desperately as he staggered toward the stairs that would lead up to the street level. His vision grew blurry with tears, his eyes flooding involuntarily.

His insides screaming in pain, sticky blood on his fingers, Omar finally understood his role as the Mahdi. He was to deliver pestilence upon this world—starting by eliminating his own sins.

"*¡Perdón!*"

Marta Medellín scoffed as the young man bumped into her roughly. He appeared to have little to no regard for others on the street. As he approached, dead-eyed and shuffling, his left shoulder dipped and collided with hers, and she hissed out a harsh, "Excuse me!" in Spanish. Yet he paid her no mind and continued on.

Having raised two boys herself, Marta was no stranger to calling out rude behavior. The way this boy staggered suggested he might have been drunk, and yet he looked to be barely an adult! *Shameful,* she thought.

Ordinarily she would not have given the rude youth a second glance—he didn't deserve her attention, bumping into her like that and not apologizing—but then she heard a cough; a deep, chest-rattling, hawking hem of a cough that, to someone in her position, drew immediate and acute notice.

Marta turned at the sound of it just in time to see his legs give out. He collapsed onto the pavement as passersby cried out in surprise or jumped back. She, on the other hand, rushed over and knelt at the boy's side.

"*Señor, ¿puedes escucharme?*" Sir, can you hear me? His breathing was shallow, coming rapidly through his open mouth. His face was ashen and his eyes half-closed. She checked his pupils—fully dilated. His forehead was burning up; his temperature must have been at least a hundred and two, maybe higher.

Several people had paused, gathered in a semicircle to see what was going on. "Someone call an ambulance!" Marta demanded in Spanish. Hospital de l'Esperanca was very close. She knew the EMTs could be there in less than two minutes. She shrugged out of her thin fleece jacket, balled it, and placed it under the boy's feet to promote circulation and hinder shock.

"Sir," she said again, "can you hear me?" He said nothing. He was younger than she had first guessed, a teenager at best, too skinny, practically swimming in an oversized sweater. But he did not seem feeble enough to be incapacitated by an ordinary disease. *Could be the flu,* she thought. It hit harder in some than others, even otherwise healthy men and women.

She put her hand in his. It felt damp and clammy. "Please squeeze my hand if you understand me." In response, the boy turned his head to the side and let loose another violent, racking cough.

"Sir, I need to know if you have any preexisting conditions, or if you are taking any medications," she said as clearly as she could. At the same time she checked his wrists and neck for a medical bracelet or necklace and found none.

He murmured something softly, something that Marta could not hear. She bent over, close to his mouth, as he said it again.

"Imam…" said the boy in barely above a whisper. "Imam Mahdi…"

"I'm sorry, I don't understand," she told him. "Is that your name? Do you speak Spanish?"

Sirens screamed down the block and traffic parted as the ambulance approached. Marta stood as two men jumped out of the vehicle. One of them prepped a gurney while the other hurried over, seemingly surprised to see her.

"Marta?" he said. "You made the call?"

"He collapsed right next to me on the street, Ernesto. He's burning up, barely responsive. We need to get him to the ER." The EMT, Ernesto, knelt beside the boy and checked his vitals. "BPM is around one-ten," Marta told him. "Airways unobstructed. Pupils dilated, temperature is at least one-oh-two."

Ernesto attempted to get a response out of the young man, but he too was unsuccessful. He and the younger EMT, Nicolás, strapped him to the stretcher and secured it into the back of the waiting ambulance.

"Marta, need a lift?" Nicolás asked as he headed for the driver's seat.

"Thanks." She climbed into the back with Ernesto. Ordinarily that would be frowned upon, but as an emergency room nurse she was in a position to assist if necessary. "Let's get him on a fluid bolus right away. Do you have antivirals handy?"

Ernesto shot her a grin as he prepped an IV line. "Did you want to take this one?"

She smirked back at him. "I'm sorry. It's habit. Please, go ahead."

The sirens came alive again, shrieking their warning as they roared toward the ER entrance of Hospital de l'Esperanca. Ernesto pushed fluids as Marta peered into the boy's face. Whatever he was in the grips of had his face contorted, every line and wrinkle showing—a sign of pain. As his muscles slackened and his face smoothed, it was all the more apparent that he was just a child.

"What do you think?" Ernesto asked.

She shook her head. "At first I thought flu, but now...it may have gone ignored and progressed to pneumonia. He was coughing before, a deep, awful cough. There is certainly some fluid in his lungs—"

Suddenly the boy coughed again, a single sharp bark that sprayed spittle over Marta's face. Her hand instinctively reached to wipe it.

Flecks of red smeared on her fingertips.

"*Dios mio,*" she murmured. "He has blood in his lungs. Call ahead, let them know."

The ambulance screeched to a halt outside the ER and the rear doors were immediately pulled open by a pair of nurses, both surprised to see Marta clambering out. "Take him in, I'll be right there." She stepped aside and let them work; policy was still policy, and she was not yet on the clock.

She took her balled-up fleece jacket and wiped her face thoroughly. She was fully vaccinated, by mandate, so she doubted she needed to worry. Even so, it wouldn't hurt to get a booster once the boy's illness was identified.

Marta frowned. The parking lot seemed busier than usual, more active. To her left, a middle-aged man was approaching, supporting a woman who seemed barely able to walk. Her face was ashen, her eyes barely open. The man, presumably her husband, spotted Marta standing there in her scrubs and badge, and called to her.

"*Ayudame,*" he pleaded. "*Por favor.*" Help me. Please.

She rushed toward him, and then leapt back with a cry as an oncoming car sped past, screeching to a halt beside the parked ambulance.

What is going on? she thought desperately.

She heard another screech of tires, and then a loud, startling crunch—a car entering the ER lot had hit another, slamming into its rear bumper as they both raced toward the hospital.

Marta paused and scanned the parking lot. Cars were pouring in. People shuffled across the pavement, coughing and moaning in pain. An elderly man, not twenty meters from her, wiped blood from his lips.

"My God," she said again. Her fingers absently touched her face. It was clean of the boy's blood, but that was the least of her concerns right now. She knew what this was.

This was an outbreak.

CHAPTER EIGHT

Deputy Director Shawn Cartwright glanced at his wristwatch as he strode quickly along the carpeted West Wing corridor. It was just after five o'clock; less than twenty minutes earlier he had been sitting at his desk at Langley, finishing some paperwork and hoping he might make it home in time for dinner for once.

Then he received the urgent call, and then came the police escort, and then the White House.

Walking along a pace in front of him was Director Mullen, head of the Central Intelligence Agency. Mullen was fifty-six, his shining bald head ringed with a ridge of gray hair. Ordinarily the director was very good at obscuring his mood, but this afternoon he seemed keen not to waste any time on pretense. His posture was rigid and his gait quicker than Cartwright would have imagined it could be.

The black high heels clacking against the floor behind him belonged to Assistant Director Ashleigh Riker, a former intelligence officer who had worked her way up the chain. Mullen had brought her along because she was being vetted for the position of deputy director, specifically to head up Special Operations Group—an idea that Cartwright was very keen to enact, since Spec Ops had been temporarily absorbed into his jurisdiction, Special Activities Division, ever since the former deputy director, Steve Bolton, had been outed as a traitor. He had also been missing for the past month. Cartwright presumed—no, he *hoped*—Bolton was dead. He deserved nothing less for what he had done.

Cartwright had no idea what this emergency meeting was about, but he was smart enough not to ask. He knew he wouldn't be told anything outside of the Situation Room.

The three CIA superiors paused outside a pair of oak double doors, guarded by two stoic Secret Service members in sunglasses who checked their credentials before granting them access.

As they did, Cartwright leaned toward Riker and said in a whisper, "Mouth shut and ears open. You're about to meet a whole lot of important people."

She nodded as Mullen led the way into the John F. Kennedy Conference Room, a five-thousand-square-foot center of command and intelligence in the basement of the White House's West Wing, known more commonly as the Situation Room.

Seated around the twelve-person conference table were several faces familiar to Cartwright—White House Chief of Staff Peter Holmes, Press Secretary Christine Cleary, Secretary of Defense Quentin Rigby, and the Director of National Intelligence John Hillis. There were a few others that Cartwright didn't immediately recognize, likely National Security Council members. Regardless, the very presence of those he knew lent to the potential gravity of whatever situation they were about to be told.

At the head of the long, dark table was a man whom Cartwright had met on a handful of occasions before, and not one of them ever pleasant. At forty-six years old, President of the Unites States Eli Pierson was fairly young for his office, with a head of thick brown hair that had not yet been grayed or thinned by his three years in office. President Pierson was not a career politician, but rather a business magnate who had been elected on a platform of significant trade reform and a viable plan for sustaining the United States' nonrenewable resources.

"Mr. President." Mullen briefly shook hands with Pierson, who did not rise from his chair.

"Sir." Cartwright greeted him in turn, as did Riker.

"Have a seat," said the president. "Thank you all for coming so quickly. As this is an urgent matter, I'm going to turn it directly over to Director Hillis for briefing."

"Thank you, sir." DNI Hillis rose and buttoned the top button of his dark blue suit jacket. He was an older man, in his mid-sixties, and Cartwright definitely noticed that his usually sharp eyes looked weary. Hillis pressed a button on a small black remote and the widescreen monitor mounted on the furthest wall of the Situation Room flickered to life, showing an office elsewhere with two men seated side by side, patched into the briefing via satellite. On the wall behind them was the blue and white logo of the CDC, the Centers for Disease Control and Prevention in Atlanta, Georgia.

A slight shiver ran up Cartwright's spine. The involvement of the CDC could mean only one thing—a biological agent. *But where? I haven't heard anything.*

"Ladies and gentlemen," Hillis began, "at approximately oh-two-hundred local time, a viral outbreak occurred in Barcelona, Spain, which is ongoing as we speak. The World Health Organization is on-site and working to contain the outbreak. The first known case, or what the CDC would refer to as 'patient zero,' was admitted to Hospital de l'Esperanca about"—he glanced at his wristwatch—"three hours and fifteen minutes ago. As of about twenty minutes ago, the entire city is undergoing lockdown. All airports are closed; all roadways are being blockaded. Federal law enforcement in Spain is under pressure from the European Union to temporarily close their borders."

"Is this an isolated event?" asked President Pierson.

"So far, yes sir," Hillis replied. "No other reports have come in from anywhere except Barcelona."

General Rigby cleared his throat. "Was this an attack?" Cartwright had no doubt that was the question on everyone's mind. It was certainly on his.

"Details are unclear at the moment," Hillis told the room. He hesitated a moment before continuing, "However, the speed with which the infection spread, and the concentration in a major metropolitan area, suggests that this is not a natural occurrence."

Cartwright was beginning to see what the CIA's involvement in the matter would be.

"Sir?" Riker raised her hand. "Assistant Director Ashleigh Riker, CIA. Do we know what it is?"

Cartwright narrowed his eyes at her. Hadn't he just told her to keep her mouth shut? She was the lowest rung on this ladder by far. Riker had a reputation for being smart as a whip and taking no grief from anyone, the latter of which she honed by virtue of being a woman in a traditionally male environment—which Cartwright respected, and he spoke highly of her whenever he had the opportunity, but this was not the time for posturing.

"I'll let our friends at the CDC answer that, Ms. Riker." Hillis gestured toward the monitor and the two men tuning in via satellite from Atlanta.

The older of the pair wore a dark suit under his salt-and-pepper hair. "For those that don't know, I'm Dr. Thomas Fitzgerald, Director of the CDC. With me is Dr. Edwin Barnard, our lead virologist and expert in toxicology."

Dr. Barnard nodded once. He wore a beige suit and his black hair was long, slicked back over his head and tied in the back in a stubby ponytail. Upon his nose was a pair of round, silver-rimmed eyeglasses and Cartwright thought he was in dire need of a shave.

Dr. Barnard adjusted his eyeglasses and cleared his throat. "I'll begin with the only good news we have. The WHO believes it can contain the outbreak. They are establishing makeshift hospitals for anyone experiencing symptoms of the disease. As of the last report, just before this meeting, we have one hundred and sixty-seven confirmed cases.

"The lab at l'Esperanca has done some imaging and sent them to the WHO, with whom we have been in constant contact. I've had the chance to thoroughly review them myself, as well as some video of the virus's effects. Here, take a look for yourself." Dr. Barnard tapped a few keys, and their perspective shifted from the two men in the office to a grainy, shaky video that appeared to have been taken with a cell phone.

In the video, doctors tended to a man lying on a gurney, the color drained from his face, as he suffered through a seizure. As his limbs fell still and the doctors eased their grip, the patient turned his head to the side and vomited a liberal amount of dark blood onto the floor.

The press secretary gasped in shock. Cartwright's own stomach turned at the sight. *Jesus*, he thought. *He could have warned us.*

"Apologies for the graphic nature," Barnard said flatly as he switched off the video. "But I have little doubt about what we're seeing here. Symptoms and cursory imaging are aligned with that of a mutated strand of *variola major*."

"Smallpox," Riker murmured.

Cartwright raised an eyebrow. *How did she know that?*

"Have there been any fatalities so far, Doctor?" President Pierson asked.

"Only one, Mr. President—our patient zero, a teenager."

"So the virus is fatal?" the Secretary of Defense asked.

"I'm afraid it's not quite that black-and-white, General." Barnard pushed his eyeglasses up the ridge of his nose. "It's too early to know the level of lethality, but we can definitely say that the virulence is much higher than that of naturally occurring smallpox."

"But smallpox was eradicated." Peter Holmes, the chief of staff, finally spoke up. Cartwright had always thought of him as something of a soft touch compared to Pierson's no-nonsense tactics and straight-shooting. "Wasn't it? Like polio, or Spanish flu."

"Yes, Mr. Holmes, the WHO declared smallpox eradicated in 1980," Barnard explained. "Since then there have been a few natural cases, but nothing we would consider outbreak level... until today."

"What about vaccines?" Holmes pushed. "Surely there must be some preventative measure—"

"Modern vaccines would be completely ineffective against this strain," Barnard interrupted. "This is unlike anything we've ever seen before. Which brings us to the crux of the matter: As I mentioned, this strain has been mutated—not by nature, but by human hands. It is a process known as mutagenesis, in which the RNA sequence of the virus is purposely altered as a means to an end. In this case, we're looking at something that is much more virulent than ordinary smallpox, with effects that reflect the more severe hemorrhagic smallpox—which, naturally occurring, is quite rare, only about two percent of cases."

A headache was beginning to form in Cartwright's skull. If what Dr. Barnard was saying was correct, someone had done this on purpose—not just mutated the virus, but released it as well, which meant that the deputy director would soon be dispatching agents in search of a biological weapon.

General Rigby's cell phone rang and he answered it, speaking in a hushed tone.

"So far no one has come forward to claim responsibility for this," said Hillis. "Dr. Barnard, Dr. Fitzgerald—should we assume that the perpetrators have more of this virus?"

The two doctors exchanged an uneasy glance. Dr. Fitzgerald, the head of the CDC, cleared his throat. "Yes," he said hesitantly. "The samples were stolen from a WHO excavation site in Siberia. We have to assume they may have *much* more."

"Can a vaccine be developed?" asked President Pierson.

Dr. Fitzgerald adjusted his tie nervously. "Well…yes, Mr. President. But it would take some time, and we would require samples of the virus. But while that is entirely possible, the mass production and dissemination to the entire developed world would be an enormous undertaking. It took the WHO years to eradicate smallpox. I don't believe we have that kind of time."

Cartwright understood immediately what the doctor was suggesting. If whoever did this had more, then Barcelona was only the beginning, and without more information they couldn't begin to guess where they may strike next. *Weaponized smallpox*, he thought. *What a goddamn nightmare.*

General Rigby ended his call and turned to the president. "Sir, I've just received word that Spain is barring all international travel, under orders from the EU. France, Andorra, Portugal, and Morocco are temporarily closing their borders. The European Commission is currently convening to decide if the outbreak warrants the closure of all airports and seaports." The Secretary of Defense paused for a brief moment before adding, "Until we know more, I would suggest we do the same."

"Jesus," murmured the chief of staff. "We can't afford to incite a panic—"

"And we can't afford to assume the US is *not* a target," DNI Hillis interjected. "Barcelona could be a shell game, and we have very little information."

"Do you have any idea how much closing international trade and travel would cost us, even for a day?" Holmes fired back. "We're already teetering on another recession. We should wait until we have more information before we make such a brash decision—"

"Mr. Holmes, I think you're mistaking brashness for cautiousness," Hillis said heatedly. "If something like we're seeing in Barcelona were to strike any major US city, the economy would be fairly low on the list of concerns…"

"*Gentlemen.*" President Pierson stood and the bickering men fell silent. Cartwright had to admit, though he didn't care much for Pierson's politics, the man could command a room. "We have to keep in mind that as a world power, the decision we make right now is going to affect other nations. We will be setting an example that others will likely imitate." He rubbed his chin as he thought for a moment. "For now, we follow suit with the European Union's edict. Close travel from Spain and all neighboring countries. If the situation escalates and the EU decides to close all international ports of entry… we will too." The president directed his last comment directly to his chief of staff.

Holmes folded his arms, but said nothing.

"Dr. Fitzpatrick." Pierson addressed the screen at the far end of the room opposite him. "The CDC has plans prepared for situations like this. What measures can we take to minimize disruption of international trade and travel?"

"Uh, well." The doctor cleared his throat. "We can work with the WHO to establish exit screenings of all passengers bound for the US. Enhanced risk assessment at all ports of entry, heightened security, and education material for TSA, law enforcement, and emergency services."

"Good," Pierson replied with a single nod. "Get on it."

"Sir, perhaps we should use the NTAS..." Hillis suggested.

"No," Pierson said sharply. The National Terrorist Advisory System, Cartwright knew, was Homeland Security's replacement for the former color-coded terror alert levels. "I don't want the word 'terror' mentioned at all, anywhere. Does everyone understand that?" The president glanced around the Situation Room, meeting each pair of eyes as murmurs of assent rose.

"As far as the American public is concerned, a dangerous viral outbreak occurred in Europe, and we are simply protecting our nation from potential exposure," the president continued. He turned to Press Secretary Cleary. "Christine, get on the podium and tell the press exactly that. If any rumor mills start up, you quash it. If any reports come out of Europe about this being an attack, our position is that we don't have enough information to confirm it."

"Yes sir." She nodded.

"We'll put the National Guard on standby," General Rigby offered. "And send out a bulletin to medical staff, law enforcement, and emergency services. Let them know how to recognize the symptoms, and what to do in the event that anyone is believed to be infected."

"That sounds like we'd be inviting a thousand cases of Munchausen's," Chief of Staff Holmes muttered.

"Maybe so," the general countered, "but we need to consider the possibility that the virus is already here."

"Rigby is right," Pierson agreed. "Dr. Fitzgerald?"

"The only solution at the moment would be immediate quarantine," the head of the CDC said without hesitation, "along with anyone that they may have come in contact with."

"And a containment plan?"

"The CDC is actively working on one," Fitzgerald replied. "But I should advise you, Mr. President, that if a major metropolitan area is hit, like New York or Boston, I just don't know that we would have—"

Pierson held up a hand sharply and silenced the doctor. "I really don't want to hear the words 'don't know' again in this conversation. We need answers. Figure it out." At long last he turned to the three CIA members seated to his left. "Director Mullen, I don't think I need to tell you your role in this."

"If this was an attack, we'll find them," Mullen confirmed.

"Before it happens again," the president added sternly.

"We need this kept tight, quiet, and quick," said General Rigby. "Interpol is already on this, as is Spain's National Police, but we can't assume their success and we have to protect American interests. You have people at the ready for that?"

Mullen turned to Cartwright expectantly; as the head of Special Activities Division, he was in the direct position to assign agents to covert international ops. But before the deputy director could say anything, Riker spoke up.

"We do," she said clearly. "We have a specialist."

Cartwright shot her a glare. Not only was it not her place to suggest anyone for this case, but he knew precisely who she meant as soon as she said it. But Riker did not return his gaze.

"Director Mullen," Dr. Fitzgerald spoke up, "given the extremely sensitive nature of the virus and the mutation, the CDC would like to request that Dr. Barnard accompany your agents. His expertise includes not only viruses, but biological weapons as well."

"With all due respect, Dr. Fitzgerald, I think it would be unwise to send a civilian along on this op," said Mullen.

"I have field experience," Barnard interjected. "I spent two years assisting US Special Forces in identifying bioterrorism agents in Afghanistan and Iran."

Cartwright almost scoffed. He had difficulty believing the owlish, long-haired Barnard had much of what anyone would call "field experience." He shot Mullen a dubious glance, but the director ignored it.

"Fine," Mullen agreed. "If you believe you can pull your own weight, get on the first plane to Dulles. We'll send a car."

President Pierson stood and buttoned his jacket. "All right then. We know our position and we know what we need to do. Get to it. Dismissed."

As soon as Cartwright was in the West Wing corridor outside the Situation Room, he spun on Riker. "Strange," he said quietly, "I'm fairly certain the agents of Special Activities Division are *my* people."

"You know there's no one better for this," she shot back. "We need someone smart enough to handle this right, brazen enough to get the job done … and reckless enough to take it on in the first place."

"It's been a month and he hasn't given us an answer about his reinstatement. I don't think he has any intention of coming back."

"Well then," said Riker, "maybe it's time we give him an ultimatum."

"Good luck," Cartwright remarked. "He has a history of being somewhat headstrong."

"From what I understand," said Riker, "he doesn't know a whole lot about his own history…"

"That's enough out of both of you," Director Mullen said sternly, coming up from behind Riker. "Were we not just in the same room? Do you understand what's happening out there—what could happen here?"

"Yes sir," Cartwright muttered.

"Riker, consider this your proving grounds," said the director. "You'll work directly with Cartwright to oversee the op."

"Mullen." Director of National Intelligence Hillis strode up to the trio. "We've gotten word that Interpol has established a temporary command center near Barcelona. They're working with the WHO to try to back-trace the virus to a source. Have your agents rendezvous there; hopefully by then they've got some good news for us."

"Yes sir." Mullen turned back to Cartwright. "Make the calls. We brief at Langley as soon as humanly possible."

The deputy director nodded. He didn't want to admit it out loud, but Riker was right; there was no one better for the job, but he was not at all looking forward to making the call.

But push had come to shove, and it was time to force Agent Zero to make a choice.

Chapter Nine

After the near-anxiety attack during his lecture, Reid called it an early day. He texted Maya that he wasn't feeling well and had headed home; she replied that she would be going to the library after classes were out. He wasn't far from the campus, so he could pick her up when she was ready. Sara was in an after-school art club, so currently he was alone in the house, upstairs in his office, and sitting on the floor with a box before him.

Alone with his thoughts and a cardboard box, Reid let his mind return to the question that Maya had asked him earlier. *"Did Mom know?"*

The formerly repressed memory of Kate's anger and the discovered gun had him doubting his answer. *What if she had?* he thought. What if Kate had found the gun and the argument in his memory was the catalyst to his eventual confession of his real vocation? On the other hand, though, he had trouble believing that Kate would have been okay with that sort of revelation. He remembered her right up to the time of her death; they had been happy and in love, raising their two girls together. He doubted it would have been so easy if she knew the truth, that her husband and the father of her children had been keeping such a dangerous secret from them.

He couldn't remember, and anyone he could have asked about the truth was dead.

Reid opened the box that sat in front of him on the floor. Inside this box was an envelope, and within that was a photo and a letter. The photo was of him and Alan Reidigger, standing before the Fontana delle Tartarughe in Rome, Italy. His arm was around

Alan's shoulders, and they were both smiling, maybe a moment or two from bursting into laughter.

Of course, he didn't remember this photo being taken. He didn't remember ever laughing with Alan Reidigger, the man who had been sent by the CIA to kill him, his best friend. Instead, Reidigger had sought a solution—an experimental memory suppressor that the CIA had been secretly developing.

The accompanying letter was handwritten in Alan's neat, legible print. Reid didn't need to read it again. Even though he hadn't looked at it in three weeks now, he had it nearly memorized. Its words crossed his mind often, whenever he stopped doing anything for more than a few minutes and allowed himself to dwell on his situation.

In the letter Alan disclosed the name of the neurosurgeon who had implanted the memory suppressor, Dr. Guyer in Zurich, Switzerland. Alan believed that the doctor could bring back everything, all of Reid's memories, if he wanted to.

Many times, more times than he could recall or even count, he had thought about this mysterious Guyer. Reidigger had chosen the doctor himself—obviously he was someone whom Alan trusted to open up Reid's head and mess around inside it. He couldn't be hard to find; even a simple internet search would likely yield some result, a phone number or an email address. But that was just the first step of many, and even taking that first step felt like a leap into the void. There would be no going back.

His cell phone rang, startling him in the otherwise silent office. He chuckled at himself for his jumpiness and checked the screen. The caller was unknown. He let it go to voicemail.

A moment later his phone chimed with a text message. Again it was an unknown sender. The message simply said: *Answer the phone, Zero.*

Reid groaned. He knew exactly who it would be when the phone rang a second time. It seemed that someone had gotten tired of waiting for his answer.

"Hello, Cartwright," he said flatly as he answered the call.

"Zero," said the deputy director by way of greeting. His voice was low, lacking any sense of joviality. "You should know you're on speakerphone. I'm here with Assistant Director Ashleigh Riker. She'll be heading up Special Operations Group."

"Congratulations, I suppose." Reid was immediately suspicious. It would be one thing if Cartwright was calling for his answer. It was a different story with another director on the line. He waited for the other shoe to drop.

"Thank you," said Riker. "Though I wish we were being introduced under better circumstances."

Reid held back an audible groan. Something was definitely amiss. "What do you want?"

"Straight to the point," said Cartwright. "Good old Zero." He sighed. "There's a crisis situation. Come to Langley. Let's talk."

"We can talk now," said Reid. He knew that going to CIA headquarters would mean giving them leverage to convince him to do whatever it was they were going to ask of him.

"I'd rather not do this over the phone," said Cartwright. "There are things you should see."

"What sort of things?" Reid asked. "What kind of situation?"

"Agent, you know we wouldn't have called if this wasn't important," said Riker. "We understand your position, and your predicament—"

"Do you?" Reid said bitterly. "I'm not sure you know much at all about my 'predicament,' Assistant Director."

"…And that's why we haven't bothered you for your answer yet," Riker finished. "But it's been a month. So we need you to come in now, or tell us you're not coming back at all."

"Look, Kent, people are going to die," Cartwright said somberly. "If you don't believe me, get online and look at what's happening in Barcelona. We have reason to believe it may be just the tip of this iceberg."

Reid frowned. He hadn't been in front of a computer all day; he had no idea what was happening in Spain. Had there been some sort of attack?

"Fine," he said finally. "I'll come. I'll listen. But I'm not making any promises."

"That's all I'm asking," said Cartwright. "Be here as soon as you can. We're briefing in forty-five minutes." He hung up.

Reid sighed in defeat. Langley was only a thirty-minute drive; he had some time to look into whatever was happening in Barcelona, and…

He looked up and blinked in surprise to see his elder daughter standing in the doorway.

"Maya! When did you get home?"

She stared at the floor, avoiding his gaze. "Few minutes ago," she said. "I finished early and took a bus."

"Jeez, Maya, you should have let me come get you—"

"That was them, wasn't it?" she interrupted.

He frowned. "How much of that did you hear?"

"Enough."

"That was nothing," he said quickly. "It was just…" *No more lies*, he reminded himself. He wasn't going to offer up information, but if she asked, he wasn't going to lie to her anymore. "Yeah," he admitted quietly. "That was them."

"You're going, aren't you?"

"Just to Langley. It doesn't mean I'm taking an assignment."

"But you will. You're not the kind of person who stands by if you could help."

Reid didn't know what to say to that. He rose and hugged her tightly, and she squeezed him, and though she didn't look up at him he could have sworn he heard her sniff once. He knew that she was scared for him, even if she thought she had to be strong and not show it.

When he released her, Maya wiped at her eyes before he could see if there were tears in them or not. "Does this have anything to do with what's going on in Spain?" she asked.

Reid was taken aback that she was more informed than he was—but then again, she was a child of the tech generation. "What's going on over there?"

"They're not entirely sure yet," she told him. "Or they're not saying. I heard some kids in the library talking about it. Here, take a look." She pulled out her cell phone and brought up a video. "This was taken less than two hours ago."

Maya held her phone up sideways as a news broadcast played. The sound was muted as a female reporter stood in front of what appeared to be a hospital. Behind her, a small crowd had gathered at the entrance. People in bright yellow hazmat suits scurried about, some of them on crowd control while others erected some kind of medical tent in the parking lot.

As Reid watched, a member of the crowd staggered and keeled over, collapsing right there outside the hospital. Two yellow-clad workers rushed over and loaded the man onto a wheeled gurney while other would-be patients shoved past them, trying to get into the ER.

Reid's mouth fell open slightly. *It looks like a war zone.* The news broadcast played like something out of a movie, something too horrific to possibly be reality.

On the video, the reporter's eyes suddenly widened in shock as she pointed at something out of frame. The cameraman panned just in time to see a sedan T-bone their news van, spraying broken glass in every direction.

"Oh my god," Reid murmured. "What is it?"

"It's some kind of viral outbreak," Maya said. "But it doesn't seem like anyone knows what yet." She glanced up at him. "You didn't answer me. Is this what they need you for?"

Reid barely heard her question. *A biological weapon,* he thought. *Spreading fast in a civilian population.* No natural disease would just blindside a major city like that, and it would be far too much of a coincidence that the call from Cartwright came mere hours after the infection began.

Moreover, he knew that his daughter was right. Before he even got to Langley—before he even got in his car—he already knew that if his help was needed, he wouldn't be able to stand idly by, even if it meant putting himself directly in harm's way.

CHAPTER TEN

Reid entered the George Bush Center for Intelligence, the headquarters of the CIA in the unincorporated community of Langley, Virginia, and stood for a moment on the marble floor. Beneath his feet was a large circular emblem, a shield and eagle in gray and white, surrounded by the words "Central Intelligence Agency, United States of America."

No specific memory manifested, but he had an acute feeling of familiarity. He had been here many times before. His feet seemed to know precisely where to go of their own volition, even if his brain hadn't the foggiest idea.

He didn't even need the comfortable, well-acquainted sensation to know he'd been here. When he pulled up to the gate, the security officer took one look at him, nodded, and granted him access. No badge, no identification needed.

"Thanks, Mel," Reid had said instinctively as the guard tipped his hat. Reid surprised himself; he knew the guard's name despite not recalling ever having met him before.

At the arcing semicircle of a front desk, a young man in a blue suit sat answering phones and checking badges. *Brent*, Reid's brain told him. *Twenty-five years old. Wants to be a field agent but suffers from minor dyslexia and colorblindness.*

"Good morning, Brent," Reid said, testing his recovering memory. Aside from the bizarre recollection of the argument with Kate, he hadn't recouped much as of late.

"Agent Steele!" The young man smiled broadly, seeming genuinely pleased to see him. "Go right on through. You're expected."

"Thank you." Reid nodded to him and continued past the desk. The further he went the more memories flooded back—meetings, debriefings, pleasant days and dark times. He realized suddenly that he had no idea just how long he had been a CIA agent. Years, it seemed, but he had no definitive notion. He wondered again if Kate knew about his past. It was gnawing at him, not knowing his own reality.

Reid turned a corner and abruptly paused. So did the other man, who had been approaching from the opposite direction at the same time.

Shawn Cartwright smirked with one side of his mouth. "Gotta be honest," he said, "I wasn't sure you'd actually come." He held out his hand and Reid shook it.

Cartwright was young for his position, only forty-four, though his hair was turning gray at the temples. Even so he had a smile and demeanor that would have been just as well suited for politics as espionage—though Reid suspected that diplomacy was certainly part of the deputy director's job description.

"I'd ask about the kids, but we're going to have to skip the usual pleasantries," Cartwright told him. "They're waiting, and we don't have much time." He led the way hastily down the corridor toward a conference room. Reid didn't bother asking who was waiting. He would find out in a moment.

"I looked into Barcelona," Reid said instead as they walked. "We know what it is, don't we?"

"We," Cartwright repeated thoughtfully. "Almost sounds like you're putting your hand in already, Zero."

"That doesn't answer my question."

Cartwright shrugged. "I know."

The two men entered a small conference room with an eight-seat oblong table. The first thing Reid noticed, with some dismay, was that Maria was not among them. He assumed she was on the trail of Rais—hopefully closing in, if she hadn't caught up with him already.

Of those present, only one was a familiar face. Agent Watson was a tall African-American field agent with whom Reid had shared very few words, but for whom he had a great deal of respect. Back in February, it was Watson who had rescued his girls from a pair of pursuing terrorists on a New Jersey boardwalk.

There were two people he did not know, but Cartwright quickly made introductions.

"Kent, this is Ashleigh Riker, interim head of Spec Ops." The woman rose from her seat and shook his hand. Reid glanced over her, noting details—*mid-forties, natural brunette, five-eight (five-six without the heels). Married; there's slight discoloration on her ring finger, though she doesn't wear it to work. She's a woman in power and wants people to know it. Doesn't wear perfume.*

Reid almost smiled. Not five minutes back in CIA headquarters and he was already settling back into Kent Steele mode. Then he noticed that she was doing the same—sizing him up, noting details. He wondered if she had been a field agent previously.

Cartwright gestured toward the other unknown in the room. "And this is Doctor—"

The man stood quickly, interrupting Cartwright. "Dr. Edwin Barnard, virologist and bioterrorism expert with the CDC," the man rattled off. He shook Reid's hand limply and did not smile. The doctor looked like he didn't get out of the lab often. His black hair was pulled tight off his forehead and collected into a thin ponytail at the back of his head. He wore round, silver glasses and his chin was stubbled in dark hair. But the most important detail Reid noted was that the doctor clearly seemed as if he was in a rush.

Virologist and bioterrorism expert, Reid thought. Barnard's position confirmed what he had already conceived earlier; the events transpiring in Barcelona were an attack.

"All right," said Cartwright, "you've all seen what's going on in Spain, so you know why we're here. Doctor, you want to give us a quick rundown?"

"By all means." Barnard stood and cleared his throat as Reid took a seat beside Watson, nodding to the other agent. "The two agents are the only ones who are not fully aware of the current predicament, so I will try to make this as brief as possible." He took a breath and said, "An unknown perpetrator has infiltrated a research expedition in Siberia, murdered four scientists, and made off with a sample of a very old strain of smallpox unearthed in the tundra. This person, potentially with the aid of cohorts, then mutated the virus to reach a startlingly high virulence, and has now released it upon the city of Barcelona."

Reid blinked in shock. Any single part of Dr. Barnard's statement was jarring enough, but put together into such a rapid, rambling speech was downright bewildering. If Agent Watson was thinking the same, he didn't show it. He merely sat, staring straight ahead at the tabletop, with his hands in his lap.

"I'm sorry," said Reid. "But did you say smallpox? That's what's infecting people in Barcelona?"

Barnard nodded. "Indeed—well, in a manner of speaking. Initial symptoms are similar, but manifest much more quickly."

Reid balked. He was well aware of how horrifying of a disease smallpox was back in the days when it ran rampant among native populations. During the Franco-Prussian War in 1870, French soldiers triggered a five-year epidemic that claimed nearly half a million lives in Germany and other parts of Europe. He didn't want to imagine what a faster-moving, mutated strain could do.

"We have reason to believe that someone out there has more of this virus," Cartwright announced, "and until we know who it is, we have to assume that the next target could be anywhere—even American soil. This is an all-hands-on-deck situation. Interpol is already on the case in Europe. The FBI is working domestically. International travel to and from affected nations is closing as we speak, and every federal law enforcement agency in the developed world is getting the information that we already have. But we have a duty to protect not only ourselves but whoever else we can, and time is a factor. We're keeping this op small, we keep it tight, and we make it fast."

"What have we got to go on?" Reid asked. "Leads, intel…?"

"You'll be briefed on the plane." Cartwright avoided Reid's gaze. "We'd like to be wheels-up in thirty minutes."

"Thirty minutes?" Reid blurted out. He felt a familiar knot of dread tighten in his stomach. This was exactly what he had feared coming in here, that once they had him in a room they would corner him. But at the same time, he already knew that he wasn't going to be able to say no, and he would soon have to explain to the girls that he was leaving again.

"Give us the room a moment," said Cartwright to the other three present.

"Time is a factor here," Riker countered. "We can't afford indecisiveness right now—"

"Our fastest plane will still take five hours to get them to Europe," Cartwright interrupted. "I think you can give us one minute."

Riker's nostrils flared, but she didn't argue. Instead she stood forcefully and marched out of the conference room, her heels clacking against the floor. Watson and Dr. Barnard followed.

"Jesus, Cartwright," Reid groaned as soon as they were alone. "It's been a month, and now you give me thirty minutes?"

"No, Zero." Cartwright folded his arms, standing across the table from him. "I'm not giving you thirty minutes. I need an answer *now*, because a plane is leaving in thirty minutes, whether you're on it or not. You saw what's going on in Barcelona. People are dying. What if New York is next? Or DC? It could be if we do nothing. You want to walk away, go ahead. You have no obligation here."

Reid scoffed. Cartwright was calling his bluff. The deputy director knew damn well that Agent Zero couldn't walk away from this.

"I need you, Kent. This is a by-whatever-means-necessary situation, and you're my by-whatever-means-necessary guy. No one has a more creative interpretation of the phrase than you. This won't be like last time. You're not going to be running all over Europe alone. You'll have the full backing of the CIA and its resources. You'll have a direct line to me and Riker. You need something, you call it in. And you'll have Agent Watson."

"Where's Johansson?" Reid demanded. He didn't want to let on that he was aware of Maria's op or Rais's escape.

"We got a bead on an Amun assassin in Slovenia. She's on the trail. But we'll pull her in an instant if you need backup on this. And Thompson will take care of your girls. I'll put in the call and let him know. He can tell them that—"

"You talk to Thompson. I'll talk to my girls," Reid said quickly. He didn't want to disappear and have some third party being the ones to tell them he'd suddenly left again.

"Fine. But we need you. If this CDC doctor is right, a lot of people could die, and we have no idea where it could happen next."

Reid ran his hands through his hair and sighed. "We both know I can't say no to something like this. But I don't want this to mean I'm back. We still need to talk about that."

"Of course," Cartwright agreed. He started to turn toward the door but then thought of something. "Oh, and the doctor, Barnard, he's going with you."

Reid blinked. It was one thing to have a trained CIA agent at his side, but to tow around a scientist seemed downright perilous. "Do you really think that's wise?"

"It's nonnegotiable," said Cartwright simply. "He calls himself an expert, so use his expertise. Now grab Watson and go see Bixby."

"Who's Bixby?"

"Right, I guess you haven't seen him since the memory thing." Cartwright smirked. "Seems you'll be meeting all sorts of new people today." The deputy director pulled the door open and left him in the conference room alone.

Reid heaved a sigh into his hands. Just that morning he had been giving a lecture on biological warfare, and now he was back in the service of the CIA, racing against time to find a completely unknown person or persons who possessed a biological weapon of potential mass destruction.

CHAPTER ELEVEN

Immediately following the small conference, Reid quickly followed Agent Watson to a bank of elevators. Dr. Barnard had agreed to meet them at the plane; he had research equipment to gather. Once they were in the elevator car, Watson swiped his ID badge and pressed the down arrow.

Odd, thought Reid. *We're on the first floor.*

Watson was extremely quiet on the downward ride. The tall, stoic agent had barely said two words to him since he arrived.

Reid cleared his throat. "So. Looks like it's you and me."

"Mm-hmm." Watson stared straight ahead, his hands clasped in front of him.

"Have, uh, you and I ever done an op together?"

Watson shook his head slowly. "Not directly."

Reid frowned; that wasn't really much of an answer. The elevator dinged and the doors open onto a hall with cinderblock walls painted gray, windowless and lit with fluorescent lights. Definitely subterranean. Watson led the way.

"Hey," said Reid, "I don't think I got the chance to properly thank you, in person, for what you did for my girls."

"Just doing the job." Watson smiled, but somehow he managed to make it seem flat and empty; not sarcastic, but not exactly pleasant either.

Reid was puzzled. Had he done something to wrong Agent Watson in the past? Something he couldn't remember, perhaps? The man wasn't being outwardly hostile, but at the same time he was making no effort to be friendly.

Reid could hear machinery whirring from somewhere nearby as the two agents strode quickly down the corridor. *Pneumatic drill,* his brain told him. *You know that sound. It means someone is tinkering.*

Watson paused at a steel door and again slid his keycard badge to gain access. The door opened inward, and he gestured for Reid to enter first. "As far as most are concerned, this is Research and Development," Watson told him as the door closed behind them. "But around here we just call it 'the lab.' "

Reid blew out a breath as he entered "the lab," feeling very much as if he had just stepped onto a movie set. The walls and floor were stark white, shining as if recently polished. Overhead, powerful halogen bulbs burned bright as daylight. Arrays of machinery were arranged symmetrically in the long, almost warehouse-sized room in the pattern of an enormous H. Reid admitted that he wasn't the most tech-savvy, but he had no doubt that whatever he was looking at was not for public eyes, machines the likes of which he had never seen: sleek black stealth drones, AI-powered robotic arms welding parts onto targeting computers, and, in the far corner, two white-coated engineers worked on what appeared to be an advanced bomb-defusing robot.

As Reid glanced around, taking it all in, he got the same familiar sensation that he had felt when walking into CIA headquarters—he had been here before, plenty of times. The sights and scents were like returning to an elementary school classroom; he could barely remember it, but somehow he knew it, and even felt at ease there.

"Bixby?" Watson called out. "You down here?"

"Welcome, Agents!" called a cheerful male voice. "Cartwright called down just a couple of minutes ago, said it was urgent, and there'd be two suiting up, equipment for three, and, uh ..."

The man trailed off as he came around the corner from a branching room, drying his hands on a microfiber cloth. He was older, pushing sixty, but he looked healthy for his age. His gray hair was parted neatly and he wore black horn-rimmed glasses. He was well dressed in a white shirt, gray vest, and a red tie knotted at his throat. His sleeves were rolled up to the elbows and his forearms were dotted in grease marks.

"Well." His face broke out into a wide grin as his gaze locked on Reid. "I'll be damned. I heard the rumors, but…" He strode up to him and clapped a hand on his shoulder. "It's really good to see you, Zero."

A brief memory flashed across Reid's mind.

This man, Bixby, stands beside you as you prep for an op. An array of equipment lies out on the table before you. He tells you a joke as you check the magazine on a pistol.

"A guy walks into a gas station covered in blood. He pays for his fuel and starts to leave. The bewildered attendant calls out, 'Hey man, are you okay?' The guy smiles. 'Oh yeah, I'm fine. It's not my blood.'"

Bixby told me that joke, Reid thought. He knew this man; he was a CIA tech, one of the best and brightest. *You two used to exchange jokes.*

"It's…good to see you," Reid said. "I'm sorry. I don't remember everything…"

"Right. Yeah, of course." Bixby smiled pleasantly. "The memory suppressor."

Reid was surprised to hear the tech speak so cavalierly about it. "How do you know about that?"

"Oh. Well. I, uh, helped create it." Bixby fidgeted with his tie.

Reid blinked in astonishment. "You did?"

"Oh, yeah. I mean, it was a team effort. We never got the go-ahead from upstairs to go to human trials, but then I heard what happened to you and, I gotta say…" Bixby chuckled. "It's pretty exciting."

"Exciting." Reid scoffed. *I barely know who I am half the time.*

The older man pulled an LED penlight from his vest pocket and clicked it on. "You know, speaking of, I'd really love to get a look at the exit wound, if you don't mind…" He leaned in, shining the white light on the jagged scar at Reid's neck.

Reid's reaction was instinctive. He stepped back with his left foot as his hand came up and, in a single swift motion, snapped the penlight from Bixby's hand.

"I do mind," Reid told him.

"Whoa, hey. Sorry." Bixby put up both hands defensively.

Agent Watson took the opportunity to step in. "We're on a tight schedule here."

"Of course," Bixby piped up again. "I'm getting some gear together for you. I'll just be a moment. Why don't you two suit up, pack a bag."

Watson nodded and gestured for Reid to follow him. "He can be a bit eccentric," Watson said once they were out of earshot. "But he's the best engineer the agency has ever seen."

"Sure." Reid hadn't meant to come off as confrontational; it had been entirely instinct, but he didn't like the way that Bixby, one of the suppressor's creators, spoke about it as if it were "exciting." "What did he mean, pack a bag?"

"I'll show you." Watson quickly led him across the lab—*This must be what the inside of a space station looks like*, Reid thought—and through a doorway that opened into another chamber. The halogen bulbs overhead buzzed to life as soon as they entered. Inside was the size of Reid's living room, but it looked more like a giant walk-in closet.

"Wow." Reid was impressed. The walls were lined with rack upon rack of clothing items, from civilian wear to military uniforms from every country, cold-weather gear and scuba suits, jackets and boots and hats, both men's and women's wear in a variety of sizes. "This is . . . thorough."

"You'll want this side over here." Watson motioned to the eastern wall. "Civilian clothing, all reinforced. I'm guessing you're a medium? Thirty-four waist?"

"Thirty-two." Reid plucked a shirt from the rack, plaid with a collar, and rubbed the material between his fingers. It felt like an ordinary shirt. "Reinforced with what? Kevlar?"

Watson smirked. "We haven't used Kevlar in years. No, this is all graphene."

"Graphene," Reid repeated. *Composite carbon fiber mesh, the width of a hundred atoms. Imperceptible, but stronger than steel. Could stop a point-blank shot from a nine mil, so long as it's not hollow point. The impact will hurt like hell—maybe even crack a rib or two—but it won't penetrate.* As soon as he said the word aloud, the information was suddenly there, as if it had been waiting behind a door that had just been opened.

The two changed quickly and quietly. Watson chose a black T-shirt, a dark brown leather jacket, and jeans, while Reid opted for a gray polo and a light suede jacket. Then they each stuffed a black duffel bag with a couple changes of clothes. It was a silent process, and Reid took the time to digest everything that had happened in just the last fifteen minutes. He was leaving again, this time to hunt down a terrorist who might be the bearer of an impossibly deadly virus. It had all happened so quickly that it seemed surreal. He couldn't help but wonder if this was what his life was like before; getting a call, leaving at a moment's notice to track down and apprehend some threat to the nation or even the world.

It definitely felt familiar, however odd it might seem when he stopped to consider it.

One thing was certain. He didn't care much for the way that Cartwright and this new woman, Riker, had been so self-assured he would come back. They knew Kent Steele well, or at least his mindset; they didn't seem to have any doubt that they could get him on this op.

The more he thought about it, the more he felt like property.

Once they had packed their bags, they returned to the lab's floor where Bixby had laid out an array of implements for them.

"All right, gentlemen," he said, clapping his hands together once. "I understand there's a time crunch, so let's see what we got here. First up: cell phones." He handed them each what looked like an ordinary rectangular smartphone. "These are off-network; instead of relaying by cell tower, they're linked directly to US satellites. You can make a call or get a call anywhere, anytime, to anyone."

At the mention of a call, Reid thought of his girls at home, and how he needed to call them before he left. He hoped Thompson hadn't yet been alerted and gone to his house. He wanted them to hear it from him.

"Lithium-ion batteries are fully charged, so you shouldn't have to worry unless you're gone for more than a week," Bixby continued. "These are both preprogrammed with numbers to Langley, Zurich, and your fellow field agents, and outfitted with just the necessities—calling, texting, camera, GPS, and internet. There is a secure cloud-storage drive that is being uploaded with all intel on the case as we speak. Oh, and radio. Speaking of which, here." He held up something tiny, pinched between his index finger and thumb. It was nearly transparent and about the size of a kidney bean. "Earpieces," he explained. "Entirely plastic and almost invisible. These link to the phones—frequency is already dialed in, you just have to switch it on. You'll get a two-mile radius out of these, so the three of you can communicate freely." He frowned. "As long as there's not a mountain in the way or something."

Reid took one of the earpieces in the palm of his hand and gently pushed it into his ear. It was a bit uncomfortable at first, but once again he had the sensation that it wasn't his first time with a piece of plastic in his ear.

"Now these," said Bixby, "are really cool." He opened a black oblong case and took out a pair of black-framed sunglasses. "Remember a few years ago, the tech companies were pushing those 'smart glasses'? Never really caught on with the public, but we've kept at them. These link to the phone via Bluetooth, so as long as you're within twenty feet of your cell you can use these to take video, photos, and even send messages, all hands-free." He cleared his throat and added, "They're also sunglasses. If it's bright out."

Reid tucked the glasses case in his inside jacket pocket. It was beyond strange, being outfitted like this in a CIA basement by an eccentric older man who knew him better than he knew himself. He wondered how many times he had done this before.

"Now let's talk serious hardware," said Bixby. "Zero, I know you're partial to the LC9, complete with ankle holster." He handed Reid the Ruger, a small black snub-nosed pistol in a nylon holster with an elastic strap. The weight of it felt good in his hand.

"That one's got the nine-round box magazine, fully loaded, and an extra clip on the side."

Kate's words from his newfound memory rushed through his head suddenly: "*Why do you have this, Reid? What if one of the girls had found it?*" Suddenly he realized this was the gun that Kate had found behind the air vent, a Ruger LC9.

Did I tell her? Did she know about me?

He shook the memory from his head as Watson strapped a holster to his own ankle. "We have to get moving," he told Bixby.

"Yes, of course." Reid had the distinct impression that Bixby was not privy to the details of their op; he doubted the engineer would be quite so casual and pleasant if he had any idea what they were heading toward. "This is the *pièce de résistance*, as it were." Bixby held up a digital tablet and presented it to Reid. "Would you press your right thumb in the center there?"

Reid raised an eyebrow, but he did as Bixby asked, pressing the pad of his thumb against the tablet screen. When he lifted it, his thumbprint remained, glowing blue.

"Great. And your left, just in case. Wonderful. Just a moment…" Bixby's fingers flew across the tablet. "*Et voilà.* Perfect. Here you go." He handed Reid a second pistol—a black Glock with a silver slide. "I know you're used to the Glock 22, but we're transitioning to the 19. Larger magazine, seventeen with one in the chamber, and a bit more durable. It's the new sidearm of choice for Navy SEALs, if you didn't know. Plus, it's got this nifty feature." He pointed out a small, smooth rectangular pad on each side of the pistol, just behind the trigger guard. "Biometric fingerprint recognition. There is no safety on this gun; the trigger is locked unless one of your thumbs is on a pad. Don't worry too much about positioning. It'll pick up a partial print."

Reid was impressed. "I didn't even know this kind of thing existed."

"Oh, it's been around for a couple years," Bixby said. "I can't take credit for it. A nineteen-year-old from Detroit invented it. Just another one of those things that never caught on with the public. Shame, too; just think what it could do for gun safety—"

"Bixby," prodded Watson. "Let's wrap this up."

"Right, right. Sorry. My point is that with this gun, if you lose it, they can't use it." He grinned.

After Watson went through the same fingerprinting process, they loaded their equipment and took up their bags.

"Ah, just one more thing!" Bixby called after them.

Watson groaned. Reid had the feeling that this was a usual routine with the eccentric tech.

"Take this." Bixby handed Reid a small, thin black object, about the size of an AA battery. "I call it a sonic grenade. It's not quite field-tested yet, so I'm eager to see how it does."

Reid turned it over in his hands. "What does it do?"

"Keep it in your pocket, and if you find yourself in a jam, depress the buttons on each end of the cylinder," Bixby explained. "Squeeze hard; they don't depress easy. It emits a combination of high frequencies that cause immediate nausea and loss of equilibrium for anyone inside a twenty-five-foot radius—except you, as long as it's close. Keep it on your person."

"Impressive." *If it works*, Reid thought. Reid examined the tiny black cylinder. "How is that possible?"

"Oh, we've been doing a ton of research with sound waves, Doppler effect, pressure cones...I mean, I could explain it, but I doubt it'll do much good to—"

"*Bixby*," Watson said sharply. "We're going."

"Right. Of course." Bixby smiled as they headed out of the lab. "Break a leg, fellas."

The two of them walked briskly down the corridor toward the elevators again. Watson was silent and strode a pace ahead. Reid couldn't help but wonder if this was how Agent Watson was all the time, or if there had been some sort of history between them. It certainly felt as if there was a tension, but it might have just been him creating it in his head.

Halfway to the elevator, Bixby called out to them.

"Hey, Zero, sorry, real quick before you go." Reid paused as the man jogged up to him. "Listen, when you get back, uh, I'd really like to run a couple of tests."

"Tests?"

"You know, head MRIs, maybe some gadolinium contrast retention... all noninvasive, I promise," Bixby assured him. "But I think with some analysis that maybe, best-case scenario, I could help to restore some of your memory."

"We have to go, Zero," Watson murmured.

"I know. Just one sec." Reid fully understood the gravity of their situation, but if he had the opportunity to learn more about what was going on in his head, he was interested. "You really think you might be able to recover anything?" he asked Bixby.

"Possibly. I mean, it would help a great deal if I could talk to the person who actually implanted it." Bixby raised an eyebrow hopefully.

Reid shook his head. "Sorry, I don't know that." He wasn't about to incriminate the Swiss doctor, Guyer; for one, he didn't know anything about the man other than his name, and besides that, Bixby couldn't make any promises. Guyer could still end up being Reid's only hope of ever getting his full memory back.

"Well... give it some thought, okay? Come see me again when you're back."

"I will." Reid nodded. He got into the elevator, where Watson was already waiting, and the two of them silently headed up to ground level. They had to meet Barnard at the airstrip, and then pursue the harbingers of the deadly smallpox mutation.

CHAPTER TWELVE

It was half past midnight before Adrian returned to the flat. He had been working tirelessly the entire day on completing the RNA restructuring to prepare the rest of the *variola major* samples, and now he shuffled through the door, his feet dragging. The batch was nearly ready, but exhaustion and hunger had set in. He assured himself he would finish tomorrow.

Claudette was not yet home; she worked at a local bar, often late into the night. Adrian casually flicked on the television and then went into the kitchen to pour a glass of wine.

He heard the news report before he saw it. The mere mention of a deadly outbreak sent him dashing back into the living room, nearly stumbling, and skidding to a halt on the carpet in his socks.

He held his breath as he watched the Spanish broadcast, dubbed in French for the network. On the screen, a reporter in a respirator mask stood outside an enormous yellow tent as WHO workers behind him, each looking identical in yellow decontamination suits, wheeled patients in on gurneys.

A viral outbreak in Barcelona had claimed more than fifty-five lives in the course of a single day. One hundred ninety-five more were in critical condition.

The Imam had released the sample of the virus publicly.

As he watched, the reporter crept closer to the tent, the camera aimed into the makeshift hospital. Rows upon rows of bodies were lying upon cots, some spasming, coughing, bleeding from their lips. Others were not moving at all.

Near the entrance to the WHO hospital was a child, no more than eight or nine years old, lying prostrate on her back. She was unmoving, but her eyes were wide open.

"*Mon Dieu*," Adrian said breathlessly. My God. Sheer horror gripped him tight as a closed fist. He clamped a hand over his mouth and took deep breaths through his nose, stifling the urge to vomit.

This was not what was supposed to happen. In all his fervor to complete the virus, he had never once considered that children might be among its targets. Of course that was naïve of him; a virus was indiscriminate, unwavering, and unselective. Yet the Imam had filled his head with notions of the demons of the West, those driven only by greed and cupidity.

Furthermore, Barcelona was not one of the intended targets that Khalil had shared. It was a mere five hundred kilometers from his own home, for God's sake.

This was a nightmare. And he, Adrian Cheval, had created it.

He was out the door an instant later, leaving it wide open as he tore down the sidewalk in just his socks. The tailor's basement, from which he had just come, was not far. The exhaustion and hunger from only moments earlier had melted away, replaced by panic, fear, and resolution.

The entrance to the tailor's basement faced a rear alley, an ancient wooden door recessed in a concrete stairwell that led down to the earthy-smelling cellar where he kept the stolen equipment, decontamination suit, and smallpox samples. He fumbled with the keys and nearly dropped them as he unlocked the steel padlock, his fingers trembling. Finally, mercifully, the lock sprang open.

As he tugged it free, a soft feminine voice reached his ears. "My love."

He spun quickly, nearly panting, to find Claudette standing in the alley behind him. She wore a black shirt and still had a white apron tied around her waist over a denim skirt; she must have come directly from the bar. Her fiery red hair was pulled up into a messy bun. Yet she had never been a more welcome sight.

He ran into her arms, holding her for a long moment. She returned the embrace, her fingers gently caressing the back of his neck, giving him a moment to compose himself. His shoulders heaved with the threat of a sob, yet he held it back.

"To say I've made a grave error is the understatement of my lifetime," he said at long last. He spoke quietly, barely above a whisper.

"Darling, no." Claudette pressed her head into the crook of his neck. "No, you've done wonderfully."

He recoiled, pushing away from her, his face a mask of confusion and dread. "How can you say that? Claudette, I have made a mistake somewhere in the RNA sequencing, a mistake that should have rendered the virus useless but by some infinitesimal coincidence it... it made it worse." The words broke free from him like a burst dam. "The lethality is higher than it should be, and the virulence, it's off the charts. The incubation period is mere hours..." He was trembling by the time he finished. "If you saw what I just witnessed, you would understand."

Claudette bit her lip. She appeared to be sympathetic to his plight as she stroked the side of his face, but her words suggested otherwise. "Darling," she said softly, "you've done exactly what you were supposed to do."

He pushed her hand away. How could he get her to comprehend? "Children, Claudette! There were *children* infected. They are innocent—"

"Innocent!" Claudette scoffed. "Adrian, do you not see? None are innocent! Not you, not me, not even the Imam. We are *all* sinners."

He frowned and blinked several times, utterly confused. "What are you saying? Khalil had his targets in the West, that's what he said. But he released the sample in Barcelona. If it cannot be contained, it will spread like wildfire. It will reach France, it will reach *here*..."

She nodded slowly, like a patient teacher prodding a student to an epiphany. "Yes, Adrian. Of course it will."

He took a step back, his heart threatening to leap from his chest. His love, his Claudette, was scaring him. He had let himself be manipulated by the Imam—no, that was not right. He had only accepted Khalil's teachings because he had allowed himself to be manipulated by *her*. She had taken him in when he had no one, and he had allowed himself to be molded to her liking.

"Adrian," she said gently, "please do not look at me like that. I love you. And you are the Mahdi, the Redeemer, and in order to redeem—"

"To hell with the Mahdi!" he growled scornfully. This time she took a step back, as shocked as if he had slapped her. "Khalil lied to me. He has *used* me, Claudette. Can you not see? This is not a jihad! This is… this is genocide!"

She narrowed her eyes. "I understand your emotions have the better of you. You don't know what you are saying. But Allah is listening, Adrian. And it is too late for a sudden change of heart—"

"You're wrong about that." He spun angrily and pulled the padlock from the door. "I cannot undo what has been done, and God willing, the WHO will contain it. But I must fix what I have broken." He tugged on the old wooden door. Sometimes it would stick in the jamb, having warped over years of disuse, but on this night it was being particularly stubborn.

"Adrian! What will you do?"

"Destroy it," he said simply. He tugged on the door again, harder, but it would not pull free. "And then we will leave, tonight, and never look back. There will be no more Imam, no more jihad, no more virus, and I will spend the rest of my life atoning for what I have done—*oomph!*"

Adrian stumbled backward, nearly falling over as the door finally pulled free. As he recovered, he felt a hand on his shoulder, tugging him, and when he turned to face her Claudette slapped him with an open palm across his mouth.

He gasped in shock. His lips stung from the blow and when he touched them his fingers were smeared with blood.

"How dare you." Her voice was dangerously quiet. "You would forsake all we have worked for here? This is not about you or me or even the Imam. This is about higher purpose! This is about the betterment of the world!"

Adrian licked his bloody lip as he shook his head. He did not know what to say that could make her see. "Claudette, I love you more than you know. More than life, more than the air I breathe. But you must see that this is *not* the way."

In response, she folded her arms and pushed out her chest in defiance, a scowl on her lips. "Destroy it, Adrian, and you will never see me again," she warned. "I will leave tonight. I promise you, this is not a bluff."

He stared at the dirty alley beneath their feet. He did not know who he was anymore without Claudette. He did not believe he could survive without her. But what she was asking of him was more than he was capable of. He thought again of the tiny girl on the cot from the news broadcast. Unmoving, her eyes wide open. No older than his own niece, Alice, living in Bordeaux with his older sister. *What if it was Alice on that cot?*

"Then leave," he told Claudette quietly, barely above a whisper. "I will do what must be done…"

The roar of an engine interrupted the moment. They both glanced up instinctively to see a dark SUV rumble past the nearby mouth of the alley. Then, an instant later, brakes screeched and the SUV came back, in reverse. It turned at the alley and the two of them were awash in bright halogen headlights.

It was too late. They had come. Even if Adrian ignored the decontamination suit and made a run for the samples, he would risk not getting to them before the Arabs caught up to him—or worse, he could risk accidentally releasing the virus on Marseille.

The headlights died and two men climbed out of the black SUV. The driver was familiar, one of the two Syrians who had visited his flat to obtain the sample. But instead of his usual comrade, he had with him a lean-faced man, wiry and wearing a perpetual scowl.

The two Arabs nodded at Adrian, thin smirks upon their lips. He recognized it as a nod of validation. *My god*, he thought. *These monsters approve of what has been done.*

The wiry Syrian held out a cell phone. *"Patron,"* he said in French. Boss.

Adrian took the phone and put it on speaker. "Khalil?"

"Adrian." The older man's smooth, quiet voice came through the phone, singsong. "You have done *superb* work, my brilliant young friend." The Imam's French was nearly flawless.

"Why Spain?" he demanded. "You had your targets, you promised me—"

"We had to ensure that your virus would work," Khalil said simply. "And releasing it upon our true targets would tip our hand. Barcelona was merely a testing ground, Adrian."

"Children, Khalil." Adrian nearly choked on the words. "Children have perished…"

"And many more will before this is done." The Imam spoke dispassionately, as if he was discussing the slaughter of ants and not human beings. "Do not fret. They are with Allah now, in the glorious hereafter."

Adrian swallowed the lump in his throat. Even before he made his plea he already knew all too well there would be no changing the Imam's mind. "Please, listen to me carefully," he said slowly. "I made a mistake. The virus is too fast. The incubation period is far too short. There is the possibility of instability and further mutation. This cannot stand—"

"A mistake?" Khalil said. "Adrian, what you have done here has exceeded my expectations! You, Monsieur Cheval, are an artist, and this is your masterpiece."

"Masterpiece!" Adrian scoffed. "What I have created is an incomprehensible horror! Khalil, if this was to get beyond WHO containment, the fallout would be catastrophic. We would be facing an endemic the likes of which has never been seen…"

"Yes, yes, Adrian, I'm aware." He could not believe his ears; Khalil almost sounded bored by the conversation. "It is precisely what I had hoped of you."

A wave of panic washed over him. He had to destroy it. There was no other option. His own life was not worth the potential of what he had accidentally created.

Khalil sighed through the phone. "Have you lost the faith, Adrian?"

Adrian looked at Claudette. Her eyes were large in the moonlight, hopeful that his answer would be what both the Imam—and she—wanted to hear.

"I'm not sure I ever fully had it," he admitted quietly. "I had love, and in my desperation I clung to it. I allowed myself to be influenced. But this... this is too far, Khalil. I cannot allow it. I cannot be your Mahdi."

"I was afraid something like this might happen," said the Imam. "You see, Adrian, in faith, as in life, things are rarely black and white. Sometimes, in order to accomplish our goals, we must do that which seems the moral antithesis to what we should. To wit..." He snapped an order in Arabic. The Syrian driver surged forward suddenly and clamped a hand around Claudette's bicep. The fingers of his other hand grabbed her by the hair, yanking her head back.

She shrieked. Adrian stepped forward in her defense, but the wiry Arab produced a silver pistol and shoved it into the young Frenchman's face, pressing the barrel against his nose. Adrian dropped the phone as he put both hands up in surrender. It clattered to the alley, but Khalil's voice still came through.

"You must uphold your end of the promise, Adrian. Claudette will stay with one of my people. The other will follow you into your basement lab. I assume you have a second suit for him." Khalil chuckled. "If you attempt to destroy the samples, or tamper with them in a way that diminishes their efficacy, my people will kill Claudette in front of you. The man holding a gun to you currently? I brought him in because he is something of a specialist. He likes to start with the eyes. It's quite horrible."

Claudette squirmed in the Syrian's grip, her neck at an odd, painful angle. Adrian held his gaze on hers, his eyes wide and terrified. He could not bear it if they did anything to her. Even with her zealotry, her insistence, her blind faith, he still loved her deeply. He was vaguely aware that the Imam had continued speaking, but he heard none of it. He was petrified at the thought of them killing her before his eyes.

"Adrian? Have I made myself clear?"

"Help me," Claudette implored him, her voice a whimper. "Please, Adrian."

Adrian chewed his lip for a moment. "Yes," he said finally. "You are clear. I will do what you ask." *I will find a way out of this*, he told himself desperately. But at the moment he had no choice but to comply with the Imam's demand. He was deflated, defeated, unable to accept a fate for Claudette so long as he had the power to change it.

"Thank you," said Khalil gently. "How long?"

"I will have to work through the night," Adrian told him.

"Get it done." Imam Khalil ended the call.

The Syrian tugged Claudette's hair. She cried out in pain as he dragged her toward the dark SUV. The wiry thug shoved the barrel of his silver pistol in Adrian's face and barked, "Go!" in French.

The last thing he saw before being forced down into the darkness of the basement was her forlorn expression as the other Syrian pulled her toward the car. "I will free you," he promised. "I will make this right." He would conceive of a way, any possible way, to avoid putting the active virus into the maniacal Imam's hands and save Claudette, even if it meant his own death.

As soon as the basement door of the tailor's shop was closed tightly again, Claudette shook out her hair and winced. "That hurt," she scolded sharply in Arabic.

"I'm sorry." The Syrian man, Abad, appeared genuinely remorseful. "Do you think he believed it?"

"Yes," she told him. "I am quite certain he will do whatever is necessary to keep me from harm." She had had the feeling Adrian would lose the faith when he saw the effects of the virus. He was too soft, not fully indoctrinated; his infatuation was far more with her than with the Imam's teachings. That was why she made the call to Khalil and had his men threaten them both.

Although, she thought, *perhaps Adrian was right to lose the faith.* After all, Imam Khalil had told her himself: Adrian was not the Mahdi. It was she who would bring redemption to the world.

CHAPTER THIRTEEN

Immediately following his meeting with Bixby, Reid was ushered from CIA headquarters in Langley and directly into a waiting black sedan with Watson and Dr. Barnard. A Virginia state trooper paved their way, its lights and sirens blaring to part traffic for the pair of agents and the virologist as they headed toward the airstrip and a waiting jet.

It was oddly silent in the car, despite the screeching wails of the siren ahead of them. Reid noted that Dr. Barnard, sitting in the front passenger seat, seemed pensive yet fidgety; he knew more about the situation than the other two, and Reid did not at all like the agitated condition that the doctor appeared to be under. Beside Reid in the rear of the car, Watson sat stoically, which Reid recognized as his seeming natural state.

Reid spent the short drive from Langley to Dulles familiarizing himself with the details of the case, reviewing the encrypted drive on his phone to which Bixby had uploaded all relevant data. He quickly read over the details of the Siberian research expedition, led by a Greek virologist named Dr. Konstantin Cicero. He and his team were found dead, all five of them killed by gunshot. Their camp was burned. Four days prior, a grad student from Stockholm University named Bastien Renault had joined the expedition as an intern. The real Renault had been found murdered in his apartment near the university.

It had taken authorities a week to find the dead student. Everyone he knew assumed he was in Siberia.

Stockholm University had also confirmed that someone used Bastien Renault's ID to gain access to their virology lab, and several pieces of equipment were stolen. The video cameras outside the lab had been disabled, so they were unable to identify a perpetrator.

Reid winced. Whoever had done this was thorough. They had planned carefully and intelligently. Even so, there were at least a few minor things that he could surmise. Whether or not they were chinks in the perpetrator's armor, he didn't yet know.

The car reached the tarmac and slowed as it approached the plane. The small, private airstrip was just outside of Dulles, government owned and kept secure for politicians, visiting dignitaries, and situations like this one. A white Gulfstream G650 waited for them, its ramp lowered. As soon as they were out of the car the engines slowly whirred to life.

Reid had not had a single moment alone since he had first stepped into the conference room with Cartwright; he had gone straight from there to Bixby's lab and into the back of the waiting car, so he used the brief interim from sedan to plane to pull out his phone—the one Bixby had given him, as he had to leave his civilian cell behind—and dialed Maya's number.

"Hello?" she answered cautiously.

"Maya, it's Dad."

"Dad? Why are you calling from a blocked number? And what is that noise in the background?"

"Sweetie, listen, I only have a minute and I need to tell you—"

"Oh god, you're on a plane, aren't you?" she interrupted.

"…About to be. Yes." He didn't know if the CIA would be listening in on his calls or not, so he chose his words carefully. "I…went and did the exact thing you told me I would go and do."

Maya was silent for a long moment. "How long?"

"A couple of days at worst. It won't be like last time," he promised. After another long pause he asked, "How's your sister?"

"She's fine," Maya said flatly. "She fell asleep in front of the TV. Should I wake her?"

"No, no. Let her sleep."

"What should I tell her then?" Maya asked.

"Tell her, uh…" He hadn't even had time to think up a proper alibi.

"I'll tell her you went on a last-minute weekend getaway with Maria. She'll buy that. She likes the idea of you getting yourself out there again."

Reid smiled. He was grateful that Maya could think up a good excuse on the fly—so long as she didn't try anything like that with him. "Perfect. Thank you. Mr. Thompson is going to keep an eye on you, okay?"

He expected an argument, but Maya simply said, "All right. How can I reach you if I need to?"

"I can't give you this number, but I can text you," he said. Chances were good that even if the CIA wasn't monitoring calls, they would be monitoring activity—but to hell with them. He would talk to his girls if they needed him. "It'll show up as 'unknown,' but at least you can message me."

"Good," she said. Then, quieter, she asked, "You'll be careful, right?"

"Of course."

Agent Watson hung his head out from the door of the Gulfstream. "Zero," he called out, "let's go. Wheels up in one minute."

Reid nodded to him. To Maya he said, "I have a, uh, 'mutual friend' of ours with me." He knew she would understand who he meant. Maya and Sara had spent a few days in a safe house under the watchful eye of Agent Watson.

"Be safe," she told him. "I love you."

"Love you too, sweetheart." He ended the call, hefted his black bag, and boarded the Gulfstream. He took a seat beside Watson, across the aisle on the eight-seat, sixty-five-million-dollar aircraft. It had a max speed of nearly seven hundred miles per hour, which would put them over Europe in less than five hours' time. As the plane began to taxi he took out his phone again and texted Maya's number: *Reply here if you need to reach me.*

Two minutes later, the small jet roared into the sky.

Watson twisted halfway in his seat to address his companions. "Our first destination is Barcelona," he told them. "Interpol has established a temporary presence there in a quarantine zone. They believe the perpetrators may still be in the country; it's coastal, and with international travel shut down, they would need a way to get the virus out of Spain. We're to rendezvous with Interpol and, with a little luck, gain a lead from their intel."

Reid shook his head. "I don't think that's the way to go about this." Something about the Barcelona attack felt strange to him; the target itself was seemingly random, unless the people responsible had some sort of vendetta. But since no one had claimed responsibility for the attack, he could not help thinking that Spain could very well be a red herring.

"Well, those are our orders, straight from the Secretary of Defense," Watson retorted.

Barnard, seated behind Reid, leaned forward with interest. "What makes you say that, Agent Steele?"

Reid thought for a moment before he said, "The researchers in Siberia were expecting a specific someone." He opened the cloud storage drive on his phone and pulled up the grad student's profile. "Bastien Renault, twenty-five years old, medium build, of French nationality. Furthermore, the gun used at the expedition site was a MAB PA-15...a French handgun that hasn't been in production since 1982. I believe the perpetrator, the person who took Renault's place, is likely a Frenchman, mid-twenties or passable as such. He obviously knows enough about virology to masquerade as an intern for four days, regardless of whether or not he performed the actual mutation."

Barnard nodded slowly, his eyebrows raised—he nearly looked impressed. "All right, Agent, Let's say we're looking for a young Frenchman, as young as mid-twenties, with the knowledge and skills to have mutated *variola major*. While that is certainly a profile, it's also still quite a needle in a haystack."

"Besides," Watson added, "there's no lead to follow or thread to pull on the virologist. Swedish law enforcement has already turned over every stone—the university, the dead student's apartment, all of it. They've got nothing, which means we've got nothing. Barcelona is where it started; Barcelona is where we're headed. If we do our jobs right and coordinate our efforts with Interpol, the trail will lead back to the virologist."

Reid sighed. He thought back to that same morning, which already felt like several days ago, in the classroom at Georgetown. He suddenly sat up straight, his mind racing. "What makes you think our guy was ever in Barcelona?" he asked. "Why would he risk his own neck to release the virus?"

"Who in the hell would be willing to do it for him?" Watson asked.

"That I don't know." *Siege of Kafa*, he thought. He had just been lecturing about a similar topic. "You know, Genghis Khan was an early adopter of biological weapons—namely, the bubonic plague. He was known to send infected soldiers into native populations who refused to yield, in order to spread their illness and thin their numbers."

Dr. Barnard scrutinized Reid. "That is true. And sometimes he would catapult their infected bodies over walls. It's very interesting, but what do thirteenth-century Mongolian conquest tactics have to do with modern biological weapons?"

"My point is that if I was the virologist, assuming he's the mastermind behind all this, I'd be as far away from Spain as possible. And based on what we know, I'd be willing to bet he isn't in France, either," Reid explained. "If I was him, I'd be in hiding. I would have sent someone else to release the virus, whether wittingly or not."

Barnard stroked his chin stubble. "Send an infected soldier in," he said slowly, "to spread the illness. It's plausible—particularly with the rate of infection we're seeing."

"You've mentioned the speed of this strain a couple of times now," Watson noted. "How fast are we talking?"

"The WHO is still working to round out a definitive profile of the virus, but..." The doctor paused to remove his glasses and clean them on his shirt. "From what they can tell so far, incubation from initial infection to symptomatic is between one and two hours. The first symptoms to manifest are headache, fever, and mild nausea, each of which compounds exponentially over the very brief life cycle of the virus. Internal temperatures are rising about one degree per hour. Then acute tussis begins, or coughing from fluid in the lungs. All bleeding is internal; there are no external sores as seen in traditional smallpox cases and *variola minor.*

"From what they're seeing in Spain, it's typically the lungs that bleed first, making it difficult to breathe. That, in conjunction with high fever, has been commonly causing unconsciousness or at least disorientation. Bleeding of other internal regions is next, generally the abdominal cavity, and eventually internal hemorrhaging until death."

Reid closed his eyes as the doctor spoke. He had no desire to see any of that for himself, not after the description and seeing Barnard's slackened features. "How long does it take?"

"The WHO's current profile of the virus is an average of seven to eight hours from infection to mortem."

Reid's stomach turned at the thought. He couldn't imagine how horrifying it would be to fall sick in the morning and be dead before sundown—without any hope for a cure.

All three of their phones chimed simultaneously. Watson checked his. "An update," he announced. "Assistant Director Riker says Interpol's got something. Whatever it is must be sensitive. They won't upload it to us for fear of a leak, but they're saying it's urgent."

Reid almost scoffed. He couldn't shake the feeling that Spain felt like a ploy, a way to throw the authorities off the scent, but it didn't matter now; Barcelona was where they were headed. And even though he thought it could be a waste of time, time that they could be spending tracking the virologist, he was morbidly curious about what Interpol had discovered.

Dr. Barnard sighed deeply, trying to contain the anxiety that was clearly scrawled across his face and brow. "Ground zero," he murmured. "Let us hope to whomever you pray to that we won't have to one day say, 'Where it all began.'"

CHAPTER FOURTEEN

Reid glanced out the window as the Gulfstream descended over El Prat Airport in Barcelona. Local time was six thirty in the morning. The sun was just beginning to rise, casting a purplish light over the transitioning sky.

It was an eerie sight. El Prat was shut down, void of life. No planes arrived or departed, and the tarmac was silent and empty. As they touched down, Reid could see that most of the lights inside the airport were on, but through the large plate glass windows the place was a ghost town.

Watson opened the door and lowered the staircase as the G650 came to a stop. Out on the runway the weather was chilly and a slight breeze blew. Birds chirped from nearby, nesting atop the glass terminal.

Strange, Reid thought. *I've never seen a silent airport before. This is what the end of the world would look like.*

A single man jogged over to them. He wore a charcoal gray suit and loafers, and sported a pencil-thin mustache on his tanned face. Despite the current situation, Reid couldn't help but grin fiercely as the man approached. He held out his hand to greet the Interpol agent who had helped him and Maria stop Amun's plot in Switzerland.

"Baraf," Reid said. "It's good to see you again."

Agent Vicente Baraf warmly returned the smile. "You as well, Agent Steele. Though I do wish the circumstances were better."

"Agreed," said Reid. "This is Agent Watson, CIA, and Dr. Barnard from the CDC."

"Yes, your director told me you were coming. Please, follow me." Baraf led the way as the four men walked hastily toward the terminal. "Interpol is working with the WHO to contain the outbreak and using the airport as a temporary base of operations while it's shut down," he explained. "El Prat is about twelve miles from the city center, so we're outside the known infection radius. The WHO has established a quarantine area in the long-term parking lot on the other side of the building—"

"I'd like to see it," said Barnard suddenly.

"There's no time," Watson replied just as quickly. "We're here for intel, and that's all."

"What I would like to show you is extremely sensitive," Baraf continued. "We cannot risk it getting out to the public."

Reid understood right away what that likely meant—Interpol had found some solid evidence of this being a biological attack. If the public was aware, it could incite a mass panic. *And hopefully,* he thought, *it includes a lead.*

Baraf led them to one of the airline lounges, which Interpol had turned into a makeshift command center. Nearly every available horizontal surface was taken up by computers, radios, and communications gear. A dozen or so suited Interpol agents scurried about or sat at temporary workstations, working feverishly on their assigned tasks.

"This way." Baraf showed them to the far corner of the room, where a stout, round-faced man sat before a dual-monitor display. On each screen was some sort of footage, which he seemed to be scrutinizing intensely.

"Sawyer," said Baraf, "these are Agents Steele and Watson of the CIA. Agents, Mr. Sawyer is the best technical analyst at Interpol's disposal."

Sawyer blinked at them. His eyes were bloodshot and circled; the man had clearly been up all night. "Agents," he nodded, his voice thick with a London accent. "I wish I could say it's a pleasure."

"Show them what you and your team have found," Baraf prodded.

"Right, of course." Sawyer rubbed his bleary eyes. "As you know, the first wave of patients came to Hospital de l'Esperanca yesterday evening. The medical staff there interviewed them as best they could—those that were coherent, anyway. Eventually a common thread emerged: many of them had ridden the subway earlier in the day. Not just the subway, but the very same *line*." He toggled to another tab on his computer, and the left-side monitor switched from the security footage to a map of Barcelona's subway system. "This line here, the red line. My team and I have spent hours poring over camera footage from the subway stations, and finally, we found this."

Sawyer switched the right monitor to another video and played it. On the screen, a small crowd of citizens waited for the approaching train to come to a stop, and then stepped aboard as the doors opened. The tech analyst paused the image.

"Right here," he said. He pointed to a young man among them, barely more than a child, it seemed. He looked a bit derelict; his hair was long, climbing over his ears, and his cheeks were patchy with dark hair. He wore a thin sweater and, admittedly, looked out of place among the Spanish citizens.

"Who are we looking at?" Watson asked.

"That," Sawyer answered, "is the first reported case of infection, as well as the first fatality of the outbreak."

"Our patient zero," Barnard murmured.

"Now, here's the thing," Sawyer continued. "He gets on the train and rides the line up and down for a while. Then he staggers off the train, obviously ill. He manages to get to the street before he collapses, and an emergency room nurse on her way to work helps him to the hospital."

Reid nodded gravely. "So the first infected, this kid, he carried the virus into the city. He rode the subway on purpose to infect commuters." His hunch had been right.

"Precisely," Baraf said quietly. "Already the WHO has received reports of infection from outside the city, in Manresa, Tarragona, and even one alleged case in Carcassonne."

Reid balked. "It reached France?"

"Why didn't we know about this?" Barnard insisted.

"It has happened only inside the last hour, while you were in the air," Baraf explained. "The WHO is doing everything in its power to stop the spread of the virus, but their resources are drawing thin. Since you've left the US, every airport in the EU has been shut down. International travel is currently prohibited, and anyone exhibiting symptoms is undergoing immediate quarantine."

"You were right, Agent," Dr. Barnard murmured to Reid. "Our perpetrator sent an infected into the city, just like the Mongols."

Reid was in no mood to muster an "I told you so." He couldn't imagine what the potential ramifications might be if such a deadly disease was released in the United States, especially on the East Coast. It would spread like wildfire. "Watson," he said quietly, "report back to Cartwright and Riker with all this. They'll want to know what's going on, if they don't already."

Watson nodded and excused himself to make the call.

"Agent Steele," said Baraf, "I'm afraid there is more I must show you. Sawyer, if you would please."

The Interpol tech switched the feed on his right monitor to a black-and-white video. He recognized the scene immediately as the inside of a hospital, with four doctors and nurses crowded around a bed as they worked on a patient. As one of the doctors stepped aside, Reid saw the patient's face—it was the boy, the first infected. They had cut away his thin sweater. His chest looked hollow, almost skeletal, and it heaved up and down rapidly. He was struggling to breathe.

"This is security footage from the emergency room of Hospital de l'Esperanca," Baraf explained. The Interpol agent picked up a pair of thick noise-canceling headphones from Sawyer's desk and held them out to Reid. "Please."

Reid fitted the headphones over his ears and immediately heard the shouts and demands of doctors issuing orders in Spanish. The boy thrashed on the video, coughing violently, his body racked with spasms.

Then he heard something else, barely above a murmur yet still audible, coming from the boy on the bed. Reid wrinkled his brow. It sounded like a soft moan, a series of monosyllabic "mm" sounds.

"Turn it up," he asked Sawyer. The tech cranked up the volume to the point that it was nearly deafening. The audio quality of the security footage was poor and white noise screeched defiantly in his ears, but Reid could still just barely make out what the boy might have been saying.

"Im…" he heard. "Im…Imam…ma…"

Reid furrowed his brow. It sounded as if in his feverish delirium, the boy was murmuring "Imam"—he was calling out for his spiritual leader, perhaps the head of his mosque or a pillar of his community. He immediately understood why Baraf did not want the video leaked; anyone who heard the boy speaking Arabic would automatically assume the worst.

Yet as he listened, there was something else, another word the boy was trying to get out. Reid could just barely distinguish a hard consonant sound as the boy attempted to say, "Ma…Ima…dee…"

"Play it back," he demanded. The English tech started the video over and Reid closed his eyes, focusing on the murmurs coming from the boy.

Mahdi, Reid discerned. *Imam Mahdi.*

His eyes widened in shock as the realization struck him. He yanked the headphones from his ears and pushed them into Barnard's hands. He needed confirmation, or at the very least, a second opinion. "What does this sound like to you? What is the boy saying?"

Barnard listened intently to the audio as Sawyer played it back, his narrowed eyes focused on nothing as he tried to make out the words. Then he too tore the headphones from his ears.

"Did he say…?" The doctor did not seem to want to say it first.

"Imam Mahdi," Reid confirmed.

"What does this mean?" Baraf asked.

"It means we can assume the worst," Reid said quietly. Countless wars had been fought in the name of religion, so Reid had educated himself fairly thoroughly on the major faiths of the world. He knew well what the Mahdi was—and what it meant.

"In some Islamic sects, Imam Mahdi is a redeemer figure," Barnard explained. "It is said he will be the last of the Muslim holy men, and he will bring about Judgment Day…"

"The end of the world," Reid finished. "The cleansing of the earth of sin."

Baraf blew out a breath. "We are dealing with Islamic militants."

"There's little doubt," Reid murmured. He thought back to Barnard's remark on the plane. *A virus is dispassionate. It does not target enemy soldiers or politicians or persons of interest.* If this boy had been indoctrinated into an insurgent group, then he had indeed carried the virus willingly into the city… which meant that this was a jihad, plain and simple.

"What do you think, Agent?" asked Barnard. "ISIS? Some Daesha faction?"

"It's not their MO," Reid replied. The "usual suspects" of Islamic subversives tended to be very vocal about their attacks, stepping up to claim them and even going as far as filming it for the world to see. This felt different to Reid; quiet, covert, well-planned.

And worse, the fact that they remained quiet after the attack on Barcelona signaled to him that they had more in store for the world.

"We're still missing a link between this boy and the virologist," Reid said in frustration. "We need something more to go on." He turned expectantly to Barnard. "You're the bioterrorism expert here. What aren't we seeing?"

Dr. Barnard was busy scrolling quickly through his phone, his eyes flitting back and forth behind his owlish glasses.

"Barnard…" It didn't seem as if the doctor was listening.

Suddenly he looked up sharply from his phone. "Agent Baraf, do you have a medical report on the boy from Hospital de l'Esperanca?"

"Uh, yes, we do." Baraf sifted hastily through a stack of paperwork beside Sawyer's computer. "They faxed a hard copy to us last night...Here." He yanked out a sheaf of collated pages and handed them to Barnard.

Reid peered over the doctor's shoulder. The report was in Spanish, yet Reid was not at all surprised to learn that he could read it as easily as he could English. He had previously learned that he could speak Arabic, Russian, and French, all of which had returned to him simply by being exposed to the language.

Apparently the CDC doctor could read it as well. "Right here." He pointed to a paragraph describing the boy's physical state upon arriving in the ER. "This boy, he passed in less than three hours of hospitalization," Barnard said rapidly. "Add to that Mr. Sawyer's observations from the train, and it's still less than five hours total; much faster than any other infected patients. But why? If you look here, the admitting doctor wrote that an MRI showed scarring on his lungs."

"A boy speaking Arabic with scarring on his lungs," Reid thought out loud. "Most likely the product of breathing something in...a toxin, and more than just average pollution..."

"It would be something strong enough to weaken his respiratory system and allow the virus to take hold much quicker," Barnard added.

Reid sucked in a breath as he realized what the doctor was suggesting. "Sarin gas. You think this boy survived a sarin attack."

Barnard nodded. "Agents, I don't believe this boy was picked from a crowd. He was chosen for a reason—a compromised system that would disseminate the virus faster than an ordinary human adult. And if sarin is the culprit, there is a good chance he is..."

"Syrian," Baraf finished.

"Baraf, every country in the EU keeps a registry of Syrian refugees, right?"

The Italian agent nodded to Reid. "Yes, but we have no background on this boy, no name to search—"

"We do," Reid countered. "Mahdi. M-A-H-D-I. This was carefully planned, and whoever the missing link is between the boy and the virologist would likely not want his identity known. Search the registries for anyone who entered Europe from Syria under that name. Start in Spain and work east—France, Italy, Greece, any country that opened its borders to refugees."

"Can you?" Baraf asked the tech.

Sawyer rubbed his bleary eyes. "It'll take a few moments... but yes. It would be faster if we had a full name, though."

Barnard and Reid exchanged a glance. He could tell they were thinking the same thing. "Muhammad," Reid told him. Barnard nodded in agreement. "Muhammad Mahdi."

Sawyer's fingers flew across the keyboard. Reid found himself chewing anxiously on a thumbnail. It was a long shot, he knew; or perhaps the perpetrator did not assume that the likes of Barnard and Reid Lawson would be on his trail. He glanced over at the doctor and could tell that he too was emotionally fraught.

"The registry will only tell us where he entered Europe," Barnard said, his voice hushed behind a closed fist over his mouth. "He may not still be there."

"Maybe not," Reid replied, "but if he's still using the alias, we might be able to track his last known whereabouts. And with international travel shut down, they would have to already be in the next place they plan to release the virus..."

"Or," Barnard offered, "somewhere far, far from it."

Reid didn't respond, but the doctor was right. Finding this alleged Mahdi did not necessarily mean finding the virus—but all they needed was someone with information. Kent Steele had proven tactics for extricating it.

The rapid clacking of the keyboard stopped suddenly as the English tech's fingers froze. "We have a match," Sawyer said, sounding somewhat surprised. "A Muhammad al-Mahdi entered the refugee registry in Athens, Greece, by way of Turkey fourteen months ago. According to this, there hasn't been any movement since—at least not registered."

Athens. It would make sense, Reid reasoned. A coastal city, close to an airport and a major trade route via the Mediterranean. This al-Mahdi must be the link, he was sure of it. "Thanks for your help," he said to Baraf. "We have to move. Barnard, let's go."

The two of them started across the floor of the airline lounge, but Baraf trotted after them. "Agent, wait! Wait a moment. Where are you going? You don't even have a precise location."

Reid paused. "We're going to Greece. It's a two-hour plane ride from here; we'll have the CIA start scouring databases in Athens for al-Mahdi's whereabouts. You should have your people do the same—housing authorities, hotels, property deeds, anything you can find with his name on it. Hopefully we'll have something solid by the time we arrive."

"I should send agents," Baraf insisted, "and we should alert the Greek authorities. If the virus is in Athens—"

"We don't know that yet," Reid argued. "This is all speculation until there's evidence—"

"Agent Steele, we have an obligation to make them aware!" Baraf said loudly. Other Interpol agents in the lounge looked up from their work, surprised by the outburst.

Reid lowered his voice. "Baraf, you remember Davos. It only took three of us to take that bomber down. If we had more, we might have spooked him, caused him to act early. Well, this is Davos all over again. We can't even be certain that the virus is in Athens; if I was al-Mahdi, I would want it far away from me. But if we find the man, we can us him to find the virus. If we go in there with cops and agents storming the building, and he *does* have the virus, we could have much bigger problems."

Baraf sniffed, but he too lowered his voice. "So you suggest that I allow two CIA agents and a doctor to handle this by themselves?" He shook his head. "Not only would that be flagrantly ignorant, but it would go against every code by which Interpol conducts itself."

Reid thought for a moment. Baraf was too virtuous to see this by any other angle—but maybe his perspective could be parried with the same tactic.

"You said it yourself," Reid told him. "We don't know a precise location. We don't technically have a lead to follow. The CIA is in full cooperation with your office, so as soon as we know something, you will too. Then you can notify Greece and send your agents."

Baraf raised an eyebrow. "You're suggesting I give you a head start."

"I'm suggesting you hold off on thinning your resources until you have something concrete." *Which is just a loophole to give us a head start*, Reid thought.

"If I may," Barnard interjected. "A potential compromise: Agent Baraf's concern is that the active virus is in Greece. We can alert the WHO to the potential threat of smallpox in Athens and have a team on standby in case of infection."

Baraf clearly didn't like it much, but he nodded tightly once. "Rest assured, Agent Steele, as soon as we have a location pinned down for this al-Mahdi, my agents will be there and Greek authorities will know about it."

"Of course. Thank you, Baraf. I hope the next time we see each other is under better terms." He briefly shook hands with the Interpol agent, and then he and Barnard hurried from the airline lounge. "Seems you have a knack for diplomacy, Dr. Barnard," Reid mused.

"It would seem," Barnard agreed. "And while we're at it, it seems you and your Interpol friend are breaking about a half dozen international laws."

"Yeah," Reid muttered. "Apparently I have a knack for that. Let's find Watson and get in the air as soon as possible." He wondered where Watson had gone. Updating Cartwright and Riker should have only taken a few minutes.

He didn't have to wonder long. As they left the lounge and stepped out into the hauntingly empty terminal, they were greeted by three people—Watson, and two newcomers, though both were familiar faces. One was a tall man with angular features sporting a blue baseball cap and brown jacket; Agent Carver, Watson's former partner and the other man who had helped saved Reid's daughters from Amun hands the month prior.

The other face was a most welcome one, with slate-gray eyes and blonde hair. Just seeing her sent a warm sensation through his limbs. Even with her hair tousled, no makeup, a white sweater and jeans with a black bag slung over one shoulder, she looked beautiful.

"Kent," she said. Maria took a step toward him, and in that moment he hoped she would run to him, but her gaze flitted to the other agents present and she stopped herself.

"What are you doing here?" he asked. He knew their presence could mean only one of two things, and he hoped the news was good.

"Riker had us rendezvous with you here," she told him. "This op is top priority right now."

He nodded; he was glad for the assistance, though he had some burning questions. "Your timing is perfect. We're heading to Athens."

Watson frowned. "What's in Athens?"

"If we're lucky? The man who knows where the virus is, who made it, how much they have, and where it's going to be released," Reid said simply.

Apparently that was as much of an explanation his new partner needed. "Let's go." Watson led the way hastily down the length of the terminal, filling Carver in on the details of the op. Barnard came next, while Reid slowed his pace to walk beside Maria.

As he did, he noticed there was a small line of blood on the right sleeve of her sweater. "What happened?" he asked quietly.

She shook her head. "Nothing good. We got a lead on Rais headed east, into Slovenia. The trail ended at an Amun safe house that we didn't know about. We were jumped by two members." She gestured toward the blood on her sleeve. "One of them grazed me, but I'm fine. He's not."

"And Rais?"

Maria sighed. "Trail went cold. I'm sorry, Kent. I would have kept going, you know that. But Riker contacted us and filled us in on what you guys were up to, had us meet here." She scoffed bitterly. "I can't believe they pulled you back in for this."

"I sort of volunteered," Reid said, even though it wasn't quite the truth. "Anything else on Rais?" Despite their situation—pursuing the bearers of a virus whose goal might have very well been to end humanity—he still found himself irrationally concerned about the assassin.

"Intel suggests he's heading to Russia. We just couldn't catch up with him." Her fingers touched his as they walked, though she didn't quite hold his hand. "Hey. That means he's heading farther away from you and your family. So let's put that out of our minds for now, because we've got way bigger things to worry about."

She was right. He needed to stay sharp, focused on the task at hand, if they were going to stop this al-Mahdi before he did whatever he was planning to do. He could only hope they would find answers in Greece.

CHAPTER FIFTEEN

Rais was careful to maintain the legal speed limit as he drove the SUV southbound on an otherwise empty Swiss avenue. He kept his eyes open and alert and listened keenly for the sound of sirens, which he expected to begin their telltale scream in the night at any moment.

The first thing he had done after his escape, after killing the two Swiss officers and the hospital guard, was take the guard's truck. He knew he could not keep it long, but he also knew that the authorities would expect him to get on the highway immediately and put some distance between him and Sion. Instead he drove up the road from the hospital until he found a gas station that was still open at that late hour.

He looked the station over from across the street before pulling in. There would be cameras at the pumps; he spotted two in the front, each angled toward the entrance, and another in the rear. However, the western-facing façade, a brick wall with no point of egress, had no cameras and no lights.

Rais secured his seatbelt and drove the truck into that wall at twenty-five miles an hour.

The impact was not enough to even deploy the airbags, but the crunch of steel on brick was definitely enough to alert the attendant, who came running out a moment later.

"Sir!" he said frantically in German as he rounded the truck. "Are you all right? Should I call an ambulance?"

Rais pointed the gun, the Sig, from the driver's seat. "Put your hands up," he said in German, "and take one step back."

The terrified attendant did as he was told, though it did not look like the first time he had been held at gunpoint. Rais climbed out of the truck. He noted with some dismay that even the minor impact against the brick wall had left him sore. He had to remind himself that he was not fully recovered; he could not act too brashly.

The attendant was a couple of inches taller and stockier than Rais, but it would do better than the thin, ill-fitting scrubs he had taken from the Swiss nurse Elena. "Remove your clothes."

"Excuse me?" said the bewildered attendant.

Rais sighed irritably. It was not a difficult request, yet so many seemed to have trouble understanding it. "Take off your jacket, your shirt, and your pants, or I will kill you."

Threats will get you everywhere, Rais thought with minor satisfaction as the attendant, jarred into action at the notion of being murdered that night, tore out of his denim coat, dark gray shirt, and jeans. He stood there, shivering in a pair of boots and white briefs.

Rais flipped the Sig in his hand and brought it down on the attendant's head in a powerful blow. The man crumpled, unconscious and bleeding from a gash on his forehead. His skull was likely cracked and he would need stitches, but he was alive. Probably.

Rais dressed quickly, pulling the jeans over the scrub pants (it was still cold in Switzerland in March, and the layers would be helpful) and then the shirt and jacket. In the pockets of the pants he found a cell phone, a disposable lighter, a wallet, and a ring of keys. He kept the lighter. There was no cash in the wallet, so he tossed it at the man's unconscious body. The phone he crushed under a boot heel. The ring of keys led him to a pickup truck parked behind the gas station.

In the distance the sirens began to scream. They were growing steadily louder. The police would be looking for the guard's stolen car.

He pulled the truck out of the parking lot, across the road, and down a side street that led into a residential neighborhood. Driving slowly, he looked left and right until he found what he was seeking—a home with a long driveway and two other cars parked in it. Rais switched off the headlights and backed the truck up the drive, alongside the other two cars.

Once the police discovered that the SUV had been crashed into the side of the gas station—which would be only a matter of minutes—they would look for the attendant's stolen car. But they would be looking for it on roads and highways, not parked in someone's drive. It was nearly two in the morning by then; with any luck it would be hours before the residents would wake and report the strange truck on their property.

Rais set out on foot, striding down the road at a pace that was not too fast yet what he hoped looked like someone simply eager to get home. Sion was not a large city; he doubted they had a sizable police force at their disposal. Even so, it was quite late at night and there were very few people on the streets. Whenever he saw headlights approaching he quickly ducked into hiding until they passed.

Even he had to admit that Sion was an attractive town, sprawled at the base of the Alps as if it had slipped off the mountainside. From nearly anywhere in the city he could look up and see the Valère Basilica, the twelfth-century fortified cathedral that sat upon a hill overlooking Sion's downtown. Most tourists mistook it as a castle.

The town proper was a mélange of narrow, winding streets arranged in no discernible pattern, as if the city planner had been a child with a crayon in their fist. It would be easy for him to lose the authorities here, if need be, but he was eager to be off the road. He hid out in the courtyard of a small hotel and waited until morning, catnapping on and off for fifteen to twenty minutes at a time.

He didn't realize how exhausted he was until he stopped moving, hiding himself between two shrubs with his back to the hotel's brick façade. His limbs ached and his wounds still pained him. If he could have risked only a few more minutes during his escape at the hospital, he might have grabbed some narcotics to assuage his pain.

No, he thought. *I must stay sharp.* He needed his mind keen if he was to get out of Sion.

Twice during the five hours before sunrise the phantom nerve pain gripped his body, what the doctors had called stingers. The first time was while he was napping, and the pain was so intense that he clamped both hands over his mouth to stifle the scream that lurched from his throat. The second time he was awake when they came on, but no less surprising. He bit the inside of his cheek, hard enough to taste blood, until the pain subsided.

Eventually the horizon turned pink as the sun began to rise— as did Rais, climbing carefully from his position and stretching in the dim light of morning. It was no coincidence that he had chosen this small hotel at which to hide.

On the southern-facing exterior wall was a loose brick, about a foot above eye level. To see it was not to think it loose, but he knew it was there. He worked his fingertips into the crevices and tugged the brick out. Behind it was a single, small gold key.

A month earlier, when the city of Sion had hosted the Winter Olympics, Rais had plotted to kill Agent Kent Steele. He would have gladly given his life for his mission to be a success—but even so, he had planned for the contingency of his survival, which would have required the necessary means to escape without notice. His circumstances may have changed, but his plan remained viable.

Across the street from the hotel was Sion's largest post office, with a revolving door entrance and a sign that read *Sion Hauptpost*. It opened at seven a.m. At four minutes past the hour, Rais hastily crossed the street, entered the building, and strode straight to a bank of steel-door PO boxes just beyond the foyer. He avoided eye contact with anyone and resisted the urge to glance over his shoulder. Doing so would only attract attention.

Instead he went straight to his rented box, number 0276. He slid the key in, opened it, removed the only item inside—a brown leather satchel—and then closed the door again. He was in and out of the Hauptpost in less than two minutes.

As he crossed the street once again, he pulled the satchel's strap over his shoulder. Then he entered the small hotel to find a young female clerk at the front desk.

"*Hallo*," he said pleasantly. "I apologize; my Swiss-German is not good. I am checking in as a guest here later today. For now, may I just use your restroom?"

The young woman smiled warmly. "*Na sicher.*" Of course. She directed him down the hall and to the right. He smiled graciously and followed her instructions.

As soon as the bathroom door was locked behind him, he set down his satchel and got to work. He was no stranger to altering his appearance; going incognito was a requisite for one whose job had been traveling frequently with the intended goal of committing murder. He took out his implements, one by one, and laid them out on the closed seat of the toilet.

Rais began by cutting off his hair, first with a small pair of silver scissors and then buzzing it down to short bristles with an electric shaver. He did the same with his facial hair. Next, he inserted brown contact lenses to hide his emerald-green eyes.

In his satchel was a German passport—not a fake, but a legitimate one sold to another member of Amun by an unscrupulous citizen of Hamburg who needed a thousand euros to post his brother's bail. The man was of a height and build similar to Rais, but the passport holder was eight years his senior and had a much different facial aspect.

Rais only had to get close enough for a believable match.

In the passport photo, the man's hair was shorn short, as Rais's now was. His eyes were brown, and he had a fairly substantial beard up both cheeks and hanging down about five inches. The prosthetic in Rais's satchel was of an approximate length—convincingly real, made of horse hair, and easy enough to find on the internet. The color of it was a shade or two darker than the one in the photo, but it matched Rais's natural hair color enough to (hopefully) avoid scrutiny.

He used spirit gum adhesive to attach the beard to his shaven cheeks, applying it as carefully and evenly as possible. He used the scissors to trim and fray the ends of it—it looked too perfectly sculpted, he thought—as well as his own sideburns to blend in with the edges.

Rais looked at the passport photo again. Next would be the difficult part; the obvious age gap between his face and the photo. After studying it for a moment, he took a tube of rubber cement from his bag and carefully pinched the skin at the corners of his eyes. He beaded the rubber cement into the pinched crevice and held it for a few minutes. His skin burned at first, but he held it fast and the pain eventually subsided to a tingle. When he released it the pinch remained, effectively creating wrinkles around his eyes. He repeated the process twice on each side.

For additional effect, he removed the denim jacket, T-shirt, and scrub top, and then put the shirt and jacket back on. The scrub top he balled up and tucked beneath his shirt, partially tucked into the hem of his jeans, smoothing it out to create a small paunch.

Rais took a step back and inspected his new appearance in the mirror. He barely looked like himself anymore. Though, he noted with some concern, the false wrinkles around his eyes looked puckered and forced. He would have to affect a slight squint if he wanted to maintain a natural mien. No easy task to hold for hours, to be sure, but he was nothing if not methodical.

In the bottom of the satchel was a wallet with a photo ID (this one was a fake, created using the passport's photo and information) and a few thousand euros in cash. There was also a burner phone, the battery likely dead, but he would not risk attempting to reach any of his contacts in Amun anyway. They were probably detained by now or on the lam. Besides, they would be little help in what he was planning to do. He was alone now, and he would do things in his own way.

I endure, he thought.

He pulled the battery from the phone and tossed it in the bathroom's trash.

Satisfied with his new appearance, he collected his tools, cleaned up the hair as best he could, and flushed it down the toilet. He could affect a German accent fairly well, but still he stood in front of the mirror, squinting his eyes and murmuring phrases to be sure he still sounded the way he ought to. Satisfied, he slung the satchel back over his shoulder. The entire process had taken less than thirty minutes.

He left the bathroom and, instead of returning to the main entrance, walked further down the hall to a side exit. He could not risk walking past the young lady at the front desk. His appearance was altered, but he was still wearing the same clothes.

Back out on the streets of Sion, the sun was up and people were filtering out from their homes, on their way to jobs or errands or whatever it was that ordinary people did with their lives. Rais walked among them freely, not warranting a second glance from anyone. As he walked, he dropped the PO box key into a storm drain. He wouldn't need it anymore. The burner phone, void of a battery, he slipped into a street-corner trash bin three blocks further.

As he suspected, the police were watching the train station (as they would be the airports and bus depots, and had likely set up roadblocks on major points of egress from the city). First he entered a public restroom. He made sure he was alone before he pried open a paper towel dispenser and hid the Sig P220 in it. He was not happy to leave it behind—it was an excellent gun—but he could not risk trying to get it past security. Then he went into a stall and dropped the second gun into a toilet tank. With any luck, it would be a few days before either was found.

Rais got on a train to Zurich without incident. He did not speak to anyone; instead, he pretended to be sleeping in order to not be bothered. Once during the train ride he rose and went to the restroom to check his wounds. They were closed, but some stitches remained. He would have to cut them out himself.

From Zurich he could take a plane to the US, but first he needed to take some precautions to avoid obvious flags. His first stop was to a thrift store, where he found an old suitcase and bought enough items of clothing to make it seem as if he was on a trip. He couldn't very well get on a plane without luggage.

Next he went to a pharmacy and purchased a prepaid debit card. The maximum allowable load was two thousand euros, which was most of his cash, but he put it on anyway. At an electronics store on the same block he picked up a new burner phone and paid for a few megabytes of data. The first thing he did was check the internet. Sure enough, Interpol had established a hotline for the public to call in with any potential leads on Rais's whereabouts. He wasn't mentioned by name, but his connection with Amun was well noted.

Next he downloaded a Chinese calling app that would generate international phone numbers for a small fee. He created two accounts, one with an Italian phone number and the second Slovenian. He paid a homeless woman fifty euros to call the Interpol tip line from his Italian number and report, in English, that a man bearing Rais's description had stolen her car at gunpoint near Bormio, just over the Swiss-Italian border. She told them that the "horrible man" had said something about Ljubljana, the capital of Slovenia.

Lastly he visited an internet café and booked his flight using the prepaid debit card. To pay for an airline ticket in cash at the counter would be highly suspect—and even more so for someone with a German passport to book one-way travel. He saw that a flight to JFK in New York was departing in less than three hours' time, with a connection in Madrid, for just under six hundred euros. He booked a return flight for seven days later to Hamburg, to make it appear as if he had traveled first to Switzerland, then to the US, and then to home. He ended up spending about twelve hundred euros on the flight; most of his money was gone, but it would be worth it if it got him where he needed to be.

Of course there was a police presence at Kloten Airport, but once again his disguise proved worthwhile as he boarded a plane without incident.

The flight from Zurich to Madrid was just under two and a half hours. While waiting in the terminal at Madrid-Barajas Airport for his connecting flight, he made two more calls. The first was to leave a message with the Interpol hotline. He called from the Slovenian number and used his fake German accent to report that Rais was heading to an Amun safe house about fifty miles outside of Ljubljana.

He even gave them the address.

Immediately after ending the call, he made another to a number he had dedicated to memory. He wasn't sure if anyone would pick up, but on the third ring the line was answered. But whoever did said nothing.

"As Amun, we endure," Rais said in plain English, quietly so that no one else in the terminal would hear him.

"Who is this?" a male voice hissed. His accent sounded Serbian.

"A brother," Rais replied. *At least I was.* "Agents will soon be en route to your location. Be prepared."

"How do you—"

Rais hung up before the man could finish his question. If Amun members were hiding out in the Slovenian safe house, they would either have to vacate or attempt an ambush. It didn't matter; what was important was that the CIA and Interpol believed him to be heading east.

He deleted the calling app from his phone and pulled the battery. In the restroom, he broke the phone in two and disposed of its pieces in three different receptacles.

Rais did not pause as he stepped off the second plane. He did not hesitate and he did not linger. He simply nodded politely to the flight attendant at the exit and followed the long line of weary passengers as they disembarked. He was, after all, incognito, and he had never been much of one for sentimentality.

Even so, it was the first time he had stepped foot on American soil in nearly two years.

As he made his way toward customs, he ran a hand over his shorn hair, cut close to the scalp. He casually patted at the dark, prosthetic beard, as if scratching an itch, to ensure it was still adhered firmly. He made sure to keep the omnipresent squint at the corners of his eyes (no easy task to maintain for a nine-hour flight) to give him the appearance of being several years older.

He had gotten quite lucky, it would seem. As he made his way toward customs he heard the collective groans and complaints of would-be passengers awaiting their flight. International travel was being shut down in the United States. Intercom announcements and digital boards scrolling through rows and rows of canceled flights told him that something was definitively amiss in the world. He did not know what, and it didn't matter. He had reached his destination.

On the eight-hour flight from Madrid to New York, Rais slept fitfully in a window seat beside a polite middle-aged Spanish woman who, thankfully, had little interest in talking with him. In between catching bits of sleep, Rais plotted. He had no resources at his disposal, and only a bit of money to get where he needed to be. But he had his wits, and he had his knowledge, and his body was, for the most part, back in working order.

It would have to be enough.

Much like his long nights in the hospital, Rais plotted every scenario he could conceive of how to find Kent Steele's residence. Finally he landed upon an idea that, if done correctly, he was confident would work.

At John F. Kennedy International Airport, his ears filled with the gripes and outcries of irate travelers whose flights abroad were being canceled. Yet he was hardly curious. It did not concern him.

At the customs desk, a blasé security official inspected his German passport and asked if Rais had anything to declare. He told the man no.

Internally, however, he had much to declare.

I endure.

I will find Kent Steele.

And he will suffer in unimaginable ways.

CHAPTER SIXTEEN

Reid's phone chimed as the Gulfstream descended from the sky toward Athens.

It was Langley.

"You're cutting it awfully close," Reid answered. "We're about to set down."

"Well, it wasn't easy to find," Cartwright replied somberly. "Outside of the Syrian refugee registry, there wasn't a single mention of a Muhammad al-Mahdi." Reid's heart sank for a moment, thinking Greece a dead end, until the deputy director added, "But we did locate an M. Mahdi. He's had a suite reserved at the Athens Grand for eleven days now."

Reid frowned. *The Athens Grand is a five-star hotel*, his brain told him. He had been there; he had a sudden and keen recollection of marble floors, vaulted ceilings, white columns, and suited bellboys. The way his memory was coming back was interesting, different from last time; while before he would get brief flashes of memories, like scenes cut from a movie, he was now getting names, images, and full recollections, as if the pieces of the puzzle were falling into place the more he was able to recover.

"The Athens Grand seems like kind of a posh place for a displaced Syrian, don't you think?" he said.

"It's why it was checked last, but lo and behold. The hotel isn't far from the airport, so you should be able to get there quickly." Cartwright sighed. "Listen, this lead was discovered by our friends at Interpol. They shared it with us, but you can bet that agents are en route right now, and that Greek police are going to know in minutes. You've got a very narrow window of opportunity."

"There's nothing you can do to keep them at bay?" Reid implored. "We should keep this covert. If this guy is here, I don't want him spooked."

"We're already sticking our necks out big-time," Cartwright replied. "Our hands are tied. Get there fast and see what's what. And remember, this is one of those situations that might be worse for us if you're right than if you're wrong…"

"So we'll proceed with extreme caution," Reid interrupted. He was beginning to feel like Kent again, the way he had back in February. A nervous excitement bubbled within him, and try as he might to stifle it, he had to admit that he enjoyed the thrill.

"You should know, Steele, the president has ordered a cease on all international travel into the US," Cartwright told him. "As has the entire EU, Morocco, and Mexico. Reports of infection are coming from as far north as central France…"

Reid's breath caught in his throat. "Another attack?"

"We don't think so; seems like it's still fallout from the Barcelona outbreak. All the same, it doesn't bode well if the WHO can't contain it. And word is starting to get out on this. There are some in the media that are reporting suspicions of terrorist activity."

"We'll get it done," Reid promised. It was more of a vow to himself than to the CIA.

"Report back with an update…"

"Wait, one more thing," Reid said hurriedly. He bounced slightly in his seat as the wheels of the Gulfstream touched down on the Athens tarmac. "That Amun assassin, Rais, he's still out there. I'd like my girls moved to a safe house until I get back."

The deputy director was silent for a moment. "Kent, your girls are safe. We need you concentrating out there—"

"I won't be able to concentrate unless I know they're okay," Reid interrupted. It came out harsher than he expected. Two rows in front of him, Dr. Barnard twisted in his seat to throw a quizzical glance Reid's way. He lowered his voice. "If anything were to happen to them…"

"Kent, listen to me. Our latest intel suggests he's moving towards Russia. Besides, with ports of entry shut down, there's no way for him to get into the country. Your girls are fine. As soon as we hang up, I'll call Thompson myself."

Reid's nostrils flared. It wasn't an outlandish request, nor was it a difficult thing for Cartwright to do. But he also understood the severity of their current op, and he imagined that the deputy director, much like himself, wanted to stay focused on the task at hand.

"Fine," he said finally. "But if we have any reason to believe otherwise…"

"We'll move them in a heartbeat," Cartwright promised. "I'll handle it myself. We're a little short-handed right now as it is, but as soon as we have an agent available I'll send them over and have them picked up, all right? Now get to it. Athens Grand, room 405. Quick, quiet, and keep it clean." Cartwright hung up.

The plane slowed to a stop and Agent Watson lowered the exit ramp. "We have a destination?"

"Athens Grand Hotel, room 405," Reid told them. His team exited the plane—Watson, Carver, Maria, Barnard, and himself. There was a dark SUV waiting for them on the tarmac, another arrangement by Cartwright and Riker.

As they climbed in, Carver asked, "We have anything to go on here? A description, an age, any distinguishing features…?"

"Outside of being Syrian, no." Reid got into the backseat, Maria beside him and Barnard at the window. Watson drove, with Carver in the passenger side. "So our target is whoever is in room 405. We keep this non-lethal. Our aim is to detain, search, and question."

Watson punched the Athens Grand into the GPS console of the car. Cartwright was right; the onboard computer told them it was only a six-minute drive to reach the hotel.

"Johansson, Carver, I want you to take the stairs up," Reid instructed. It was strange to him how just being around the familiarity of an op could bring back his nature as an agent. It was almost as if he'd never left. "Watson and I will wait in the lobby, in case anyone tries to make a run for it. Radio down to us when you're in position and we'll take the elevator up."

"What should I do?" Dr. Barnard asked.

"You're going to stay in the car until this is over," Reid told him frankly.

"Excuse me?" Barnard frowned. "Agent Steele, I assure you I have been trained with firearms, rapid intervention, strike-team protocol—"

"Are you an agent?" Reid interrupted. "Or are you a doctor?"

Barnard stared straight ahead, clearly unhappy but not arguing.

Beside him, Maria's fingers surreptitiously found Reid's and gave his hand a reassuring squeeze. "You ready to get back into this?" she asked quietly.

He nodded. "Yeah. I am." And it was true; his muscles were taut with anxious energy, craving a thrill, a chase, a release of adrenaline and endorphins. It should have scared him, how easy it was to settle back into his Kent Steele persona. But it didn't; it excited him. He couldn't help but wonder how he managed it before, when he had all of his memories. How did he go from being Professor Lawson, loving husband and father, to CIA Agent Kent Steele? Was it like flicking a switch? Was he able to leave the terror and bloodshed at the door? He had failed to do that after Davos; perhaps whatever part of him was able to keep up the subterfuge with his family was still locked away in his mind.

"Radios on," Watson said as they approached the hotel. "Keep the line of communication open." He pulled the SUV into the roundabout that led to the valet service.

The first three floors of the Athens Grand had been built to mimic ancient Greek architecture, with huge white Ionic columns supporting the stone awning over the hotel's main entrance. Beyond that, another twelve floors stretched skyward in a simple gray high-rise, a bizarre but beautiful blend of contemporary and past, situated on the edge of the city proper.

Watson parked the SUV just beyond the valet stand. "Barnard, keep the engine running and don't let anyone move it. We'll keep in contact."

The doctor murmured his assent, and the four agents climbed out of the car. A young parking attendant in a red vest chattered at them in unintelligible Greek—*I guess I don't know Greek*, Reid mused—but they ignored him and hastily entered the hotel's spacious white lobby.

"Stairs." Maria gestured towards a white door to the right of the bank of elevators and Carver followed her. She threw a glance over her shoulder at Reid. "See you soon." She and Carver headed up to the fourth floor.

Watson and Reid stood in front of an elevator, waiting for Maria and Carver to reach their position and scope it out. The two of them would look like an ordinary couple staying in the hotel; the four of them together might startle anyone paying too close attention.

Reid's foot bounced against the marble floor as they waited.

"Nervous?" Watson asked casually.

"Anxious," Reid replied. "And…yeah, maybe a little nervous. For all we know, a potentially world-ending supply of mutated smallpox could be forty feet over our heads. Let's make sure we play this cautiously, all right?"

Watson scoffed lightly. "Agent Zero is telling *me* to play it cautiously?"

Reid frowned. "What's that supposed to mean?"

"Nothing." Watson shrugged one shoulder. "Just 'cautious' isn't usually your way."

This time it was Reid's turn to scoff. Was *that* what this was about, Watson's aloof attitude toward him? Because he didn't care for the "Kent Steele way" of doing things?

"I'll remind you that I barely remember what 'my way' might be," Reid told him. Although, he thought, despite not having his memories as Agent Zero, when things got rough his instincts tended to kick in—often with very bad results for the person on the receiving end.

Maria's voice suddenly came through the radio, directly into his earpiece. She spoke quietly, her words feathered with an edge of white noise. "Fourth floor," she confirmed. "Hall is empty. We just passed four-oh-five. Door is closed. If anyone is in there, they're silent. There's an ice machine just around the corner where we can keep eyes on the stairs; we'll wait there for you."

"Got it. Be there in a minute." Reid pressed the up button, and both agents watched the red-lit display above the elevator as it descended to the ground floor.

The doors opened and Reid stepped aside as five people got out, scattering in different directions. Agent Watson stepped forward, but Reid paused, his brow knitting in the center in a deep frown.

Two of the people who disembarked from the elevator were men, dressed casually, walking slowly toward the exit. Their skin was an olive hue that might have been Greek. There was nothing to immediately suggest that there was anything amiss about them—except that they were speaking Arabic to each other, and Reid understood them as easily as if they had been speaking English.

"It is taking too long," the first man remarked to his companion as they brushed past Reid. "It should have been ready by now."

"Kent, let's go," Watson prodded, holding the elevator door.

Reid held up a hand sharply and took a few quick steps after the men, just in time to overhear one's words to the other.

"Patience," the man told his companion. "The Imam says today is the day."

The Imam.

"It's them," Reid called to Watson. "The Syrians!"

"What?" Watson stepped off the elevator, clearly confused. The two Arabic men heard him and spun quickly. Reid suddenly realized his mistake; he had been listening to an Arabic conversation, and he had unwittingly shouted to Watson in Arabic.

The pair of Syrians wasted no time; they took off at a sprint toward the hotel's exit. Reid gave chase, Watson not far behind him. A pair of British tourists stepped into Reid's path as he ran, and he plowed into a hapless middle-aged man, sending him sprawling across the floor.

"Sorry," Reid grunted. Watson caught up to him and the two agents burst through the doors, just in time to see the Syrians climbing into a silver sports car. A young valet, the same one who had shouted at them upon their entrance, was lying on his back and holding his bleeding forehead.

The sports car's tires screeched loudly and it rocketed forward, the back end fishtailing around the roundabout and onto the street.

It was them. There was no doubt in Reid's mind as he leapt forward toward their waiting SUV.

CHAPTER SEVENTEEN

Reid slid into the driver's seat of the still-running car. Watson jumped in beside him.

"Was that them?!" Dr. Barnard practically shouted from the back seat. He had witnessed the two men assault the valet and steal the sports car.

"Yes," Reid said breathlessly. "Buckle up." He slammed the gas and the SUV lurched forward onto the city street, barely missing an oncoming car.

"Jesus, Kent!" Watson shouted from beside him. "How do you know that for sure?"

Reid swerved expertly in and out of traffic. The roads in this part of Athens were tight, two lanes wide and lined with storefronts and cafes. "They were speaking Arabic," he said calmly. "They mentioned the Imam."

"Imam can mean a lot of things," Watson countered. He gripped the handle over his door with white knuckles.

"They ran, Watson! They stole a car!" Reid resisted the urge to shoot his partner a sidelong glare and focused on the road. He blew through a red light, inviting a slew of honks and Greek profanity.

Where are they? They couldn't have gotten too far ahead. The silver sports car the Syrians had hijacked could certainly outpace the SUV on the open road, but on the busy streets of Athens it would be more of a level field of play and come down to the more experienced driver.

Reid kept his eyes on the road, not blinking, his hands expertly maneuvering the steering wheel smoothly. His heart was pounding harder than it had in a month, and his mind was racing with the possibility of losing the terrorists, but his hands—his hands were steady.

You've done this before. Plenty of times. Again the familiar sensation crept into his mind; just like realizing he could speak Arabic or speed-load a pistol clip, Kent Steele handled the SUV like a rally car driver. And he was not going to allow them to get away.

Up ahead he caught a flash of silver as the sports car weaved in and out between lanes. "There you are," Reid murmured. He jerked the wheel slightly to the right. The passenger side tires bounced up onto the sidewalk as he skirted around traffic. Passersby cried out and leapt aside, though he was careful of pedestrians.

"Take it easy, Kent!" Watson scolded from the passenger seat. "This is an urban area!"

Reid said nothing. The sports car had a good lead on them but the SUV had a better engine—a five-point-seven-liter Hemi, by the sound of it. If the Syrians wanted to lose them, they would have to find a highway or a stretch of road with no traffic.

"Kent?" Maria's voice crackled in his ear. "What's going on? Where are you?"

He had forgotten for a moment about Maria and Carver, still at the hotel and awaiting their arrival. He pressed a finger to his earpiece. "We're in pursuit of a pair of Arabic men that jacked a car. They must have been coming down in the elevator as you were going up the stairs."

"Ten-four. Carver and I are going in to see what we can find in the room."

"Be careful," Reid told her. "There might be more than just two." Only static hissed in his ear. "Maria?" No response; they must have exceeded the two-mile capability of the radio.

Not more than thirty yards ahead, Reid saw the back end of the silver sports car drifting sideways as they attempted a tight left turn. The light was changing, so Reid slammed the gas, jumping to nearly sixty. "Hold onto something!" He did not slow down as he approached the turn; instead, he yanked the emergency brake up as he jerked the wheel. The SUV slid sideways into the intersection and Reid counter-steered. He held his breath for a moment as the driver's side wheels came off the road for a moment.

"Christ, Kent!" Watson shouted.

Then he straightened the steering wheel and the tires met ground again. The smell of burnt rubber filled his nostrils as he slammed the gas anew to catch up to the Syrians. Pedestrians scattered; he could hear their surprised cries even through the closed window and over the roar of the engine.

His heart was pounding a mile a minute and adrenaline coursed through his veins. Reid had to fight to keep the grin off his lips. This was the hunt, what he missed most about being in the field. This was his runner's high, his endorphin release, his drug of choice.

Twice more the sports car turned wildly, trying to lose them, but the Arabic driver was not as skilled. The car's tires skidded in protest, slowing them, and Kent's expert driving closed the gap between them. Watson continued to protest from beside him, but Reid ignored it. Behind them, Barnard muttered quietly to himself, though at least once Reid could have sworn he heard the phrase "Please God..."

Funny, he thought. *I guess we all get a little religious when we think we're going to die.*

They hit a straightaway with only tight alleys as turn options. Reid rode the line at sixty-five, praying that no one jumped out from the narrow side roads. The Syrians would have to try to turn again eventually; Reid had closed the gap to between thirty and forty feet from bumper to rear fender.

"Good, that's close enough," Watson said breathlessly. "Let me get a license plate number, and... What the hell are you doing?!"

Reid reached into his coat and unholstered his Glock 19, keeping the car at speed and driving with his right hand. *Time to see if Bixby's biometrics work*, he thought as he rolled down the window.

"Kent... just hold up a second..."

Any moment now… He wrapped his hand around the Glock, with his thumb naturally positioned over the biometric pad. Something inside the gun clicked; the trigger lock sprang open.

"Kent!" Watson barked angrily.

The silver sports car careened to one side as the Syrian driver attempted a left turn. The driver's side wheels came off the ground slightly. They were taking the turn too tight and too fast. Reid didn't even try to follow into it.

Instead he leveled the gun out the window, aimed, and fired off two shots.

Barnard gasped from the back seat at the sharp report of the Glock. The first shot missed, but the second found a home in the rear tire. As rubber shredded, the sports car lost traction with the ground and rolled. Time seemed to slow as the vehicle flipped twice on its side, each impact with the road sending a sickening crunch echoing into the air. The car crashed into the storefront of a deli with a stupendous racket. Glass exploded outward. People on the street screamed and scattered as the sports car came to a sudden stop upside-down on its roof.

Reid slammed the brakes and the SUV skidded sideways to a halt. Watson breathed hard beside him. He wasn't sure if Barnard was breathing at all. Gun in hand, he jumped out of the car and headed toward the crashed car.

Two Greeks emerged from the deli. A cursory glance told him they had only minor cuts and scrapes. "Go," he told them in English. "Get clear." They clearly understood his gesture, if not his words, and they did not have to be told twice.

He kept the Glock pointed at the ground as a figure crawled from the wreckage—the driver, inching forward on his knees and one elbow. Blood ran down his face from a gash across his forehead, and his left arm was certainly broken. Even so he managed to pull himself from the crash and then carefully climbed to his feet. As soon as he was up, he stumbled and fell again, crying out in pain at his broken limb.

"Stay on the ground," Reid told him in Arabic. "Do not get up."

The Syrian glared at him furiously, a snarl on his lips. Despite the warning, he tried to rise again, cradling his broken arm with his good one. Reid saw a glint of metal as the man yanked a small gun from his jacket. Before Reid could even react, the Syrian fired off two shots.

The man was disoriented, unstable, and the shots went wild. Reid leveled his gun, aiming at the Syrian's shoulder, but another shot rang out. From behind him.

The man's body went rigid as the bullet hit center mass. Blood flowered from the Syrian's chest as his heart emptied, and he crumbled to the ground.

Agent Watson stood behind Reid, his pistol leveled. Watson had taken the shot. Reid had the Syrian dead to rights, about to disarm him, and Watson had put the man down.

"Why did you do that?" he demanded angrily. "We could have gotten information out of him!"

"Are you out of your damn mind?!" Watson shouted back. "He almost got the drop on you!"

"I had him…" Reid argued.

"Jesus, what part of 'covert op' do you not understand?" Watson slid his Glock back into the shoulder holster under his coat. "What if you had hit a pedestrian? What if one of his shots had gone through a window and hit a kid?"

"What was I supposed to do?" Reid shouted back. "Let them get away?"

"No, Kent. You were supposed to get close enough for me to get a license number, a make, and a model." Watson lowered his voice. "Because then we could call it in and track the vehicle. It's a new enough car to probably have GPS. We could have watched where they went and followed them."

Reid scoffed. "We don't have time for that."

"Well, you may not remember this, but that's what an intelligence agency does, Kent. We gather intelligence, and we act intelligently. Not… *this*." He gestured to the dead man in the road, the overturned sports car, the destroyed deli storefront.

Reid didn't have a good response for that. He had simply acted out of instinct, and if he was being honest, the thrill of the chase took over. Stopping the Syrians was the only thing that mattered in the moment. And now the fact that he didn't have a logical response to Watson's rebuttal only made him angrier.

"So that's it then," he said forcefully. "That's your problem with me, isn't it? That I do things a little differently than what you're used to?"

"A little differently." Watson chuckled bitterly. "Sure. Just a *little* differently. Good ol' Ground Zero." He approached Reid and lowered his voice to nearly a whisper. "And what if they had the virus on them, Kent? What then?"

"They don't." Neither of the Syrians had been carrying anything out of the Athens Grand, he was sure of it.

"All it would take is a vial," Dr. Barnard said quietly. He too had gotten out of the SUV, still trembling slightly from the high-speed chase. "The tiniest amount could do untold damage."

Reid stared at the ground. *Jesus*, he thought, *he's right*. He had been so intent to catch them that he had neglected to think clearly.

"I'm going to go see if anyone's hurt." Watson sighed. "Search the body for ID or leads."

Watson hurried over to the broken storefront as Reid approached the dead Syrian. He rolled the man over and checked his pockets, finding only a wad of euros and a cell phone. No virus, thankfully. He took the findings, along with the man's gun, and stowed them in the SUV.

He turned his attention to the overturned sports car and knelt beside the passenger side. A face stared back, eyes wide and mouth slightly open. Reid winced; the second Syrian looked like he was barely into his twenties, and he hadn't been wearing his seatbelt when they crashed. His body was upside down, head at an odd angle with the ceiling. The impact had broken his neck.

Watson ushered two more people out of the deli, a woman and an older man—the latter of whom was presumably the proprietor, since he was wearing a white apron that was slightly spattered with blood. At the sight of civilians exiting the now-destroyed deli, Reid felt a deep pang of remorse and hurried over to make sure they were all right.

"Superficial injuries, mostly," Watson told him. "Nothing serious and no one killed. Luckily."

Even though Reid was thankful for that, he was certain he was going to hear about this.

Sirens wailed in the distance; it was the police, either on their way to the Athens Grand or to their location. Maybe both.

"Let's go," Watson said. "Cops and Interpol will be all over that hotel any minute, if they're not already. We'll need to see if Maria and Carver came up with anything."

Reid didn't argue, even when Watson climbed behind the wheel. The three of them were silent as they headed back to the Athens Grand. Once they were within radio range again, Reid tried Maria. "Johansson? You copy?"

"I'm here," she said quietly over the radio. "So is Interpol, and Greek authorities. They're not happy. They said there was a car crash…?"

"In a manner of speaking. We're fine. Did you find anything?"

"Oh yeah," she said, but her voice sounded tight and anxious. "We found something. Get back here as fast as you can."

CHAPTER EIGHTEEN

"**A**re you nearly finished yet?" the Syrian asked irritably. The thin, wiry man—the one that Khalil had labeled a "specialist"—had been sharpening a wickedly curved hunting knife for the past thirty minutes, rubbing the blade back and forth on the edge of the rough-surfaced worktable, much to Adrian's irritation.

"Nearly," Adrian told him. Both men wore decontamination suits in the basement of the tailor's shop in Marseille, Adrian Cheval's makeshift laboratory, as he completed the necessary containment of the smallpox samples.

"You told Imam Khalil you would need only until morning. It is nearly ten a.m. What is taking so long?" The man spoke much better French than his partner, the one who was holding Claudette hostage. Adrian wondered if she had been taken somewhere, if she was okay in the hands of that monster.

"I said *at least* morning," Adrian replied sharply. "Impatience is a fatal shortcoming in my line of work."

"And restlessness is one in mine," the man grunted.

Adrian looked up from the RNA model displayed on his laptop screen. "You must know that this is not the way. What Khalil is planning to do with this is an abomination—"

"It is none of my business," said the man brusquely. "As long as I am paid."

Adrian scoffed. "And what happens when your friends and loved ones are dying around you? When you feel yourself growing nauseous? When you cough and there is blood in your hands? What will your money do then to save you?"

145

The man simply shrugged. "It will get me to Borneo."

"Borneo. You think you will be safe there?"

"I suppose we'll see." The wiry man returned his attention to his knife.

Adrian could see there would be no changing the man's mind. It was not the first or even the second time during the night and morning that he had tried, but it would be the last. He typed away on the computer's keyboard, attempting to look busy, but really he was only feigning progress. The samples had been ready for hours—in fact, they had been prepared even before Imam Khalil's men had returned and taken him and his beloved Claudette hostage. But the sadist standing guard did not seem to have a clue what Adrian was doing, so he pretended to still be at work.

He was wasting time in an effort to come up with a plan.

The longer they remained down in the lab, the more time Adrian had to think, and he had come to some conclusions that had previously been muddled by his emotions and concern for his misguided love.

The most important of his conclusions was also the simplest. There was no reason for Khalil and his people to keep Adrian alive once he was done.

He had argued the usage of the virus. He had told them that the lethality and virulence was unintended. He had begged Khalil against using it. He had, effectively, doomed himself and probably Claudette already. He put himself in the shoes of the Syrians; if he were them, he would fear that as soon as they left with the virus he might call the authorities, even anonymously, and report it.

Any way that he considered it, any angle at which he took the facts, it was clear that he had outlived his usefulness as soon as the virus was prepared. And Claudette, his dear, sweet beautiful Claudette, she knew too much.

And so Adrian delayed for as long as he could, pretending to work while his captor grew more and more impatient. Soon, however, he would have to act. The problem was that while he knew the virus had to be destroyed, even if it meant his life, he refused to subject Claudette to the same fate.

But maybe I don't have to. The Syrian sadist had a knife and a gun. The knife hadn't left his hands since they had put on the clean suits. The gun, the silver pistol he had stuck in Adrian's face in the alley, sat upon the far edge of the long wooden workbench, within arm's reach of the man.

If he could distract the Syrian long enough to get the gun, he could shoot him. But the report would be loud—loud enough not only to alert those upstairs, but also the Syrian's partner. Adrian would not have enough time to kill the man and then destroy the virus; it would have to be the other way around.

He had a failsafe for destroying the virus, if necessary, and as most things go, the simplest answer was generally the best one. High on a shelf to the right of the workbench was a glass bottle filled with a yellowish fluid—pure chlorine in liquid form. It would kill the virus the instant it was exposed to the toxic chemical, but was also incredibly dangerous; to open the bottle in an enclosed space like the basement without the aid of the respirator would cause unconsciousness in seconds, and death in under a minute…

That's it, Adrian thought. *The chlorine.* It would be, as they say, two birds with one stone. He quickly formulated a new plan in his mind: Distract the Syrian. Open the chlorine. Tear the man's mask from his face. Confirm he is dead. Destroy the virus. Take the gun. Kill the other Arab, and free Claudette.

It was remarkably simple—but again, he realized, the right answer often was.

Even so, it took him another ten minutes to gather his courage and remind himself that he was capable, intelligent, and strong-willed. "I need assistance," he told the sadist.

The man raised an eyebrow. "Doing what?"

"I cannot manipulate the strain and watch for the proper mutation at the same time," Adrian said. That was, of course, a pseudo-scientific lie, but the Syrian would not know that. "All I need you to do is look through the microscope as I alter the RNA sequence, and describe what occurs."

The sadist groaned irritably and made a big show of rising from his stool. "And then you will be finished?"

Adrian nodded. "Yes."

"Fine." The man bent at the waist and put his face to the lens of the microscope. What he was seeing was a slide of inert *variola major*. He could stare for decades and nothing would happen. "That is what it looks like up close?"

"Yes," Adrian confirmed, "and I want you to watch the leftmost edge of the cells, the bubble-shaped end of what looks like a barbell. Do you see that?"

The man hesitated a moment, but nodded. "I see it."

"Good." Adrian tapped a few useless keys on his computer, pretending to influence the virus in some way (and hoping that the man did not realize that a laptop computer could not, in fact, mutate a virus). "Anything?" he asked.

"No," said the Syrian. "Not a thing. What will it do? Will it move?"

"You'll know when you see it." He tapped a few more keys. "It may take just a bit of time … don't take your eyes from it." As soon as he said it, he twisted and reached up over his head for the bottle of chlorine on the shelf to his right.

There was one thing that Adrian Cheval did not account for. Ordinarily, with his face pressed to the microscope lenses, the Syrian's entire field of vision would have been obscured. But with the respirator mask over his face, he had a small margin of periphery, and he saw Adrian's movement.

At the same time that Adrian turned for the poisonous gas that would destroy the virus, the Slav twisted as well, away from the microscope with the hunting knife still firmly in his fist. As Adrian reached, he knelt, and in one fluid motion he slid the knife into the meaty back of Adrian's thigh and out again.

The Frenchman's fingers grazed the glass bottle of chlorine as a pain like a thousand angry wasps seized his thigh. He cried out sharply as his leg crumpled beneath him and he collapsed to a heap on the floor, bleeding amply.

Both his hands clamped desperately around the wound as blood eked between his fingers. His sliced thigh stung acutely, but even more worrisome was the hole in his decontamination suit. Desperately he realized that he would not be able to open the hermetically sealed vials of smallpox to destroy them, or he would risk putting himself at jeopardy.

The Syrian sadist stood over him, the blade of his knife wet with blood. He shook his head sadly. "The Imam was right," he said in French. "You are brilliant. But that is the flaw with people such as yourself; you assume everyone else is an idiot." He chuckled lightly. "I assumed you would make a move. But to do so in such glaring fashion, Adrian, it's just... well, honestly, it's just disrespectful."

Adrian sucked sharp breaths through his gritted teeth, through the burning pain in his thigh. The Syrian knelt beside him.

"Move your hand. Let me see," he instructed.

Adrian did so, sliding one hand just slightly from the wound. As soon as he did, a thin stream of blood spurted forth. He gasped and quickly clamped down on it again.

He knew precisely what that meant.

The Syrian clucked his tongue. "Hmm. It looks like I nicked your femoral artery. That's not a good sign. One moment." He rose and crossed the basement, where the tailor stored old clothes with stitching errors and suits that customers had never returned to retrieve. He picked out a white shirt and tore the sleeve from it.

"Lucky for you," said the Syrian, "I am ex-military. A field medic, if you can believe it." He tied the sleeve around the bleeding thigh in a tourniquet. Adrian yelped as he yanked it tight. "There. Now, that will curb the blood loss, but it won't stop it. I imagine you have about thirty minutes at most—probably less—to finish your work. If you do, I will take you to the hospital. If you don't, I will let you die here."

Adrian breathed hard. His hands were sticky with blood and his leg throbbed angrily. "You won't," he said quietly. "You won't take me anywhere. We both know I die down here."

The Syrian nodded. "Like I said. Brilliant. You're right; you will never see the light of day again. Since you understand that, let me put it another way. If you don't get up and finish, then I will have my associate bring your girlfriend down here. We don't have a suit for her, but that won't matter, because she will not live long anyway. I will remove both her eyes in front of you."

Adrian's lower lip trembled, the terror of Claudette's death washing over him anew.

"And this...oh, what is it called?" He pointed vaguely at his own throat. "The thing that hangs, I've lost the word...ah, uvula! The uvula. It is completely unnecessary, did you know that? But if you cut it off, it bleeds and it bleeds. Claudette will drown in her own blood. Would you like that to be the last thing you see before you die, Adrian?"

"Don't," Adrian stammered. "Don't. Please don't."

"Calm down now," the Syrian said. "An elevated heart rate will only decrease your remaining time." He took Adrian by the arm and hauled him to his feet. "These samples...they are finished, aren't they?"

Adrian leaned on the workbench, keeping his weight off his leg. He closed his eyes and said nothing. *I could tear off this tourniquet. Let myself bleed to death. It would be over fast. Like falling asleep.*

"All right then. I will retrieve Claudette." The Syrian moved toward the stairs.

Adrian lurched forward, leaping on his one good leg, and grabbed up the man's gun. It was still sitting on the end of the workbench, unattended. He lifted it in his shaky fist, smearing blood on the grip as he aimed and pulled the trigger.

Click.

He tried again. Nothing. He turned the gun over in his hand. There was no clip. It was not loaded.

The Syrian grinned wide. "I've been waiting for you to do that for the last nine hours." He turned back toward the stairs.

"No!" Adrian cried out. "Wait... wait. Yes. They are done. The virus is done."

The Syrian paused. "Good." He approached Adrian, holding his hand out expectantly. Adrian slowly handed him the gun again. The sadist reached under the workbench and pulled out the clip that he had ejected earlier. He pushed it into the gun and cocked it. "For what it is worth, I missed your femoral. I was bluffing. It would take a very long time to bleed out from that cut." He twisted a suppressor onto the end of the pistol.

Adrian closed his eyes. He thought of Claudette. He thought of the very first morning with her, waking in her bed with filtered sunshine framing her perfect face as she smiled down at him and told him, "I know exactly what you need."

I'll see you in the next life, he thought, right before the bullet entered his forehead.

CHAPTER NINETEEN

Reid was astonished to find the Athens Grand Hotel completely barricaded by the time they returned. Their pursuit of the Syrians had taken no more than twenty minutes, yet in that small window of time the five-star hotel had turned into an absolute madhouse.

Greek authorities had shown up in force, no doubt tipped off by Interpol about the suspected presence of the virus and Syrian terrorists. Several police cars choked the valet parking area, lights flashing. A WHO containment unit was on-site, donning containment suits as police evacuated angry guests out of the building and ushered them across the street.

"Well," said Dr. Barnard quietly from the back seat, "I suppose the proverbial cat is out of the bag now." He pointed; several members of the media had already shown up, reporting on the incident.

Watson double-parked the SUV and the three of them hurried to the entrance to find it swarming with bodies. It took three minutes to find Maria and Carver, the former of whom seemed to be in a heated discussion with a man in a blue suit. *Interpol*, Reid assumed. They likely wouldn't be happy that the CIA had somehow made it here first.

"They showed up just minutes ago," Carver told them as they approached. "The police right after them." The voices of frustrated guests nearly drowned him out. All of Europe had temporarily shut down international travel, and there seemed to be plenty of irate people wondering where they were supposed to go if not home or the evacuating hotel.

Maria stormed over to them, obviously irritated. "So much for cooperation between agencies," she muttered. "Interpol charged in here and took over the place like we were nobodies. I tried to tell them we found no evidence of the virus, but they're insistent on sweeping the entire hotel."

"I'm betting they're not too happy with us right now," said Watson, shooting a glance Reid's way.

He ignored it. "Did you get into the room? What did you find?"

"Let's get out of here first." Maria started toward the waiting SUV.

"So you found something?" Reid pressed.

"Tell you on the road."

"And what about sharing what we know with Interpol?" Watson asked.

Maria paused, annoyed. "We'll share with Baraf. We know him and we trust him. Look around you. Interpol shows up with the WHO in hazmat suits? There won't be any misconceptions about what this is or what it could be, and I don't want to be standing here when this crowd becomes a mob."

Reid hurried after her. She was right—and, he had to admit, so was Cartwright. This was why he wanted to keep the op small and quiet. People tended to start asking questions, if not panicking, when a dozen agents showed up … let alone the police and the WHO.

Watson drove, with Barnard between Reid and Carver in the rear. "What'd you find?"

"There wasn't anyone else in the room," Carver told them. "And I checked the guest log at the front desk; there were only two people registered for the suite."

"The two we went after," Reid guessed.

"And?" Carver asked.

"They're dead now," he replied flatly.

If Carver had anything to say about it, he kept it to himself. He was Watson's former partner, so Reid had few misgivings that they might share the same mentality.

"But I got this." Reid pulled the Syrian's phone from his pocket. It was a simple flip phone, no internet connectivity or GPS—likely a burner, but that would hardly be a hindrance. He flipped it open and navigated the menu with a thumb. "There's nothing saved in here, no contacts or names or messages ... but there's a number. Just one, and it looks like it called them once a day for the past eleven days."

"The student from Stockholm, Renault, was murdered eleven days ago," Barnard noted.

"Exactly." Reid passed the phone to Carver. "Send that number to Langley to trace." If the caller was also on a burner phone, they wouldn't be able to get a name—but they could trace the last call to a location, and as long as the phone was on, they could find it using cell tower relays.

Reid almost smirked. Ordinarily he could hardly figure out how to program a new contact into his cell phone, but a working knowledge of call-tracing was suddenly there when he needed it. *Curious,* he thought. He would have to test the returning knowledge when he had a moment. *After we find the virus, and the jihadist behind it, of course.*

"So we've got two dead Syrians and a cell phone number." Watson sighed. "It's not much, but I guess it's something."

"We also have this." Maria reached for the small of her back and pulled out a folded sheet of paper. "We tossed the room before anyone else got there. There was hardly anything out of the ordinary—but there was one thing that stood out. Here, take a look." She passed it behind her to Reid.

The page was folded in thirds, well-worn and crinkled as if it had been opened and closed several times. Barnard peered over Reid's shoulder as he unfolded and scrutinized it.

On the page were a number of black circles, drawn in marker, in no discernible pattern or order. There were no labels or words or numbers; just small circles, hand-drawn in such a way that to Reid it looked like a game of connect-the-dots. There were twenty-five in all, many of the circles crowded closely together in the lower left corner of the page, with a number of others spanned further out along the right side.

"What is this?" he asked.

"No idea," Maria told him. "Like I said, it was the only thing that looked strange, so we took it."

"Did you share that with Interpol?" Watson asked.

"Not yet. I snapped a photo; I'll send it to Baraf." She twisted slightly in her seat and added, "But if we happen to figure out what it is first, that would be very helpful."

"Barnard?" Reid murmured. "What's your take?"

"I can honestly say I am at a loss, Agent." The doctor pushed his silver glasses up his nose. "Perhaps the dots connect to form a shape, or a symbol, or ... or a map?"

"A map." Reid stared at the page until his eyes lost focus. *Dots on a map.* "Like the Manstein Plan," he muttered.

"Sorry?"

"In the early forties, German war plans were transmitted in pieces," Reid explained quickly. "If any single piece was intercepted, it wouldn't make any sense. But together, they formed a complete plan of attack. This could be a piece of their attack, their jihad." He shook his head. "But if this is a map, it's not anywhere I recognize. Once we're on the plane, we could try overlaying it against maps of Europe, start with the Iberian Peninsula where the first outbreak began and see if we come up with anything that makes sense—"

"Good lord," Barnard interrupted suddenly. His eyes widened behind his owlish glasses. "Agent Steele ..." He snatched the page from Reid's hands and flipped it around. "What does this look like to you now?"

Reid lost his breath for a moment. Suddenly the arrangement of the dots made a lot more sense—but not at all in the way he had hoped. "It's the western half of the world," he said quietly.

Maria twisted again in her seat. "What?"

"Here." Reid traced his finger along the cluster of dots now in the upper-right corner. "Europe. If this dot is Barcelona, then this would be Paris, London, Brussels, Berlin ..." He ran his finger along the page to the other side, now on the left, over the dots that were spanned further apart.

"The United States." Barnard's voice was slightly tremulous, and for good reason. Fourteen of the twenty-five dots were focused in what would be the US on the map, from Miami up to New York, and several more on the West Coast.

Reid's throat ran dry. He couldn't tell if it was coincidence or purposeful, but the largest of the dots was unmistakably over where the nation's capital would be. Washington, DC, was a target—and only a twenty-minute drive from his new home, just over the Potomac from his daughters. He didn't want to imagine the horror of his girls falling ill with such a fatal virus. His mind reeled back to Barnard's description of the symptoms—fever, nausea, internal bleeding. *Fall sick in the morning and be dead before sundown.*

If the virus found its way to the United States before he could stop it, and it was released in DC, his own children could be dead before he even returned.

"Maria, we need to get that photo to Langley and to Baraf," Reid said suddenly. "Every city on this map needs to be aware that they're a target."

"Already on it."

"Barnard, I want you to get on the phone to the CDC and tell them what we've found."

"Of course." He gulped. "What…what should I tell them? We don't know when this will happen, or how—"

"I overheard the two Syrians in the hotel right before they ran," Reid explained. "One of them mentioned the Imam, and said that 'today is the day.' Now I don't know what that means exactly, but we have to assume the worst."

"Another attack," said Watson.

"Right. So we can only relay what we know and try to be ready for anything…"

"And now we have a deadline to find our Mahdi," Maria added ruefully.

Carver's phone chimed. "We've got a location. The last call came from Marseille."

Reid blinked in surprise. "Southern France?" He shook his head. "No, that can't be right." Marseille was barely three hundred miles from Barcelona. Reid had assumed that the perpetrators would be as far away from the virus as possible, and that the virologist would have long fled from France. Either he had been wrong, or they were being fed another red herring, much like his suspicions with Barcelona. Was this Mahdi just that smart, or simply a lunatic?

Maybe both, he thought. If that was the case, they had mere hours to locate and interrogate an intelligent psychopath armed with twenty-four vials of a deadly virus he intended to unleash on the entire western world.

CHAPTER TWENTY

Claudette returned to the flat in Marseille to find a most welcome sight. Imam Khalil sat on her sofa, wearing a soft brown suit, his legs crossed at the knee. In the kitchen were four other followers, the Imam's entourage that had accompanied him from Greece three days earlier.

She beamed as she hurried to him, dropping to her knees and taking his hand.

"Darling girl," he said, gently squeezing both her hands in his. "Is it finished?"

"It is." She gestured behind her, where the Syrian driver Abad followed into the flat carrying the steel containment box that held twenty-four hermetically sealed vials of the mutated smallpox virus. Behind Abad came Rami, the wiry, lean-faced killer. She did not like Rami; he took pleasure in the pain of others, but the Imam had assured her that he was nothing more than a means to an end, and would not be following them into utopia.

"You have done so well." Khalil gently stroked her cheek with the back of his hand. "And Adrian?"

"He is … also finished." Claudette had not yet processed her feelings about Adrian's death. She had grown fond of him over their year together; perhaps she had even loved him, in her way, but he had lost the faith. He had turned his back on not only the Imam and Allah, but on her as well, and had tried to unmake his promise. And that was simply unforgivable.

"Abad, the kitchen." Khalil switched from French to Arabic. "Bag them both. Use caution."

Abad carried the steel box with both hands as he crossed into the small kitchen. Upon the counter was an identical box, emblazoned with the biohazard symbol, and two brown leather tote bags. The Syrian carefully lowered the box with the virus into one bag, and the second box into the other.

Claudette watched him curiously. "Two, Imam?"

"Yes, my dear." He turned to Abad and the other four Syrians mulling about in the kitchen. "Leave us," he ordered them. "Wait outside." The five filed out wordlessly, followed by Rami.

Once they were gone, Khalil sighed and lowered his voice. "Regretfully," he told Claudette, "the news has reported a false alarm in Athens. Two of ours were killed in a chase."

She gasped. "Marwan and Hilal? Dead?"

"I'm afraid so. But do not weep for them; they are with Allah, peace be upon Him."

"But... the map..." If the authorities found the two men at the hotel, they would likely have found the map of the Imam's intended targets.

"Yes, I'm certain Interpol has it. We cannot concern ourselves with that now. Our people are in place; the virus is ready. The plan continues. There is only one thing that can stand in our way now."

Claudette furrowed her brow. "What is it?"

Khalil smiled sadly. "Me, dear girl. They will come looking for me, and they might even find me. That is why we have prepared two identical boxes. I will take the empty one and lead the authorities away from here, to the coast. You will take the virus and carry out our plan." His warm gaze met hers. Though his eyes were a soft brown, nearly the same hue as the suit he wore, she had always found it difficult to hold his stare. "Do you know why?"

"Because I am the Imam Mahdi," she said quietly.

"Yes. You and you alone can bring redemption to the world. Bringing Adrian Cheval to me was the first step; now this is the last, and only you can take it." He leaned forward and gently kissed her forehead. "I must leave soon to divert the authorities from you. This is the last time we will see each other, Claudette. But before I go, will you pray with me?"

She gripped his hand tighter, holding back the threat of tears for this selfless man who would give himself for her, for the cause. "Yes, Imam. Of course."

Khalil lowered himself from the sofa and sat on his knees in front of her, facing her, as they each closed their eyes and prayed silently. Claudette prayed for the strength and fortitude to do what she must. She prayed for the safety of the Imam, and for the success of their holy mission.

"Thank you." Khalil opened his eyes and smiled once more at her paternally. "Go with God, peace be upon Him—and peace be upon you, Claudette." He rose slowly to his feet, and then crossed the carpet to the kitchen, where he hefted one of the two brown bags Abad had prepared. "Wait thirty minutes after I leave, and then depart. You will go alone; Abad and the others have their instructions. Remember, under no circumstances should you open this box. The virus must arrive intact."

"Of course, Imam. And...and thank you." Her voice was nearly a whisper.

He smiled at her once more, for what she knew would be the final time, and then left the flat. Claudette remained on her knees on the carpet for several minutes. She would never again see the man who had saved her life, who had brought her back from the brink of suicide and gave her purpose. But soon, it would not matter. They would be together again in utopia.

At long last she rose, planting her hands on the sofa for an assist—and she felt something hard between the cushions of the sofa. It was the Imam's cell phone, a simple and outdated flip phone that he used to communicate with his followers. It must have fallen out of his pocket when he sat, she reasoned. For a moment she panicked, thinking he might need it, but he was already gone. There would be no way to contact him now, and the plan was already in action.

She left the Imam's phone on the coffee table, and her own beside it. Neither of them would need it anymore. Then she headed up the stairs to the loft, changed her clothes, and prepared for the final step. When she was ready, she took one last look around the flat before lifting the brown tote bag and slipping the strap over her shoulder.

Then she too walked out the door, leaving it unlocked, and heading for the railroad yard where she would enact the last stage of the plan.

CHAPTER TWENTY ONE

"All right, listen up." Riker's commanding voice came through the speaker of Watson's phone so that the five of them on the Gulfstream could hear her. Reid glanced down at his own screen as an update came through, an ID photo of a pretty young woman with fiery red hair.

"You've just received a photograph of a Ms. Claudette Minot," Riker told them. "The cell signal of the number you found in Athens traced right back to her apartment in Marseille."

Reid frowned. The young woman did not fit into their profile of the virologist, other than being a French citizen. "What does she have to do with this?"

"Ms. Minot is a former aid worker with the *Service de l'Action Humanitaire*, a French humanitarian organization," Riker explained. "A few years back she signed on for a year-long stint, and they sent her over the Syrian border to help with the displacement crisis. According to her profile with the organization, she witnessed a sarin gas attack on an elementary school and it affected her to the point of attempting suicide. But it would seem she recovered, and converted to Islam."

Barnard nodded knowingly. "She fell in with our missing Imam."

"That's correct, Doctor," Riker confirmed. "Ms. Minot has an estranged brother in Paris; he says she came back from Syria a completely different person, indoctrinated by someone that she referred to only as 'the Imam,' some self-proclaimed holy man peddling a tailor-made offshoot of Islam. Minot mentioned the Imam several times to her brother, even tried to convert him. When he resisted, they stopped talking."

"Whatever the Imam had to say must have been exactly what she wanted to hear," Maria reasoned. "Do we have any bead on him at all?"

"I'm afraid not," Riker admitted. "It's not enough to go on, and getting anything from the Syrian government is near impossible."

"But I think it would be safe to assume that our Mahdi and the Imam are likely the same person," Reid offered. "The missing link between the Syrian boy in Barcelona and the virologist."

"Exactly," said Riker. "And speaking of, Ms. Minot has had a flatmate for the last year or so—a young Frenchman named Adrian Cheval, former virology student of Stockholm University who was expelled for forgery and unsafe practices."

Reid let out a long sigh. Time was running short, but the pieces were beginning to fall into place. "So the Imam indoctrinates the girl, and she involves the virologist." *There were two missing links*, he thought.

"Right. And all three phones are active," said Riker. "The mystery number and Minot's trace back to her flat. Cheval's is showing as three blocks east. We're uploading coordinates to GPS currently."

The intercom overhead crackled and the pilot's voice resounded through the small cabin. "Five minutes to wheels-down in Marseille."

"Does Interpol have all this info?" Carver asked. "The French police?"

Riker hesitated. "It took a bit of digging to find this out," she said. "We've only just gathered the intel now." Reid understood precisely what she was suggesting—that they were purposely holding back the information, even if only temporarily. But he didn't have to say it aloud because a moment later, Deputy Director Cartwright's voice came through the line.

"What happened in Athens was a complete disaster," he said. His tone was not friendly. "The media is having a feeding frenzy with it and Islamic terrorist involvement is on everyone's lips. To compound matters, we're shutting down mass transit and establishing

CDC presence in every city on your target map. Police and emergency services are on the highest alert, and that makes people nervous. Simply put, things are not good here. A whole lot of folks are panicking, and we can*not* afford another mess on our hands. There are five of you and three of them. Get in there, immobilize, interrogate. Find the virus. Put an end to this, quickly and quietly. Got it?"

"Yes sir," Watson murmured.

"Yes," said Maria.

"Good." Cartwright paused a moment. "Now let me talk to Steele."

Watson passed him the phone. Reid almost groaned aloud; he knew he was about to catch hell for his stunt-driving in Greece.

He took the phone off of speaker before answering. "Yes?"

"Zero." Cartwright suddenly sounded a lot less stern and a lot more tired. "You give me ulcers. You know that?"

"I know Athens could have been handled better," he said by way of answer. He stood and made his way to the rear of the plane's cabin as it dipped lower in altitude.

Riker scoffed, and then her irritated voice boomed through the phone. "Could have been handled better? That is quite an understatement, Agent."

"I'm sorry," he said halfheartedly. "We needed intel, and—"

"Do you have any idea," she interjected, "how difficult it is to convince Interpol to continue cooperation with us when we're killing key suspects? Do you know the effort involved in keeping the CIA's name out of the media when something like this happens?"

"I ... can't say that I do."

"People watch the news, Agent Steele, and people talk," she continued harshly. "Our perpetrators may have seen it. And when you leave a trail of bodies behind, it's only a matter of time before they realize that the trail leads back to them. Then they panic. I don't think I need to describe what could happen after that."

Reid gritted his teeth. She was right, but he wasn't at all willing to admit it. He was a professor, a CIA agent, a father of two, and in no way appreciated being spoken to like he was a petulant teenager who had crashed the family car.

"I was told to handle this by whatever means necessary—" he began.

"Not by me," Riker interrupted again. "I won't tolerate this kind of behavior on my team. Are we clear?"

Reid felt his face flush with anger, but he stifled it and managed to grunt, "Yes."

"Good," she said simply. "Then we're done here. Get to work."

"Wait." Reid threw a glance toward the front of the plane. No one seemed to be paying him any attention—but three of his four companions were CIA agents, trained to make eavesdropping not look like eavesdropping.

He ducked into the small bathroom before he continued. "My girls. Have they been moved to a safe house?"

Silence reigned on the other end of the phone. For a moment he thought that perhaps Riker had already ended the call. "Cartwright?"

The deputy director cleared his throat. "Kent, I spoke with Thompson myself. Everything is fine there. But we don't have an agent to spare. All hell is breaking loose here, and now we have a list of targeted cities... we just can't spare the resources."

Reid closed his eyes and again shoved down the urge to protest in anger. "But you're evacuating VIPs, right? The president, the cabinet, high-level officials... they're getting out of Dodge, I bet." He knew that protocol for a suspected attack on American soil was to first secure the heads of state. "It wouldn't be any big issue for you to put them on a plane..."

"Agent Zero." Riker spoke up. "While I appreciate your concern for your daughters, our focus right now needs to be on the well-being of every American. As much as I would like to make caveats for you"—Reid very much doubted that she would—"it would be irresponsible of us to use resources to make exceptions. Your fellow agents have families. I have people back home. Deputy Director

Cartwright, Director Mullen ... none of us expect anyone to go out of their way for our loved ones."

Reid squeezed his eyes shut and leaned his forehead against the mirror. There was no way he would be able to get Riker to understand that the perceived threat to his daughters was more than just a disease.

After a moment of silence she said, "Do you understand?"

"Yes."

"Good. Thank you. Report back with your findings." She abruptly ended the call.

For a brief moment, Reid felt the intense need to shout, to hit something, to find some quick and violent outlet for his anger. Kent Steele did not like being talked down to, and it seemed to be Riker's specialty. But he forced himself to take a breath. *That's not who you are. You've learned patience. You screwed up. Accept it.* He nodded, as if affirming it to himself.

When he pulled open the bathroom door he was surprised to see Maria standing directly on the other side of it.

"Oh," he said. "Sorry, I was just, uh ..."

She put a hand on his shoulder. "They're going to be okay," she told him, her gray eyes fixed on his.

"You heard that."

Maria nodded. "Rais has no way into the country. Travel is shut down. Intel suggests he's heading east. The virus is what's important right now, Kent. That's the threat to their safety. So let's stop one international risk before we move on to the next. Okay?"

He nodded. "Okay."

The plane bounced as the wheels touched down at Marseille Provence Airport. Reid gripped the headrest of the seat next to him to keep from falling over. The sudden jolt took him out of his own head for long enough to snap out of his feelings of anger and helplessness. Maria was right, as usual; the virus took precedence. Rais was two continents away, and Thompson was capable. It was time for him to focus.

"All right," he said to his team. "There are five of us and two locations. Dr. Barnard, if the virus is here in Marseille—and we can't assume that it's not—I think the virologist would be the most likely to have possession of it. Agree?"

Barnard nodded. "He would be my candidate of the two, yes."

"Then Barnard and I will go after the virologist. The three of you take the flat. Like Cartwright said, quickly and quietly. No one fires a shot unless absolutely necessary. If the virus isn't here, we'll need someone who can still talk." Reid turned to Watson and added, "And yes, that's *me* telling you that. I'll be sure to take my own advice this time around."

A corner of Watson's mouth twitched. Reid could hardly believe it—it almost looked like Agent Watson was going to smirk.

Much like El Prat in Barcelona, the French airport of Marseille Provence was utterly empty and quiet. This time there was no Interpol agent to greet them, no car waiting for them. They were alone in this.

The five of them hastily crossed the tarmac to a car rental agency opposite the main terminal. Watson pried open the lockbox that held the keys and grabbed the first two rings he found.

Dr. Barnard glanced up nervously at a security camera directly over them. "Is this legal?" he asked.

"Matter of international security, Doctor." Carver grinned. "Don't worry. We'll bring them back."

Watson passed off a set of keys to Reid. The electronic key fob led him to a dark blue sedan that looked reliable and swift. Not that it mattered; Reid did not plan on getting in another car chase in Marseille. Maria, Carver, and Watson were in a white mid-sized SUV.

"Be careful," she called to him before they parted ways.

"We will. Keep your radios on." Reid and Dr. Barnard climbed into the car and sped off in the direction of the coast. They were both silent until they were clear of the airport. "Switch your GPS on," Reid told him.

Barnard scrutinized his phone screen. "The virologist hasn't moved."

"Do you think that bodes well for us?" Reid asked.

"Hard to say. It could mean he lives there, or he works there. Or … or he's working on something else." Barnard didn't have to say more, because Reid was thinking the same thing. The virologist could be making more of the deadly virus. He could be working with active, mutated smallpox in the heart of a highly populated area.

"Why did you choose me?" Barnard asked suddenly. "To accompany you, that is."

Reid shrugged, taken aback by the question. "You're a virologist and a bioterrorism expert. If we're going to apprehend a virologist, I figured you would be the best person to have with me."

"I've seen and heard a lot of strange things in the last twenty-four hours," Barnard noted. "But you, Agent Steele, you are the strangest of them all. You're like a …" He thought for a moment, searching for the right word. "A polarity, existing inside a single person."

Reid almost laughed. "You have no idea," he muttered.

"Despite that, I think I might have grown some sort of admiration for you." The doctor stuck a finger in the air to punctuate his point and added, "Maybe. It's still too soon to say."

"Let's get through this alive and find the virus and we can talk again about if we like each other or not." Reid smirked. It was probably the closest he was going to get to a compliment from Barnard anyway. "Here." With some difficulty and driving one-handed, he reached down for his ankle and pulled free his sidearm, the Ruger LC9. "I don't know what to expect here, and you said you were trained."

Barnard took it reverently with both hands and turned it over, as if examining a specimen. "Thank you, Agent. I'll act responsibly."

"All I ask is that you don't accidentally shoot me."

"Turn here," Barnard said suddenly. He did so, and suddenly the road opened enough for them both to have a view of the sea.

Reid let out a low whistle. Marseille was an utterly beautiful city, its buildings almost entirely white and beige with orange roofs along the coastline, none of them more than six or seven stories high, as if not to overshadow any other. It was the type of uniformity that was rarely seen in modern times.

Barnard stared out the window. "It would be quite a shame if this was no longer," he said quietly.

"Then... let's make sure it still will be."

The doctor directed him toward the GPS signal, several tight turns as they headed slightly away from the coast and inland, heading uphill. The signal led them to a particularly narrow street in a business district, surrounded on all sides by little shops, mom-and-pop stores, small cafes, and restaurants that had stood there for decades.

Reid parked in the first available spot and they both got out. The air smelled like the sea and the passersby seemed generally pleasant. He desperately wished he was not there on business—and "business" was putting it lightly.

Barnard frowned. "It's a tailor's shop."

"Well, this is where the virologist's phone traced back to," Reid said, "so it's here, even if he's not. Come on, let's check it out." He led the way inside. The door creaked and a bell rang as they entered.

The tailor's narrow shop looked ancient and smelled somewhat musty, the walls lined with rack upon rack of classic clothing in browns and blacks and beige, suede and wool and cotton. They were the type of clothes that Professor Reid Lawson would have loved, but that felt like another life in the moment.

"Can I help you gentlemen?" An old Frenchman hobbled toward them from the rear, wearing a starched white shirt and a gray vest with a measuring tape around his wrinkled neck.

"I hope so," Reid replied in French. "We are looking for someone named Adrian Cheval."

"Oh, Adrian." The old tailor smiled. "A pleasant young man. He lives only a few blocks from here, down that way..."

"We know," Reid said. "But he's not at home. We were told he might be here."

"Ah." The old man leaned back onto a stool with a grunt. "Excuse me, my knees are not what they used to be. Yes, Adrian uses my basement for his research … something to do with genetics and DNA. It's all far beyond me." He chuckled. "The entrance is in the alley around back. I can show you …" The tailor grunted again, attempting to rise.

"No, that's all right." Reid smiled and put out a hand. "Please, sit. We'll find it just fine."

He nodded. "All right then. Have a nice day."

Back out on the street, Reid surreptitiously checked the clip on his Glock 19. He had only fired two shots in Athens; he was still nearly full.

"I thought you said no shots fired unless necessary," Barnard noted.

"I did," Reid said. "But it might become necessary." He replaced the gun in his jacket, and then touched the earpiece in his left ear. "Our location is a tailor's shop on Rue de Concorde. The proprietor told us the virologist uses his basement for 'research.' We're about to check it out."

"Ten-four," Watson responded quietly through the radio. "We're at the apartment, getting into position to infiltrate."

"Should we hold?" Maria asked.

"No," Reid replied. "The sooner this is done, the better. We'll be fine." He put a finger to his lips to gesture to Barnard for silence, and then waved him to follow down the adjacent alley. As they crept closer to the rear of the building, Reid's heart again started racing with the thrill of the hunt. *Restraint*, he reminded himself. *If the virus isn't here, we need this man alive.* And though he fully realized it was an insane thought for anyone to have, he very much hoped they did find the virus there, because it would mean an end to all of this.

They had nearly reached the mouth of the alley when Reid heard a car door slam, just around the corner from them, followed by the bark of a husky male voice.

"Leave the body. We'll take it last."

The voice spoke in Arabic.

Reid shoved Barnard backward against the brick façade of the tailor's shop. The doctor's eyes widened in surprise and his breath caught in his throat.

"Shh. Stay right here," Reid said as quietly as possible. He slowly pulled his Glock from its holster and rested his thumb against the biometric lock. The internal trigger guard sprang open with a small click.

He took a breath, his heart pounding, and then swung around the corner into view.

CHAPTER TWENTY TWO

Reid leveled his pistol as he stepped around the corner and caught sight of the two men in the alley. Neither of them, however, took any notice of him—not at first. They were seemingly Middle Eastern, wearing street clothes. The larger of the two carried a wide white cylinder, what Reid could only guess was a centrifuge. The other hefted a microscope in both hands as they carried the equipment toward a waiting van parked diagonally across the alley, effectively blocking it off to cars, and blocking them from a westerly view.

They're emptying the basement lab. And they mentioned a body. Neither of those things boded well at all for him.

"Stop!" Reid said sharply in Arabic. The two men turned slowly, seeming to be more confused at the sudden appearance of an Arabic-speaking Anglo than frightened of the gun. "Put down the equipment," he said carefully, "and put your hands on your head."

Neither of them spoke. Instead they exchanged a brief glance with one another, and then did as he asked—they dropped the equipment. The microscope's lenses shattered as it struck the pavement, and the centrifuge sent a jarring boom in the air.

The larger of the Syrians immediately reached for the small of his back. Reid didn't wait to see if it was a gun or not. He aimed and fired a single shot into the man's hip, high enough to avoid his femoral artery. It did the trick; the man yelped as his body spun and collapsed to the alley. The second Syrian scurried away and leapt behind the van for cover.

Reid surged forward; the downed man was holding his bloody hip with one hand, but still struggling to free his pistol. He managed to yank it loose, but Reid was upon him. He kicked the gun from the Syrian's hand and sent it skittering across the alley and under a dumpster.

He heard feet pounding against stairs and turned to his right just in time to see a thin, wiry Syrian charging up the stairs from the basement, flicking open a switchblade.

"Kent?" Maria hissed in his earpiece. "Was that a gunshot?"

It just became necessary, he thought, but he had to ignore her for the moment. Instead of running from the charging Syrian, Reid met him halfway; he leapt down the first few stairs toward him.

"*Allahu*—" The man's cry choked in his throat as Reid planted a flat boot into his chest, kicking him back down the way he came. The Syrian tumbled down the stairs, landing with a sickening crash on the concrete below.

He quickly turned his attention back to the two in the alley. "Stay down," he ordered the one lying on his back, grunting in pain from his shot hip.

"To hell with you, American," he hissed through gritted teeth.

Reid kept low as he approached the white cargo van. All the doors were closed and the windows were tinted; he couldn't see the man on the other side. Instead, he lowered himself to the alley and peered beneath the van. He could see a pair of brown shoes and the hem of the Syrian's khaki pants, hiding on the other side of the van just behind the passenger-side tire.

Reid took careful aim and fired. The bullet tore through the man's right ankle and he dropped immediately, letting loose a high-pitched scream that set Reid's teeth on edge.

Then he stood at the top of the stairs and waited. One Syrian was down behind the van. Another, only a few feet from the basement entrance. The third, at the bottom of the stairs. All three still alive, but he had no idea if there were more. He waited for a full ten seconds, but heard nothing except the anguished cries of the ankle-shot Syrian and the groans of pain from the other two.

He pressed a finger to his earpiece. "Shots fired," he confirmed. "Three down, all Arabic-speaking. We're both fine. No sign of the virologist yet—"

"*Mon Dieu!*" Reid glanced up to see the kindly old tailor, now wide-eyed in horror as he hobbled around the corner from his shop. He no doubt heard the shots and came to investigate. "Wh-what is happening here?" he asked in French.

"Monsieur," Reid replied, "please go back inside. It might not be safe to—"

The back window of the van exploded outward as a fusillade of bullets tore through the air, buzzing dangerously close like angry bees. Reid threw himself forward onto his stomach and covered his head with his hands. *A fourth, inside the van, with an automatic. You didn't clear the van,* he screamed at himself internally.

He dared to glance up, and in that moment time felt as if it stood still. The old tailor faced him, the same shocked expression on his weathered face. Blood slowly blossomed from several places on the old man's chest.

Then time resumed, and the tailor crumpled into a heap.

That was your fault. You didn't clear the van. His death is your fault.

Reid pressed his palms against the asphalt to push himself up, but a voice barked from the van behind him. "Your gun. Push it away." The surprise attacker in the van spoke rough, accented English. "Do this, or you die slowly."

Reid huffed a frustrated breath. He was on the ground and facing the wrong direction; the Syrian had the drop on him, and presumably a gun aimed at his back. After a moment of hesitation, Reid shoved the Glock several feet away.

"On your back," the attacker barked. "Do not rise." Reid did as he was told, turning over slowly so that he was lying on his back. The assailant had been in the rear of the van; the back driver's side window was blown out, and the bearded Syrian leaned partially out of it with the stock of an AK-47 against his shoulder. "Who are you?"

Reid shook his head slowly and said nothing. *We don't talk, ever.*

"How did you find this place?" The angry Syrian shook his rifle, as if it might prompt a response. "Answer me!"

Again Reid did not answer. Instead his mind raced. *They're not finished yet,* he realized. The Syrian would not be so concerned with who he was and how he found them unless he thought there was a chance their plot might fail. *They haven't finished enacting their plan.*

"Have it your way," the Syrian growled. "Death to the infid—"

Three roaring shots split the air suddenly, but they were not automatic gunfire. The Syrian's body jerked wildly backward and thudded against the opposite wall of the van. Dr. Barnard stood only a few feet from the unfortunate tailor's body. His hand trembled as he lowered the smoking LC9.

Reid leapt to his feet, retrieved his Glock, and stuck the pistol into the shot-out window to clear the rest of the van. Satisfied there were no others, he hurried over to Barnard.

"You okay?"

The doctor stared at the ground. "I-I've never shot anyone before," he murmured.

"Hey. You just saved my life, you understand?" Reid gripped the doctor's shoulder. The man was clearly shaken. "We probably don't have more than a few minutes until police arrive, so I need your head clear. Come on." He tugged gently on Barnard's shoulder and the doctor followed him to the entrance of the basement. "I'll go first. Stay alert."

Each man kept a firm grip on his pistol as they slowly descended into the makeshift laboratory. The wiry Syrian at the bottom of the stairs spat curses at them in Arabic, but Reid ignored him. The man had badly broken his leg in the fall; the bone jutted at a nauseating angle and blood soaked his denim jeans just below the knee.

Reid carefully cleared the area first—a simple task, since it was a single open room with a concrete floor—and found no one else. At least no one else alive.

He hurried over to the yellow-suited man lying prostrate on his back on the concrete. The respirator's facemask was cracked, and when Reid tugged it off, he saw the smooth features of a young Frenchman, and the bullet wound in his forehead.

"I think it would be safe to assume this is Adrian Cheval," he noted grimly. "The Syrians were done with him. They must have the virus. We should double-check the van ... Barnard?"

The doctor was hardly listening. He glanced around in wonder at the half-disassembled lab. "This man mutated one of the deadliest viruses known to mankind in a dirty French basement." He shook his head sadly. "What a waste of immense talent. Imagine what he might have done if he hadn't been brainwashed by these ... *animals*."

Barnard suddenly sucked in a breath and rushed to the far end of the basement, where a closed laptop computer sat upon a workbench. He pushed the lid open and the screen awoke, displaying Cheval's work: a cyclical RNA strand awash in vibrant hues, labeled with colorful tabs of notations in French. "My god," Barnard sighed. "This was his process, his mutagenesis. If we can transmit this to the WHO, it will make a vaccine significantly faster." He spun toward Reid. "The battery is dying. I need the power source, the plug ..."

Reid looked around quickly but saw no power adapter for the laptop. "No time. Use these." He reached into his jacket and produced the glasses that Bixby had given him. "There's a camera in the lenses." Reid took out his phone and opened the CIA drive. "Put those on and record whatever you can. It'll upload to the CIA."

Barnard did as Reid told him, slipping the glasses over his own round frames and frantically clicked through every available file that Adrian Cheval had left on the computer. Reid set his phone on the workbench next to the computer and had a quick look around for himself. The Syrians had taken most of the equipment; there was little to find besides the laptop and a few items on a shelf beyond it.

Or maybe there is. Reid retrieved the fallen Syrian's switchblade, even as the man continued to hurl curses his way, and used the blade to cut open the side of Cheval's decontamination suit. He carefully slid his hand in, retrieved the virologist's cell phone, and slipped it into his own pocket.

As he rose again, he heard the telltale whoop of approaching sirens. "Time to go, Barnard."

"Just one moment, Agent—"

"*Now*, Barnard." Reid pressed a finger to his earpiece. "We found the virologist. He's dead. The Syrians have the virus." There was no answer. "Maria? Watson?" No one responded. "Come on, Barnard…"

It was too late. He heard the screeching of tires above him as sirens screamed into the alley. A moment later the wailing klaxons were accompanied by slamming car doors and at least a half-dozen urgent voices shouting to each other in French.

"Dammit," Reid murmured. They couldn't afford to waste time explaining what had happened to the police and getting their story verified. He needed to know what the others had found—and why they weren't responding.

The thin Syrian on the floor grunted. "You are American, yes?" he asked in Arabic. With some difficulty he pushed himself up onto one elbow, his other arm pinned beneath him. "C-I-A?" He enunciated each letter carefully and in English.

Reid ignored him, keeping an eye on the doorway above at the top of the stairs. A figure appeared there, silhouetted by the sunlight behind him. "If anyone is down there," the officer called out in French, "show yourselves slowly, and come up with your hands above your head."

"Dead," Barnard muttered. The laptop's battery had depleted. "I believe I got enough to be helpful."

"We've got other problems at the moment," Reid told him. "Let's go. I'll do the talking."

The wiry Syrian on the floor, his leg bleeding amply, laughed hoarsely. "Your people and the French, they are not always so friendly."

"What is he saying?" Barnard asked as he pulled off the high-tech sunglasses.

"Ignore him. Listen, we show them credentials and we tell them the truth about what happened here. Do *not* mention the virus though. It's not here, and I don't want to cause a panic…"

"How will they feel," the Syrian continued in Arabic, "when they discover their deaths were on your hands?"

Reid spun on him angrily. "What are you talking about? Whose deaths?" Only the tailor and a single terrorist had been killed, and neither at his hand.

The Syrian laughed again as he worked his other arm free from beneath his body. Clutched in his fist was a cell phone, and his thumb hovered over the send button.

"No!" Reid lunged forward, but not in time.

The Syrian terrorist pressed the green button, and the van outside exploded.

CHAPTER TWENTY THREE

The detonation sent a jolting shockwave through Reid's body. He felt it before he even heard it, a deafening explosion that filled the doorway above them in a roiling fireball. Flames licked the stairs, and he felt the intense heat on his face, even as he covered it with his hands and fell to the ground. Debris showered down the basement stairs.

Dr. Barnard sat up on the concrete floor, swaying slightly and working his jaw as if trying to speak. He *was* trying to speak; Reid could hear nothing but a ringing in his ears.

Are you okay? he asked—or he tried to. He couldn't hear his own voice over the high-pitched whine in his head. He tried again and coughed on dark smoke.

He crawled over to the doctor, gripped his arm, and pointed upward. Barnard nodded vaguely and followed along, stumbling slightly, as they made their way to the now-charred stairs.

The Syrian was either unconscious or dead. In the moment, Reid didn't care which. He climbed the wooden stairs carefully, fearing that the explosion might have weakened any one of them.

The van was wired. Probably in case of this exact situation, if any authorities came around with knowledge of what they were doing. That was why the Syrian in the van had attempted to interrogate him. He wanted to know if they would be expecting others. The terrorist in the basement could have detonated earlier and killed both him and Barnard, but he waited.

He waited until he would have the most casualties. Not unlike the Imam's virus-bred jihad, striking the most populous cities around the globe.

Slowly but surely he and Barnard made it to the top of the stairs, though Reid immediately wished they hadn't. The scene was utterly horrific. The van still blazed, engulfed in orange flames. Several bodies lay in the alley, some charred beyond recognition, and others bloodied from the bomb's force.

"...beyond heinous," Reid heard Barnard say behind him. The ringing in his ears was subsiding. "I cannot believe that any people would want to do this to others."

"We have to call this in," Reid said hoarsely. He reached into his pocket for his phone—but the device he pulled out wasn't his. It was the virologist's. His phone was still in the basement, on the workbench where he had set it while Barnard recorded screenshots of Cheval's computer. "I have to go back down there—"

"Agent, wait!" Barnard grabbed his arm. The southern façade of the building, the one closest to the van, was blown inward, and the second floor threatened to topple. Wood groaned as it bent, and there was only so far it would give. "You can't. It could collapse. Take mine, but don't go back in there."

The building groaned and shuddered. This time Reid grabbed the doctor's arm, pulling him back as the entire roof of the two-story building slid slowly off its peak. It crashed into the burning van, sending a shower of embers that had both men shielding their faces.

If the Syrian in the basement wasn't dead yet, Reid reasoned, he would be soon when a few tons of rubble came crashing down.

"Give me your phone." Barnard handed it over, and Reid brought up the number for Langley. He had to report what had happened here before French authorities, or anyone else, got the wrong idea. No one alive outside of Virginia had any idea that he and his team were in France.

He was about to hit the green send button when a thought struck him so hard he nearly dropped the phone. "Jesus," he murmured. *If the van was wired, it was because they were expecting trouble. And if that's the case… Claudette Minot's flat might be wired too.*

Reid broke into an immediate sprint.

"Agent Steele!" Barnard followed as best he could. "Where are you going?"

He didn't have time to explain. It was only three blocks away. "Try to raise them on the radio!" he called back to Barnard. He ran as fast as he could, struggling to bring up the GPS on the doctor's phone at the same time.

"Agent Johansson? Agent Watson?" He heard Barnard's strained voice behind him as he gained a longer lead on the CDC doctor. All the while the mantra ran through his head, *Please no, please no, please no…*

He rounded a corner and practically skidded to a stop. Maria and Watson were there, standing on the sidewalk outside a row of connected homes, both looking bewildered. Maria's expression dissolved into relief when she saw him—and then immediately into concern.

"Kent, what was that?" she asked quickly. "Are you okay?"

"What did you find?" he demanded.

"Not much. The two phones, but only one man, and we don't think he's the Imam…"

One man. That's all it would take. *Why else would they leave someone there?*

"Which unit?" He sprinted past them. "Which one?"

"Kent, will you stop for just a second and tell us what happened?" she insisted.

He didn't need an answer; only one of the units had a wide-open front door. He bounded through it to see Agent Carver standing over a Middle Eastern man, who was seated calmly on the sofa of the living room.

Carver glanced up at him and frowned. "Zero, what the hell was that noise?"

Reid didn't answer. There were two cell phones on the coffee table—and with Carver's attention on Reid, the Syrian lunged forward suddenly, reaching for one of them. Reid leapt and tackled the man off the couch in a tangle of limbs. The phone skidded across the floor. Reid clambered to it while Carver put his knee into the Syrian's back.

He tore open the burner phone and yanked out the battery. Then, for good measure, he did the same with the other, a modern smartphone.

Watson and Maria stood just inside and watched for a moment as he dismantled the two phones. Barnard appeared in the doorway, panting and leaning against the frame.

"What the hell happened?" Watson asked.

"You're sure you didn't find anything else in here?" he asked.

"We tossed the whole place," Maria said. "There was nothing. No virus, no evidence . . ."

"No bombs?"

She blinked at him. "No, Kent. We didn't find any bombs. Jesus, is that what happened out there?"

Reid rubbed his face and his fingers came back with gray streaks. He couldn't imagine how he probably looked to them, half-crazed and covered in soot and dust. "The virologist is dead. The lab was being dismantled by the Syrians. They had a van, and it was wired. It must have been two pounds of C-4, maybe more. They detonated . . . just after the police showed up."

Maria covered her mouth with a hand.

"How many?" Watson asked quietly.

Reid shook his head. "I don't know for sure. Three cruisers, I think . . . maybe six people, not including three terrorists."

"Christ." Watson paced the length of the living room and back again. "And you couldn't stop them?" he asked. "You let them blow it?"

"I didn't *let* them!" Reid nearly shouted. "I didn't expect them to—"

"Didn't expect it." Watson scoffed. "Did you at least search them? Detain them? How did they blow it if you did what you were supposed to do?"

"I did what I was supposed to do," Reid said slowly. His fist balled instinctively. He very much wanted to hit something, to find an outlet for his frustrations and adrenaline and failure, and Watson was standing right in front of him, bristled and agitated.

"No, Zero, what you're *supposed* to do is avoid international crises when we've already got one on our hands. Since we've been out here, you've caused two—"

Reid had just about enough. He had just watched the tailor die, saw the bomb explode, and averted another near disaster, yet they were no closer to finding the virus. He didn't have the patience or tolerance to stand there and take any more abuse.

He took a step toward Watson and nearly raised his fist, but Maria intervened. She stepped between them, facing Reid, and stuck a finger in his face. "Calm down," she ordered.

Her slate-gray eyes bored into his as he stared down at her. His nostrils flared and he opened his mouth to protest, but she glared right back. "I said, calm down."

He let out a long breath that he didn't realize he had been holding. Some of the tension eased from his shoulders.

"This is not the time for us to fall apart," Maria told the room. "Now obviously we've hit a dead end, so there are two things we need to do: report to Langley with what's happened, and chat with our new Syrian friend." She turned to Reid. "Will anyone be looking for us?"

He shook his head. "I don't think so."

Maria raised an eyebrow expectantly. "You don't *think*?"

"No. No one will be looking for us." Everyone who had seen him and Barnard at the tailor's shop and the basement were now dead.

Outside, emergency sirens screamed as fire and rescue personnel dealt with the fallout of the explosion a few blocks away.

"It was a mistake coming here," Watson griped. "We should get clear before the French authorities come around."

"I said no one knows we're here," said Reid. "Look, don't you see? This was a setup. The Imam is smarter than we gave him credit for. He left his phone at Claudette Minot's flat for a reason. It was the only way we had to track him, if we could. And if we found the girl, we would find Cheval. No one had bothered to remove his phone either. That van was wired as a failsafe. Maybe they weren't expecting trouble, but they had a way to slow us down if we came."

"But we didn't find any bombs here," Carver said. He hefted the Syrian man off the carpeted floor and shoved him roughly back onto the sofa. "Only this guy."

Reid thought for a moment. He glanced down at the dormant halves of the two phones lying on the floor where he'd tossed them. If their speculation was right, one of them belonged to the Imam, and the other to Claudette Minot.

"What if he wasn't trying to blow anything?" Reid suggested. "What if he was trying to warn someone? The trail led back here. The van was carrying explosives. Maybe they didn't expect us to catch up this quickly. The bomb in the van could have been intended for elsewhere."

"One way to find out." Maria stooped and picked up the battery and the two parts of the burner phone. "I can check and see if there are any numbers in here."

"No way," Watson interjected. "We could be wrong. That thing could still be a trigger to a bomb somewhere else."

"Well, there's one way to find out." Reid strode into the kitchen and looked around, searching through cabinets and drawers.

"Hey." He felt a hand on his shoulder and spun to find Maria behind him. "You seem a little shaken."

"I'm fine." He didn't find much; a roll of duct tape under the sink, along with some cleaning chemicals, and a set of knives on the counter next to a gas stovetop. *That's all I need.*

"We tried to radio you when the bomb went off," she said quietly beside him. "You didn't answer."

"I lost my phone."

"Where?"

He hesitated. "Under a building."

She nodded slowly, as if that explained everything. *In our line of work, I guess it does.* Then, to his surprise, she took his face in both her hands and kissed him gently. "We're going to find it, okay?"

"You're damn right we will," Reid said. "Give me ten minutes with that guy and we'll know everything he does."

They returned to the living room, where the other three were standing over the seated Syrian.

"We managed to upload a video of the virologist's work," Barnard was telling Carver and Watson. "Assuming the CIA received it, it should help considerably in the manufacture of a vaccine."

"But you said it yourself, Doc," Watson replied dourly. "It could take months to mass-produce and distribute it."

"Well...yes," Barnard admitted. "I just thought...it could be helpful."

Reid could tell that Barnard was making an attempt, in his own way, to diffuse the tense mood. Their lead had been a bust; they had a single person to interrogate, and no further leads. Whatever the man on the sofa had to tell them would have to be their next step, so Reid vowed to make sure that it was the truth—by whatever means necessary.

"I got a good look at our former virologist," Reid announced. "It appeared he's been dead for no more than a couple of hours. That means it is entirely possible that whoever has the virus is still in France. We'll talk to Langley and let them make the call on whether or not they alert French authorities. But my concern right now isn't how it's getting into where it's going. It's how it's getting *out* of France."

"I'll put the call in to Cartwright and Riker," Watson said.

Reid grabbed the Syrian man by an arm and pulled him to his feet. "Come on," he said in Arabic. "You and I are going to chat in the kitchen." He half-dragged the man through the doorway. "Ten minutes," he told his team.

Though not directly responsible for what happened at the tailor's shop, this man knew about it. And Reid was sure he knew other things, too.

And I'm going to make sure you tell me everything you know.

Chapter Twenty Four

"Some people might start something like this by saying that there's an easy way, and a hard way." Reid spoke in Arabic for the benefit of his captive as he twisted the dial to turn on one of the rear burners of the gas range. It clicked twice and ignited in a ring of blue flames. "I'm not going to say that. There's only one way: *my* way."

The Syrian sat in one of the dining room chairs, facing away from the table. His hands were bound at the wrists by duct tape, his ankles taped to the wooden legs and another strip over his thighs, lashing him to the chair. Yet his face was passive. If he was concerned, he didn't show it.

"Here's how my way works," Reid told him, his voice low. "I'm going to hurt you. And then I'm going to ask you a question. Then I'm going to hurt you some more, but worse. There's no way around it, and there's only one way through it. That's for you to answer quickly and honestly. Do you understand?"

The Syrian's lips curled into a slight smirk. "I am not afraid of you. I am not afraid of pain, or death. Only one can judge me. And I will meet Him soon enough."

Reid knelt so that he was face to face with the man. "They all say that. Usually right before the screaming begins. Speaking of." He took a balled-up sock, one of Adrian's he had found in the loft upstairs, and stuffed it into the Syrian's mouth. "We don't want to wake the neighbors."

The last time Reid could remember torturing anyone for information was a Russian man, whom he waterboarded for intel on the

186

terrorist organization Amun. At the time it had sickened him to do it. All the while he kept thinking, *This is not what Reid Lawson would do.*

He was wrong then, and he wasn't thinking like that now. Reid Lawson was Kent Steele, and vice versa. He was not two minds in the same body. He was one man who, until he got his memories fully restored, was simply confused about who he was. But at the moment, he knew exactly who he was—and what he was capable of.

If the map they had found in Athens was correct, then Washington, DC, was a target. And despite the fact that millions could die if the virus was unleashed, Reid could think only that his two little girls were a mere stone's throw from the nation's capital.

This man and his cohorts, they had unknowingly threatened his family. And that made torture *precisely* the kind of thing that Reid Lawson would do to protect them, if he needed to.

"Barnard, you're probably not going to want to watch this," Reid said in English. The doctor stood in the doorway, possibly to satisfy some grim curiosity, but at Reid's warning he nodded and turned away. Maria stayed, leaning against the refrigerator with her arms crossed. She was no stranger to this sort of work.

Reid took a steak knife from the block he'd found and held it near the man's throat. But he wasn't slicing skin. Instead he swiped it downward on the collar of the Syrian's T-shirt, and then tore it open, exposing his chest.

"Nnggh." The man was trying to speak, but Reid wasn't interested in what he had to say—yet. He had already outlined his method, and the first step was not questions.

He held the head of a teaspoon over the blue flames on the gas stove. "I don't have time right now to explain the different degrees of burns to you," he said in Arabic. "Suffice it to say that what you're about to experience is going to be a second-degree burn."

He pressed the head of the spoon to the man's left pectoral muscle. His eyes widened and the sock in his mouth muffled his cry. When Reid pulled the spoon away, the skin was red and already beginning to blister slightly.

He yanked the sock from the man's mouth. "What is your name?"

The man sneered up at him, panting slightly. "Your friend in there...he called you 'Zero.'" Though he spoke Arabic, he said "Zero" in accented English. "You are the Agent Zero?"

"Yes. I am. And if you know that name, then you know that this is going to get so much worse for you."

"The fact that I know that means I will not make it through this alive anyway. I have nothing more to say." The man opened his mouth wide—but not to speak. He was inviting Reid to stuff the sock back into his mouth. ·

Reid obliged. The Syrian seemed confident, already knowing that this was going to end in his death and believing he had no reason to talk. *But he will. To stop the pain.*

He pulled on an oven mitt and held the spoon over the flames again, longer this time, until the head of it glowed orange. When he pressed it to the man's chest, the skin sizzled and immediately bubbled in angry, gray blisters.

The Syrian threw his head back and let loose a gurgled cry, drowned by the cloth in his mouth.

"That was still a second-degree burn," Reid told him, tossing the spoon and mitt in the sink. "To get to third-degree, we have to do something a little more drastic." He lowered himself to his knees. "Maria, hand me that bottle of floor cleaner."

She passed him a plastic jug of amber-colored liquid, and Reid splashed it liberally over the man's shoes. It stank of ammonia and artificial pine scent.

"I'm going to set you on fire now," he said soberly. "Starting with your feet. It's going to take a long time. You're going to watch as the fire melts your shoes. It won't hurt—at first. Not until the flames eat the rubber. By the time you feel your skin scalding, it will be too late. Your pants will catch fire. Your legs. It will slowly creep up and engulf you. And I will let it."

Reid took a strand of pasta he had found in a cupboard and held it over the blue flames until the end caught like a makeshift match. Then he lowered the flame toward the terrorist's feet.

"Mmm!" the man shrieked. "Nngh!"

Reid blinked at him. "I'm sorry. You made it clear you had nothing more to say to me."

The chemicals ignited quickly, orange fire spreading over the man's black shoes. The Syrian screamed in fear. He tried to thrash in the chair, to kick his legs, but the duct tape held him still. He whimpered and whipped his head left and right as the leather soles curled and the acrid scent of burning rubber filled the kitchen.

Reid glanced over his shoulder. Dr. Barnard stood in the doorway again, watching, one closed fist held tightly over his mouth as the flames licked the tops of the Syrian's shoes, threatening to spread to the hem of his pants. The panicked noises emitting from his throat were like that of some dying animal, vacillating between brays, grunts, and muffled screams.

After several seconds Reid leaned close to his ear and repeated his previous question. "What is your name?"

He pulled the sock from the man's mouth. "Please! Please, make it stop!"

"Your name."

"Put it out, I beg you!"

"You have less than a minute before your flesh begins to burn," Reid noted. "Your name."

"Abad! My name is Abad!"

"Who has the virus, Abad?"

"She does, the girl!"

"A name, Abad! What is her name?!"

"Claudette! Claudette! Please, stop this…" Abad squeezed his eyes shut, whimpering incoherently.

"Where is Claudette taking it?"

"I don't know! I swear to Allah, I don't know!"

"What *do* you know, Abad?"

"North! I know she went north…" Abad winced. The fire was burning through his shoes. "Please, it hurts, make this stop…"

"What were you trying to do with the phone? Warn her?"

"No!"

"Is there another bomb?"

"A car, outside ... black ..."

Reid glanced over his shoulder at Maria. She stepped forward and asked in Arabic, "And the Imam? What is his name?"

Abad was near hyperventilating, his chest heaving as the flames caught his denim pants. Every breath was an intense wheeze, his teeth gritted in agony. Reid knew that the pain of even a mild burn was intense, torturous—and Abad had not even begun to feel what might actually happen if they let the fire continue.

"The Imam!" Reid demanded. "Who is he?"

"Khalil! His name is Khalil."

Reid grabbed a towel from a hanging rack and threw it over the flames, patting them out. The smell of burnt rubber and hair was atrocious. Abad hung his head, sweat pouring from his brow as he continued to whimper softly. The terrorist was undoubtedly in a lot of pain, but the actual damage done was minimal—far more psychological than physical.

Reid leaned in again, very close to the man's ear, and whispered. "That still was not a third-degree burn, Abad. I'm not going to kill you today, because I'll know your face. If I ever see you again for the wrong reason, what you experienced today will seem like mercy."

Abad muttered something incomprehensible as his head lolled to one side. Reid and Maria left him like that, passing Dr. Barnard in the doorway.

"Claudette Minot has the virus," he told Watson and Carver. "She took it north."

Watson shook his head. "The whole of France is north of Marseille."

"She'll need to get it out of the country somehow," Reid said. "Planes are all grounded."

"Seaports are closed," Maria added. "And she can't just drive it across the border."

"The trains aren't running," said Carver.

"That...might not be entirely true." All eyes turned to Barnard, still standing in the threshold between the kitchen and living room. "*Passenger* rails are all shut down. But what about freight lines?"

"Freight trains only require one driver, sometimes two," Watson offered. "They're all background-checked and vetted."

Reid stroked his chin. *Freight lines in France. Of course.* He cursed himself for not seeing it before. "Jesus, Barnard, you're a genius! The Marseille-Ventimiglia line!"

"The what?" Maria asked.

"It's a railway established in 1859," Reid explained quickly. "Two hundred and sixty kilometers long, one of the only international lines that runs from Marseille, and it goes from here to Italy..."

"But Italy has a travel ban in place," Watson countered.

"Right, but if Claudette can ride the freight rails east, she would just have to keep going until she reaches a country that doesn't have a ban in place. Or it could be a rendezvous point. Either way, it's our best shot."

"You know where we need to be?" Watson asked.

Reid nodded. "Marseille-Saint Charles, the railway station."

"Let's go." Watson led as the five of them hurried out of the flat, leaving Abad in the kitchen. They piled into the white SUV with Watson behind the wheel.

As they sped down the street with Carver directing him, Reid held his hand out to Maria. "Let me use your phone." She handed it off and he called Langley.

"Riker." She sounded exhausted.

"It's Steele."

"You are the *last* person I want to hear from right n—"

"We need to find out if France has shut down freight lines," he interrupted. He was in no mood for a lecture. He still felt incredible remorse for what had happened at the tailor's shop.

"Freight lines," she repeated. Her tone suggested she understood. "I'll get someone on it." He heard her snap her fingers and bark an order at someone in the background. "You think whoever has the virus is stowing away on a freight train?"

"Yes. It's our French girl, Claudette Minot."

"Find her fast."

"We will. Our missing Imam's name is Khalil. We have no idea where he is or what he's up to, but it seems that he's intent to let others do his dirty work for him."

"We'll look into it ASAP and gather whatever we can," Riker assured him.

"There's more. French authorities need to know that there's a black car outside Claudette Minot's flat wired with explosives. Inside the flat is a terrorist involved in the smallpox plot."

Riker was silent for a moment. "We'll make them aware. Tell me about the other bomb."

Reid almost groaned. "We have more pressing matters—"

"Seven, Agent Zero. Seven dead French officers. That is *dizzyingly* incompetent. At the moment, French authorities have no idea about any CIA involvement, but eyewitness accounts from neighboring buildings saw two white men fleeing the scene."

"No one else spoke to us," he said. "No one else knew."

"Even so, we can't keep lying to allies to cover up your mistakes, especially when they involve people dying—"

"I wasn't the one that triggered the bomb," he argued.

"No, but it was within your power to stop it—"

"You weren't there," he said defiantly. "You don't know what you're talking about." He was keenly aware that he was crammed into a vehicle with four other people who could all hear the conversation. He was almost afraid they could hear him thinking. *You could have stopped it. You could have searched that man.*

"What I do know, Agent Steele, is that you are a liability. If we could afford to, we would take you off this case. I assure you, there will be repercussions for your actions—"

Reid ended the call, hanging up on the assistant director before he had the urge to say something he might later regret. He handed the phone back to Maria and shrugged. "Call dropped."

"ETA is twelve minutes," Carver announced.

Reid's knee bounced against the floor of the car. This was it, he was sure of it. The end of the line. They were going to find Minot, and the virus, and put an end to the crisis. He could only hope they reached her before she reached a train.

CHAPTER TWENTY FIVE

"**H**ello, Restorations Department."

"Yes, good morning." Rais did his best to affect a professional yet friendly tone. "My name is Charles Rothstein, from the law firm of Holbrook & Leary. I'm calling in the hopes of obtaining some information on a past employee."

"Who are you calling about?" He could hear the frown in the woman's voice.

"Well, admittedly, it's something of a sensitive subject," he told her. "This particular employee was a woman who passed away suddenly about two years ago..." He trailed off slightly and let the woman take his bait.

"Oh. You must mean Kate. Kate Lawson."

"Yes, that would be her." *Kate Lawson.* He hadn't known the woman's name; only what she looked like and that she worked at the Smithsonian American Art Museum in Washington, DC.

In fact, it wasn't until afterward that he learned she was Kent Steele's wife.

"What sort of information are you looking for, Mr....?"

"Rothstein," Rais said pleasantly. It was nauseating him to act so...so *American*, but it was a necessary step to find what he needed to know. He was certain that Kent Steele would have relocated after the events of February, after members of Amun had revealed themselves in the States. "You see, our firm was hired on a case of potential negligence on the part of the emergency medical technicians that arrived on scene at the time of Mrs. Lawson's... untimely passing. I'm sure I don't need to tell you how long these sorts of things can get wrapped up in litigation. But I'm pleased to say that we've arrived at a fairly substantial settlement, one that I'm certain the family would appreciate..."

"I'm sure they would," the woman agreed. "Those poor girls, losing their mother like that."

"Yes," Rais agreed quietly. Sounding sympathetic was nearly beyond him. "But I've run into a problem. It seems the Lawsons have moved recently, and they did not supply us with a new address. I suppose they might have forgotten that the case was still pending."

"Well, it's no wonder," the woman said. "A single working father with two teenagers? I can't imagine the burden."

Rais almost smirked. This woman was giving him everything—except what he actually needed to know. "Unfortunately," he told her, "I can relate. I'm a single father myself. In fact, my son is right around the same age as his eldest."

"Oh, Maya?" The woman sighed. "I haven't seen her since she was probably twelve years old. It was a 'take your daughter to work' day. Such a smart, happy girl. Goodness, she must be about ready for college now."

"Yes, just about. They grow up so quickly," Rais said. *Kate Lawson. Maya Lawson. A second, younger Lawson girl. Interesting.*

"Well, Mr. Rothstein, as much as I would love to help you, I'm afraid that if the Lawsons moved, we wouldn't have that information on file," the woman told him. "Have you tried contacting Kate's life insurance provider?"

"I did," Rais said, a tone of dismay in his voice, "but it's somewhat rough terrain when you're dealing with someone deceased. Their policy is against sharing any personal details unless it's required for criminal proceedings, and unfortunately this doesn't fall under that category."

The woman scoffed. "Well, that's just strange to me. I hope you told them that you were only trying to help the family."

"I certainly did, but I understand their position. Dealing with that much money, you can never be too careful. You just don't know when someone will claim to be someone they're not for personal gain." This time he couldn't help but smirk. "I'm so sorry. I didn't get your name."

"It's Cheryl," the woman told him.

"That's lovely. I had an aunt named Cheryl. I'm going to be honest with you, Cheryl. This has been my case for nearly two years, and as I mentioned, I'm in a similar situation as Mr. Lawson, so there's a personal investment in this as well. I just want this family to have the closure they need and the settlement they deserve. If there's any way at all in which you can help me find them, I would very much appreciate it. And I think they would too."

"Hmm." The woman, Cheryl, sighed into the phone again and thought for a long moment. "You know what, Mr. Rothstein? There just might be. We would still have all of Kate's employment records in our system, and the museum requires three emergency contacts. One of them would have been her husband, but if I'm not mistaken, she had a sister, in New York…" Cheryl called to someone in the background. "Ben? Ben, do you remember the name of Kate Lawson's sister?" There was a brief pause. "Was that it? Okay, thanks." To Rais she said, "Linda. I believe it was Linda. If I can put you on hold for just a few minutes, I could check the computer and find a contact number for you. If anyone would know where Reid and the girls moved, she would."

"That would be wonderful of you. Thank you, Cheryl."

"Just one moment." There was a click, and light violin music began as she placed him on hold.

Rais was reminded of an old adage: *You'll catch more flies with honey than vinegar.* It was a part of his job that most in his position failed to realize, let alone nurture. A knife or a gun could get you to some places, but a pleasant tone, forging an emotional connection, and finding common ground could get you everywhere else.

Rais put the call on speaker while he waited for Cheryl to return with the information. The car he had rented at JFK with his fake identification was currently parked in the lot of a grocery store in northeastern Maryland, only about an hour outside of DC. He assumed that Steele would not have been relocated too far from

Langley, so he refrained from going any further until he had a destination.

And this trusting woman was going to make it easy on him. Rais had no gun, and his money was running dangerously low, but he had a full tank of gas and a rather attractive blade he had purchased at a sporting goods store along the way.

All he had to do was pull this thread a little more, and he would find Kent Steele.

CHAPTER TWENTY SIX

Reid pushed open the back door of the SUV before it came to a complete stop outside the Marseille-Saint Charles railway station. The four agents and Dr. Barnard clambered out and hurried up the white stairs to the entrance.

This is it. Reid was certain of it. *End of the line. We find the virus, we put an end to this crisis.*

"Minot is twenty-three years old, five-foot-four, with bright red hair," Reid said as they climbed the steps. "Let's split up and find her. Watson and I will take the south side of the station—"

"I'll go with you," Carver volunteered.

Reid nodded. "All right, Carver and I take the south, Watson and Maria, you take the north end. Barnard, you come with us."

They pushed through the doors of the station to find it eerily empty and silent. With the travel ban in place, the train depot was a ghost town, working on a skeleton crew of employees. Custodial workers were using the opportunity to buff the floors, while a few security guards milled about to turn away would-be passengers unaware of the shutdown.

"Good luck," Reid told them as Maria and Watson broke off, heading toward the northern section of the station. He, Carver, and Barnard headed the opposite way.

"It's unlikely she's in the station, but we still want to be thorough," Reid told his two teammates as they walked hastily across the empty floor. He didn't want to attract any undue attention from the security guards on-site. "Barnard, do a quick sweep of this side. Carver and I will head to the freight yard."

"And if I locate her?" the doctor asked nervously.

"Use the radio," Reid told him. "Don't let her out of your sight, but do *not* approach her alone." With his phone crushed under the pile of rubble, Reid's earpiece was useless, but he would have Carver with him.

"Godspeed, Agents." Barnard hurried off to a set of stairs to check the platforms while Carver and Reid headed toward a rear exit of the station.

"I'm guessing the freight yards will be behind the passenger rails," Reid ventured as they pushed out into the afternoon sunlight again. "We can only hope that she hasn't boarded a—"

"Wait a sec." Carver stopped. "Do you hear anything?"

Reid shook his head, no. Then he understood what Carver meant. He didn't hear *anything*—no chugging of engines, no warning whistles, no bells to indicate a moving train.

"Kent, I don't think the freight lines are running."

But this has to be right. It has to. They had come too far to be wrong again, to be misled by the Imam and his followers. "We're here. This fits. We're still going to check it out." He broke into a jog across the sets of empty passenger rail lines toward the freight yard.

"Kent, wait up." Carver hurried after him, putting a finger to his ear. "Langley just confirmed it with Watson. Nothing is running. This is a dead end."

Reid pressed on defiantly. He refused to believe it. They were wrong about the virologist being the mastermind behind the plot. They had been wrong about finding the Imam in Athens, and about the terrorists fleeing from France. *We can't be wrong again. It's too late for that.*

About seventy-five yards from the railway station and across more than a dozen empty sets of track was the freight yard, literally hundreds of multicolored boxcars lined end to end on the rails. As Carver had keenly pointed out, nothing moved. Everything was quiet, and there didn't seem to be anyone around.

He paused at the veritable wall of yellow, green, orange, and blue cargo containers. To go around them would take too long, so instead he dropped to his stomach and crawled underneath the nearest train car, shimmying across the gravel between the tracks. The smell of axle grease and fuel filled his nose.

He stood on the other side and waited for Carver, but the other agent didn't appear. Reid bent and looked beneath the car. Carver was gone. *Where the hell did he go? Around? Was there a radio call that I missed?* He panicked slightly; what if Watson and Maria found Minot?

He deliberated for a moment. Carver was gone and Reid had no radio. He wasn't about to go back; he was here and he had a purpose.

The tall boxcars on either side of him formed a long, shadowy corridor. He started down the length of it until he reached a section of enormous, wide cylinders sitting on the tracks—tanker wagons, hauling oil or some other type of fuel. The gaps between them were wide enough for him to slip through. He climbed carefully over the hitch of a tanker and hopped down from the other side to find yet another set of rails laden with boxcars.

This isn't a corridor. It's a labyrinth. He hastened along the length of them, trying to find another passage to the other side while also keeping an eye out for any sign of movement—not only from Carver, but potentially from a French girl carrying a cataclysmic lode of smallpox.

Jesus, this doesn't end. He squeezed himself precariously between two boxcars and found himself in yet another corridor, the sixth in a row. He had never been in a freight yard, at least not that he could remember, but occasionally driving over the Bayonne Bridge from New York to New Jersey had afforded him the view of the freight yard below it, and it was enormous. If the Marseille-Saint Charles yard was even half as big, he could easily get lost in here.

He lowered himself down from the boxcar hitch and was about to huff a frustrated sigh when he stopped dead in his tracks.

Not fifty feet from him was a figure, sitting on the ground facing away from him, her head of fiery red hair shining despite the long shadows of the train cars. She had her knees drawn to her chest and, most importantly, a brown tote bag at her side.

Reid's heart leapt with excitement and anxiety in equal measure. He had found her. And the virus.

He lifted his boot to take a step in her direction, but paused. The ground was gravel; she would hear him approaching. *Shoot her. She's alone and you have a clear shot. A single bullet would end all of this.*

His hand reached for the hilt of his Glock 19.

Then he heard a sound, possibly the last sound he would have thought to expect in the moment. Claudette Minot sniffled.

She was crying.

Reid's hand left his jacket empty. *No. You've been responsible for enough death today, and you're not going to shoot a crying young woman in the back. She's going to be apprehended, and she's going to help us find Imam Khalil.*

He took a few steps toward her, his boots crunching on the gravel. She turned suddenly, and at the sight of him she scrambled backward, pulling herself awkwardly to her feet.

"Claudette." Reid put both his hands up, palms out, as a gesture of nonviolence. "Please step away from the bag," he said in French.

"Stay back!" She stooped and grabbed the strap of the tote bag, hefting it onto her shoulder. Her eyes were moist and rimmed in red. She had definitely been weeping.

"Look around you. There's nowhere to go. There are others with me. You can't run from this." He took a few more slow steps in her direction.

Claudette looked frantically past him and over her shoulder. "I don't see anyone else." There was a nervous tension in her voice. "You're alone."

"So are you. There's no train, no rendezvous. No Imam Khalil."

Her eyes widened in shock at the mention of the Imam's name. "How do you know about him?"

"I know more than you think," Reid said. He kept his voice low, soft, nonthreatening. "I know what's in that bag. I know that you need to put it down and step away."

Her eyes glistened with the threat of fresh tears. "He...he told me the trains would be running. He told me to come here, to find the car..."

Reid's gaze flitted from Claudette to the train car that she had been sitting beside only moments earlier. It was a tanker wagon, and though it had been painted over gray, vague markings showed through where it had once been white.

Alarms screeched in his head. Something about this was very wrong. Everything the Imam had planned so far suggested he was a step ahead of the CIA, ahead of Reid. How could he make such a miscalculation?

He turned his attention back to the girl and the tote bag. "I'm not going to tell you again. Put the bag down and step away from it." She was a fanatic, and he had little hope of getting through to her. If she didn't heed his warning he was going to have to shoot her.

"You don't understand." She stared at the gravel. "I can't fail now. I can't." Her head lifted slowly, her bloodshot gaze meeting his. "I am the Imam Mahdi."

Reid froze. *Imam Mahdi.* The same words that died on the lips of the Syrian boy in Barcelona. Suddenly he understood. *The boy wasn't calling out for the Imam. He thought he* was *the Imam.*

"Claudette," he said slowly. "Think for a moment. Did Imam Khalil tell anyone else that they were the Mahdi?"

She shook her head quickly. "No. Only me. It was always me..." She sniffed again. "He...he only told Adrian to get him to mutate the virus. It wasn't true."

Reid sighed in dismay as the bigger picture came together. This Imam Khalil was no holy man; he was a con artist, luring people in with his ideologies and convincing them that they were important, a redemption figure, for his own ends—a jihad against the western world.

This girl was a terrorist, yes. She was in possession of what was currently the deadliest known weapon on the planet. But she was also a vulnerable young woman who had been indoctrinated when she was at her lowest, a pawn in a game she could barely understand.

Worst of all, Reid knew that there would be no changing her mind. He was going to have to shoot her if he had any chance of getting the bag away from her.

"I'm so sorry, Claudette. Truly I am." He reached into his jacket and pulled the Glock 19.

At the sight of the gun Claudette gasped and lowered the tote to the ground. For a moment Reid thought she might comply, but instead she dropped to her knees and tore the zipper open.

Now! he screamed at himself. *You have to do it now!* He swallowed the lump in his throat as he aimed and squeezed the trigger.

Nothing happened, not even a click.

The biometric trigger guard was locked.

Claudette quickly pulled a steel box out of the tote bag, emblazoned on each side with a biohazard symbol.

Panic rose in Reid's chest as he repositioned his thumb and tried again. Still nothing. He glanced down at the Glock; the thumb pad was smeared with black soot from the explosion and subsequent fallout. It wasn't reading his print.

No! He switched the gun to his other hand and tried again, but the damage had been done. He had no time to wipe it clean and hope it worked. The girl's fingers were unclipping the box's four metal clasps.

There was forty feet between them. Reid had no choice. He dropped the gun and charged at her as fast as his legs would carry him.

He wasn't even halfway to her as she lifted the lid. Once again it felt as if time slowed down, as if he were running in slow motion. His legs weren't moving fast enough.

Then—Claudette's jaw fell open in utter incredulity. Reid expected her to reach into the box, to pluck out a vial and release the virus.

Instead, she stood.

Her arms fell limp at her sides.

Her eyes blinked quickly several times, as if trying to process whatever she was seeing.

Reid skidded to a stop ten feet from her as she took two steps backward. He couldn't believe it. *She saw it, and she's had a change of heart.*

Her gaze met his, and in that moment he saw her—not the brainwashed fanatic, but the *real* her. A susceptible young woman, scared, bewildered, and completely alone.

"But… but I'm the Mahdi," she said softly.

A single gunshot cracked the air. Reid crouched instinctively as Claudette Minot's body convulsed once and fell to the ground.

CHAPTER TWENTY SEVEN

Reid could do nothing but watch as Claudette collapsed sideways to the gravel. Her eyes were wide and confused, her lips still working in some final, unheard utterance.

About twenty yards behind her stood Agent Carver. He slowly lowered his Glock.

Reid felt a strange mix of anger and relief. He knew he would have done it himself if he was able, but now seeing her lying dead on the ground filled him with remorse.

"She down?" Carver asked, his gun still at waist level.

"Yeah. She's down." Reid looked up at the agent as he demanded, "Where were you?"

"I told you I was going around. Didn't you hear me?"

Reid shook his head. "No. I didn't." It didn't matter now. Carver had done what he was unable to do. He snapped out of it and circled around the biohazard box to take a careful look at what had made Claudette Minot freeze like that and step away.

He held his breath as he peered inside. He had hoped, in the moment, that the woman's sudden halt meant a change of heart, but he was extremely doubtful that that was the case.

"Dammit," he said in a whisper. The steel biohazard box did not contain vials. It did not contain a virus.

The box contained nothing. It was empty.

"It's not the virus," Reid announced as Carver trotted over to him.

"You've got to be kidding." Carver glanced down at Claudette's body and shook his head. "What a waste." He held a finger to his ear. "We found Minot, but it was another goose chase. She didn't have the virus. Freight yard." To Reid he muttered, "I suppose we should be glad it's not another bomb."

"We've got to get out of here." Reid stood quickly. "If Minot was a false lead, then someone else has the virus. This was a distraction, to put us off track while they get the virus out."

Carver nodded his agreement and started to trot down the length of the freight rails. But Reid didn't. He paused. Something about this didn't feel right.

Why here? Why send Minot to a freight yard? Why would the Imam have her leave her phone behind? If she was a red herring, we could have tracked it and found her that way...

"Kent?" Carver slowed, tossing a glance over his shoulder. "What's up?"

"Hang up a second." Something Claudette had said only moments before she'd been shot. *"He... he told me the trains would be running. He told me to come here, to find the car..."*

To his left was a cylindrical tanker wagon, the one that Claudette had been instructed to find. Reid used the sleeve of his jacket to wipe away some of the dirt and grease from the side.

It had been repainted, but the former side of it was still faintly legible. The white letters that had once been large and bright on the curved tanker's side said KHALIL OIL.

He stared at the tanker in disbelief. *This isn't a red herring. It's a clue. We were led here, while the virus gets to where it needs to be.* All of this was a ploy, not just to keep them busy, but to bring them to some inevitable conclusion—not the least of which was that they were too late.

But once again he was missing a link, between the Imam Khalil and this tanker wagon, this Khalil Oil.

"Oil," he murmured aloud.

"What's that?" Carver came trotting back to see what he'd found.

But Reid didn't answer. A memory came swimming through his head, pushing hard like a fish struggling upstream.

The CIA black site in Morocco. Designation H-6, aka "Hell Six." An interrogation. You pull the fingernails from an Arab man for information about the whereabouts of a bomb maker.

Between screams and whimpers and insistences that he doesn't know, something else emerges.

A pending war. Something big coming.

There is no pending war.

A conspiracy. A cover-up. Designed by the US government.

You don't believe him. Not at first. But you couldn't just let it go. No one lies under that sort of duress.

You knew something, back then. You didn't want to believe it. Not at first. But you found more. Others that had small pieces of intel. Like a jigsaw puzzle, you started to put it together.

Then Amun happened. You got distracted. You vowed to return to it.

You didn't get the chance.

Reid sucked in a breath as a sudden, intense headache intruded into his skull. He leaned forward, bracing himself against the filthy tanker wagon with a flat palm. Thousands of miles away, in his office back home in Virginia, was the letter from Alan Reidigger. In it his old friend had told him there was something else that Kent Steele knew, something dangerous. Before the memory suppressor, Agent Zero had been onto something—something he was afraid to tell anyone else about, even Alan.

You were building a case.

You never finished.

You never told anyone.

"Kent? You okay?" Carver frowned, watching Reid's confused, almost pained expression.

"I...I don't know," he said quietly. "I can't say for sure, but...but I think there's something much bigger going on here."

"Bigger than a world-ending virus?" Carver asked in disbelief.

"No, no. Bigger in scope. Some sort of conspiracy..."

A pending war. But there is no pending war... Is there?

Carver's eyes narrowed in concern. "What sort of conspiracy?"

"Something about a war ... something to do with oil ..." Reid cut himself short. He didn't want to say more without knowing more—without knowing more. "Forget it," he said quickly. "We need to find out exactly who this Khalil is, and *where* he is, before the virus is released on the next—"

Still facing the tanker wagon, Reid felt a pressure on the back of his head. It was unmistakably the barrel of a gun.

"I really wish you wouldn't have said that," Carver said quietly. His voice genuinely sounded rueful. "Because now I have to do this. Goodbye, Kent."

CHAPTER TWENTY EIGHT

"In the back, Carver?" Reid said quickly. It was the first thing that sprang into his mind that might have given the other agent pause before pulling the trigger. "You would shoot me in the back of the head?"

The moment of silence that followed felt like it stretched for eternity, Reid fully expecting a bullet to enter his skull at any millisecond. But mercifully, the pressure of the barrel relieved slightly.

"Turn around," Carver ordered.

"At least tell me why." Reid was pushing his luck, he knew, but it was the only way he had to delay his assassination. "For knowing too much?"

"For remembering too much," Carver replied. "I saw that look in your eye. You remember what you knew back then. Now turn around."

Reid panicked slightly. He didn't remember enough to know what he knew back then, but even the little he'd said was apparently enough to get him killed. He knew now why he hadn't said anything to Reidigger two years ago.

"Who put you on this?" he asked. "Mullen? Riker? The CIA is in on it too then?" He was bloviating, trying to get Carver to give him even a half-second of an opening to react. He slowly raised his hands, as if in surrender. "Think about this a second. You know too much too. What do you think they'll do to you after you do it to me?"

"It's not like that," Carver said. "And I'm not going to tell you again." Reid felt a hand on his shoulder as the other agent pulled to spin him around.

"Carver?"

They both turned instinctively at the sound of Maria's voice. She was peering out from between two of the tanker cars, climbing over the hitch and bewildered at what she was seeing.

Agent Carver looked from her, back to Reid, and his expression hardened. In the instant his finger squeezed the trigger, Reid brought his raised arms together in front of his face.

The Glock barked thunderously and a bullet struck his left forearm. Pain seared through it and the arm fell away useless at his side. But his other arm was already swinging outward. His cupped hand struck Carver's arm just behind the wrist with enough force to send the Glock flying out of his grip.

Reid stepped into the strike for a kick, but Carver was ready for it. He twisted away from the oncoming boot, grabbed Reid's foot, and yanked him off his feet. He hit the gravel hard enough to knock the air from his lungs.

Several yards away, Maria clambered down from the tanker wagon and pulled her own pistol. Carver acted fast, leaping into a roll as she fired off a shot. The bullet struck nothing but air in the space he'd just been and he vanished, rolling lengthwise underneath the train car.

Maria sprinted to Reid, grabbing up his Glock from the ground as she did. "Here. You okay?"

He clamped a hand over his shot arm, expecting to have to stymie the blood flow—but there was no blood. He inspected the wound. There was no bullet hole, and not nearly as much pain as there should have been.

The graphene. He'd nearly forgotten that his jacket was reinforced. The sleeve had stopped the bullet from penetrating his skin. It hurt like hell, and he would most definitely have a nasty contusion, but no bones were broken and there was no entry wound. He could flex his fingers and move his wrist.

"What the hell was that?" Maria exclaimed.

"A memory. Carver turned on me." Reid dropped to the ground and searched beneath the train car. There was no sign of the sudden renegade agent. "Some kind of cover-up. No time to explain." He clambered up the steel-rung ladder of the nearest boxcar. He wasn't about to take a chance of going underneath if Carver might be on the other side with a backup sidearm.

Once on top of the car, he crouched low and frantically wiped the soot from his Glock with the hem of his shirt. He swiped his thumb along his tongue, and then pressed it to the biometric lock. The gun clicked; the trigger guard opened.

Maria started up the ladder after him. "Wait," he said. "Call Langley. Talk to Cartwright. Tell him Minot is dead, there's no virus here, and to look into Khalil Oil right away. There's a connection there with the Imam that might help us locate him."

"What do I tell them about Carver?"

"Nothing. Not a word." *Someone over there already knows.* He was certain Carver's hesitation to shoot him was because the agent wasn't working of his own volition. He was under orders.

Reid carefully peered over the side of the boxcar. He looked left and right but didn't see Carver. He didn't hear him either. The next set of cars was too far a span to jump, so instead he dropped over the side and tucked into a roll as he landed, coming up with his gun level.

There was no sign of Carver. He'd run off, it seemed.

But I remember now, at least a little bit. I was working toward something two years ago. Gathering intel. Trying to uncover it. Whatever this conspiracy was, it had been in the works for a long time, even as far back as then.

He saw a flash of movement in his periphery. He didn't look up; he spun to his right and dropped to his stomach as two shots blasted over his head. Not twenty feet away from him, Carver leaned out from behind a tanker wagon, standing on the hitch. Reid shimmied quickly underneath the boxcar as a third shot rang out. The undercarriage tugged at his jacket and sharp gravel poked his chest through his shirt, but he didn't dare move or try to climb out the other side. Carver would be waiting for him, and he had a second gun.

Carver favors the .38 Colt Cobra. Six shots. He's used three. Reid did not want to take his chances on forcing Carver to take his other three shots. He scanned the ground around him. Carver was either still standing on the hitch or had climbed another boxcar; either way, he had the upper hand. There was nowhere Reid could go, and he couldn't risk revealing himself. But Carver couldn't either. As soon as he climbed down and exposed his feet, Reid would certainly take a shot.

Stalemate, he thought bitterly. His radio was useless, since he had lost his phone in the tailor's basement. Barnard had his LC9. Reid had his Glock 19, but that did him little good in his position.

Wait a second. With some difficulty he managed to snake a hand into his jacket pocket and pulled out the one other item he had at his disposal. It was a small, smooth cylinder about the size of a battery. *The sonic grenade.* What had Bixby said about it?

If you find yourself in a jam, depress the buttons on each end of the cylinder. It emits a combination of high frequencies that cause immediate nausea and loss of equilibrium for anyone inside a twenty-five-foot radius—except you, as long as it's close.

The CIA tech had also told him it wasn't yet field-tested, and this seemed as good a time as any. He held the device between his thumb and index finger. Then he held his breath, and squeezed down on both ends as hard as he could. The buttons each depressed with a small click.

And then—nothing happened. He heard no sound, no frequency. The tiny device appeared to be inert; there was no indication that anything was going on.

A few seconds passed by, and then something hit the gravel on the other side of the boxcar. It was a .38 revolver, and it was almost immediately followed by a body.

Agent Carver hit the ground with a groan. He rolled onto his side, his eyes squeezed closed and his mouth twisted in a grimace. He tried to get up on his hands and knees, but he fell again.

Something above Reid fell too, something heavy hitting corrugated metal with a dissonant thud. *Oh, god. Maria.* She must have followed and climbed up onto the boxcar to get the drop on Carver. He heard a soft moan that confirmed his fears. If she fell off the boxcar, she could break something. A limb or worse.

Reid scrambled out from beneath the boxcar and stood with the sonic grenade still in his hand. Bixby was right; as long as he kept it close he didn't suffer any of the ill effects that the writhing Carver was experiencing. The betraying agent groaned again and retched a small amount of bile onto the gravel.

Reid hurried to him and snatched up the Colt revolver, sticking it in his jacket pocket. He realized suddenly and desperately that he had no idea how to turn the sonic grenade off. The buttons were depressed; there didn't seem to be any way to deactivate it.

Carver leapt up at him with a snarl and tackled Reid to the ground. The force of the hit again knocked the wind out of him and his Glock 19 sailed from his grip. The two men landed in a heap, but he managed to keep his fist closed around the sonic grenade.

Too close. I got too close to him. Carver straddled Reid and pummeled him with both fists. It was all Reid could do to keep his hands up and protect his face, but as long as Carver was on him he too would be protected from the frequency.

Reid bucked his hips and Carver lurched to the side. He steadied himself with one hand as the other swung at Reid's face, missing by an inch. Reid responded with a right hook that grazed across the agent's jaw as he jerked his head back. Carver swung again, but Reid blocked the strike with his forearm. He cried out as pain splintered up and down his arm from the deflected gunshot. He brought an elbow up and it connected with Carver's nose. He fell backward, blood blossoming from both nostrils.

Reid reared back to hit him again when a voice rang out from behind him.

"Stop!"

They both turned. Maria stood just a short distance behind them. Her breathing was ragged and there was sweat on her brow. Reid blinked in surprise. The sonic grenade was still in his fist, the buttons both still depressed. Bixby's untested weapon had worked, but only for a short burst.

In Maria's hands was a gun—but not her gun. It was Reid's, his Glock 19 that had fallen to the ground while the two men had grappled.

"Move aside, Kent." She had the gun trained on Carver.

"Maria, wait." Reid couldn't very well tell her that the gun wouldn't work for her, not in front of Carver. *Maybe she knows, and she's bluffing,* he hoped.

"Move aside," she repeated. He did, getting to his feet with a groan. "Why did you do this?" she demanded. "Why are you trying to kill Kent?"

Carver stayed on his knees as he wiped blood away from his lips. "You don't know what he knows," he said forcefully. "You don't know how dangerous it is."

"If you know, you're going to tell us," Reid said. "Who put you on this?"

Carver did not answer. He glared at Reid, his lips curled in a snarl.

"He's not going to say." Maria took a step closer, still keeping her aim leveled at the downed agent. "Get up. On your feet, and if you try anything, I will shoot you."

Carver nodded. He put his hands up first and began to stand. Then he threw his body weight to the right, hit the gravel, and rolled beneath the nearest boxcar.

Maria pulled the trigger—or tried to. With the biometric lock, the trigger didn't move. "What…?"

Reid lurched forward and tried to grab for Carver, but the agent kept rolling, beneath the boxcar and clear to the other side. Reid struggled to free the Colt from his jacket pocket as he quickly climbed up the ladder one-handed to the top of the boxcar. Carver scrambled to his feet and ran, sprinting down the length of the freight rails away from them.

Reid took careful aim, targeting Carver's leg. Even if he had graphene reinforcing his clothes, the impact would take him down. He squeezed the trigger.

The gun clicked. Carver kept running. He didn't look back or hesitate.

Reid popped open the revolver's cylinder and found nothing but spent shell casings. Carver had only had three shots. The turncoat agent vanished around a bend in the tracks. Reid wanted very much to pursue him, to catch him and force him to tell them why. But Carver was unarmed and fleeing, and they had something much more important to pursue.

He climbed back down and took his gun back from Maria. "Biometrics," he explained quickly. "On the trigger lock."

She scoffed. "Dammit, Bixby." Then she frowned and knelt, picking something up from the ground. It was a small piece of plastic, nearly transparent—an earpiece.

"Carver's," Reid said. "Must have fallen out when I hit him…"

"Or else he took it out on purpose," she countered. "I bet he'll drop his phone too, so he can't be tracked. That traitorous son of a bitch…"

Reid shook his head. "He didn't want to do it. Not at first, anyway."

"Kent, he pulled the trigger on you—"

"I know. There's no excuse for it. But I'm telling you, he was acting on orders. I'm sure of it. Come on, we have to go. Now." He led the way, climbing between two boxcars as Maria followed. "I'm sorry about the frequency," he told her as they hurried out of the maze-like freight yard. "Are you okay?"

"I'm fine," she said. "I lost my gun, though. Minot didn't have the virus?"

"No, but she was made to look like she did."

"Then who has it?" Maria asked breathlessly.

"If I had to bet? It's the Imam. His name is Khalil. This must be his plan, his jihad… Minot was made to believe that she was the Imam Mahdi, but she's not." *Neither was the Syrian boy. Or the virologist.* "Khalil is. And I don't think he would trust anyone else to pull off his master stroke."

At last they broke free of the labyrinthine boxcars and onto the empty passenger rails that stretched between them and the station. Dr. Barnard and Watson hurried toward them.

Watson had his gun drawn.

Without hesitation Reid skidded to a stop and raised his own Glock, aiming for Watson's forehead.

CHAPTER TWENTY NINE

"Stop right there and put the gun down, Agent Watson," Reid ordered loudly.

Watson froze in utter disbelief. "Are you out of your mind, Steele? We heard shots, we came running…"

Reid did not falter. "Put it down," he said again firmly. Barnard took two uncertain steps back. Even Maria seemed unsure of what to do, but Reid had no choice. Carver had been ordered to take him out for what he knew. And Watson was Carver's former partner.

Watson put his hands up slowly, but he did not put his gun down. "Where's Carver?" he demanded. "What did you do?"

Reid shook his head. "He's alive. He fled. Right after trying to kill me." He was careful not to mention anything about his memory or the newly rediscovered conspiracy.

"No," Watson said quietly. "No, he wouldn't have—"

"He did," Maria confirmed, her tone apologetic. "I saw it happen, John."

"And I can't risk you doing the same." Reid's hand was steady, his gaze unflinching. "I don't know you well enough to take you at your word. I believe you're a good man and a good agent, but there's still someone out there with the virus. That's my focus right now. I can't keep one eye on you and hope you don't shoot me in the back when you have the chance."

Watson scoffed. "You think I would do that, Kent?"

He shook his head. "I can't risk it."

"What do we do now then? You going to shoot me? Because I'm not putting this gun down. Not while you've got one pointed at me."

217

"No," Reid said, "I'm not going to shoot you. We're going to leave you here." He could trust Maria; if she had been under the same orders as Carver, she would have had plenty of opportunity to take a shot. Besides, he knew her. She wouldn't do that to him. And Barnard was a CDC doctor, not an agent. "The three of us are going after the virus. You do whatever it is you feel you have to do to finish this op, but you're on your own."

Watson shook his head. "That would be damn foolish of you. Johansson said it herself. We need to stick together right now, not fall apart." He turned to Maria. "You know me. You know I wouldn't."

Maria averted her gaze. "I would have said the same thing about Carver twenty minutes ago." She sighed. "I'll stay."

For a split second Reid took his gaze off of Watson to shoot her an incredulous look. "What?"

"I'll stay with him," she repeated. "We split up. You take Barnard and the car and go. Watson and I will find transportation and see what Langley finds on the Imam. If you get a lead, call us, and we'll do the same. You won't have to keep an eye on Watson. I will."

Reid bit his lip. He didn't want to leave Maria behind as well. He wanted her by his side. He wanted her watching his back. But short of leaving Watson behind entirely, he couldn't think of a better way.

"All right," he agreed finally. "Barnard, give her the Ruger."

The doctor took the small LC9 from his jacket and handed it off to Maria.

"Holster that," Reid ordered Watson. The agent slowly tucked his Glock back into his shoulder harness. Only then did Reid lower his aim, though he still kept his gun firmly in his grip. "If we find something, we'll call. Good luck. Barnard, let's go."

Reid hurried across the tracks with Barnard following. Only when they reached the station again did he holster his gun. The doctor remained entirely silent until they had reached the white SUV parked outside.

"Should I be concerned about what I just witnessed?" he asked as Reid started the engine.

"Yes," he replied candidly. "But if you're asking me to tell you, I won't." *It could be as dangerous for you as it apparently is for me.* "Take out your phone. Call this number and put it on speaker." Reid recited the phone number as he hit the gas, screeching away from the Marseille-Saint Charles station and toward the highway.

"Agent Baraf." He answered on the second ring.

"It's Kent," Reid told him. "I need to know the most recent update the CIA has provided Interpol."

"Kent? Where are you and your team? We found nothing in Athens—"

"I know," Reid replied hastily. "Baraf, time is crucial here." He highly doubted the virus was still in France. "What have they given you?"

"The CIA hasn't updated us in the last few hours," Baraf told him.

Reid slammed the steering wheel in frustration. Maria called in the update to investigate Khalil, yet the agency didn't update Interpol. He was already keenly aware that something was very wrong on account of an agent trying to kill him, and this news only furthered his suspicions.

"Baraf, have your people look into a company called Khalil Oil. That's K-H-A-L-I-L. I need whatever you can get, but don't share it with the CIA. Only me."

Baraf blew out an exasperated breath. "Agent Steele, just what is going on?"

The less you know the better. And I don't know enough to explain it to you. "Baraf, please. I need your help."

"All right," the Interpol agent agreed, though somewhat hesitantly. "Give me a minute." Baraf shouted instructions in Italian to someone. "*Adesso! Velocemente,*" he added. Now. Quickly.

"Oil?" Barnard asked. "What have you found, Agent?"

"I'm not convinced our Imam is a holy man," Reid told him.

"Khalil Oil," Baraf said suddenly, returning to the line, "was a privately held company in Syria with a second refinery in Lebanon, owned by man named Hassan ibn Khalil…"

Imam Khalil, Reid thought.

"... That is, up until 2011, when it was shut down," Baraf added.

"Why was it shut down? What happened in 2011?" Reid asked as he navigated onto the highway. They didn't yet have a destination, but he had an inkling of where he should be headed. He turned south.

"It seems that Khalil found some sort of loophole in the export tariff bill that would save him millions," Baraf read. "The Syrian government, however, saw it as stealing. They seized the company's assets and sold them off to pay what was construed as his debt, and Khalil spent the next two years in prison for it. Currently he resides in Saudi Arabia, doing bookkeeping for another oil venture."

Reid frowned, perplexed. "Wait, what?" If that was the case, then who was their Imam? "What about his family?"

"Family..." Baraf paused a moment before he said, "Let's see. Most of them moved with him after the advent of the Syrian crisis. But his eldest son, Assad, remained. Seems he had no interest in the oil business. Instead, he's made a name for himself by causing some trouble among local Sunnis—"

"Calling himself Imam Khalil," Reid finished. Assad ibn Khalil, the prodigal son of the Khalil family, was the Imam. "Recruiting followers to his cause."

"Correct, Agent Steele." There was both confusion and trepidation in Baraf's voice. "This Assad...do you believe he is the one behind all this?"

"I do," Reid told him. "And I think he has the virus. Or at least he did. If it's not here anymore, he must have found a way to get it out of France."

"France?" Baraf repeated suddenly. "Is that where you are?"

"Yes, southern France, in Marseille."

"*Dio!*" Baraf exclaimed. "Why didn't you say so? Kent, France was Hassan's loophole!"

Reid frowned deeply. "Sorry?"

"The loophole he used to exploit the export tariffs," Baraf said quickly. "Any ships that left Syria with his drums must pass by the southern coast of France, so Khalil purchased a storage facility on the Marseille Fos Port. He found that if he claimed to be exporting to France instead of the United States and stored his product there for at least four months, he could then export to the US at a much lower cost and—"

"Baraf," Reid interrupted. "Who owns the facility now?"

"Uh…" He heard the clacking of keys in the background. "No one, it seems. It is for lease and currently unused."

Reid's hands tightened around the steering wheel as he felt a spike of exhilaration and fear. "Send the address of his storage facility to this phone right away. How soon could you get agents there?"

"An hour at most by helicopter," Baraf replied.

That would take too long. He and Barnard were less than twenty minutes from the coast. "Send them," he said anyway. He had no idea if the facility would be a dead end or not, but if it wasn't, whatever might be there could be much more than one agent and a CDC doctor could handle. "And Baraf? Keep quiet on this. No one outside Interpol but me, and especially not the CIA right now. I can't tell you why. Please just trust me on this."

Baraf was quiet for a moment. Reid felt bad just putting his friend in a situation like that, but until he knew more about it, he wasn't about to put anyone else in the line of fire. "All right, Agent Steele. I'll alert you when my agents are near."

Reid ended the call. Only then did he notice he was doing close to ninety miles an hour down the highway toward the coast. He eased slightly off the accelerator; they couldn't afford to draw attention to themselves from French authorities now that they had a destination.

Barnard's phone chimed. "I have the address. GPS says we're seventeen minutes away. Should I send this to Agent Johansson?"

"Yes," Reid said. Regardless of Watson's intentions, he trusted Maria to have his back and keep a watchful eye on him. "Tell her to get there as fast as possible."

Before Barnard could punch in the text message, his phone rang in his hand. He frowned. "Unknown caller. Should I answer?"

Reid had a pretty good idea of who was calling. He didn't want to involve the CIA any further, and they had a destination, but a morbid curiosity got the better of him. "Yes. Answer it." Barnard put it on speaker, and Reid said, "It's Zero."

"Kent." Deputy Director Cartwright's voice was quiet, little more than a harsh whisper. "Jesus. Watson just reported in. Something about Carver going rogue and attacking you ...?"

"Did you put him on it?" Reid asked point-blank.

"I'm on my personal cell phone, whispering in a goddamn stairwell right now. What do you think?"

"Did you?" Reid asked again, more forcefully this time.

"No! Of course I didn't," Cartwright insisted. "But I also know you weren't the most trusting guy before all this, so I don't expect you to take my word for it."

"Well, someone did." *And there's only one other person leading this op.* Reid didn't say it aloud, but he didn't have to. Cartwright picked up what he was suggesting.

"Look, when all this is over, there *will* be an investigation," Cartwright said firmly. "If something is rotten in the state of Denmark, I'll find out about it. You understand me?"

Reid furrowed his brow. The way the deputy director said it made it sound like a threat, but the line itself drew his attention. *Rotten in Denmark?* He knew the line—it was uttered by Marcellus in the play *Hamlet*—but it seemed very uncharacteristic of Cartwright to quote a play about treachery and betrayal ...

A light bulb went off in his mind. Cartwright wasn't talking about investigating *him*; he was talking about someone else, and the only other person involved was Assistant Director Ashleigh Riker. But he wouldn't say it out loud. Reid wouldn't have been the least bit surprised if every wall in Langley had ears.

"I understand," Reid said. "Why isn't the CIA sharing the information about Khalil Oil with Interpol? They haven't been updated in hours."

"Our intel suggests that's a dead end," Cartwright said. "The company went under years ago." Dr. Barnard frowned at Reid. His mouth opened as if he wanted to protest, but Reid shook his head as Cartwright added, "But maybe Interpol knows something that we don't. Look, the virus is what matters here. Get to it. And Zero? Keep doing what you're doing." He hung up without another word, but Reid understood the message.

And apparently so did Dr. Barnard. "Did your superior just suggest that we keep the CIA out of the loop?"

"Yeah. I think he did." Reid could hardly believe it, but he found himself actually appreciating Cartwright. He still didn't quite trust him, at least not completely, but the deputy director seemed to be aware that something was amiss. The CIA was trying hard to keep the name Khalil Oil off the record and out of anyone else's hands. "So we will. If you get a call from Langley, don't answer it. Text Johansson the location."

And let's hope we're not too late.

CHAPTER THIRTY

Maya yawned as she came down the stairs, barefoot and in her pajamas. She'd stayed in bed later than she normally would; she kept waking up the night before from terrible dreams about her father. She worried for him, and even had a powerful urge to send him a text to make sure he was all right, wherever he was. But she didn't. She had told him that she would only contact him if necessary, and a text from her might make him worry needlessly when he had bigger problems to concern himself with.

She had been following the news as best she could about what was going on in Europe. Several outlets had used the term "terrorism," despite the White House's official position that they could not confirm that Barcelona was an attack. Maya was dubious about that; after all, her father had been sent at the same time that the outbreak began.

Since then, more cases of the virus had appeared in Spain, parts of France, and even in northern Portugal. Not only had the United States temporarily barred international travel, but now several cities were going on high alert, including DC, only twenty minutes from their home in Alexandria. It was almost surreal to see the news footage; her neighborhood seemed the same as always, quiet and calm, while a short drive away people were panicking and leaving the city in droves.

She wondered if they would even have school on Monday.

Maya padded into the kitchen to find Mr. Thompson, already fully dressed and bright-eyed, seated at the counter and—*of course he was*—cleaning his revolver.

"Good morning!" he said, a little too cheerfully for her taste.

"Morning." She went straight for the coffeemaker.

"Sleep well?"

"Not really," she replied flatly. She poured herself a cup and added an ample amount of sugar. She didn't care for the naturally bitter taste, and she'd never admit it aloud, but drinking coffee helped her feel more adult. "Have you heard from my dad?"

"Nope," Thompson replied with a smile. "Should I have?"

Right. Thompson was keeping up with the charade that her father was off on a weekend getaway with his new friend Maria. He had no idea that it was a lie that Maya had made up herself. She resisted the urge to tell the old man that she knew about her dad, or at least knew some things.

Instead she said, "I was just a little worried, with everything going on in the city. I hope he can make it home okay."

"I'm sure he'll be just fine. Your dad is a very resourceful guy." Thompson set about reassembling his revolver. His actions were well rehearsed, appearing almost instinctive. Maya couldn't help but watch in mild fascination. She had never so much as held a gun before, let alone fired one. "Say, how about some breakfast? I make a mean French toast. And I bet that would get your sister out of bed before noon."

Maya smirked. She couldn't imagine the grizzled old former Marine, his fingertips slick with gun-lubricating oil, making breakfast. "You make French toast? Really?"

"Sure." Thompson snapped the cylinder into the revolver. "Make it for my grandson all the time."

"You're a grandfather?"

He grinned. "I never told you that? Yeah, little guy is seven now. His name is Matthew. Let me wash my hands, I'll show you some pictures on my phone." Thompson rose from his stool with a grunt and went to the kitchen sink.

Maya smiled. It was sort of a nice change of pace to talk with their neighbor about something other than the Marine Corps.

She caught movement in her periphery, something flitting past the open blinds of the dining room window. She turned quickly, but there was nothing.

Probably just a bird.

Mr. Thompson dried his hands on a dish towel. "Matt just had a birthday party a couple weeks ago. His mama made him his own separate cake, so he could, you know, dive into it face-first." The old man chuckled. "I've got photos of the mess he made—"

Thompson suddenly snapped to attention, his gaze focused on the far window of the living room.

Maya gulped. She felt a slight knot of anxiety forming in her midsection.

"I saw it too," she said quietly. Something—or someone—had definitely just dashed past. And she was certain it was not just a bird.

Thompson snatched up his Smith & Wesson and pushed open the cylinder.

"It's probably nothing," she said, more for her own benefit than for his. Still, her voice sounded smaller than she thought it would.

"Maya, I know what you probably think of me," he said quickly. As he spoke, he loaded six rounds into the revolver. It took him only a few seconds, his thumb and fingers working far more deftly than Maya would have thought possible. "I'm the crazy old man next door that carries a gun everywhere. But believe me when I say that I have lived a dangerous life, and the only reason I'm still here is by one simple rule." He flicked the revolver sideways and the cylinder locked into place. "You can *never* be too careful. Now I'm going to do a perimeter check. I want you to go upstairs, wake your sister, and get down to the basement. Got it?"

She nodded. "Yes."

"Good. I'll be right back." He pushed open the sliding glass door that led to the deck, the revolver in his hand pointed at waist level.

Maya stood rooted to the spot. *It's nothing,* she told herself. *It could have been an animal. A package delivery. A utility worker. No one knows we're here.* Her curiosity got the better of her. She crept to the living room window and peered out through the blinds. She saw Mr. Thompson as he rounded the corner from the backyard, his gun in both hands and raised.

Her heart pounded in her chest. *He doesn't see anything. Still. Go wake Sara. Go to the basement. Grab your phone—*

An arm snaked around her shoulders. She let out a gasp of shock as she was pulled backward against someone's body. Then she froze in abject terror as something thin, razor sharp, pressed against her throat.

It was a sensation she had felt once before, but that did not make it easier; if anything, it made it worse, as the panic and dread of having a knife to her neck came rushing back.

"Do not scream," whispered a male voice. "Do not make a sound other than to answer my questions or I will cut your throat." The man was impossibly quiet. She hadn't even heard the sliding door open. "Now walk backwards." He took a step back and pulled her with him, keeping her tight to his chest. She did as he said, taking tiny steps backwards out of fear that the knife might slip against her skin.

"Are you Maya?" he asked her quietly as they moved from the living room to the kitchen.

Her breath came quickly, in short hissing bursts through her nose. "Yes."

"Is your father home?" He kept going, taking small steps from the kitchen to the corridor that led to the foyer.

"Yes," Maya said softly. "He's in the basement. And there are three other agents here too—"

Her assailant stopped in the foyer, just short of the staircase. "Do not lie to me," he whispered. "I've been here for twenty minutes. There is an old man with a Smith & Wesson Model 19 Classic. There is you. Presumably your sister is upstairs."

Sara. Maya's panic doubled at the thought of her sister, asleep and unaware. *I have to keep her safe.*

"I have killed many people, some of them women and children. I don't like to do it, but it is sometimes necessary, especially when proving a point. If you lie again, I will open your throat, and then I will do the same to your younger sister."

Tears welled in Maya's eyes. "Don't touch her." She had intended her words to come off as defiant, but instead they sounded like a plea.

"Is your father home?"

"... No."

"Is he in the country?"

"I ... I don't know."

"You said there were other agents. So you know what he is? What he does?"

Maya heard the sliding glass door open with a whoosh. A wave of relief washed over her as Mr. Thompson called out. "Maya?" A moment later she heard the familiar creak of the basement door. "Maya, are you down there?" Footfalls—then Mr. Thompson rounded the corner.

His revolver was up in an instant. "Drop the knife and step away," he ordered firmly.

"Those are .357 rounds." The assailant sounded strangely calm. "Would you risk killing her to take a shot?"

"I'm a very good shot," Mr. Thompson said, his voice low and gruff.

"Then you would have taken it by now." Maya felt the pressure of the knife ease off her throat slightly. "Don't worry. I have no intention of hurting the girl. In fact, I'm going to give her back to you." The assailant stepped forward, forcing her with him. He took another step. Thompson kept the gun level, his aim just over Maya's right shoulder.

The man suddenly shoved her roughly. She stumbled, flailing her arms for support, and collided with Mr. Thompson. He caught her and at the same time twisted his body, dropping her safely to the floor and out of the way.

But the assailant surged forward right behind her. He swung the knife in a tight arc at the older man's throat. Mr. Thompson was deceptively fast; he ducked out of the blade's way and it missed by an inch. As he tried to bring his gun up again, the assailant slashed upward, cutting into Thompson's forearm. He cried out and the gun clattered to the floor. The stranger kicked it backward, into the foyer and away from all three of them.

As the two men grappled, Maya crawled away desperately on her hands and knees, toward the kitchen. She used a stool to pull herself to her feet—her limbs still felt shaky and weak with the fear of having a knife at her throat again. She grabbed her cell phone from the counter.

Emergency plan. Text Dad. Call the police. Her thumbs trembled as she replied to her dad's text message, the one from the unknown phone number. *Reply here if you need to reach me,* it had said. So she did.

Help

She hit send. Then she opened her keypad and dialed 9–1…

The assailant lunged toward her and swiped an arm. The cell phone flew violently from her hands and clattered to the floor. In that instant, she looked up and got the first good look at him since he had slipped into their house. He was lean, his face angular, his cheeks shaved smooth. He bled from a split lip. His hair was dark and cut close to the scalp. But most unsettling were his eyes, a deep, vibrant green that was simultaneously wild and animalistic.

He snatched up the cell phone and shoved it into his own pocket.

Behind him, Mr. Thompson struggled to get up. He was on his hands and knees on the kitchen tile, his head bent low and a ribbon of bloody spittle hanging from his lips.

Maya breathed hard, not daring to move. The assailant did not seem to be in any rush; he strode to the foyer and retrieved the Smith & Wesson, tucking it into the back of his jeans. Then he picked up his curved hunting knife, the one he had pressed to Maya's throat, and stood over Thompson.

"My job," he said softly, staring directly at Maya, "was more than just assassin. It was also messenger. I will show you how I sent messages. You will watch, and this way you will know that I'm serious."

"Please, don't…" Her voice was hushed, practically a whisper.

The assassin rolled Thompson over with a swift kick from his boot. The old man grunted and lurched onto his back. One eye was swollen half-shut, and blood eked from his nose.

Maya clamped a hand over her mouth. *He's going to kill Mr. Thompson. I have to do something. I have to...*

"Maya." Thompson grunted again in pain. "Go."

The assailant straddled Thompson. He brought the knife up in both hands, and then slammed it downward.

Thompson's hand flew upward to meet it. The knife sank into his palm and out the other side. He let loose a guttural scream, but he held the knife, pushing against it with both his pierced hand and his other. The assassin gritted his teeth and leaned into the knife, pushing as hard as he could. His body jerked as he rocked onto the knife, heaving it forward inch by inch, as feral gasps and growls escaped his throat like some sort of wild beast.

"Go!" Thompson bellowed, loud enough to jar Maya into action. She jumped up and sprinted past them, into the foyer and to the stairs. She paused for a moment, and then slipped her hand into the pocket of her dad's bomber jacket that hung near the door.

It came out again holding a black pistol. Her hand shook. She had never held a gun before, and it terrified her.

In the foyer behind her the assassin leaned his body weight onto the knife, the tip of which was positioned directly over Mr. Thompson's heart. The older man's strength was failing him. If she did nothing, he would be dead in moments.

Maya couldn't leave him to die.

There was no time to examine the gun or check if it was loaded. Instead she grabbed the barrel in her fist and brought the hilt swiftly down across the back of the assassin's head. The dull smack of steel against bone resonated up her arm, turning her stomach as the assassin grunted and fell aside.

"I told you to go!" Thompson struggled to get up on his elbows, the knife still pierced through his hand. He coughed and blood stained his lips. "Get your sister—"

The assassin sat up again just as quickly as he'd fallen. His face was bright red and snarling as he flung out an arm and backhanded Maya across the mouth. Sharp pain stung at her lips and she nearly fell over. The assailant tried to climb to his feet, but Mr. Thompson managed to find a surge of strength and wrapped him from behind, around the waist, yanking him back down to the ground.

The two men grappled on the floor, smearing blood across the tile. Maya could only watch the tangled fray of limbs, feet kicking, fists flying. From the melee came only one word, in Thompson's raspy, gravelly voice.

"Sara!" he cried.

Sara. Keep her safe. Maya forced her legs to move, to get up. Her feet pounded the stairs as the two men grunted and gasped from the kitchen.

Her sister was awake, sitting up wide-eyed in bed as Maya charged into her bedroom. "I heard banging and shouting..." She saw the black pistol in her sister's hand and gasped. "What's going on?"

"Sara, listen to me." Maya knelt at the bedside. "Someone is in the house. You need to do as I say, no matter what. Okay?"

Her little sister's eyes immediately welled with tears and her lip trembled, but she nodded quickly. Their father, overprotective as he tended to be, had installed an escape ladder on a window in each of their rooms. It was two lengths of twenty-five-foot chains with rungs between them that unfurled into a ladder in the case of a fire or other emergency. They could get down it, run to the street, make a lot of noise...

Maya hurried to the doorway and listened. She heard the grunts of effort from both men downstairs. Then a deep throaty shout— no, two of them.

Then it stopped. Maya froze, listening as intently as she could. Someone panted, breathing hard from the exertion.

She couldn't hesitate and take the chance that it wasn't Thompson. She yanked the window open and pushed the rolled fire escape ladder out. It unfurled with a clatter, the far end of it thudding against the ground in the backyard.

Steady footfalls on the stairs reached her ears and she froze again. *If it was Thompson, he would have called to us. Told us it was safe.* She couldn't take that chance. If it was the assassin, they didn't have time to both make an escape out the window.

"Sara," she whispered quickly. "I want you to get in your closet. I'm going to draw him away from you. As soon as you're able, you run downstairs and you get to the panic room. Understand?"

"Maya, don't go—"

"You don't wait for me. You lock the door behind you, and you call the police. Now go. Go!" She practically shoved her sister off the bed. Sara scurried to the closet and pulled the door shut behind her.

Maya gripped the gun in her fist and hid herself between the open bedroom door and the wall. She barely squeezed behind it in time; a second later, the assassin stepped into the bedroom. She heard his soft boots against the carpet as he crossed to the window.

She dared to glance around the edge of the door. The assassin stuck his head out the window, looking out over the yard for any signs of the girls. In his fist was the knife, its blade awash in blood. Her stomach churned at the sight of it.

Mr. Thompson... His last words had been to her—for her to save her sister. Maya stepped out from behind the door and ran out of the bedroom, intentionally slapping her feet against the hardwood floor of the hall.

The assassin gave chase, but she had a lead. She ran past her own bedroom and into her father's, slamming the door shut behind her. She quickly looked over the gun in her hands; there was a safety on it somewhere, and her father was the type that would keep it on. She found it, a small black button just above the trigger, and pressed it.

The knob turned slowly and the door swung inward, the assassin standing in the frame. He blinked twice, very nearly an expression of surprise, to find himself face to face with the barrel of a Glock.

Then he smirked. "Do you know how to use that?"

Both her hands trembled, wrapped around the pistol. "If you know who my father is, then you know I do."

Over his shoulder, Maya saw Sara slip quietly down the stairs. The younger girl hesitated for just a moment, her mouth agape as she saw her sister with the assailant at gunpoint, but she did as Maya asked and hurried down the stairs. Her bare feet barely made a sound against them.

"I had a feeling I might die here today," said the assassin. "But at your hand? That would be … unexpected."

They both heard a small shriek of terror from downstairs.

Maya had forgotten to warn her sister about what she might see down there.

The assassin did not take his eyes from her. "A diversion? Well done. But you wouldn't need it if you were going to kill me."

Do it, she told herself. *Pull the trigger.* Her teeth chattered nervously. She suddenly felt very cold. *This man killed Thompson. He came here to kill your dad. He threatened your sister. He held a knife to your throat.*

Maya squeezed her eyes closed and then squeezed the trigger.

Nothing happened.

Her mouth fell open in utter disbelief. She had taken the safety off, she was sure of it…

"You have to cock it," he told her. He seemed amused. "This top slide, right here." He pointed, reaching out and touching the gun. "Go ahead. Pull it back."

Maya took a quick step backward, away from him, and yanked back on the top slide. It barely moved; it was difficult to pull. She took another step back, desperately trying to cock the gun.

The assassin stepped forward. "I suppose not even Kent Steele would leave one in the chamber when his young girls could find it."

Please, she pleaded with the gun. *Please work.* She struggled and tugged, straining with the effort, until there was a solid click as a bullet slid into the chamber. As she raised the pistol again, the assailant brought one hand up and easily snapped it from her grip.

"You have spirit. You're certainly his daughter." Quick as a flash, faster than she could even react, he brought a fist careening into the side of her head. His knuckles caught just behind her jaw. She felt the impact, but no pain, as stars swam in her vision.

Maya was unconscious before she hit the carpet.

CHAPTER THIRTY ONE

Reid drove the SUV slowly along the wide asphalt of the Marseille Fos Port. The industrial seaport was an enormous spread of cranes, dry docks, silos, storage facilities, and stacks upon stacks of colorful cargo containers. Despite being closed by the government, there was still a surprising amount of activity as workers unloaded freight from docked vessels and piloted cranes to slowly shift the enormous steel shipping containers from ships to stacks.

He parked between two squat beige silos and turned off the engine, leaving the keys in the ignition. Not more than a hundred yards past the windshield was the storage facility that had once belonged to Khalil Oil, a rectangular brick structure with partitioned windows about halfway up the walls. A wide banner over a pair of garage-door bays announced that the building was for lease in both French and English.

"Try Maria on the radio," he told the doctor.

Barnard pressed a finger to his ear. "Agent Johansson? Agent Watson? Can anyone hear me?" He turned to Reid. "Nothing."

Then they're still at least two miles away, outside the radio's range. "All right. Try to get her on the phone and get an ETA." He reached for the door handle.

"Wait, Agent Steele, you're not seriously going to go in alone, are you?"

Reid nodded. "If he's in there, I'm not going to wait around for backup. Tell Maria to approach carefully and from the rear."

"I should come with you—"

"No," Reid told him. "You stay here. I don't know what I'll find in there, but keep an eye out and a window open. If I need you I'll do what I can to signal you."

Barnard hesitated, but he nodded. "Godspeed, Agent Steele."

Reid closed the door and headed straight for the storage facility. If anyone was looking they would clearly see him approaching, his hands in his jacket pocket, trying to look as casual as possible while striding toward the entrance, but there was no way for him to make a furtive approach. The area around the facility was wide open.

His heart rate sped up as he got closer. *It'll be here*, he thought. *Khalil and the virus. He hadn't counted on this. He didn't plan for it. He thought Claudette Minot would be the end of the line for us.*

He reached the entrance, a door on the southwest corner of the building, and paused to draw his Glock 19. There were no windows at a height that he could use to see inside. He would be entering blind.

Reid tried the knob. It was unlocked. He knew that wasn't a good sign.

He knew that he should at least wait for Watson and Maria, if not Baraf's agents too.

He thought of his girls back home. He hadn't even been gone for two full days but already it felt like a week. He missed them dearly, and he would do anything to keep them safe. If there was even a chance that he could stop the virus from reaching the shores of the United States, he would do it without a second thought.

He pushed the door open and stepped inside the warehouse, his gun level in his right hand.

The empty storage facility was huge and cavernous, the concrete floors swept clean and wide, round steel columns supporting the ceiling about thirty feet above his head. It was dim inside; the only light came from the partitioned windows above him, angled to reduce the amount of sunlight.

He stepped carefully, leading with his gun. His heart slowed, but his anxiety did not. The place appeared to be empty. There was no one and nothing here.

Still he crossed the floor clear to the other side, just to be sure. As he reached the opposite entrance facing the harbor, a voice rang out, clear and male and echoing in the empty space.

"Are you alone?" the voice asked. He spoke English, but his accent was clearly Middle Eastern—in fact, Syrian.

Reid spun, tracking the barrel left and right, but he saw no one. *The columns.* It was the only hiding place in the building. There were eight of them in all, and he had no idea where the voice had come from. He stepped as silently as possible to his right so that he could see around the four on the western side of the building.

"Lower the gun, please." The voice was surprisingly gentle, calm even.

"Show yourself," Reid demanded. "Hands on your head."

Slowly an arm snaked out from behind one of the western columns, the second in the row. Brown fingers curled around an object.

A cell phone. With the thumb on the green send button.

Reid knew immediately what it meant. His glance flitted up and down, but he saw no wires, no bombs. *Where then?*

"Drop it," Reid commanded. "And come out."

"Are you alone?" the voice asked again.

Reid scoffed in frustration. "In here, yes. But the building is surrounded. There are dozens outside. There's nowhere to go."

"I'm going to step out," said the man. "But you should know what this is, and what it means. If you pull the trigger I will press this button, and half of Marseille Fos will explode. The entire port is wired. Your friends outside will die."

"I won't shoot," Reid said. *At least not until I know where the virus is.* "But I'm not putting the gun down either." Even if he was lying about the facility being surrounded, he couldn't call the man's bluff. There were innocent workers on the dock, not to mention Dr. Barnard. Maria and Watson would arrive shortly. Interpol agents were on their way.

The figure stepped out from behind the column. He was Syrian, with smooth features and a dark, neatly trimmed beard on his cheeks. He wore a clean beige suit with a red tie.

The man was not at all what Reid had expected. He thought he would find an angry, militant, bearded man in a taqiyah or turban, shouting about the glory of Allah and the death of infidels. The man standing before him looked as if he had just walked out of a corporate shareholders meeting. He looked far more like the son of a wealthy oil magnate than a holy man.

Yet his appearance made him no less dangerous.

"Assad ibn Khalil," Reid said slowly.

Khalil's soft gaze glinted as he shook his head. "No longer. These days, I go by Imam—"

"You're no Imam," Reid interrupted. "You're a con man. You exploit weak people to carry out your will." Reid had a clear shot; at this range he could bury a bullet in Khalil's skull before he heard the cap explode. But anything less than a kill-shot would risk him detonating the bombs, and Reid needed to know where the virus was.

"Not my will. The will of Allah, praise be unto Him," Khalil said plainly. "And who do I have the pleasure of speaking with?"

"They call me Agent Zero," Reid told him. He took a slow, careful step, almost imperceptibly sliding his left foot forward.

Khalil's lips curled into a smirk. "*The* Agent Zero? Well! It is an honor. I've heard your name whispered in both reverence and terror." He looked Reid up and down. "Though I have to say, I was expecting more."

That's enough small talk. "Where's the virus?" Reid demanded.

Khalil's eyes flitted left and right. "You came alone, didn't you, Agent Zero? I don't believe the building is surrounded at all. From what I've heard, you are very much the lone-wolf type."

"Where is the virus?" Reid shouted. His grip tightened around the Glock.

"Did you not find her?" Khalil asked, trying to sound innocent.

"We did. Claudette Minot is dead."

Khalil shook his head. "Shame. She was such a lovely, loyal girl."

"She died confused and alone," Reid said forcefully. "Carrying an empty box."

"She died for a great and noble cause," Khalil countered, "in the service of the one true Lord—"

"Enough," Reid interrupted. "I know why you're really doing this. This is revenge, isn't it? Your family's company was taken by force. Your father was imprisoned for two years. There is no jihad; just your half-baked revenge plot against the wrong people."

Khalil smirked. Despite the dim light of the warehouse, his eyes gleamed. "Is that what you believe, Agent Zero? The narrative you have invented for me? You know nothing. I never wanted anything from them. My family's greed and opulence sickened me ..."

"And yet here you are, using their money and resources to enact your plan," Reid countered.

"A means to an end, Agent. That is all."

"Like convincing several of your followers that they were the Imam Mahdi, the Redeemer? You lied to them. You're responsible for their deaths, as well as the researchers in Siberia and the hundreds in Barcelona." Reid shook his head in disgust. "That's not something a holy man would ever do."

Khalil licked his lips. "No? Do you not know your history, Agent Zero? Because the precedents for such things are plentiful."

Reid swallowed a lump in his throat. Khalil was, unfortunately, right; more death, war, and atrocities had been carried out in the name of religion than any other motivation in history.

But that still didn't make it right.

"Then why?" Reid insisted. "If not for revenge, if not for your family, then why are you doing this?"

"You know why," the Imam replied. "This is the jihad. The great struggle. The battle against the enemies of Islam. I will succeed where so many others have failed."

Reid couldn't believe what he was hearing. He had thought there must be a motivation, some missing link fueling Khalil's plan, his rage, his desire to see so many dead. And there was, whether it could be called ideology or spirituality or religion.

To Reid, it simply seemed like lunacy.

"You won't succeed. You're done."

Khalil shook his head sadly. "No, Agent. I'm afraid the virus is already on its way to your shores."

Reid's heart skipped a beat. The map they had found in Greece had suggested that targets were throughout the western world, throughout Europe and the Americas. "We found your map in Athens…"

"A fake," Khalil said. "A distraction. Barcelona wasn't a target; it was a testing grounds to ensure the efficacy of the virus. When it spread into France, we drew that map to cause panic. Incite shutdowns. There are not twenty-five targets. There is only one. We will destroy the United States from the inside."

The barrel of the Glock trembled slightly. "No," Reid said in disbelief. "You had no way to get it out of the port. It's still here somewhere. You're bluffing."

"I am not, Agent Zero. I promise you that. My people are in place. They know what to do and how to get it. I planned for years, and it is finally coming to fruition. And the only reason I am telling you any of this is because there's nothing you can do to stop it. Once the virus is released, there will no longer even be an America."

Reid's blood ran cold. *And with international travel closed, the virus would be contained to one country. Borders to the United States will stay closed, just on the other sides. The entirety of America would become an isolation zone if the infection couldn't be stopped…*

"Tell me where the virus is," Reid threatened, "or I will shoot you on the spot."

Shoot him, he shouted at himself in his head. *Shoot him now.*

Khalil chuckled bitterly. "I know I am going to die today. It's part of my plan. The rest of it is already in motion." His soft gaze met Reid's. "But I wouldn't be telling you any of this if you weren't going to die with me." He unbuttoned his beige suit jacket and opened it.

Reid took an instinctive step back in alarm.

It wasn't the port that was wired to blow—it was Khalil. Several pounds of C-4 were strapped to a vest around his torso in long gray bricks.

He tapped a black box on the vest, just above his navel. "All I have to do is make the call and send the signal to this transmitter, and we will both go up in flames, along with the entire building," Khalil told him passively. "I have accepted my fate. I told you it was an honor, Agent Zero, and I meant it. It is my honor to take you to the afterlife with me."

Reid kept his aim on the man. He knew the rear exit of the building was no more than fifteen feet behind him, but he doubted he could get to it before Khalil pressed the button. He didn't dare so much as glance over his shoulder.

But he could have blown it at any time. This was his intention, to kill himself and whoever he could with him. Yet he waited. He told me his story, and it couldn't have just been for catharsis.

"You've been stalling," Reid said. His rational mind screamed at him, fully realizing it was insane to call Khalil on it with his finger on the button. "You're waiting for something."

Khalil narrowed his eyes. "You are keen, Agent Zero."

"What are you waiting for?" Reid took a small step backward. "It's the last part of your plan, isn't it? You need to make sure that the virus gets to where it needs to be. Is that it?"

Khalil licked his lips nervously. "My plan is flawless. The only reason you've gotten this far is because I let you get this far—"

"No," Reid interjected. "You didn't think we would get any further than Minot, but you needed a contingency. You're only still here because you need to be. Which means there's still a chance we can stop this—"

Suddenly the southwestern entrance to the building flew open with a booming thud. Maria and Agent Watson charged through, guns aloft and both aimed at Khalil.

"Freeze!" Watson shouted. "Hands in the air!"

The Imam's head whipped around instinctively.

Reid wanted to shout to them, to warn them of the bomb, but he had no time. He dropped to one knee and took careful aim. A silent prayer ran through his head.

He took the shot.

Khalil pressed the button.

CHAPTER THIRTY TWO

The single blast from Reid's Glock 19 thundered in the empty storage facility, sounding three times louder. Its jarring report startled even him, every muscle tensed as he waited for the subsequent explosion—the bomb strapped to Assad ibn Khalil's chest.

Khalil's face contorted into abject confusion. His thumb was firmly pressed against the green button. Then the phone slipped from his fingers and clattered to the floor. His other hand touched his stomach, just above the navel, as blood ran over his knuckles.

Reid had aimed for the transmitter on the vest. His bullet had found its home and rendered it useless an instant before the Imam's thumb found the button.

Khalil fell to his knees, clutching his stomach.

"Jesus, is that a bomb?" Watson asked incredulously, his aim still fixed on Khalil.

Reid let out a long breath he didn't realize he'd been holding. "It was."

Watson blinked at him in astonishment. Then he nodded. "Nice work, Zero."

"Not quite. The virus isn't here. We still need to find…" He trailed off as the phone chimed from the floor.

Khalil glanced down at it, his breath coming in gasps. His lips twitched as they pulled into a weak grin. "You're still… too late." He collapsed onto his side with a groan.

Reid snatched up the device. The screen displayed a text message that said only one word: *Received.*

"Confirmation," Reid said quietly. He was right; Khalil had been waiting for a confirmation that the virus had gotten to where it needed to be. *It can't be far.* He sprinted out of the storage facility, leaving Khalil dying slowly on the floor.

"Kent, wait!" Maria and Watson followed as he tore the cell phone open and removed the battery. He wasn't taking any chances that there weren't other bombs around the port, as Khalil had claimed.

"Where's Barnard?" He looked around frantically. The doctor was trotting toward him from the waiting SUV.

"Agent Steele, what happened?" he asked as he drew near.

"The virus isn't here. Khalil sent it somewhere," Reid said quickly to his team. "He came here for a reason. How could he have gotten it out of France?"

Barnard shook his head. "Agent, the port is closed. No one is allowed entry or exit."

"But you heard what Baraf said. Khalil knows this place. This facility belonged to his family. He must know something … the shipping routes…"

"Through the Mediterranean," Barnard finished his thought for him. "You're suggesting he doesn't need a ship to come or go from here."

"He just needs one to pass by," Maria said. "Dr. Barnard, what would the CDC's plan dictate for the threat of a pandemic?"

"In this particular case? Closure of airports, seaports, and land borders, of course," Barnard recited quickly. "Uh, heightened security among TSA, emergency personnel, and law enforcement. Possible deployment of the National Guard—"

"But what about industry?" Reid interrupted. "What about trade? Specifically, what's the one thing that the United States would most likely *not* bar from a port of entry?"

"Oil," said Watson. "You're talking about oil transport."

Barnard's expression slackened as he came to the realization. "Good lord, I should have realized… In the emergency meeting with the president, fears were explicitly voiced about the potential cost of shutting down trade."

Reid nodded. "You know how many of people in positions of power have their hands in those pockets. Hell, even our own president." It was no secret that while President Pierson had officially stepped down from his business holdings when he took office, he still had plenty to do with the management thereof.

"You think Khalil's plan is to stow the virus on an oil tanker passing through the Mediterranean?" Barnard asked.

"He's proven himself smart enough already," Reid said ruefully. "I wouldn't doubt if he found a way." He scanned the industrial seaport. "The question is, can we?"

"We're sure as hell not going to find any speedboats around here," Watson said.

"Call Cartwright. See if he can arrange a..." Reid was interrupted by a familiar sound, faint at first but approaching quickly. He looked skyward and shielded his eyes with a hand as the steady *whump-whump* of rotors grew louder.

A black helicopter descended from the sky, landing about twenty-five yards from them in a clear span of asphalt on the port. Four suited Interpol agents leapt out, followed by a fifth man— Vicente Baraf.

Reid grinned fiercely as he hurried over. His jacket flapped wildly around him from the still-spinning blades overhead. "We found Khalil," he shouted over the noise. "In the warehouse. He's been shot, and he has an explosive strapped to him. There might be others around the port. Have your people contact French authorities and get a bomb squad down here immediately."

Baraf quickly relayed the message, and his four agents sprinted off toward the warehouse. "And the virus?" he shouted to Reid.

"We're going to need to borrow your helicopter. We need to get out to sea, and fast."

At first Baraf frowned as if he had misheard. Then he nodded once. "Get in."

Reid paused a moment, expecting pushback or questions, but Baraf smirked. "I'm quickly learning not to doubt your instincts, Agent. Let's go." Baraf climbed back into the cockpit as Maria and Barnard scrambled into the rear-facing passenger seats behind him.

Watson hesitated, glancing precariously at Reid. They didn't have to exchange any words. Reid gestured with his head, and Watson climbed up into a seat. He still didn't fully trust the other agent, not after what happened with Carver—but, he realized, he didn't fully trust anyone other than Maria. Now wasn't the time. He needed Watson with them.

Baraf spun his finger in a circular motion to the pilot, and the helicopter immediately lifted off. Reid strapped himself in and fit on a headset, drowning out the wind whipping around his ears from the open door.

"Head due south until we have a heading," Reid said as the helicopter soared out from Marseille Fos and over the Mediterranean Sea. "Patch in Sawyer from Command at Barcelona."

Baraf nodded and punched in the number on a communications console between him and the pilot.

"This is Sawyer." The familiar and still-exhausted British voice came in through the radio headset.

"It's Baraf. I'm with Agent Steele and his team from the CIA. Stand by." He flashed Reid a thumbs-up.

"Sawyer, this is Steele," Reid said. "We need to know if there are any oil tankers in the Mediterranean Sea, close to Port Marseille Fos."

"Begging your pardon, Agent, but you'll need to define 'close,'" Sawyer said. "There are likely a whole fleet of them at any given time in the—"

"The *closest* tankers to Marseille," Reid clarified with obvious irritation. "Any that might have passed by within the last hour or so."

"And quickly, Sawyer," Baraf added.

"Yes sir, tracking now. Give me just a minute." Reid could hear the frantic clacking of keys in the background.

"You can do that?" Dr. Barnard asked.

"Satellites," Watson said into his headset. "We can track anything that has GPS—phones, cars, even ships."

"I've got nothing," Sawyer said. "No oil tankers have passed near Marseille recently. Besides, anyone that's out there would be under orders from the EU to anchor offshore until the ports are open again."

Reid slammed his fist against the side of the chopper in frustration. He was certain that Khalil would have used a tanker—but no. That would be the obvious choice, given his background. Besides, a tanker could be easily stopped if they identified it as the carrier of the virus.

We can track anything that has GPS. But whoever was carrying the virus wouldn't want to be tracked, he reasoned. "Sawyer, what about something we *can't* track?" Reid asked suddenly.

"Sorry?" said the British tech in the radio.

"Something smaller, maybe…" Reid worked out his logic aloud. "Or… or something invisible, at least to us…"

Baraf frowned. "Agent Steele, I'm afraid that doesn't make sense."

Reid snapped his fingers. "What about something that was there before but isn't there now? Something unaccounted for?"

"Give me a moment." Sawyer fell silent for nearly a full minute. Then he said quietly, barely audible over the helicopter's whirring rotors, "Well, I'll be…"

"Sawyer," Baraf snapped.

"A Norwegian cruise ship bound for Italy went off the radar only twenty-five minutes ago," Sawyer announced quickly. "Seems they had already left port when the virus was released in Barcelona; their orders are to remain in the Mediterranean just off of Corsica until further notice."

"Has the crew reported in since they went dark?" Maria asked.

"Yes… the captain reported the failure as a malfunction in their positioning system."

"How far from here were they last seen?" Reid demanded.

"About forty-five miles," Sawyer replied instantly. "Sending the coordinates now."

Forty-five miles, Reid thought. It sounded far, but this was an NH-90, a twin-engine multi-role helicopter built through a partnership between France and German aeronautics. *Likely decommissioned from the military, judging by the lack of guns and obvious alterations. But it's still got ballistic tolerance and high crashworthiness. And with a top speed of 188 miles per hour we'll be there in twelve minutes, tops.*

Reid turned his attention to the chopper's pilot. "Once you reach the coordinates, continue west."

"West? The opposite direction?" Baraf said.

Reid nodded. "If I'm right, that ship has been hijacked. I'd bet Khalil's people were already on board before it ever left port, and…" He trailed off. Suddenly he understood the Barcelona attack. *It wasn't just a testing ground for the virus. It was to stall the cruise ship from reaching port.* "And his people will turn it around, head towards the United States."

"So why don't we let it?" Maria asked. "The US can stop them at port. They'd have nowhere to go."

"Think about it," Reid said. "Khalil might be out of the picture, but he's had a contingency every step of the way so far. We need to be prepared for anything."

"What might anything include?" Dr. Barnard asked nervously.

Reid didn't want to say it aloud. "Sawyer, how many people are on that ship?"

"Let me check the manifest." A moment later the tech answered. "The ship is called the *Jade Star,* and it's carrying a passenger load just shy of twelve hundred."

Reid held his breath. Twelve hundred people. *That must be Khalil's failsafe,* he thought—if the virus itself couldn't reach the shore, carriers of it could.

"ETA to coordinates, eleven minutes," the pilot said into the radio.

If they had been in any other situation, and not en route to find a virus that was intended to destroy the entire United States of America, Reid might have laughed aloud. He knew how to fly this machine. As he watched the pilot's hands move deftly over switches and levers, he knew each precise movement before it was made.

He glanced upward, over the sliding door to his left. The rappelling system had been removed; the chopper would have to land on the cruise ship.

"Sawyer can patch us in to the ship," Baraf said. "We could order them to slow, it might make our approach faster…"

Reid shook his head. "We don't want them to know they're coming. That will only give them time to prepare for us." He turned to his team. "Trust no one on that ship. Some of the crew could be Khalil's people. Expect them to be armed. Based on what we've seen, some of the ship might be wired with explosives." Khalil's words from just minutes ago ran through his head. *The only reason I am telling you any of this is because there's nothing you can do to stop it.* This was a man who had planned for seemingly every scenario. "And possibly infection," he added.

The color drained from Barnard's face. "You think they would risk releasing the virus prematurely?"

"If the alternative would be having it taken from them? Yes. I do."

"But… they would be dead long before they ever reached the United States," the doctor argued.

"And so would we," Maria said quietly into the radio. "Would the virus?"

"No." Barnard shook his head. "No, it wouldn't."

"Be ready for anything," Reid repeated.

No one spoke for several minutes as the NH-90 sped toward the *Jade Star.* Reid's knee bounced involuntarily against the floor. The minutes were feeling like a very long time.

Across from him, Maria pulled off her headset and gestured for him to do the same. The roar of the rotors was near deafening, but she leaned over and spoke directly in his ear.

"Listen," she said, "just in case something goes awry down there, there's something you should know…"

He had a feeling he knew what she was going to say. His fingers found hers and squeezed. "I do know. And I feel the same."

"No, Reid. You don't know."

He furrowed his brow. "You just called me Reid."

"That's your real name, isn't it?"

He nodded. "Yes." *Did I tell her that? I must have.*

Her lips brushed against his ear, moving, but not uttering anything. There was more she wanted to say, but she seemed hesitant to do so.

"Hey," he told her. "We're going to come out of this on top. So whatever it is you want to tell me, how about you save it for our second date?"

She gently kissed his cheek. "Okay." Then she leaned back and put her headset on. He smiled at her, trying to appear reassuring, but she stared out through the open doorway with a faraway look in her eye.

He followed her gaze. There was nothing but blue water in every direction, a vast sea spanning the distance between two continents as the chopper hurtled west.

But then, something came into view—a long shape, entirely white, growing larger by the moment.

The *Jade Star*'s deck was oblong and lengthy, the bow coming to a sharp point at the front of the boat. At its stern was a raised cockpit, white and enclosed. Reid counted the decks as they drew near; there were eight in all. Many of them would be staterooms for guests. Finding the virus would be no simple task.

"Baraf, binoculars." Reid held out his hand and the Interpol agent passed him a large black pair, military-grade and heavy. Reid peered through the lenses and leaned forward to get a better view of the ship as they made their approach.

On the top deck was a swimming pool, surrounded by deck chairs, hot tubs, a bar, and ... and much to his surprise, dozens of lounging tourists. He scanned the deck slowly, left and right, in disbelief.

No one was panicking. No one seemed to be in the grip of terror.

For a moment he felt a tinge of alarm up his spine. He was wrong; this ship was not hijacked. *But it's heading in the wrong direction,* he remembered. These people, the passengers of the cruise ship, they had no idea what was happening. Khalil's people must have carried out their plan quietly.

He directed his gaze toward the rising white tower of the control room, but the windows around it were dark. He couldn't see what might be happening beyond them.

He adjusted his focus and panned low, below the cockpit, and caught sight of a trio of figures crowded around a bizarre-looking object. Reid couldn't quite tell what it was. He adjusted the binoculars and fixed his gaze on it. The object was small, and painted sky-blue. As they drew nearer he saw that it was in the shape of an X…

No, he thought, *not an X. Those are wings. And a tail.*

He lowered the binoculars. *That's how they got it to the cruise ship.* "I've got eyes on a UAV," he said into the radio. An unmanned aerial vehicle—what most would call a drone, though this particular one was fixed-wing, built for distance. *And to carry a load.* "That's how they got the virus from Marseille Fos to here. I'm sure of it."

"They're going to hear us coming," Baraf warned. "Be ready, Agents. We need to act as soon as we've touched down."

Reid nodded. "Maria, Watson, secure the console. I don't know if the captain is in on this or not, but we need this boat stopped. Make sure to search them for weapons, phones, detonators, anything of the like. Baraf, sound the emergency alarm, and then get to the evacuation point. It looks like the lifeboats are affixed to deck four. And be careful; Khalil's men want these people to stay on the boat."

"And you?" Maria asked.

"I'll go after the virus." Reid glanced through the binoculars again. The three men were still there, surrounding the drone near the rear of the deck. *The virus is there,* he thought. *I can't lose sight of them.*

The NH-90 dipped from its low altitude and approached the cruise ship. Many of the tourists looked skyward at the sound of the blades, shielding their eyes from the sun in confusion as the chopper neared. People rose from deck chairs or left their seats at the poolside bar to watch the oncoming military helicopter.

There was little they could do to gain any further element of surprise. Reid brought the binoculars around to the drone again— but the three men who had been huddled around it had vanished.

Where did they go? He tracked left and right quickly, scanning the deck, but saw nothing. *They couldn't have just disappeared. They ran off to hide. Or to stow the virus. Or worse...*

He caught movement and focused as two figures came into view again from the base of the cockpit. They each had something in their hands. Reid almost realized it too late.

"Incoming!" he shouted as automatic gunfire tore at the helicopter.

CHAPTER THIRTY THREE

Reid ducked as low as he could while strapped in and covered his head with both hands as bullets pounded and clanged against the side of the chopper.

"Hang on!" The pilot yanked the stick. The NH-90 spun in place ninety degrees, now moving sideways as it continued to descend toward the cruise ship.

Watson reached into his jacket for his Glock 19, but a stray bullet struck him in the shoulder. He grunted through gritted teeth as blood sprayed against the seat back.

"Watson is hit!" Reid shouted.

"I'm okay," he hissed, gripping his shoulder. "Just set us down!"

The fusillade of bullets ceased, at least for a moment, and Reid hazarded a glance through the binoculars. The two men were each carrying a Sig Sauer MPX—*gas-operated submachine gun, nine-millimeter rounds, thirty-round detachable box magazine.* They were reloading. The NH-90's ballistic tolerance could handle another sixty rounds, but the people inside couldn't.

Sheer pandemonium broke out on the top deck, with people scurrying every which way, dashing below deck, trampling each other in the melee. Some dove for cover behind whatever they could while others simply ran.

Reid tore off his headset and unstrapped himself from his seat, pulling his Glock at the same time. He looped one hand into a nylon strap hanging from the ceiling and then leaned out the open door, aimed carefully, and fired down on the two assailants.

The Syrian men scattered for cover. It gave the pilot the precious few seconds he needed to make a precipitous drop down toward a now-open span of the ship's deck. The sudden loss in altitude made Reid's ears pop, but he shook it off. They were no more than twenty-five feet from the surface.

"Setting down!" the pilot announced. No sooner had he said it than another bout of gunfire ripped the air, tearing at the side of the helicopter. The pilot pulled on the cyclic and the chopper spun again.

Reid's feet lost the floor with the unexpected rotation, and for a moment his body was half outside the cabin, swinging by one arm. His pistol fell from his grip. He watched it fall the short distance to the planks of the deck below.

It's not that far, he thought. *I've fallen farther.*

He let go of the strap as the chopper came out of its revolution. For a moment he felt weightless, careening through the air in an indiscernible direction; in the next instant that direction was most definitively down. He miraculously struck the deck feet-first and immediately tucked into a roll. Pain shot up and down his bad knee, but he was able to spring back up again and flatten himself behind a round white column. The chopper roared overhead, but not loud enough to drown out the frantic screams and shouts of passengers as they dashed madcap in every direction.

The bullets stopped again. Thirty rounds went quickly in a submachine gun. These men weren't military; they were amateurs, he knew, or else they would be alternating and reloading one at a time.

He leapt out from his position and rolled again, this time grabbing his fallen pistol as he tucked. Reid came up on one knee not fifteen feet from the two assailants.

The pair of Arabic men froze mid-reload, staring at him in utter bewilderment.

Reid took only half a second to make sure no one was in his line of fire. He squeezed the trigger twice, and both Syrians fell.

Behind him the chopper set down gently on the deck and his teammates jumped out to join him. He retrieved the two submachine guns and passed one off to Maria. "Secure up top and stop this boat!" To Baraf he said, "Start evacuating!" He pointed at Barnard. "You stay in the chopper!"

Watson groaned as he climbed down from the cabin. Reid frowned, but the agent waved his hand. "Don't even say it. It's not that bad, and I'm tired of you being the only one that gets to show off. Go. Find it."

Reid nodded. He scrambled down the length of the deck as passengers shoved and found hiding places. He had spotted three men from above. Two were down. He had no doubt that the third was in possession of the virus. *But where had he gone?*

"Get out of here!" Reid shouted and waved his hands. "Evacuate! Get to the lifeboats!" His shouts were all but unheard over the chaos on the top deck. The few people who did heed his warnings cowered in fear and ran the other direction—Reid was holding one of the two submachine guns.

Reid stopped trying to plead with them and instead shoved his way toward the nearest stairs. The third terrorist had undoubtedly vanished below deck, he reasoned, to hide. And it was a large ship.

He ran past the pool and bar he had seen from the helicopter, holding the gun aloft, barrel pointed upward. Most of the passenger had only heard the chopper and the gunshots; they hadn't seen the source, so merely the sight of the gun gave him a wide berth without being trampled by the panicking tourists. He watched with dismay as one man jumped overboard, literally diving over the glass partition that separated the deck and a nearly fifty-foot drop to the sea. Another unfortunate passenger was shoved into the glass and then right over the side.

He hoped Baraf got to the alarm soon, or the entire boat would be gripped in this mayhem.

The stairs leading down into the cruise ship's decks were carpeted, the walls done in cherry wood-panel and well-lit by warm lights in the ceiling. It was designed to feel cozy and inviting, like the interior of a home—a strange contrast, he couldn't help but note, to the turmoil happening upon them. He stuck as close to the gold banister as he could, with the MPX in one hand and his Glock in the other, shouting all the while.

"Out of the way! Get to the lifeboats! Move!"

People crowded the stairs, either fighting to get down them or misinterpreting the source of the gunshots and struggling to get up. It was going to be impossible for him to run or move quickly, and even more so since he was completely unfamiliar with the layout…

As much as he didn't want to threaten anyone, he couldn't deal with this sort of disorder. Reid fought his way to the center of the staircase and fired his Glock, just once, straight up in the air. The swarm of passengers ducked as a chorus of screams rang out.

"Down!" he ordered. "Everyone down! To the lifeboats, now!"

That did the trick. No one wanted to be near the crazed gunman, or even on the same ship as one. The flood of bodies rushed downward, draining away from him like a pulled plug.

Once he had some room to move he descended the stairs and glanced down the long, carpeted corridor. Dozens of brown doors stared back at him from either side of the hall; he was on a stateroom deck.

He groaned in dismay. It would take far too long to search the entire ship for the virus. *Think, Reid. If you were them, where would you take it? Where would you put it?*

He got his answer just a moment later. A shrill, harsh tone rang out, loud enough to make him jump instinctively and level both weapons. It rang again, rhythmically, accompanied by flashing lights in the ceiling.

The alarm. Baraf had turned on the emergency alarm.

Suddenly the hall was alive with activity, stateroom doors flying open and passengers filling the corridor. Murmurs of confusion mingled with shouts—until a woman close to Reid noticed the guns in his hands and shrieked.

"Police!" he yelled in the brief space between alarm rings. He didn't have the time to explain the CIA or their presence aboard the boat. Instead he raised both his hands, the guns still in them, and shouted, "Lifeboats! Go!"

He flattened himself against a wall as passengers filed past him quickly, pushing each other out of the way to get down to the evacuation points. As he stood there, being jostled by elbows and assaulted by shouted questions that he ignored, he realized it.

The evacuation points. If he was the terrorist wielding the virus, that's where he would go—prevent people from leaving the ship while holding leverage to keep them at bay.

And if it was released prematurely, every person on this ship would die.

He followed the crowd, moving with it, keeping the guns pointed upward and keeping his eyes open and scanning as he headed back toward the stairs. The people were a mélange of nationalities, it seemed, judging by the anxious chatter he could overhear—some Scandinavian, others from the UK, some Americans, a handful of Asians. As much as he hated to admit it, he couldn't help but profile; anyone with darker skin that could potentially be Arabic got a second look, but the few he saw seemed to be just as panicked as their fellow passengers.

As the throng pushed down the stairs to the next deck, Reid noticed a tightly packed group crowded around a pair of elevators, people desperately smashing the button. He knew that in an emergency situation like this the elevators would stop running; these people were waiting for cars that would never come.

"No elevators," he shouted to them. "Down the stairs, let's go." Before anyone could inquire about his two weapons he added, "American law enforcement. Let's move, people, in an orderly fashion—"

"Just what is going on?" a woman asked him, her voice high and screeching. She was American, middle-aged, with her hair in a bun as tight as her strained words. "Is the ship sinking? Are we in danger?"

"He wouldn't have guns if the ship was going down!" shouted a male voice, British, from somewhere behind Reid. "And I'm sure I heard shots fired!"

The woman's eyes widened in shock. Several people in the vicinity gasped audibly. "Is it terrorists?" she asked.

"Please, there's no time for that," he implored them. "Just get down to the lifeboats. You'll be safe."

The American woman was clearly dubious, but with the knowledge that the elevators didn't work she didn't seemed interested in standing around. She joined the pressing crowd as they poured down the stairs.

Someone touched Reid's elbow. He spun, growing angry at the tourists' hesitation. "No more questions…" He stopped himself and blinked in surprise. "Barnard? What the hell are you doing?" he hissed. "I told you to stay in the—"

"I am a doctor," Barnard said, quietly but forcefully. "I am an expert, and I am trained. The only reason I'm here is to help you find the virus, and that's what I intend to do." He stuck a hand out expectantly.

Reid had to admit, he appreciated the doctor's courage. Just fighting his way down here was likely no easy task. He handed off the MPX. "It's a full clip, thirty rounds, but they go fast. Use with caution."

Barnard cocked the gun with a fluid motion. "We have a lot of ship to cover. Have you searched this deck?"

Reid shook his head. "I'm heading down to deck four. If I was the Syrians, I would want to cut off the evacuation. They might need people—as hostages or as carriers."

"Lead the way." Barnard slung the MPX over his shoulder by its strap and followed closely behind as Reid pushed his way through the surging crowd. On the stairs, an elderly man lost his footing and vanished beneath stampeding feet. Reid shoved people out of the way and helped him up by an elbow.

"Even if we can get these people onto the lifeboats," said Barnard behind him, "we can't promise them they'll be able to go to shore."

"And we won't," Reid said back, as quietly as he was able over the din of the crowd. "You said the profile of the virus was six to eight hours, right? They'll have to stay in the lifeboats for at least that long, until they're cleared to come into port at Marseille." At that point it would be out of his hands and up to the WHO and French authorities.

If he thought the upper decks were chaotic, deck four was utter anarchy. On any other day the deck was intended for leisure—lining a wide avenue in the center were duty-free shops, a café, two restaurants, and a number of other shopping outlets, not unlike an American mall. But currently the entire area was choked with more than a thousand writhing, angry, anxious people, shouting over one another, breaking into shoving matches, and in more than one place, actual fistfights.

At the stern of the deck was the evacuation point, a single double-wide door that led onto an outdoor balcony and, further down, the lifeboats. Each boat was a long, yellow vehicle, fully enclosed and able to seat a hundred twenty bodies—not unlike a school bus without wheels.

Reid clung close to the wall and shoved his way past passengers, shouting as he did. He quickly found that "police" was a better cognate for the multicultural crowd than "law enforcement," so he yelled out, "Police! Step aside!"

Barnard hurried along behind him. "My god," he muttered. "These people are going to kill each other..."

As they neared the exit doors, Reid spotted Baraf helping crew members to get people at the head of the crowd as orderly as possible. Baraf was shouting himself red in the face, ushering people two or three at a time through the doors while literally holding back those who tried to shove past him.

"Baraf!" Reid waved an arm to get the Interpol agent's attention. They needed help finding the virus; the crew could see to the safe evacuation. "Baraf..."

As the agent turned toward him, the man beside Baraf twisted his face into an ugly grimace. Before Reid could even wonder what was happening, the man retched and vomited onto the floor.

The crowd immediately pushed backward, away from him, forming a small clearing around the sick man.

Reid was pushed backward by the sudden retreat, his back smacking hard against the wall behind him. But he couldn't take his eyes from the sick man.

They were too late. The virus had already been released on the ship.

CHAPTER THIRTY FOUR

Reid could do little but stare in shock. There was no way the terrorists hadn't noticed the klaxon alarm blaring throughout the entire ship. They knew they'd been discovered. They released the virus.

And if the mutated smallpox had been released, everyone on board—himself included—was already dead.

While he stood rooted to the spot, Barnard sprang into action. He pushed through the crowd hurriedly and crouched beside the sick man. "Sir? Sir, look at me." Barnard forced the man's head slightly back. He felt his forehead, his throat, his lymph nodes. The doctor inspected each eye quickly and made the man open his mouth.

By the time he'd finished the cursory examination, Reid had shaken off the bombshell of the moment and joined him. "Barnard? Is it …?"

"No." Dr. Barnard shook his head fervently. "No, it's not. He has no fever. There's no blood in his bile."

"Claustrophobic," the man said weakly in accented English. "I'm sorry."

"Don't be." Barnard snapped his fingers toward the nearest crew member. "Get this man some water and somewhere to sit while the rest of the boats are loaded."

The crew member didn't move. Reid glanced up, his eyes narrowed. The man was wearing pleated khakis and a blue polo emblazoned with the cruise line's logo—the casual uniform of a crew member—but his dark eyes darted left and right. On his cheeks was a thin beard, and his skin was a few shades darker than Reid's own.

"Did you hear me?" Barnard said again. "Please, help this man!"

"Help him." This time Reid said it—but in Arabic.

Recognition lit in the man's expression at his native language. Immediately he understood he was discovered. One hand reached behind him, toward the small of his back.

Reid had the Glock up in an instant. He did not hesitate. Two shots thundered in the cavernous corridor. The first struck center mass, just to the left of the Arabic man's heart. The second found home in his forehead. His head snapped back as a cloud of blood misted behind him.

The crowd instantly surged again with screams and frantic cries at the gunshots. Reid hurried forward and pulled a Sig Sauer from the man's pants.

Crew members. That's how they were able to take over the console. They would have access to nearly any part of the ship they needed.

"Khalil's people are dressed as crew members." He handed the gun over to Baraf, and then turned to the woman beside him who had been aiding in the evacuation. She was short and blonde, wearing the same khakis and polo as the Syrian, and was clearly petrified. Her mouth hung open and she couldn't tear her gaze from the dead man on the floor. "Where are the crew quarters?" he asked her.

"I...I..."

"Look at me." He stepped between her and the body, forcing her to avert her eyes. "The crew quarters. Where are they?"

"D-deck two," she stammered. Her accent sounded Icelandic. She gulped and then added, "I didn't know him..."

"I know. This man here is an agent of Interpol, and he needs help. You need to get these people off of this ship and those boats into the water in the next ten minutes, okay?"

"There's...there's protocol," she said, her senses starting to return. "There's an order, by groupings..."

"Forget the protocol," Reid demanded. "Get these people off this boat or else more of *that*"—he gestured to the body for emphasis—"is going to happen to the wrong people."

She nodded, rubbed her face with both hands, and then turned back to the crowd to usher more people out to the lifeboats.

"I'm going to deck two," Reid told Baraf. "I don't think they would stow the virus anywhere that guests might find it."

"I'll come with you," he said immediately.

"No, you should stay here. There could be more gunmen. These people will need you." As much as he could use the help, he didn't want the ship turning into a hostage situation—or a slaughter.

Barnard stood and hefted the MPX on his shoulder. "I'm with you."

Reid nodded. "Follow close." Again he pushed his way back through the crowd, shouting mostly unheard demands for a calm and orderly fashion. He was dismayed, though not entirely surprised, to glance through a window and see more people leaping from the decks to the water below. He hoped the lifeboats would get to them in time; otherwise they would undoubtedly drown.

The stairs were much easier to navigate with most of the passengers on deck four waiting to evacuate. Still he and Barnard passed by lingering guests, people who had gone back for luggage or to find loved ones. He shouted at each person they passed, insisting they go straight to the evacuation point. He kept his eyes open for anyone suspicious and kept the Glock firmly gripped in both hands.

Deck two was the second-lowest on the ship and the first one above water level. It was a far cry from the gilded banisters and carpeted stairs of the levels above them; this deck was white-walled, the floor beneath their feet tiled, with bare pipes running the length of the tight corridors. Doors on the left and right opened onto common crew areas—a small bar, a rec room with a pool table, storage rooms, a galley, and a cafeteria.

"We need to check every room," said Reid, "including the crew cabins."

"We should split up," Barnard suggested. His voice sounded too loud in the otherwise silent hall. Reid's own ears were still ringing from the gunshots and noise of the crowd. "I'll check these areas if you start with the cabins."

He didn't want to send the doctor off alone, but Barnard was right. "When the alarm went off the crew should have gone immediately to their assigned stations. There shouldn't be anyone down here. If you see someone, assume the worst. Godspeed, Barnard."

The doctor nodded and doubled back, hurrying toward the open door of the rec room they had passed. Reid watched until he turned the corner and then he continued on his path. The tight corridor turned to the left and he balked. There were white doors spanned every six feet for the entire length of the hall. *These must be the crew cabins,* he thought.

He noted with concern that he could feel the deep rumble of the ship's engines beneath his feet on this deck. The boat hadn't stopped yet. He hoped Maria and Watson were all right.

Reid pushed open the first door and stepped inside, his gun raised. It was a closet of a room with two bunks, one atop another, and not even enough floor space for an adult to lie down. But the room was empty. He left the door open to show it had been checked, just in case he had to double back.

The next door was already partially open, by just an inch. He took a deep breath and then kicked it fully open, the Glock level.

A terrified young man stared back at him, lying on the bottom bunk. At the sight of the gun he slowly raised both hands. He was either very tan or dark-skinned, and looked like he was in his early twenties at best.

"Khalil," Reid said. He examined the boy's face for any sign of recognition, a glimmer or even involuntary twitch, and saw none. "Get up," he said in English. The boy did so hastily, scrambling from the bed with his hands still raised.

Reid searched him quickly and found nothing. "What are you doing down here?" he demanded.

"I heard gunshots," the boy answered quickly. He didn't take his eyes off of Reid's weapon.

"Go to deck four," he ordered. "Hurry up. They need help." The young man nodded frantically and scurried down the corridor the way Reid had come. He watched until the boy rounded the corner that led to the stairs.

Then he continued on his way.

The tile beneath his boots did little to muffle his steps. Anyone who was in hiding would likely hear him coming—but he would hear anyone who was on the move. He checked every room on both sides of the hall in the course of only a few minutes, each one devoid of life, before the corridor made a left turn and continued on with more cabins.

Before he could kick open the next door, there was a chugging sound from below him as the engines slowed and died. Maria and Watson had stopped the boat. At least that was something in their favor; they couldn't risk pulling into port, any port, with the active virus aboard.

Reid tensed as he heard footfalls from somewhere nearby. *Clack-clack-clack-clack*—someone walking rapidly and getting closer. He crouched, gun at the ready, as a man turned the corner at the far end of the hall.

For the briefest of moments they both froze in their positions. The crewman had dark, curly hair, a thick beard, and wore blue coveralls, suggesting he was a sanitation worker.

But most importantly, he had a box cradled in his arms, the hint of a bright green biohazard sign emblazoned on the side.

It was an exact replica of the box that Claudette Minot was carrying.

The virus. The man was carrying it in his hands right before Reid's eyes.

The shocked crewman blinked once at Reid before noticing the gun in his hands. Then the man turned and sprinted back the way he had come.

"Stop!" Reid cried, barely realizing he had shouted it in Arabic. He leapt to his feet and gave chase. As he reached the corner, he caught another glimpse of the blue coveralls rounding yet another corner. *This place is a goddamn maze!* he thought in frustration. Worse still was that even if he caught up to the terrorist, he couldn't dare

264

take the shot; he had no idea what would happen if the box fell to the hard floor. If any of the vials broke, or if the man acted brashly, it could doom them all.

Reid spun around the next corner and stopped suddenly. The man was nowhere to be seen. The corridor split off in two directions, left and right, and straight ahead was a steel staircase leading up to the guest decks.

Instead of choosing randomly, he paused for a moment and listened intently for the sound of footfalls. He heard nothing. His brow pricked; he was starting to sweat. With the engine's cut, the ship's lower decks were heating up quickly. He tightened his moist palms around the gun and pressed on, listening for any sounds other than his own footsteps and breathing.

He hid. To his right was a cabin, the door open just a few inches and the lights off inside. Reid took a breath and shoved into the room, the gun raised. He couldn't see a thing.

His free hand groped for the light switch. His fingers found it, a thin lever that toggled parallel to the wall. He pulled it.

The lights flickered to life just in time to see the knife coming down in an overhand stab. He had no time to react as the blade struck home in his chest, just above his right pectoral. He cried out as he felt the sharp pressure of it jam into his muscle.

His assailant's face was a mask of rage, a twisted, wild snarl. "Glory to the Imam Mahdi," the man growled in Arabic.

Then he looked down, and his expression contorted into confusion.

The blade had struck Reid's chest—but it didn't penetrate. The graphene in his jacket and shirt had stopped it.

Reid bent at the waist, putting his entire upper body into a vicious head-butt to the man's mouth. Lips split and teeth broke as the Arabic terrorist stumbled backward. Reid flipped the Glock around in his hand and whipped the pistol across his temple. The man struck the wall behind him and slumped to the ground.

But it wasn't the man in the blue coveralls, and the box containing the virus was nowhere to be seen.

Reid left the unconscious man there. He pulled the door closed behind him and swung the Glock down by the barrel, breaking off the steel level of the doorknob.

His chest hurt as if he had been struck with a dull projectile, but he would live. He wished he still had his phone and the radio, so that he could contact Barnard and those above deck, to see what was going on elsewhere on the ship…

A short blast of automatic gunfire echoed through the deck. Reid crouched instinctively as he tried to trace the source of the sound. *Barnard. That was the MPX.* He was certain of it.

He ran down the hall as fast as he could, back the way he had come. At the mouth of the cabin-lined corridor he nearly stumbled over a pair of dirty white sneakers. The man in the coveralls had come this way—he had pulled off his shoes to muffle his footfalls. Reid stood there for a moment, listening, waiting for another sound, anything that might tell him which way to go.

His patience wore thin quickly. "Barnard!" he shouted. In response, he heard another rapid tear of the submachine gun, only four or five shots. He cursed and sprinted down the hall toward the rec room, the last place he had seen Barnard go.

But before he reached it he saw the gun, the MPX, laid on the floor outside a doorway.

Reid hurried over to it as his chest grew tight. Someone had gotten the drop on Barnard. He peered into the doorway. It was the cafeteria, a wide austere room with tables, chairs, and a buffet-style layout of steel trays behind sneeze guards.

He tiptoed into the cafeteria with his gun raised, but there was no sign of Barnard. No sounds. Reid ducked behind the cafeteria line and entered the crew kitchen, a narrow space that looked tighter than a fry cook's station.

"Agent Steele." He heard Barnard's voice and looked up sharply to see the doctor just inside another doorway—a food storage room, it appeared to be, like a walk-in pantry of nondescript sacks and boxes.

But Barnard wasn't looking at Reid. The doctor's face was white as a sheet as he stared unblinking at something else, obscured by the partially open door.

"Please move away, Agent," the doctor said slowly.

Reid did not heed the advice. Instead he took a step inside the pantry.

Behind the door was the terrorist in the blue coveralls. His eyes were wild and his hair was slicked back with sweat. Clenched in his teeth was a single glass vial of the deadly smallpox.

Chapter Thirty Five

Reid's first instinct was to raise the Glock and shoot, but he fought it down. Any sudden violent action could make the man bite down, and the smallpox would be released on the cruise ship, endangering not only anyone who was still on board, but also everyone Reid now counted amongst friends.

Instead, he slowly holstered his Glock and showed the terrorist his hands.

"I told you to move away," Barnard said. He did not take his gaze off the man, or perhaps the vial in his teeth. The doctor stood rooted to the spot with his hands up, palms facing outward.

The biohazard box was open at the man's socked feet. Inside was a tube rack holding four rows of six vials each, save for the fourth row, which held only five, since the sixth was firmly gripped in the man's jaw.

Reid ignored Barnard. Instead he spoke in Arabic to the man in the blue coveralls. "There's no reason to do this," he said slowly. "Khalil has been caught. He lied to you, his followers. There is no holy war, no jihad."

The Lebanese man repositioned the vial to his molars so he could speak. "You would say anything to keep me from doing what I must."

"He's going to bite down," Barnard said. He had no idea what Reid was saying in Arabic, but he could read the tension on the man's face.

"You might be right," Reid told the man. "Maybe I would say anything, but I *will* say this. He told you that you are the Imam

Mahdi, didn't he? The Redeemer, the one that will save the world from its sins?"

The man said nothing, but his brow furrowed deeply.

"Please don't goad him," Barnard said tightly.

Reid pressed on. "I know that because he told others the same thing. He told them that they were the Mahdi too. He told a Syrian boy who brought the virus into Barcelona. He told a French woman who thought she was carrying the virus. He told a virologist, who created what you have there in front of you—"

"You lie!" the man snarled. His teeth scraped against the glass vial. Barnard flinched.

"Smallpox is an airborne disease," the doctor said quickly. "Transmitted via droplets in the air onto the nasal, oral, or muco-sal membranes...usually through close contact...sometimes in enclosed settings, such as the underbelly of a cruise ship..."

Reid knew that Barnard was panicked, rambling, but he main-tained his composure as best he could. "I'm not lying," he told the man holding the deadly virus in his teeth. "I was the one who found Khalil. He admitted all this himself. I'm sorry, but you have been a pawn in his game. But you don't have to be. All you have to do is put that down, and close the box."

The man's gaze flitted from Reid to Barnard and back again.

Barnard bristled as the terrorist's fingers moved.

Slowly the man reached up, and he plucked the vial from his teeth with two fingers.

Barnard let out an audible sigh of relief. Reid lowered his hands to waist level. "Now please, put it back in the box, and step away."

The man looked down at the vial in his fingertips for a moment. Then he brought it to his lips and, without hesitation, snapped down on it. Splinters of glass rained down from his mouth as the tube shattered.

"Glory to Allah!" The man threw back his head and shouted, spittle and blood spraying from his lips. "Praise be unto Him!"

Reid stopped breathing. The virus was released—and not eight feet from him.

In that moment, he knew he was likely going to die. But it wasn't his life that flashed before his eyes; it was his daughters, their faces, their smiles. Every impetuous, difficult moment and every blissful, joyous one.

And he was not about to give this terrorist the satisfaction of knowing that he was responsible for anyone's death but his own.

Reid pulled his Glock from the holster and fired a single shot into the man's forehead. Blood and brain spattered the wall behind him and he fell beside the open box of the smallpox virus.

To Reid's surprise, Barnard had reacted too. He didn't realize it until the doctor was upon him, grabbing him by an arm and yanking him out through the open door of the pantry. He shoved Reid out into the cafeteria and pulled the door closed, shoving the lever down to lock it with a resonant *chunk.*

Reid slumped down, seemingly having lost control of his legs. It was only then that he let his breath out, a long whoosh that he once again could not recall holding.

Barnard knelt beside him. "Did you breathe?"

"What?"

"Did you breathe it in?" The doctor shrugged frantically out of his jacket.

"I ... I don't know ..."

Barnard scoffed in frustration. "I told you, it's transmitted via droplets in the air onto the nasal, oral, or mucosal membranes." With a heavy grunt of effort, he tore the sleeves from his jacket and handed one to Reid. "Wrap this around your nose and mouth."

Reid did as he was told, tying the sleeve around his face like a mask. Barnard did the same, and then stuck out a hand to help Reid to his feet. "Come on. Hurry!" He led the way, striding briskly back into the corridor and toward the crew quarters. "Here." He gestured into an empty cabin.

Reid peered inside, uncertain of what Barnard was suggesting. The doctor pushed him inside. "We have to quarantine ourselves for at least three hours. If we're not infected, we won't exhibit any symptoms." The doctor started to pull the door closed behind him.

"Wait!" Reid shouted. "And if we are?"

Barnard paused. His rueful gaze met Reid's. "Then it was a genuine pleasure to know you, Agent Steele. Don't come out." He yanked the door closed. A few seconds later, Reid heard the clang of another door as Barnard quarantined himself in another cabin.

For a long moment Reid could only stand there, trying and failing to process what had happened in just the last minute. Then he noticed something—hanging on the wall, near the bunk beds, was a white phone with a curling cord. Taped to the wall beside it was a single sheet of paper, a directory to other parts of the ship, faded but legible.

He pulled the tied jacket sleeve from around his face. He would have to call and try to reach someone on his team, Maria or Watson or Baraf, to let them know that the virus had been released on deck two.

Beyond that, all he could do was wait to die, or wait to see the light of day again.

Chapter Thirty Six

Maya Lawson awoke with pain in her skull and in her jaw, radiating from both points throughout her head. She opened her eyes slowly, and then immediately clenched them shut again under the glaring white light.

Thoughts returned to her slowly. *An intruder, in the house. Mr. Thompson, dead. Sara…*

She panicked and sat upright. Fresh, jolting pain seared through her forehead and she winced, rubbing it. She worked her jaw around in slow circles. It hurt, but it wasn't broken.

She needed to get to her sister. *Keep Sara safe.* That was all that mattered.

Maya looked left and right in confusion. She was in the basement of their Spruce Street house in Alexandria. The assassin had knocked her unconscious and brought her down here. The door to the makeshift panic room was directly before her and, hopefully, Sara was safely behind it.

But the assassin was nowhere to be seen.

Hope swelled in Maya's chest. *Sara got to the panic room. She called the police. He fled.*

She tried to climb to her feet but they seemed to be stuck together. Her ankles were bound tightly with electrical tape, wrapped at least a dozen times around the hem of her pajama pants. She tore at it with her fingers while straining to pull her ankles apart.

Heavy footfalls resonated from over her head. A pair of steady, clomping boots stepped slowly over what would be the short corridor between the foyer and kitchen. Only one pair.

The hope of a moment ago dissolved. He was still here.

Maya ripped at the tape frantically as the man appeared in the doorway at the top of the stairs. He took them one at a time, slowly, like the ever-patient killer in a supernatural horror movie. Maya grunted in frustration as she pulled at the electrical tape, but she had only peeled back a few layers by the time the man reached the bottom of the stairs.

He knelt at her side and watched her work for a moment. His patience was as exasperating as it was terrifying. Maya shrieked in frustration and yanked at her bonds with both hands. Tears swelled in her eyes. Why were the police not here? Why had no one come for them?

"Shh," the man said, drawing the syllable out. "Stop." He put his own hand over hers. She flinched at his touch. His hands were ice cold.

"Don't," she warned, her voice hoarse and throaty. "Don't touch me. Where's Sara?"

The man pointed at the reinforced door, the one her father had installed to keep them safe. It was designed to be bulletproof and fireproof, with a steel core and three heavy deadbolts that locked from the inside. There was nothing the assassin could do to get to her sister.

"The police will be here any second," Maya told him quickly. "There's a phone in that room, and Sara would have called nine-one-one by now..."

"I cut the landline." The man's expression was passive, almost curious, as he watched Maya's lower lip tremble.

"She has a cell—"

The assassin held up a silver phone in a hot pink case. "She left it charging in her room when she ran. Anything else?"

Maya's breath came ragged and heavy. Thompson was dead. No one was coming.

"Yes," the assassin said, as if he was reading her mind. "You are alone." He reached for his belt and pulled loose the hunting knife, now clean of Mr. Thompson's blood. Maya's heart skipped two beats at the sight of the glinting blade.

With one smooth motion the assassin sliced through the tape that bound her ankles. "Stand up," he ordered. She did so, slowly, her legs shaky and her knees weak. The assassin pointed to a rectangular white box mounted over the door, pointed downward at them. "That camera. Does it have audio feed?"

Maya had nearly forgotten about the cameras. Her dad had two of them installed, one over the door and another on the garage outside, directed at the driveway and front walkway. Both fed to monitors inside the panic room so that anyone inside could see who was entering the house, or who might be outside the door.

"Maya," the man said again. His voice was oddly gentle. It made her skin crawl. "Does it have audio? Can Sara hear us right now?"

She nodded once. Sara would have heard the whole conversation.

"Good." The assassin grabbed Maya's right arm so suddenly that she yelped in surprise. He twisted her wrist outward and her arm behind her, away from her body so that her torso bent at an odd angle. She cried out again as the tension sent pain radiating up into her shoulder.

"Sara," the man said firmly, his gaze directed at the camera. "First you should know that no one is coming. No police are en route. Your bodyguard is dead. You have no way to contact anyone outside that room. Short of your father walking in the front door, there is no one who can help you. And believe me, I would love nothing more than for that to happen."

He paused for a moment before ratcheting the tension on Maya's arm. She gasped in pain as her muscles screamed, stretched to their limit.

"My name is Rais," he told the camera. "This is happening to you because of what your father has done. I harbor no personal resentment or vendetta against you or your sister; to me, you are instruments, the means to my end. If you do as I say, I will not harm you or your sister. If you do not, immeasurable harm will come. I don't want that. Neither of you are valuable to me injured or dead."

"Sara, don't listen—*aah!*" Maya shrieked as the assassin twisted just a little further. Her shoulder burned as muscles began to tear. Just the slightest bit more pressure on her wrist would snap it.

"Sara," the assassin Rais said to the camera. "I want you to open this door and come out. I will not hurt you. I will stop hurting your sister. If you don't come out, I will stand here in front of this camera and break each of your sister's limbs, one at a time. If you think I'm bluffing, then do nothing and watch."

"Don't," Maya gasped, barely able to get the word out. "Don't." She did not think the assassin was bluffing at all. *Don't open the door.* All Sara had to do was stay put.

Bones could heal. But she did not believe for a second that no harm would come to them.

Unplug the audio feed. Don't watch. Maya had the distinct feeling that they would not come back from whatever he was planning to do with them.

"So be it," the assassin said quietly.

Maya gritted her teeth and waited for the bones in her arm to snap. She had broken her arm once before, when she was eight, by falling off her bike.

She hadn't cried then. She wouldn't give this psychopath the satisfaction now.

He twisted further. Her mouth opened wide, her eyes clenched tightly shut, but she did not cry out. She did not scream.

There was a dull, heavy click as one of the deadbolts slid aside in the door.

No!

The pressure on her arm relieved slightly, only enough to keep her wrist from breaking. Several seconds passed in complete silence. Then, a second deadbolt opened.

"Sara, no!" Maya cried.

The third deadbolt clanked to the side, and the door pushed outward slowly. Standing in its frame was Sara. Her lips trembled and tears ran down both cheeks. Her eyes were bloodshot and puffy. Her wide, fearful gaze was fixed on Maya.

The assassin released Maya's arm and she fell to her knees. Her shoulder burned and her wrist ached terribly, but nothing was broken. She scrambled to her feet and hugged her little sister with her

275

good arm, pulling her close as Sara sobbed. Maya wanted to scold her, to tell her she never should have opened the door, but in the moment all she could do was hold her.

"Thank you," the assassin said quietly behind them. "Upstairs now. Your neighbor's truck is already in the driveway."

Maya spun on him. *How did he know Mr. Thompson was our neighbor?*

Rais dangled a set of keys in the air. *The key fob.* He must have taken Mr. Thompson's keys and used the fob to find his vehicle.

He pulled out the hunting knife again and showed them the blade. "I have two guns, thanks to your neighbor and your father," he told them. "But I prefer this. I've just cleaned it of blood. I'd hate to have to do so again. The three of us are going upstairs. You are both going to put shoes on. Then we will go outside and directly into the truck without a sound."

He knelt so that he was about eye level with Maya. "You care for your sister, enough to try something brash. If you do, she will pay for it. If you make a noise, I will cut something off of her. If you try to run or to let her run, I will catch her, not you. You will stay like this, close to her, and if you separate even an inch, it will be her that I hurt. Am I clear?"

Maya's nostrils flared as feelings of both fury and fear washed over her. This man had done this before, maybe several times. He seemed to know that Maya would try something; even as he threatened them she had been formulating a plan in her mind, to jump him and let Sara run.

Her sister sobbed harder, pressed against her chest. She couldn't risk it. Where he might take them she didn't know, but she would find an opportunity. Bide her time and form a plan.

Maya nodded once. She hugged Sara tighter as she thought of her text message that she sent to her father—just one word, *help*. He got it. She just knew he did. He was on his way now.

"Shh," she whispered to her sister. "Dad is going to find us. I promise."

"Yes." The assassin said quietly, more of a hiss than a word. "I'm counting on it."

Chapter Thirty Seven

R eid wiped sweat from his brow with a sock and groaned. He
felt awful. Even not moving at all he was still sweating, and
mild nausea had risen in his gut. He had spent much of his time in
the tiny crew quarters thinking of his girls back home, wondering
what they were doing at that same moment, and if they were thinking of him too. He desperately wanted to hear their voices. But he
couldn't. He had no line of communication to them.

The faded white phone on the wall rang with two dull electronic
tones that had really grown to irritate him. He answered it quickly.
"Steele."

"Hey."

He smiled. "We just talked fifteen minutes ago."

"I know," Maria said. "I just wanted to check in again and see if
you were dead yet."

He laughed. "Still kicking, at least for now. But someone has got
to get me some water. I think dehydration is setting in."

For six hours he had been quarantined in the crew quarters
Barnard had shoved him in. The first two hours had been fraught
and nerve-racking, but when he hadn't developed any fever or nausea after hour three, his tension eased. His breath had caught in
his throat when the terrorist in the blue coveralls bit down on the
vial. He hadn't breathed anything in, and the ventilation system
in the cruise ship had shut off when the engines were cut off. The
smallpox virus was cordoned to the pantry and cafeteria.

But while the ventilation system remained off, the air grew stuffy
and stiflingly hot. There were no windows or other points of egress

in the tiny cabin. Reid had stripped down to his T-shirt and boxers and was still sweating, wiping his forehead with his socks. It was torturous, but the WHO demanded that he remain where he was until they had swept the ship and cleaned up any remnant of the virus.

"The least they could have done was stick us in the same room," Maria griped. "I'm dying of boredom in here."

"I'm pretty sure that would defeat the purpose of a quarantine," Reid remarked. After Maria and Watson had stopped the boat, they radioed Interpol, who sent a helicopter of yellow-suited WHO scientists to their location. By that time the passengers and most of the crew had been loaded into the enclosed yellow lifeboats, which were currently doing laps around the inert ship. For those still aboard, the WHO had demanded that everyone be quarantined separately to ensure that no one was exhibiting symptoms of the active virus.

Thankfully, Reid had the white service phone in his quarters, an internal communications system to most of the compartments on the ship. Maria had found it particularly useful, calling him no fewer than six times in the last three hours. She had closed herself into a room on deck seven, just below the top deck—a spacious and pleasant stateroom, by her own admission.

"How's Watson?" Reid asked.

"He's fine. They won't be able to patch up his shoulder until the quarantine ends, but it's not like he would complain anyway." She laughed lightly.

"I think I might owe him an apology," Reid said quietly.

"No. He understands," Maria told him. "He might have been confused and angry in the moment, but after what happened with Carver you were right to distrust him. I wouldn't have blamed you if you didn't trust me after that."

"You're the only one I *can* trust. If I didn't have that, I think I might go crazy." And it was the truth. Ever since rediscovering his CIA identity, Reid felt extremely distrustful of nearly everyone around him. He couldn't help but wonder if that was a symptom of his unique background and situation or of being a secret agent in general.

He very much wanted to talk to Maria about his fragmented memories, the conspiracy, the alleged pending war and Carver's motivation for attacking him—but he didn't dare talk openly about it. Apparently his distrust had spread to more than just people.

Instead he asked, "By the way, what did you want to tell me on the helicopter? You seemed kind of troubled by it. Now's as good a time as any."

"Hmm." He could hear the smile in Maria's voice. "Like you said, I think that can wait until our second date."

"Fair enough." Reid looked up suddenly as he heard a click. A moment later the door to his cabin swung inward and a figure in a yellow decontamination suit stood on the threshold. "Hey... I have to go. Someone's at the door."

"All right. See you soon, I hope." She hung up.

The figure took a step into the room, holding a rectangular package sealed in plastic in one hand and a bottle of water in the other. Reid couldn't see past the respirator mask; the white lights overhead glinted off the glass. But when the figure spoke, Reid smiled.

"Agent Steele," said Dr. Barnard. "I believe you might be part cat."

Reid raised an eyebrow. "Nine lives?"

"I was going to say you always land on your feet. But I suppose either way works." He tossed the water bottle to him, and then the plastic package. "Decontamination suit. Put it on and come up to the top deck."

Reid unscrewed the top and downed the bottle's contents in a few seconds. *Much better,* he thought. "Why the suit? It's been six hours. I'm not sick."

"The active virus is still on the ship," Barnard said. "You may not be exhibiting symptoms, but until we're off this boat and cleared, no one is above scrutiny. There is still the possibility of infection."

It was another nine hours before Reid felt a breeze on his face. At six in the morning local time, he pushed through the double glass-door entrance of the boxy WHO facility and took a liberal breath of fresh air.

Despite the early hour, the place was already bustling with white-coated researchers and doctors in suit jackets. Reid felt oddly out of place in the white V-neck scrub top and pants they had issued him, plastic slips over his feet. It made him feel more like a patient than an agent, but that was fairly accurate for what he had been through.

He had been allowed on the top deck of the *Jade Star*, wearing the decontamination suit, and had watched with his teammates as a tugboat pulled the cruise ship toward Valencia. They anchored about a mile off the southern coast of Spain so that the World Health Organization could facilitate transport of the equipment necessary to scrub the ship clean of the virus.

Reid, Baraf, Maria, Barnard, and Watson had been taken by helicopter, under the cover of night, to a WHO facility in northern Spain. They were taken to separate clean rooms, where they stripped out of the yellow hazmat suits and scrubbed thoroughly with near-scalding water, emulsifiers, and decontaminants. Their graphene-reinforced clothing had been left behind on the ship, along with their shoes, guns, and phones. Reid was issued the white scrubs, and then blood and saliva samples were taken. Finally he was led to an all-white room with three walls made of glass. Despite its bright and clean appearance, it felt like a cage.

But the cot was comfortable enough, so he caught a few hours of much-needed and well-deserved sleep. When he awoke it was to the sound of his door sliding aside as a young technician told him, "Congratulations, Agent. You've been cleared." As the tech turned away he added, "Though you are a bit hypoglycemic. You should probably eat something."

It was good advice; Reid was starving. But the first thing he did was find the nearest exit, gulp some fresh air, and enjoy the Spanish sunrise. It was not a warm morning, but the chill in the air was welcome after the last fifteen hours. He stretched as he wandered around the grounds. Along the side of the building he found a few stone benches, and as he headed toward them he was quite surprised to see that the only person seated there was a very familiar—and very welcome—face.

Maria was dressed in plainclothes, not the white scrubs that he had been issued, and sat on the bench poking randomly at a phone as he approached. There was a black duffel bag under the bench, behind her feet. It looked like she was leaving.

"Hey."

She looked up and smiled wide. "Hey yourself."

"They let you out before me?"

She shrugged. "I wasn't the one caught in the pantry with a virus-wielding terrorist."

He chuckled. "Did you get an update? On what's happening out there?"

"I talked to Cartwright." She sighed. "Where do I begin?"

"The virus...?"

"Sealed and safely remitted to WHO headquarters in Geneva," she told him. "By now it's probably locked away in an underground vault, I bet. They'll work on a vaccine, in case there's more of it out there."

"Good." Reid took a seat beside her. "What about the outbreak?"

"Mostly contained. There are still a few reported cases as recently as a couple hours ago, but the WHO is on it. Since we've found the virus, several countries in Eastern Europe have lifted their travel bans, with increased security at ports of entry. The US hasn't yet reopened, but it's only a matter of time."

"And Khalil?" Reid asked. He wanted to know if the Imam had survived the gunshot to the stomach. "Is he...?"

"In custody. They have him in Morocco, giving us everything."

Morocco. The CIA black site, Hell-Six. Reid knew the sort of interrogation tactics that went on there, had even been a part of them, and despite how horrific they could be he had no remorse for Khalil. Not after what he had done, what he had tried to do.

"Based on his info," Maria continued, "Interpol raided a Lebanese facility about, oh, three hours ago and detained nine

more of the Imam's followers. And soon we should have the locations of any associated terrorists in the States."

"Huh." It seemed that while Reid was in quarantine, the agencies around the globe were quite busy. "So, what…all's well that
ends well, then?"

"You don't sound so pleased for someone who gets to go home,"
she noted.

Home. He wanted desperately to get back, couldn't wait to see
his girls again. "But that's not where you're going," he said, gesturing toward the bag beneath them.

"I was going to tell you," Maria said softly. "Rais is still out there.
Russia didn't close their land borders."

Reid scoffed. "I can't believe they would send you right back out
after everything we've been through …"

"I volunteered," she told him. "It's important. To you, and to me
too. As long as he's out there, no matter where he is, he's still a threat."

"Let me come with you." He said it quickly, almost reflexively.

"No." She smiled. "You need to go home to your girls. I can see
it in your eyes."

He nodded, not saying anything. She was right. He wasn't ready
to jump into another op.

"Are you going to call them?" she asked.

"I can't. A building fell on my phone."

She smirked and held out hers. "Go ahead. You know you want
to hear their voices."

"Thanks." Reid took the phone and dialed Maya's number. The
line rang once, twice, three times, and then went to voicemail. He
frowned—but then reminded himself that he had promised not to
be so overbearing. There were a thousand reasons she wouldn't be
right near her phone at that moment. He resisted the urge to call
again and instead he typed out a text.

It's Dad. I'm okay. Coming home soon. Love you both.

As he handed the phone back to Maria, it chimed with a new
text. She read it to him. "Glad to hear it. We're fine here. Hope

everything is okay." Maria scrunched up her nose. "What does that mean, 'hope everything is okay'?"

Reid frowned. Maya knew, or at least partially knew, why he had to leave—but he couldn't very well admit that to Maria. "Well, they, uh…" He cleared his throat. "They think I'm on a weekend getaway with you."

Maria laughed. "Good cover. Maybe sometime we can make that actually happen?"

"Yeah. That would be nice."

Her phone chimed again. She checked it and said, "That's my ride. I have to go. But I'll see you around, Reid." She leaned in and kissed him, only briefly.

"You'll keep in touch, right?" he asked. "Especially about Rais?"

"Of course I will."

As she rose and headed toward the front of the building, he called out to her. He couldn't let her leave without at least mentioning the thing that had been gnawing at the forefront of his mind. "Hey… I remembered something."

She paused questioningly.

"And it's something that… well, it might spell trouble for a lot of people. Maybe most of all for me."

Maria regarded him evenly. "This job teaches you a lot of things," she said at last. "But number one of them all is that you can't trust anyone but yourself."

"Even you?" Reid asked.

She shrugged one shoulder as if that was an answer.

"But… what if I find something worth saying?"

"Then you take it straight to someone who can do something about it," she told him. "Two years ago you knew all this. Now I'm just reminding you. Don't talk to anyone about it. If you go digging, do it alone. And if you find something, you make damn sure the people you tell are people in your corner."

He hesitated to ask, but he needed to know. "Are you in my corner?"

"Always." She winked, gave him a small wave, and disappeared around the building.

Reid swallowed the lump in his throat. He had wanted nothing more for the past fifteen hours of near-isolation than to talk to someone, Maria or Watson or even Cartwright, about the conspiracy, about his memory, and about Carver's actions.

But once again he felt alone.

CHAPTER THIRTY EIGHT

Ashleigh Riker's heels clacked rhythmically against the concrete of the parking garage as she paced slowly, waiting for her meeting. She was at the furthest end of the third deck, where there were the fewest cars and a convenient blind spot from cameras.

She heard footfalls echoing and glanced up to see the director striding toward her. He took his time, intentionally not looking as if he was in a rush to get anywhere.

"I just got off the phone with DNI Hillis," Director Mullen said as a greeting. He kept his voice low to keep from reverberating in the largely empty space. "The president thanks you personally for your involvement. Spec Ops Group is yours. Congratulations, Deputy Director."

Riker smiled with half her mouth. The promotion was welcome, but not at all unexpected. "Thank you, sir."

"But I'm guessing that's not why you asked me to meet you here and leave my phone behind," Mullen mused. This was not the first time they had met like this.

"Agent Carver called in," she told him. "On my personal line. He claims that Steele remembers."

If Mullen had any reaction, he didn't show it. "How much does he remember?"

"Unclear."

The director was silent for a moment. "Let's stay alert for any chatter. We've got a few friends in the NSA that can help with that. Have Carver stay dark until we can clear the air—a few weeks, maybe more. Where's Zero now?"

"On his way back here with Watson and the CDC doctor."

Mullen nodded solemnly. "Debrief him and see if he'll talk about it."

"And if he doesn't? If he keeps quiet and digs deeper?"

"Make a contingency," Mullen told her. "Something here, on our turf, something we can control." The director shrugged. "Terrible accidents happen every day." He turned and walked away, back the way he had come.

⚜ ⚜ ⚜

The other two men were already buckled in when Reid boarded the Gulfstream. He took a seat across the aisle from Watson and in front of Barnard. The engines whirred to life as he strapped himself in.

"How's the shoulder?" He gestured to the blue sling around Watson's neck and arm.

"I've had worse."

Reid nodded. Then he leaned over again. "Listen...I think I owe you an apology."

Watson abruptly held up his good hand. "You don't owe me anything. Not an apology, nor an explanation." He settled into his seat and closed his eyes.

"What about you, Barnard?" Reid twisted in his seat. "We made a pretty good team. Have we inspired you to volunteer for more bioterrorism ops with the CIA?"

"Actually, Agent Steele," Barnard replied as he shifted in his seat, "considering the events of the last forty-eight hours, I plan to apply for the very next laboratory position that opens with the CDC. With any luck, I'll spend the rest of my career in very quiet and very *un*surprising conditions."

Reid laughed. He settled into the plush, inviting chair and closed his eyes.

He was going home. It would still be Sunday by the time he got back; even with the debriefing, the six-hour backward leap in time zones would likely put him home—and back to his daughters—by lunchtime.

Maria pushed open the door to the ladies' room at Boryspil International Airport in Kiev, Ukraine. It was a brief stopover to refuel the plane; she had slipped away under the pretense of getting something to eat. And she was famished, but that wasn't the reason for her visit to the main terminal.

She entered a stall and opened her purse, removing her CIA-issued phone and a plastic waterproof baggie. She sealed the phone inside it and placed it gently into the toilet's rear tank for safekeeping. It would only be for a few minutes.

Then she casually made her way to gate nineteen and sat, choosing a plastic chair a decent distance from the passengers waiting to board their flight.

Less than a minute later she felt a pressure at her back as someone sat in the opposite-facing chair behind her. The man cleared his throat loudly and opened a newspaper in front of his face.

"Marigold." He spoke in Ukrainian and his voice was husky, as if he was perpetually getting over a cold.

"Don't call me that," she muttered in the foreign tongue.

The man chuckled to himself softly. "Report."

"He remembers," she said simply.

There was a very pregnant pause before the man asked, "Steele? Are you certain?"

"He didn't say so. Not overtly. But I could see it in his eyes. And another agent attacked him, out of nowhere."

The man sighed. "This could spell trouble for us."

Maria hesitated. "Or... he could be an ally."

The man behind her scoffed loudly.

"He nearly had it figured out before," Maria said in a harsh whisper. "He just needs to remember, and to retrace his steps..."

"He is CIA."

"He didn't trust them before, and even less now," she argued. "He has no allegiance to them."

"And where do his allegiances lie, hmm?" the Ukrainian man asked. "With you, I suppose?"

Maria huffed. "Possibly."

"You're letting your emotions get the best of you," the man warned.

She felt her face grow hot with anger. "I am perfectly in control of my emotions," she hissed. "And I'll remind you that I've gotten a hell of a lot farther than anyone else." She took a deep, calming breath. "Look, I'm on the trail of the assassin. If I bring him in, I believe I'll fully gain Steele's trust. He already believes I'm doing it for him, to help keep his family safe."

Aren't you? she wondered. But she kept it to herself.

The man did not speak for a long moment. "Prove you can do it first," he said finally. "Then we will consider it. But if this fails, it will be on your head." He abruptly folded his paper, stood, and stalked away.

Maria sat there alone for a full minute, her hands tented at her mouth. She sighed. "I'm so sorry, Kent." *But it has to be this way.*

Then she stood and hastily went to retrieve her phone.

Chapter Thirty Nine

Reid got into his car in the CIA parking deck and just sat there a moment with his hands on the steering wheel. His limbs ached. His forearm hurt where he'd nearly been shot, and his chest hurt where he'd nearly been stabbed. Both spots were badly bruised, particularly his arm, which was swollen and dark purple. He had so much running through his head that he feared his skull might split in two.

The debriefing with Riker had lasted two and a half hours. It had started out well enough—a call from President Pierson to personally thank and congratulate Agent Steele on a job well done—but immediately following that was a thorough grilling from Ashleigh Riker. He painstakingly detailed the entire ordeal twice to her, only to circle back around to Agent Carver's bizarre attack.

Reid was careful not to make any mention of his memory or any conspiracy theories. He simply stated and restated that Carver's attempts on his life were sudden, mysterious, and unjustified. Riker assured him that they would find the renegade agent and bring him to justice.

Despite her promises, Reid was fairly certain that Riker at least knew about the cover-up, and was possibly even in on it. Either way, she was not to be trusted. She would be keeping her eye on him, he knew.

And for the foreseeable future, he would have to keep glancing over his shoulder.

He considered just packing up again, taking the girls, and leaving. *Tell no one. Just go somewhere.* But he knew he couldn't do that. The agency would have little trouble finding him if they wanted to.

And he needed answers to the dozens of questions that were swimming in his head.

Reid sighed as he powered up his personal cell phone, the one he'd left behind at Langley before the op, for the first time in two days and waited a minute or so for it to boot up. He had a few emails from students—*right*, he remembered, *I have to give a lecture tomorrow*—and only one voicemail, from Kate's sister, Linda, in New York.

He didn't really feel like speaking with Linda at the moment, but he listened to the voicemail as he pulled out of the deck, just in case it was something urgent.

"Hey, Reid!" Linda's cheerful voice said through the phone. "Just wanted to let you know that I got a call from a lawyer in New York, something Rothstein, who said that you were entitled to some kind of settlement from back when, uh, Katie passed…"

Reid smiled sadly. Linda had trouble saying the word "death" when it came to her little sister. He could relate; he did too, even after two years.

"He couldn't share details, but it was about the medical personnel who tended to her. Apparently some money's coming your way? It sounded like good news, so I gave him your info. I wanted to follow up and make sure he got in touch. Give me a call when you can, and give my love to the girls. Bye!"

"Hmm." He couldn't remember anything about a settlement. *A class-action suit, maybe?* Had he opted into something around the time that Kate passed, and forgotten about it? It was entirely possible; everything had happened so quickly that it was all a blur in his mind. And it wasn't that long thereafter that the memory suppressor was installed in his head.

Either way, he didn't have any missed calls or voicemails from any lawyers. Besides, it was the weekend; if he was going to hear anything, it would probably be on Monday.

But as he got on the highway, taking the quickest route home, he found he couldn't get the thought of Kate out of his mind—and the memory he'd nearly forgotten about for the last two days.

"Why do you have this, Reid?"

That's what she had asked in his memory about the gun she'd found. He hadn't stopped long enough to think about it while on the hunt for Khalil and the virus, but now it came creeping back into his brain, along with the question that had been doing laps in his conscious three days ago. *Did she know about me?*

"It's just for protection," you lied to her.

"I'm sorry, Katie," you told her.

After she left for work that morning, you retrieved the other eleven guns you'd hidden through the house.

Reid's grip tightened on the steering wheel. Traffic was light, but he felt tension brewing in his chest.

It was guilt.

You kept three. Found better spots for them.

That night, when she came home, you cooked her favorite meal and lit candles. You kissed her forehead and apologized. She tried to stay mad.

She couldn't. She smiled.

"Imagine it," she joked. "You, shooting a gun." She laughed.

You grinned. "I know. It was a dumb idea."

"Your heart was in the right place." She put her hand on yours. "But we don't need it."

"You're right."

"They cause more harm than good. You know that, right?"

"I know that."

He did know that. She had definitely been right.

Reid blew out a long breath and relaxed his white-knuckled fingers from the wheel as the memory faded. She didn't know. Kate didn't know about him, because he lied to her. And he kept up that lie right until the end. And now he was continuing it with his daughters—or one of them, anyway.

"It was to keep them safe," he said to himself aloud. "You only lied to keep them safe." *And you keep lying. Did that keep them safe in February?*

He shook the thought from his head. This was fatigue, nothing more. He turned onto Spruce Street and eased down the block until a familiar and most welcome sight came into view. He turned into the driveway and parked.

He reached for the door handle but paused, frowning. Thompson's truck wasn't in the driveway. *Maybe they went somewhere?* It was just before noon on a Sunday; where would they have gone?

Reid laughed at himself. Hadn't he made a promise to try not to be so overprotective? Thompson obviously ran an errand. *Good, maybe I can surprise the girls without a Smith & Wesson getting pulled.*

He pushed his key as quietly as possible into the front door and turned it. He slipped inside the foyer and pushed the door closed again with his palm. He didn't need to worry about the alarm as long as someone was in the house and had set it...

His keys fell out of his hands at the sight of the blood in the foyer.

He ran, sliding to the tile beside the body as his knees weakened.

He checked for a pulse. But he already knew by the look of the face that there hadn't been one for hours.

Thompson was dead. He had been beaten and stabbed in the chest.

"No," Reid said hoarsely. "No, no, no, no, no..." He was back on his feet, sprinting down the basement steps as fast as he could, half-stumbling down them and gripping the banister for support.

Sara's cell phone, in its hot pink case, sat on the floor of the bottom landing.

The panic room door was wide open.

No one inside.

"God, no, please, no..." His fingers were trembling as he dialed 911 on his own phone, smearing the screen with Thompson's blood. "Y-yes, my name is Reid Lawson, 241 Spruce Street. There's... there's been a murder..."

He told them that his two teenage daughters had been kidnapped, even as tears welled in both his eyes. Even though he shook so hard the phone threatened to fall from his hand.

He didn't remember going back up the stairs, but suddenly he was in Maya's room, tearing her comforter off the bed, looking beneath it, flinging open the closet, because she was here. She wasn't gone.

She was here somewhere. She was smart. She had hidden. It had to be true.

In Sara's room he saw the open window, the fire escape ladder unfurled, and his heart leapt. *They got out. They used the ladder. Thompson gave his life to save theirs. They're out there, safe, somewhere.*

He convinced himself of it. He was certain of it. When his brain told him that they would have contacted him, called his cell phone, sent a text, called Linda, called the police, he swatted at the air in front of him as if he could physically push those thoughts away.

They're safe. They're fine. They got away.

Sara's phone chimed in his hand.

He hadn't realized he was still holding it.

His breath came in ragged gulps as he swiped across the screen to unlock it and checked the text message that had just come through.

It was a picture. And it came from Maya's number.

The photo was of his girls. They were in their pajamas, huddled together in the backseat of a vehicle. Maya was holding her little sister. Both their faces were red, puffy from crying.

There was a message with it. *They are still alive. For now. Come find me.*

He dropped the phone as if it was on fire. The screen cracked.

As the sirens outside screamed, Reid did too.

NOW AVAILABLE!

HUNTING ZERO
(An Agent Zero Spy Thriller—Book #3)

"You will not sleep until you are finished with AGENT ZERO. A superb job creating a set of characters who are fully developed and very much enjoyable. The description of the action scenes transport us into a reality that is almost like sitting in a movie theater with surround sound and 3D (it would make an incredible Hollywood movie). I can hardly wait for the sequel."

—Roberto Mattos, Books and Movie Reviews

In HUNTING ZERO (Book #3), when CIA operative Agent Zero finds out his two teenage girls have been kidnapped and are bound for a trafficking ring in Eastern Europe, he embarks on a high-octane chase across Europe, leaving a trail of devastation is his wake as he breaks all rules, risks his own life, and does everything he can to get his daughters back.

Kent, ordered by the CIA to stand down, refuses. Without the backing of the agency, with moles and assassins on all sides, with a lover he can barely trust, and being targeted himself, Agent Zero must fight multiple foes to get his girls back.

Up against the most deadly trafficking ring in Europe, with political connections reaching all the way to the top, it is an unlikely battle—one man against an army—and one that only Agent Zero can wage.

And yet, his own identity, he realizes, may be the most perilous secret of all.

HUNTING ZERO (Book #3) is an un-putdownable espionage thriller that will keep you turning pages late into the night.

HUNTING ZERO
(An Agent Zero Spy Thriller—Book #3)